Readers love
ROWAN McALLISTER

Power Bottom?

"I have to say with all honesty that this book completely blew me away."
—Gay Book Reviews

"*Power Bottom* was nothing like I thought it would be—it turned out even better!"
—Alpha Book Club

Water and Fire

"Once I picked up this book, I could not put it down. I literally devoured it in a matter of hours."
—MM Good Book Reviews

Green the Whole Year 'Round

"Definitely a heartwarming and wonderful holiday novella!"
—Boys in Our Books

"If you are a sucker for Christmas tales of love the way I am, I can't recommend it enough."
—Prism Book Alliance

By Rowan McAllister

Cherries on Top
Cuddling (Dreamspinner Anthology)
A Devil's Own Luck • Never a Road Without a Turning
Feels Like Home
Grand Adventures (Dreamspinner Anthology)
Green the Whole Year 'Round
Hot Mess
Lost in the Outcome
My Only Sunshine
Power Bottom?
A Promise of Tomorrow
We Met in Dreams

ELEMENTAL HARMONY
Air and Earth
Water and Fire

Published by Dreamspinner Press
www.dreamspinnerpress.com

We Met in Dreams

Rowan McAllister

Published by
DREAMSPINNER PRESS

5032 Capital Circle SW, Suite 2, PMB# 279, Tallahassee, FL 32305-7886 USA
www.dreamspinnerpress.com

This is a work of fiction. Names, characters, places, and incidents either are the product of author imagination or are used fictitiously, and any resemblance to actual persons, living or dead, business establishments, events, or locales is entirely coincidental.

We Met in Dreams
© 2017 Rowan McAllister.

Cover Art
© 2017 Anna Sikorska.
Cover content is for illustrative purposes only and any person depicted on the cover is a model.

All rights reserved. This book is licensed to the original purchaser only. Duplication or distribution via any means is illegal and a violation of international copyright law, subject to criminal prosecution and upon conviction, fines, and/or imprisonment. Any eBook format cannot be legally loaned or given to others. No part of this book may be reproduced or transmitted in any form or by any means, electronic or mechanical, including photocopying, recording, or by any information storage and retrieval system, without the written permission of the Publisher, except where permitted by law. To request permission and all other inquiries, contact Dreamspinner Press, 5032 Capital Circle SW, Suite 2, PMB# 279, Tallahassee, FL 32305-7886, USA, or www.dreamspinnerpress.com.

ISBN: 978-1-63533-295-7
Digital ISBN: 978-1-63533-296-4
Library of Congress Control Number: 2016915167
Published February 2017
v. 1.0

Printed in the United States of America

This paper meets the requirements of
ANSI/NISO Z39.48-1992 (Permanence of Paper).

To all those who fight a daily battle that no one sees.
Fight on.

Chapter One

A LOUD clatter and frightened shout from beyond my door jolted me out of a fitful doze and left my heart hammering in my chest. Nestled in my warm cocoon of blankets on the floor, frozen with my heart still in my throat, I blindly searched the darkness until my mind at last supplied a name for that voice. It was only Tom, the footman my uncle had hired last year to replace John.... At least I was fairly certain the previous footman had been John, although that could have been Henry. I couldn't quite remember, because neither John nor Henry had lasted long. Tom had made it almost an entire year thus far. He must've been made of sterner stuff than the others... or my uncle had offered him a higher wage.

Fully awake, I frowned into the darkness around me and pulled my blankets higher atop my shoulders.

What is Tom doing in the upstairs hall at this time of night?

I strained to hear more but was rewarded with only the creaks and pops of the house and the rattle of shutters from an errant breeze outside my window. Perhaps I had imagined it, after all.

Still curious but no longer alarmed, I slipped from the comfortable nest of blankets I'd made in front of the hearth and crept to my door. I had nothing better to do. My fire had died too low to read by, but perhaps I might have a bit of a diversion yet.

Placing my ear to the heavy wood, I caught the sound of hushed whispers some distance away, but I couldn't quite make out the words. Relieved I wouldn't be subjected to another round of the pitiful moans and tortured wailings that often plagued me at night, I strained against the door until I felt sure my cheek would bear the impression of its carved surface. The voices were familiar and comforting, even if the words were unclear.

Then the whispers stopped abruptly, and the silence was broken by the quiet rattling of doors being opened and shut and the scuffle of hurried footsteps up and down the hall. I felt the vibrations through my cheek and hands as each door was opened and closed, and I huffed in frustration at not knowing what was going on. The light from a lamp grew through the gap beneath my door, only to fade away again shortly after. Then the sounds and vibrations ceased entirely, and all was still and dark again.

I waited, but when nothing else happened, I sighed and straightened. With only a token glare for the ever-present lock on my door, I shivered and shuffled back to my little nest. The novel I'd been reading before I fell asleep tumbled free as I tugged the blankets about me again, and I tucked it close to my chest and settled in for another long night. I was awake now, with no fire to read by and nothing but my thoughts to keep me company. That usually boded ill for my state of mind.

As the supposed master of the house, I could've kicked up a fuss and demanded to know what had occurred outside my door. I could've pulled the bell rope and forced Pendel, my butler, to return and explain his and Tom's presence abovestairs at this hour. But, as always, I hated to be a bother. If the disturbance had been of any real import, I trusted Pendel would have come to me on his own. A little mild irritation over my curiosity going unsatisfied wasn't worth all that. And besides, the chill January air had crept beneath my nightshirt and dressing gown after only that brief excursion outside the warmth of my nest—despite my nightcap, mittens, and wool stockings—and I was loathe to leave it again.

Running my fingers over the cloth binding of my novel, I turned from the dull orange glow of the dying coals in the stove and peered forlornly through the darkness toward the heavily curtained alcove hiding my window seat. Regardless of the cold, I might have been tempted to move my nest there if even a scrap of moonlight were to be had, but I knew I would find only a deeper darkness beyond the thick green velvet brocade. For months, everything outside the rippled glass of my windows had been draped in a fog so dense and unending, I feared—in my darker moments—that the world beyond might have disappeared entirely, save the odd laborer or tradesman who would suddenly appear on the grounds beneath my rooms as if conjured out of the mist.

The newspapers had commented almost daily on the pernicious fog that had shrouded all of London, so I knew it wasn't just our little corner of Kensington that suffered. But as the bleak months dragged on, the dense fog and cold were taking their toll on my spirits, and I ached for even a glimpse of sunlight or moonlight to cut through the unending gray beyond my prison.

Hissing in disgust, I turned away from the thick darkness behind me and returned my gaze to the coals in my hearth. I couldn't allow myself to think like that. This was not a prison but a haven to keep me safe and to keep others safe from me. I belonged here. I was well taken care of. This was my home.

I took a deep breath of frigid air and blew it out forcefully, counting to three on the inhale and another three on the exhale, as I'd been taught. I flexed my frozen fingers in my mittens to get the blood flowing, drew my shoulders back, and lifted my chin. I was a Middleton, heir to a long and illustrious line, and I could not allow myself to be beaten by melancholia or any other manifestation of my illness.

The voices in the hall had been real. I'd recognized the footman, and I would know Pendel's gruff whisper anywhere. I could still tell the difference between reality and those other sounds and voices that plagued me. Someday soon the sun would return, and I would shake off this new and unwelcome addition to my troubles, just as I did the rest. Someday I would be well and no longer need these rooms. I had to persist in that belief.

I held my rigid posture for only a few moments before I shivered and wrapped my arms more tightly around myself as a wave of hopelessness threatened to crash over me again. I was so weary of fighting. The melancholia, the visions, the voices, all of it was that much harder to overcome when the world seemed determined to keep me in the dark and dreary gray forever.

Agitated and unable to distract myself with my novel, I tossed the volume on the nearby chair, collected the blankets around me like a cloak, and moved to my pianoforte. I could play by feel in the darkness, after countless nights of practice, and music often soothed me when the forced confinement and solitude of my existence became too much to bear. If I played quietly, I would not disturb anyone's slumber. The servants' hall was too far away for them to hear me unless I truly made an effort.

I had just reached the bench and was fussing with my blankets so I could settle comfortably, when another sound reached my ears, this time from the stairwell leading up to my rooftop conservatory. My uncle had commissioned the conservatory for me so I might have the fresh air and sunshine Dr. Payne recommended without having to leave my house. I barely had to leave my rooms, in truth. No expense had been spared for my convenience. The finest of materials and skilled craftsmen had been hired to construct it, but the staircase just on the other side of the wall my pianoforte rested against still creaked whenever someone trod upon it.

Tom used a second door from the hall to access those stairs daily, stocking the coal stove up there so the more delicate of my plants wouldn't suffer too badly in the bitter cold. But he'd already seen to that duty before the rest of the house turned in for the night, and I hadn't heard a key rattle in the lock on the hall door. I couldn't imagine Pendel allowing him to have the key on his own, at any rate. Perhaps Pendel was the one using the stairs after whatever the disturbance in the hall had been.

I froze, straining for more, and heard two more quiet creaks as someone ascended the stairs. My heart racing despite the myriad explanations for the sound, I crept on slippered feet to the door that separated my rooms from the stairwell, drew the heavy insulating velvet drapes aside, and pressed my ear to the wood. A slight draft brushed my cheek from the gap between the door and its frame, as if the outer door at the top of the stairs had been opened, but no lamplight penetrated those spaces. I couldn't imagine any of the servants taking the stairs in the dark, particularly not Pendel, now that he was getting on in years.

Holding my breath, I carefully turned the knob and poked my head through the opening. I saw nothing as I squinted into the deeper darkness, and no more stairs creaked or latches rattled no matter how hard I listened. The air was still and cold, and I shivered in my dressing gown. But I'd already stirred myself, and, my curiosity piqued for the second time that night, I crept up the stairs and eased the outer door open.

An inky gray-black, barely lighter than the darkness behind me, stared back at me as I searched in vain for the source of the sounds. The glass walls and roof of the conservatory were of little help due to the thick fog outside. I gripped the doorframe and strained but saw and heard nothing. I was on the verge of dismissing the whole thing as another trick of my mind when the faint tinkle of something metal falling to the stone tiles and a muffled curse stopped me.

"Hello? Is someone there?" I asked breathlessly.

My words were met with silence, but a spot of darkness, deeper than the rest, detached itself from the far end of the conservatory and moved toward me. Instinctively I retreated.

"Hello? Who is it? Who are you?" I croaked.

The shadow said nothing, only continued to follow me as I retreated down the stairs and through the door to my rooms. I stopped in front of my hearth, still cloaked in my ridiculous mound of blankets, and waited with my heart beating frantically. Then my heart stopped altogether when I heard the rustle of the thick curtains being pushed aside and saw the faint outline of the shadow as it stepped into my rooms.

I had to swallow against a sudden dryness in my throat before I whispered, "Say something. Please."

The shadow finally halted its silent advance. This close, in the faint light of the coals, the dark shape resolved itself into a man, looming over me. I was about to repeat my somewhat shaky demand, when the shadow finally spoke.

"Don' cry out. I mean ye no 'arm."

His accent was strange to me. I couldn't place it, but that was hardly surprising, given the limited number of people I'd been allowed to interact with in my life. His speech lacked the elocution of a gentleman, but he spoke in a pleasant baritone I found quite soothing to my nerves nevertheless. My anxiety melted by slow degrees as I let his voice wash over me, and I forced myself to think the situation through instead of giving in to my fear.

I had never heard that voice before. He was a stranger. A stranger could not possibly have just appeared in my conservatory in the middle of the night. Campden House resided in a respectable neighborhood surrounded by a large park that rarely ever received visitors beyond tradesmen. My rooms were on the third floor. No one but Pendel, Tom, Sarah the maid, the doctor, and on the rare occasion, my uncle ever came to the third floor or into the house at all. And Pendel kept the place locked up tight at all times. Surely if that little disturbance in the hall a few moments ago had been about an intruder, Pendel would have notified me.

These were all things I knew to be true. Because of my illness, I could trust in those facts better than I could trust my own senses. Therefore, I could only conclude that this shadow was not real. It was simply another creation of my illness, another vision sent to plague me in the dark of night when I was unable to sufficiently distract myself or too weak to fight.

"Have ye nothin' to say?" the shadow asked, and I smiled for the first time in weeks.

It seemed this hallucination might be different from the others—the ones that hovered silently and menacingly over me until I was fit to scream or pull my hair out. This one almost sounded put out that I hadn't spoken again. I couldn't remember the last time I'd had a vision I could talk to.

I worried my lip as I pondered the shape in front of me. Dr. Payne would doubtless see the appearance of another hallucination as very concerning—and perhaps I should as well—but I had to admit I was relieved more than anything. This one seemed like it might just be amusing. I was so very tired of being alone and fighting my illness day after day. One night of surrender would not be so bad, particularly if I remained fully cognizant of the fact that he was not real.

What harm could it do to talk to it just this once?

I turned my back on it and made my way to my bed. The fire no longer gave enough warmth to offset suffering the hardness of the floor, and if my hallucination were going to bless me with some conversation, I could at least make myself comfortable.

After settling my blankets over the bed, I crawled beneath them, relaxed against the stack of pillows, and waited. The apparition had been silent and still through all of this. If it had a face, I could not see it, but it shifted slightly, giving it an air of puzzlement before it spoke.

"Ye're not gonna bring the 'ouse down on me 'ead?"

I chuckled. "Why would I do a thing like that?"

"'Twould seem the natural thing to do… under the circumstances."

I frowned at it in suspicion. "Is that what you want, for me to bring the whole house down on us? To shout them awake from their beds?"

"O' course not. I'm just surprised, is all."

Its rather peeved grumble made me smile again. "The days of me making a spectacle of myself over my visions are long gone," I said loftily, "at least as long as I can help it. You've no need to worry about that."

"Yer visions?"

I rolled my eyes. "Yes. My visions, my fancies, my hallucinations. You are not the first, nor will you be the last, I fear. But I've learned to live with you. And if you're actually willing to talk, then I am more than willing to listen and while away the hours until I fall asleep again. I could use the distraction, since I've no light to continue reading my novel and the winter nights are so damnably long."

Silence fell as the shadow seemed to ponder my words.

"Are ye sayin' ye think I'm not real, then?" it asked, hesitating as if it were choosing its words carefully.

I laughed. "Of course you aren't. You arrive in my rooms in the middle of the night, a dark specter in the heart of winter, without so much as a cloak or a hat to shield you from the cold—without even a jacket, as far as I can see in this blasted darkness. My rooms are on the top floor of the house, and Pendel checks the locks on all the doors and windows every night as part of his routine. Has done for ages. What else could you be?"

This time the vision chuckled too. "I s'pose that makes as much sense as any. So what are ye gonna do, then, if not call down the guards?"

"I'm going to sit here comfortably and listen to whatever it is you've come to tell me, obviously."

The silence that fell after my proclamation was soon broken by the sound of footsteps in the hall. A quick glance in that direction revealed the flickering light of a lamp beneath my door. The added light revealed more of the shape of the man before me but still no detail and no face.

"My lord?" Pendel called quietly from the hall. "My lord?"

"Yes, Pendel," I answered, turning my attention to the door again.

"Forgive the disturbance, but I happened to be on the stairs, and I thought I heard you speaking. Are you well? Is anything amiss?"

I glanced toward the apparition, but the shadow had vanished.

Damn.

Sighing in disappointment but not surprise, I answered, "All is well here. Is there something wrong?"

"No, my lord. So very sorry to disturb you at this hour."

"But I thought I heard you in the hall earlier."

"Yes, my lord. The footman, Tom, thought he saw someone, but we've searched the rooms and found no sign of any disturbance and all the doors and windows remain locked. I will check them again, to be sure, but I expect he saw only his shadow or a trick of the light."

"Perhaps he saw the headless spirit of the first Viscount Campden," I teased as I scanned my rooms for my visitor.

"Perhaps, my lord."

I could almost see Pendel's frown of disapproval from his tone, and I hung my head. I had to find humor in such things as visions and specters or I might have collapsed under the weight of my illness long ago, but poor Pendel had enough of a burden caring for me without me making light of such things. I cleared my throat and asked, "Did Tom say why he was up here in the first place?"

My question was met with a brief silence in which I could almost see the stern twist of Pendel's lips. "No, my lord. But that is a question I will have answered soon. I promise you."

Pendel had been with my family since my father was a lad. Loyal to his core, no matter how unhinged I might be, Pendel would not stand for anyone treating me as some sort of carnival attraction to be gawked at or whispered about. Campden House would need a new footman in short order if Tom couldn't provide a more convincing story for his presence where he should not have been.

"I'll leave you to it, then. Good night, Pendel."

"Good night, my lord."

His footsteps receded, along with the light, and I was left to my solitude again, wishing I could have had some excuse to keep him there longer.

"Is he another of your visions?"

The softly spoken words from close beside my bed nearly made me jump out of my skin, despite the veiled humor in them. I'd thought my visitor had dissolved into the ether, as they so often did when the real world intruded, but perhaps this one was more real than the others. Tom had heard something. But if all the doors and windows were still locked, a stranger couldn't have entered the house.

Wrapping my arms around myself, I frowned at the shadow. "No. No. Pendel is real. He's been with my family for years."

"Perhaps he is, and perhaps he isn't," the voice teased.

"He is," I insisted.

"But if you can see and hear me, as you can see and hear him, how is he real when I am not?"

Before I realized what I was doing, I reached beneath my cap and pulled a few hairs from my scalp. I could feel them in my palm, along with the slight sting, and I gritted my teeth. A real intruder would hardly hang about simply to tease and torment me. He had to be another vision conjured by my own mind to make me miserable. I rubbed my temple seeking to ease the growing ache behind my eyes as anxiety and frustration formed a vise around my chest. When I caught myself reaching for my hair again, I fisted my hands and forced them beneath the covers, keeping them firmly in my lap so I wouldn't do my scalp any more damage.

"I know the difference between what is real and what isn't. *I know it*," I asserted, mostly for my benefit. "If you've only come to upset me, I want you to leave. Leave now, please."

I clamped my lips shut against their trembling and breathed deeply as Dr. Payne had taught me. The icy air hurt my nose and throat, but it was good for the body.

"Fresh air, quiet, and exercise are the keys to continued good health," Dr. Payne always intoned.

I closed my eyes to blot out what little I could see of the shadow in the darkness and continued my breathing exercises, hoping it would go away.

"Wait. Forgive me. I didn't mean to upset you so. I'm very sorry. Please, don't cry." The words came at me in a rush, almost desperate in their pleading as I heard him move closer to me.

"I'm not crying," I insisted between labored breaths. "I'm breathing."

"Oh. Well. Good, then."

The hints of confusion and amusement in his voice didn't startle me as much as the change in his accent. Earlier, despite my not being able to place it, his accent had been undeniably working class. Now, his English was crisp and proper as any gentleman's. The change was enough to startle me out of my attack of nerves, and I stopped my exercises and frowned at him.

Did I alter his speech to ease my distress or so I would put a higher value on his words?

I'd never considered myself so much the snob before. I was hardly one to cast stones on what was right and proper in this world—wretched creature that I was. But I learned things about myself from my visions, after the trauma of their presence receded and I had hours and hours alone to reflect.

"Can you forgive me?" the shadow asked into the silence. "Truly, I did not mean to upset you."

With effort, I unclenched my palms and allowed the rest of my body to relax against the pillows again. A flicker of movement and flash of murky white light in a far corner to my right tried to distract me, but I ignored it in favor of the more solid and unfamiliar vision at the foot of my bed. "Yes, I can forgive you. Only please don't ask me such things again. It's upsetting enough to have you here, without my own hallucinations questioning my sanity."

The shadow chuckled, but the flicker and flash to my right caught my eye again, and I couldn't help but turn toward it. The hazy apparition I'd seen so many times before struggled to take shape in the corner by my window seat. It glowed with an eerie light, though that light didn't touch anything around it. It writhed in place, almost taking a form reminiscent of a woman in a diaphanous gown, but it never quite solidified. Like the darker shadows that plagued me, this vision never spoke, only hovered for a while before fading away again. It wasn't as bad as some of the others, but her appearance often preceded worse.

"What's wrong?" the shadow asked, and I chuckled helplessly at the lunacy of it all.

Perhaps there was some harm in not rejecting this new vision, after all. Perhaps it only opened the door to more.

"Someone else is competing for my attention, I'm afraid," I said, forcing a laugh. "I'd be flattered at my popularity, if I weren't merely flattering myself."

I heard the faint rustling of cloth as the shadow turned this way and that. "You see them now?"

"Yes." I sighed tiredly. "My visions always get worse the more unsettled or distressed I become. I'd take another dose of my medicine, but I don't wish to disturb Pendel again, and I really do hate the stuff. Besides, if I took it, I'd probably fall asleep and you'd disappear again, and then where would we be?"

"I see."

His tone said clearly he did not, in fact, see, but he was no longer baiting me like before, and the nervous ache in my head and chest lessened.

"Is the other vision still there? Where is it?" he asked.

I glanced toward my window seat, but the apparition had disappeared along with the worst of my anxiety. "No. She's gone."

"She?"

"She, it, I don't know." I sighed my irritation. "It reminds me sometimes of a woman in a flowing gown, but mostly it's just a floating kind of mist."

"Do you see her often?"

"Not so very often of late. I see her more when I'm feeling unwell, either in body or spirit."

"And you are feeling unwell now?"

I rolled my eyes, though I knew he could not see it in the dark. "Perhaps," I hedged, wishing he'd change the subject.

"Is there anything I might do? Would a lamp help? I could light one for you if you tell me where it is."

"No. I'm not allowed a lamp or a candle."

"Why?"

"For fear I may set the house ablaze and burn everyone in their beds, of course," I bit out irritably.

"And would you?"

"Of course not, at least not intentionally."

"And yet someone thinks you might?"

"No—I mean yes." I growled in frustration. "I don't know. I suppose they must, at least a little."

"How about a gas lamp? Surely such a grand house as this should have had them installed by now."

I lifted my chin. "Of course. After the fire several years ago, my uncle had them installed, but none in here, I'm afraid. I think they fear I might have another bad spell and blow the house up for good and all." I forced a chuckle.

"But I can see the faint glow from the hearth," the shadow argued. "You're allowed that obviously."

This subject had been done to death already, long before tonight. If the damned vision was going to quibble with me all night about things that hadn't changed in over ten years, then he could bloody well be on his way.

"The stove is filled and locked before the servants go to bed and then refilled in the morning when they wake," I explained through clenched teeth. "But really, this conversation is becoming tiresome. The least you could do is talk of something interesting, if you are going to plague me in the middle of the night." I sounded haughty and peevish, but I didn't care. This wasn't the kind of distraction I wanted.

The shadow let out a bark of laughter. "Of course, *my lord*. Forgive me, *my lord*. I should hate to think you aren't being sufficiently entertained."

"I thank you, good sir. It *is* a terrible tragedy to be without proper diversions," I threw back at him, choosing to ignore the acid in his tone, and I was gratified to hear him chuckle again.

He had a nice laugh, a laugh that warmed me and made me smile. Perhaps I could allow myself to be teased a little, after all, if it meant I could hear him laugh again.

No one else ever dared tease me. Pendel loved me in his own way, but he would be scandalized if I were to suggest a greater intimacy than we already shared as master and servant. The underservants rarely spoke a single word to me, let alone in jest. And my uncle and I talked on his monthly visits, but he was always so careful with me—as if I were made of spun glass—hesitant to speak of anything beyond estate business and the exchange of the usual pleasantries for fear of upsetting me. I'd read so many books and plays where the characters traded witty barbs and dueled with words, the results quite hilarious, but I'd never had the chance myself.

I liked this vision, despite his annoying propensity to discomfit me. For once, I found myself wishing I knew how to make him stay, rather than begging him to leave me in peace. If only my traitorous mind had given a face along with that laugh.

My mattress shifted under me as the shadow settled on the end of my bed, startling me a little. He was not the first of my visions to have substance, though I shivered at the memories of the others. During the worst of my spells, early in my illness, my visions had terrified me. Phantom hands had held me down, their weight smothering me until I fainted dead away in my fear. I hadn't had such an episode in many years, and I hoped to never experience that again.

I caught my hand reaching for my hair, but forced it down and bit my lip instead. Such thoughts could twist my visions into something ugly and fearful if I dwelled too long in the past.

"If I am to amuse you, I will require amusement in kind," the shadow said, his voice thankfully teasing and light as he broke in on my dark thoughts.

"What kind of amusement?" I croaked gratefully.

"Satisfaction of my curiosity, I think—an answer for an answer. I will answer your questions, if you will do the same for mine."

"What kind of questions?"

"Impertinent ones, I'm sure."

"How impertinent?" I asked, tensing again.

The shadow shifted on the bed and chuckled. "Oh no. I've answered one for you. It's my turn now. What is your name?"

Whether I agreed that I owed him an answer or not, at least the question was an easy one, and one I wasn't at all ashamed of. Without even thinking about it, I sat up straighter, lifted my chin, and drew my shoulders back. "I am Arthur Phillip James Baptist Middleton, Viscount Campden."

"My word, that's certainly a mouthful. I think I'll call you Arthur, then."

I felt a brief jab of pique at such familiarity, before I was reminded that I was speaking to a creature of my own creation and to demand it use my title seemed the height of absurdity.

"And what is your name, pray?" I asked wryly.

"Hmmm. I feel I should not reveal too many of my secrets, lest you lose interest too quickly. You may call me Fox."

I frowned at him. "That hardly seems an answer. I feel I'm being cheated somehow."

"I said I would give you an answer for an answer. I didn't say it would be a good one." He laughed, and I couldn't help but join him. His laugh did strange things to my stomach.

"I like you," I blurted out before clamping a hand over my mouth and blushing in mortification.

How ridiculous. I was in my own rooms, with only an apparition for company. I should not have been embarrassed. But years of always saying the wrong thing at the wrong time and shaming myself and my uncle in the few social situations I'd been allowed as a youth—before we'd given up and had to lock me away completely—had taken their toll.

Fox's laughter died, and he was quiet for a time before he said, with mild surprise in his voice, "I like you as well, Arthur."

"Well… good," I replied stupidly, shifting uncomfortably but unable to stifle a smile. If anything, my blush deepened under the warmth in his voice, and I thanked the darkness that he could not see. I cleared my throat. "I suppose with that out of the way, we could continue our question and answer, then?"

"We could," Fox agreed hesitantly. "But I fear my time here grows short. It won't be long before the sun rises, and though the fog still seems thick enough to cut, I'd rather not risk discovery. I'll need to leave before dawn to avoid being seen."

I lurched forward, clutching blindly for his sleeve. My grasping hand encountered smooth, padded silk, and I twisted a desperate fist in it, grateful his substance didn't dissolve beneath my grasp.

"Don't go, please. I'm the only one who can see you. There's no need."

Realizing again that my reaction was wholly inappropriate to the circumstance, I released his sleeve as if it had burned me and shrank back again. "Forgive me. I—it's just… we've only begun talking."

How pathetic was I that I was willing to get on my knees and beg a figment of my own imagination not to leave me alone?

Fox sighed as I began my breathing exercises again and clenched my fists in my lap.

"I can spare a few minutes," he replied, "but not much more. I'm sorry."

Other shadows skittered and writhed around the edges of my vision, but I kept my gaze focused on the dark outline at the end of my bed. "At least tell me a little about yourself," I pleaded quietly trying to regain my calm.

Fox chuckled. "If I am indeed merely a product of your fancy, shouldn't you be the one to tell me who I am?"

"It doesn't work like that. My mind has a way of surprising me. You might be a character from a novel or a play I've read. You might be one of the infamous ghosts that local gossip claims haunts this house. You might be someone barely remembered from my childhood, before…. Well, you might be a combination of people or things really. I never know."

Fox was silent for a few moments before he leaned back against the post at the foot of my bed. The wood creaked quietly under his weight, and the heavy bed-curtains rustled in the darkness. "All right. If I can be anyone, then, I will entertain you with my tale… which may or may not be the truth."

His teasing tone had returned, and I smiled as I felt my desperation ease. If I could keep him talking, perhaps he would forget this nonsense about leaving.

"I am a thief," he began. "But no lowly brute on the smash-and-grab am I, for I am also a gentleman… well, *mostly*. I slipped into your beautiful and grand house this night, fully intending to slip out again with as much treasure as I could carry, but instead of the upper halls being dark and empty—as they had been every night for the past week—I nearly tripped over a great lumbering oaf in your hall and had to dash into what I thought might be a bedroom before I was seen. I tried to wait him out, but the oaf and another man blocked the stairs, so I had to think of some other way to get out of the house. I believed God had smiled on me when I discovered the bedchamber I'd hidden in was in actuality a stairwell. The stairs led up instead of down, but I still counted myself lucky. Except the fog that was supposed to obscure my departure made it near impossible for me to see my own hand in front of my face, let alone the locks I needed to pick to carry out my escape. I was fumbling with my tools when a quiet voice called to me. I thought I was done for, but the owner of that voice simply backed down the stairs, climbed into bed, and ordered me to tell him a tale, as if thieves in his house were an everyday occurrence. Apparently my luck held true, after all." Fox's arm moved in the darkness in what I thought might have been a dramatic flourish, and then he chuckled. "So what do you think about that, Lord Campden? Entertaining enough for you?"

Smiling, I clapped my hands vigorously. "Yes, very much so. I suppose I should be flattered you chose to sit and chat with me during all that excitement. I truly had no idea."

"You should be flattered. I wouldn't do such a thing for just anyone. In fact, you're lucky I didn't simply bash you on the head and make a run for it."

"Oh yes, I'm very lucky," I teased back a little breathlessly.

The slightest edge to his voice sent a thrill through me, but whether of fear or excitement, I refused to name it. An apparition Fox might be, but he was solid enough to my fractured mind, and I had made him several inches taller than myself, perhaps to add to that delicious hint of danger I must somehow be craving.

I was not a large man, but I was no milksop either. Though I never left the confines of my rooms and rooftop conservatory, I kept myself fit with the forms the doctor had taught me. Compared to the laborers and deliverymen I'd seen from my windows, I thought I measured up well enough. Fox had to be larger than myself to give him any of the deliciously menacing qualities I'd read about in my novels. A gentleman thief indeed—what on earth could I be thinking? Perhaps Dr. Payne had been right to caution against the influences of such stories. Still, boredom and loneliness could lead to their own kind of madness in time. I was very grateful Pendel chose to not look too closely at the packets of books Wallace Fuller, the bookseller, sent me every two weeks.

Fox cleared his throat, drawing my wandering thoughts back to him. "So now I have answered you. I believe it is your turn to tell me a story."

"What kind of story?"

"Tell me about yourself, of course. Quid pro quo. Tell me how is it that the Viscount Campden came to be locked in a room in his own home with no light to see by and a dying fire he's not even allowed to stoke with his own coal?"

I shifted uneasily at the edge in his voice, my discomfort returning. "I already told you that."

"Not really," he pushed. "You said you are ill, but not how. Have you always been ill? How long have you been confined to these rooms? Where is the rest of your family? You spoke of an uncle making decisions for you, but why is he not here in this enormous house with you? I watched the house for days and only saw a few servants moving about. That's why I picked it. I assumed the family was away."

"I don't wish to speak of it. Not now, please," I replied quietly, twisting my hands in my lap.

After a pause, Fox sighed and stood. "Perhaps that should be all for tonight, then. I should go."

I ruthlessly smothered my first inclination to grab for him again. My pride wouldn't allow another lapse in dignity, even if I feared he'd never return. "If you must," I murmured. And even though I knew it to be pointless, I couldn't help but add, "But you will come back, won't you?"

"I don't know," he replied. "It seems I upset you more than I entertained you. I can't think why you'd want me to call on you again."

"But I do… please." I didn't bother concealing the need in my voice this time.

"Well, if all you've said is true, and I am a thing of your creation, then that is entirely up to you now, isn't it?" he asked teasingly, his voice receding as he moved away from me.

I stuck my tongue out at him. He couldn't see that brief lapse in decorum, but it made me feel better nonetheless. "Possibly," I replied with as much hauteur as I could manage. "But it is only polite to ask." When he made no reply, I grew nervous again. "Will you?" I pleaded.

I heard the distinct click of a door latch, and a slight draft of colder air rustled my bed-curtains. "I will try. Good night, Arthur."

I had to swallow a slight lump in my throat before I could reply. "Good night, Fox."

After a brief moment of silence, I assumed he'd gone, evaporated into the ether like the others, but then his voice drifted to me again, quiet and hollow, as if from a long way off. "Arthur, if I do come again, I should like to be able to see your face when we talk. No matter your illness or the story behind it, the lord and master of the manor should not be kept in the dark in his own house, particularly if he does not wish to be."

Chapter Two

I MUST have managed to fall asleep after he left, for when I next opened my eyes, the drab light of another fog-shrouded day filtered through the heavy velvet brocade over my windows and Pendel was knocking on my door.

"My lord?"

"Come."

Pendel's key rattled in the lock, and then he entered. The lumbering bulk of Tom the footman followed, and then mousy little Sarah the housemaid came after, looking that much smaller next to Tom.

When Pendel saw that I was in my bed, his thin lips curved ever so slightly, the closest his craggy face ever came to a smile. "You slept, my lord?"

I rarely slept at night anymore. It wasn't entirely the fault of my illness. The laudanum potion Dr. Payne had prescribed for me every day—to help keep me calm—left me soporific for hours, so of course, I slept much of the day away and lay awake most nights. Though I hated to agree with anything Dr. Payne said on principle, since I detested the man, I found the night more soothing for my nerves at any rate, with less stimulation to become overwhelmed by, fewer distractions outside my window to agitate me. But I knew Pendel disapproved of my sleeping in my nest on the floor, and he'd be cheered by any sign of my returning to some sort of normalcy. I would not begrudge him that today.

"Yes, Pendel, I did sleep a little."

"Excellent, my lord." His smile remained, warming me with his approval, and I couldn't help but return it.

I could feel the weight of the furtive, nervous glances Sarah and Tom shot in our direction as we spoke, but I chose to ignore them as always. Even after months of working for me—years in Sarah's case—they still eyed me as if I might, at any moment, have some sort of fit and leap on them in mad abandon. I had never done anything of the kind, but that truth never seemed to matter. I was still watched with wary eyes at all times, as if I were some dangerous caged animal.

I was certain the impertinence of their looks would have earned them a dismissal in any other great house, but this was no ordinary great house, and I was no ordinary master. Efficient and discreet help was difficult to find, and after one early incident I didn't like to think of, paying off servants to ensure their silence about my condition once they left my employment was an expensive proposition.

Pendel's constant supervision of the other servants wasn't strictly necessary. Tom and Sarah knew their duties, but I supposed all parties felt better with Pendel there to handle me should I become "overwrought," even if it pricked my pride.

With haughty unconcern I continued to focus my attention on Pendel while Sarah poured hot water into the basin and Tom shoveled hot coals from a bucket into my stove and then locked it again. Pendel was the only one who wasn't afraid of me, and thus his presence was soothing. The sad truth was, the more I knew someone disliked or feared me, the worse my illness became in reaction, thus substantiating their fears—a truly vicious circle I was powerless to escape.

"Your medicine, my lord."

He held out the silver tray bearing the small crystal cordial glass containing my daily potion, and I took it dutifully. The bitterness of the preparation clung to my tongue, despite the initial sweetness of the brandy, but Pendel always had my tea ready to wash it down.

"Thank you, Pendel," I said, taking the cup and saucer.

"My lord," he replied with a customary bow of his head.

I sipped my tea as Sarah collected my clothes from the day before and laid out fresh ones. She coughed several times while she worked, ducking her head and throwing apologetic glances in Pendel's direction, and as soon as she was given leave by Pendel, she scurried from the room with her hand covering her mouth. I waited for Tom to follow her before I spoke again.

"Is Sarah ill?"

"She assures me it is only a flare-up of her asthma, my lord, nothing to concern yourself over. The doctor told her all of his patients with respiratory ailments are suffering more than usual this winter. He believes it may have something to do with the fog."

"If she needs to rest, we can certainly do without her for a few days."

"Thank you, my lord. We have all encouraged her to rest, but she insists it isn't necessary. We will keep a close eye on her, however."

"Good. Did Tom give any reason for his presence in the upper hall last night?"

"He said he was chasing a rat when he saw what he thought to be a man going into one of the rooms."

"And you believe him?"

"I did not say that, my lord, but he did seem quite shaken by whatever it was he saw."

I sighed, not as interested as I should be in what happened in my own house, but I could blame at least some of that on the soporific effects of my medicine. "Will you dismiss him, then?"

"I wished to know my lord's thoughts on the matter first."

I struggled with the lethargy that stole over me, trying to remain present in the conversation for Pendel's sake. I loved that he fought so hard to preserve my dignity, but we both knew I had no real authority. My uncle made all the decisions that mattered, and Pendel would consult him before taking any action, no matter what my feelings were. It was only a token gesture to ask my opinion.

But what was nobility, if not some grand illusion that the world subscribed to? Pendel would continue to hold true to that illusion until the day I died, and I supposed I would play my part if only for my love of him.

"I think we should give Tom another chance… after, perhaps, a reminder of his position in the house," I replied with all the authority I could muster, though it was spoiled by a yawn I could not stifle.

"Very good. Is there anything else you need?"

"No, thank you. I still have the books from Mr. Fuller's packet to keep me company. I'll ring if I need anything more."

"Yes, my lord."

As I struggled to keep my eyes open, I saw the sadness creep into Pendel's countenance that often showed itself when he thought I couldn't see. As always, I wished I could erase that sadness and be the man worthy of Pendel's loyalty and dedication, but I was not. I was damaged. I was a man who could not trust his own mind, no matter how hard I wished it weren't so.

After Pendel left and locked the door behind him, I spent many hours hovering in the half sleep my medicine provided. The wash water Sarah had brought turned cold in the ewer before I managed to struggle out of bed. Even then, I passed over it and the fresh clothes she'd brought me with barely a glance. I shuffled to my armchair in front of the hearth and settled beneath a lap quilt, still in my midnight blue velvet dressing gown and nightshirt from yesterday. I tried to read more of my book, but the letters swam in the cold gray light, and I must have fallen asleep again. I didn't wake until the great clock in the downstairs hall chimed two in the afternoon, along with the faint ringing of the Great Bell, Big Ben, in the distance.

Feeling a little less lethargic, I moved to my washstand and bathed with the icy water. Shivering, I donned clean stockings, underclothing, striped wool trousers, shirt, braces, waistcoat, lounge jacket, and tie before pulling my dressing gown over the lot again. Now properly dressed, I rang for the servants, and Pendel arrived soon after with a lamp and a tray of sandwiches and fresh pot of steaming tea. I gratefully warmed my hands on the teacup he gave me while Tom fed the fire, Sarah collected my soiled nightclothes and wash water, and Pendel cleaned up my mostly untouched breakfast tray.

As always, I waited until the two underservants left before I conferred with Pendel. This time, when he asked if there would be anything else, I gathered my courage and said, "Yes. I'd like you to leave the lamp. What little sun there is beyond the fog will be gone in only a few hours. My eyes are a bit tired, but I'd still like to read this evening."

To his credit, Pendel only hesitated a moment before he nodded. "Of course, my lord. If that will be all?"

"Yes, nothing more until dinner. Thank you."

He bowed his way out and locked the door again, but the room was a little less depressing with the warm flicker of lamplight to keep me company. Fox, whatever he was, had been right. I shouldn't have to languish in the dark. It was such a simple thing to ask for a lamp to read by in the evenings, particularly in winter when the sun went down so early. I wasn't sure why I hadn't done it before, and that lapse bothered me.

I tried to read for a time, but my visitation from the night before kept intruding on my thoughts. Fox's voice, his very solid weight on my bed, the warm silk of his sleeve under my fingers, and his ridiculous and strange tale all replayed in my mind. He'd made me laugh for the first time in longer than I could remember, and I smiled as I strained to recall every detail of our conversation. Try as I might, though, I could not stop his last words to me from overshadowing all the rest, and my smile soon fell away as I stared raptly at the lamp by my side.

"The lord and master of the manor should not be kept in the dark in his own house."

The words began as barely a whisper but eventually rang out in a continuous refrain in my head, no matter how I tried to distract myself. The flickering light from the glass globe danced over the rich red and gold tones of my Aubusson rug and the midnight folds of my dressing gown. It played across my perfectly appointed bookshelves, where every volume had been wrapped in identical gold-embossed paper, and every delicate porcelain figure and bit of statuary had been placed with exacting precision. All of this should have comforted me. Everything was in its place and as it should be.

"The lord and master of the manor should not be kept in the dark in his own house."

Forcing myself not to look at the lamp again, I began reciting the titles of the books on my shelves. The paper they were wrapped in disguised their bindings, but I knew every one of them by heart in the exact order I'd placed them—that being the order I'd received them, so I didn't have to change it with each new edition Mr. Fuller sent in my packet.

Starting with the books my mother and father had given me, I recited, "*The Children of the New Forest* by Captain Marryat, *The Little Duke* by Charlotte M. Yonge, *Hans Brinker, or The Silver Skates* by Mary Mapes Dodge, *Alice's Adventures in Wonderland* by Lewis Carroll...."

Why shouldn't I have a lamp at night as well?

I haven't had an "unfortunate episode" in many years.

I might not be well, but I should think I could be trusted not to burn down my own house after all this time. The master of the house shouldn't be left in the dark. That's not right. I'll ask Pendel to leave the lamp. I must do it tonight.... I should not be kept in the dark in my own house.

With a growl of frustration, I dragged my hands down my face. Clearly my little recitation ritual would not be enough to distract me. After throwing off my lap quilt, I stood and removed my dressing gown and jacket. I strode to the small open space in front of the door that Fox had disappeared through the night before and began my daily exercises. Breathing forcefully, I pumped my arms and kicked my legs high. I bent and touched my toes and twisted at the waist. I even jogged in place until I was quite out of breath, but I could not escape the flickering light of that lamp. It caught my eye at every turn, and my anxiety grew along with my frustration.

Finally I donned my jacket and dressing gown again and moved to my pianoforte, hoping to lose myself in music. It often worked when all else failed. I pounded on the keys for what seemed like hours, moving erratically from composition to composition. Agitated and restless as I was, I must have played too loudly, for Pendel arrived early with my dinner, startling me out of my state and sending me in a near panic because I was not yet prepared for the confrontation over the lamp.

I sat frozen on the bench while Pendel fussed with my dinner tray and Tom nervously tended my fire. As soon as Tom finished his duties, he scurried out of the room, barely waiting for a nod from Pendel and moving surprisingly quickly for someone so large.

But with Pendel hovering anxiously over me and the looks Tom had given me before he left, my nerves were at their limit. I barely contained myself until Tom was gone. The instant he stepped outside the door, I shot to my feet and paced in front of my newly stoked fire. Pendel's countenance was as indecipherable as ever, but his eyes watched me as if I might sprout fur and teeth at any moment, which only made my nerves worse. Add to that the fact that my current state would by no means help me make my case, and I almost gave up the scheme entirely. The only thing that stopped me was Fox's voice in my head.

Stuffing my hands into the pockets of my dressing gown to keep from pulling my hair, I clenched my teeth and took several deep breaths.

"Thank you, Pendel. Give my compliments to Mrs. Peeble," I managed by rote, my voice betraying only the tiniest of tremors.

"Certainly, my lord."

Pendel bowed, seeming content to forgo mentioning my obvious state, but when he reached for the lamp, I lurched forward.

"No. Leave the lamp," I ordered breathlessly.

He froze with his hand on its base and turned concerned brown eyes toward me. "My lord?"

"The lord and master of the manor should not be kept in the dark in his own house," I repeated mechanically from the litany in my head.

Pendel's expression grew pained. He lifted a hand as if to touch me but stopped halfway. His aborted gesture and strained countenance sent a stab of regret through me for making his work more difficult than it already was, but I *needed* the lamp.

It was all I could think about.

His hand dropped to his side, and in a quiet voice filled with regret, he said, "Forgive me, my lord, but I thought you, the doctor, and your uncle agreed it would be safer and more calming for you not to have a lamp at night, when the rest of the house was asleep."

He chose his words so carefully I began to think I might just be the wounded animal he took me for. I worried my lower lip and fisted my hands in my pockets. Clenching my jaw to keep from shouting at him, I took a few more deep breaths through my nose—as I'd been taught—and tried to reason beyond the litany in my head.

If I didn't have the lamp, it wouldn't be the end of the world. Tonight would only be as every other night. I didn't *need* it. I wanted it. The lamp was only symbolic of a greater discontent with a life I had so little control over. I didn't have to let the voices win. I was a Middleton. I was made of sterner stuff than this. I was a gentleman, and gentlemen didn't fall to pieces over something so common as a lamp.

"Perhaps I should fetch another draught of my lord's medicine if he is feeling unwell?" Pendel asked with great care, his faded brown eyes pleading with me.

Over his shoulder, a shifting gray-white shape caught my eye as the lady in white materialized in the corner by my window seat, but I shut my eyes against her. The last thing I needed was another of my visions plaguing me.

I was frightening the one man in the world who put my welfare above anything else, even his own. The poor man was constantly torn between keeping me happy and keeping me safe, without me making the task more difficult. The appearance of the lady usually heralded the arrival of others. I needed to put a stop to this madness now or it would only get worse. The medicine quieted the voices and the visions… for a while, anyway. I would sleep if I took it, and that wasn't such a horrible thing.

After a few more careful breaths, I nodded in defeat.

"Perhaps my lord might do some of his exercises while I prepare it? I shall leave you the lamp and return shortly?"

"Yes. Thank you, Pendel," I replied shakily and with as much dignity as I could muster.

He left and locked the door behind him as always, and I loosened my necktie and began the forms I'd done that afternoon. By the time I'd begun jogging in place, counting off the seconds to drown out the voices in my head, Pendel returned with my glass of laudanum.

I couldn't look him in the eye as I drank the potion, but I did manage to mumble a shamed apology for my behavior, once I'd finished the draught.

"You have no reason to apologize, my lord. You should perhaps eat some of your dinner before it turns cold, though. I'll leave you the lamp for a little while longer and return for it before I go to bed, if that is acceptable?"

After the drug puts me to sleep, you mean.

I blew out a weary breath and smiled for him. "Yes, thank you."

Before he closed the door behind him, Pendel said, "I believe we expect your uncle's visit tomorrow. Perhaps you could discuss the matter with him, and he can consult the doctor."

"Yes, perhaps. Thank you."

Pendel would more than likely tell my uncle of my lapse the moment he entered the house, and the doctor would be forthcoming whether I willed or no.

I ate mechanically, forcing down each bite. Pendel would worry even more if I left my plate untouched. I was certain the glazed chicken and roasted root vegetables Mrs. Peebles had prepared were delicious, but I hardly tasted them. The medicine frequently ruined my appetite, and I ate as a matter of course rather than finding any true enjoyment in it. I did not finish my plate before my eyelids became so heavy I couldn't keep them open. I must have made it to my bed before I fell asleep, because that is where I woke sometime later in the dark.

Judging by the healthy orange glow from the stove, my fire had been restocked with coal and my dinner had been removed, but the lamp was gone. Having taken a second draught of my medicine, I could not dredge up much vexation over its loss. The potion made any emotions I might have had dull and meaningless and filled my head with cotton. I supposed that was all to the good. I couldn't distress anyone else in this state, nor could I harm myself.

LATE IN the night, my medicine wore off enough that I managed to drag myself from my bed to make my nest by the hearth. The faint glow of the coals gave me just enough light to read by, if I used the bellows from time to time, but again my novel could not hold my interest. Listless and melancholy as I was, every little creak and moan of the old house made me set the book aside and search the darkness for any sign of Fox's return. Of all the visions I'd had over the years, Fox was the only one I'd ever actually wanted to return. He hadn't frightened me or made me feel ashamed, even when he'd pushed for me to talk of things I didn't want to.

And he'd made me laugh. It was such a simple thing, but I'd forgotten how good it felt to laugh.

I was truly ill. I had to be where I was. The outside world terrified me, after all these years alone. I could not manage in society as I was, but I was still a man beneath the madness. I still felt loneliness. Perhaps, if the only companionship I could have was that created from my own mind, that wasn't the end of the world. I harmed no one by talking to myself in the confines of my rooms. And as long as I understood that it was all a fantasy, surely I could be forgiven that one little lapse.

Why did Fox not come?

Chapter Three

THE NEXT morning, I was still in my nest of blankets by the hearth when Pendel arrived with my breakfast and my medicine. In my obsession over my latest vision, I'd forgotten Pendel's reminder of my uncle's visit and thus that Pendel would be attending me earlier than usual. On visit days, we timed my dose so the medicine would have worn off enough for me to be coherent by the time my uncle arrived but still lingered enough that we wouldn't have to worry about me suffering too many emotional outbursts should I become agitated.

I rose swiftly and stumbled to my chair, feeling disgruntled and still a bit muddled from the little sleep I'd managed. I dutifully swallowed the draught Pendel offered and tried to infuse a little dignity in my manner while I sipped my tea and waited for Sarah to remake my bed and Tom to tend my fire. Pendel's concerned frown seemed more for me than Sarah's cough as he also waited for them to finish, but I pretended not to notice until the other two servants had made their exit.

"I am well enough, Pendel. Do not concern yourself," I said, giving him as reassuring a smile as I could dredge up. "I am only a little tired. I shall eat my breakfast and retire for a while. Please have Tom bring up more hot water an hour before tea, and I promise you I will be dressed and ready to meet with my uncle when he arrives."

"Very good, my lord."

The crease between his brows did not ease, but he bowed and took his leave. After the lock clicked in place, I shuffled to my newly remade bed, kicked off my slippers and collapsed for another few hours of floating in oblivion. I must have slept, but I hardly felt as if I'd closed my eyes before Pendel was knocking on my door again with Tom in tow.

The faint chime of the front bell echoed through the house a quarter of an hour after I'd finished dressing. I tugged my waistcoat to straighten it, grabbed the small leather ledger I kept for my uncle's visits, and moved to my door to await my servants. Like Pendel, my uncle preferred to maintain the illusion that I was still master of my house, and so he rang instead of simply entering as surely was his right. I thought it a bit silly, but the bell did give me some warning to expect Pendel's knock.

"Your uncle has arrived, my lord, and he is awaiting you in the library."

My smile was genuine this time as Pendel unlocked the door and held it open for me. Uncle Oscar did not like to meet in my rooms, preferring instead the downstairs library, despite Dr. Payne's cautions about overexcitement. I didn't know why my uncle disliked my rooms so much, but his visits occasioned the only times I was allowed to leave them, so I was hardly going to protest the welcome change of scenery. The library had an open fireplace, no bars on the windows, and no locked doors—a welcome change indeed.

Pendel and Tom fell into step behind me as I trod the familiar path. The doors I passed on the way to the stairs were all closed, the rooms long ago shut up and the furniture draped in white cloth. The hall was dark but for the lamp Pendel carried. The wavering light made the shadows dance, and I did my best to ignore the ones that moved without benefit of lamplight, in hopes they would ignore me as well.

At the top of the stairs, the gloom was only partially alleviated by the great, three-storied bank of windows above the front doors. The fog had still not lifted, and I could see nothing but shifting pearly gray and white beyond the enormous glass panes. With nothing much to see there, I had to content myself with following the glint of lamplight off polished carved oak banisters, railings, and paneling. As a rule, I avoided the paintings that adorned nearly every square inch of the stairwell. The figures in them tended to shift and move with a general air of menace or disappointment when I looked too closely, and I hardly needed the added strain on my nerves. I already knew I was not the pinnacle of Middleton breeding. I had no need of their frowning faces to remind me of that fact.

Despite the chafing presence of Tom hovering nervously behind us—in case I decided to make a mad dash for freedom, I suppose—I smiled happily when Pendel opened the library doors and announced me. I had wondered if word of my outburst from yesterday might make my uncle change his mind about our meeting today, but it had not, and I was very glad to see him.

Uncle Oscar levered his bulk out of one of the comfortably overstuffed leather chairs by the fire and came forward to take my hand.

We were of a height, which was neither tall nor short, though Oscar had begun to thicken considerably around the middle as the years passed. We shared the same blue eyes and unruly blond hair that marked us as Middletons. His was thinning at the crown now, but he'd made up for it by growing a truly magnificent mustache. It gave me hope that I, one day, might have more than a few thin wisps of dark blond hair on my chin and above my lip for Pendel to shave.

I wasn't allowed the razor on my own.

"Arthur, my boy, good to see you. You are well?"

If not for the slight faltering of his smile and quick dart of his gaze to Pendel, I could have almost believed we were any other uncle and nephew about to enjoy tea together. The hovering bulk of Tom in the hall also somewhat damaged that illusion, but I lifted my chin and pressed on as cheerfully as I could with the words I knew I was supposed to say. I could manage that much with family at least.

"I am well, Uncle. And you?"

"Quite well. Quite well. No need to hang about in the doorway when there's a warm fire waiting, eh?"

He turned and hurried back to his usual chair by the hearth, and I gratefully followed and took mine, while Pendel rang for our tea.

"So, my boy, have you read anything truly riveting or educational since last we met?" Uncle Oscar began our conversation as he always did. He and I both knew he had no real love of literature, either low- or highbrow, but it was our little ritual just the same, familiar and comforting.

"I've nearly finished *Natural History Rambles: Lakes and Rivers* by Charles Napier. I'm finding it quite edifying."

"Good. Good."

It wasn't a lie, exactly.

I was slogging through it, page by page, and I did enjoy reading about birds and plants in hopes I might one day see them for myself. I merely omitted any mention of the hours I'd spent immersed in the penny horribles and novels Mr. Fuller included in my weekly packet, which Pendel conveniently overlooked. Dr. Payne had been quite adamant about limiting my exposure to anything that might "upset" me, and while my uncle had insisted I be allowed access to newspapers so I would not be completely ignorant of the world, I doubted he would defend my penchant for novels with the same zeal. Still, neither Pendel nor Uncle

Oscar questioned what my packets contained, and Uncle Oscar did not look too closely at the bill from Mr. Fuller's shop—as long as I remained happy and calm.

To fill the silence, I rattled away about the book, the unrelenting fog, and interesting bits from *The Times*. While I spoke, Sarah arrived with the tray, and Pendel poured our tea. As always, Uncle Oscar mostly nodded and grunted between bites of sandwiches or cake but said little of note. He was not simple by any stretch of the imagination, but he was a man of few words. He was more keen on action than conversation—a true country gentleman in his love of hunts and horses and hounds. He was content to listen to me prattle away, as long as I took a few bites of the aforementioned sandwiches and cakes to assure him that I was eating properly. I had so little conversation that I'm sure I overdid it whenever he came, but he never censured me for it.

With long-practiced ease, Pendel knew the exact moment when Uncle Oscar finished eating and was ready for our tea to be removed. At Pendel's silent signal, Sarah took the tray away, and Tom moved the small table closer, onto which Uncle Oscar placed his ledgers. I retrieved my ledger from beside my chair and the business portion of our meeting began. I listened dutifully and copied down all the relevant information as he reviewed the estate's finances and then moved on to a detailed account of all the changes in our investments since last time. In truth, they were *our* investments only in as much as I held the title and my name and signature were needed on the documents, but the effort was all my uncle's. He could have long ago had me declared *non compos mentis*, had me locked in an asylum—as Dr. Payne had frequently recommended—and taken over everything. His life would have been so much easier if he had. But he hadn't, and I was grateful for that every day. Even on the days when the walls of my room closed in on me and I cursed God for the way I was, I never cursed my uncle.

"*You* are Lord Campden! The estate is yours, not mine. The capital for these investments came from that which your father left you. I am merely custodian of it until you are well enough to take your rightful place," he had insisted, the one and only time I'd been brave enough to give voice to the terrible guilt and shame inside me. His face had been quite purple, his breath uneven, and his frown thunderous. I'd never dared to broach the subject again, but we both knew he was the one and only architect of our estate's successes. If it had been up to me alone, there would likely not have been an estate left for anyone.

"As I said last month, the rail shares continue to perform quite well, and with the good harvest last fall and increased income from your tenants, we should be able to proceed with the improvements we planned on the house as soon as the weather allows," Oscar finished with a pleased smile.

I nodded dumbly and tried to return that smile. I hadn't seen my estate in nearly a decade. I had a few fond memories of it as a child, but with all my uncle had done to it since then, I probably wouldn't recognize it now. It was his country home, no matter what the official record said.

Uncle Oscar's smile faded, and after a quick glance at his pocket watch, he snapped his ledgers closed, levered himself out of his seat, and cleared his throat.

"'Tis time I must be leaving you, lad. I have calls I must make, now that I'm in town," he said rather quickly as he patted his ledgers, indicating what most of those calls would be concerning, before heading for the door. Pendel opened it, but Uncle Oscar hovered on the threshold. He turned back to me and cleared his throat again. "Am I right in understanding that a visit from Dr. Payne may be in order?" he asked, not quite looking at me.

He always waited to bring up any uncomfortable business until just before his departure. I suppose I couldn't blame him for that. If I could, I'd want to run away from me as well.

Straightening my shoulders and lifting my chin, I said, "I don't think so, Uncle. I was a little out of sorts the other night, but nothing an extra dose of my medicine couldn't cure." My palms were damp and my chest tight as I drew on what little courage I had left to broach the subject calmly. "I… I did want to ask… that is to say, I have not been overly unwell for some time now, and given that my medicine makes me sleep so much of the day away and the nights are so very long, I thought it might be better if I had some light to read by, so I need not strain my eyes reading in the dark."

I had rehearsed what I would say to him several times as I'd dressed that afternoon, but when the time came, I stammered and gibbered like the madman I was. Clenching my fists and my jaw in frustration and disappointment, I waited while my uncle exchanged a worried glance with Pendel.

"Dr. Payne—"

"I know what Dr. Payne recommended, Uncle," I interrupted breathlessly, trying my speech again, though I could feel my cheeks flaming. "But I cannot sleep all the time. And if I must have the medicine to keep me calm during the day and I'm left with hours and hours of darkness to while away… don't you see, any man would go m—" I drew in a quick breath. "Any man would have difficulty filling those hours without light to see by, especially with this damned fog covering the sky, day after dreary day."

I held my breath as my uncle pursed his lips and slid his glance first to Pendel and then to the open door next to him. He clearly wished to be anywhere but where he was, and shame knifed through me.

Silence fell heavy and thick in the room, and I had to tuck my thumbs in my waistcoat pockets to keep from reaching for my hair or hugging myself like a chastised child.

"Perhaps I might make a suggestion, my lord," Pendel interjected quietly.

Uncle Oscar blew out a breath and turned to Pendel, his relief palpable. "Yes?"

"Perhaps I might suggest a similar contrivance to his lordship's coal stove be found for a candle lantern, thus diminishing any concerns should the lamp or candle get knocked over or left to burn if he falls asleep. We could try it for a short time, and if nothing untoward happens, and his illness is not exacerbated, we might continue. Or if his troubles are aggravated, of course, we could then send for Dr. Payne."

And if I become unhinged and decide to set the drapes afire, I'll have a damnable time getting at the flame.

I hoped my smile showed only relief as I turned hopeful eyes to my uncle and waited.

"That sounds just the ticket, Pendel, thank you. You have my leave to procure such an item. Worry not over the cost," he said with a negligent wave of his hand as he hurried through the door.

In his relief to be done with the conversation and away from me, my uncle did not make even the pretense of including me in the decision, but I didn't mind. I would have my light, and I wouldn't have to upset either myself or anyone else over the subject again. I might've hugged

Pendel in that moment if I didn't know the poor man would've been scandalized by such a gesture.

I followed my uncle down the great entry hall to the front doors, where I waited while Pendel brought Uncle Oscar's coat, hat, scarf, and gloves and helped him into them. My heartbeat was still a little erratic, my clothes clammy against my skin, but the tightness in my chest was gone, and my smile was genuine as I shook his hand and then watched him descend the front steps and climb into a waiting carriage. My smile remained even as the waiting mist swallowed the carriage, despite the fact that it signaled the end of his visit and I would be returned to my rooms.

Tom hovered nervously behind me while the door remained open. I could hear him shifting from foot to foot as if ready to leap into action at the slightest provocation, but I was too happy to pay him much mind. I had managed a victory of sorts. It was a small one and owed most of its success to Pendel, but I would get what I wanted, and I hadn't made a complete spectacle of myself in the bargain.

Bravo, Arthur, you didn't fall apart. Just imagine what you won't do next.

I resisted the urge to roll my eyes at myself as I led the way back up the stairs to the dark, lonely hall that harbored my rooms.

Chapter Four

My happiness faded over the next two nights spent alone in the darkness. I tried to be patient and understanding, but anticipation and the endless cold and dreary fog wore on my nerves. I soon began to question whether I would receive my lanterns at all, or if Pendel and my uncle were lying to me merely to put me off in hopes I would forget.

The thoughts were ungenerous, and I knew them for what they were—my illness at work—but that didn't lessen their volume nor the weight on my chest as I prowled my rooms like a caged animal all night, seeking distraction.

"Still nothing?" I bit out through clenched teeth on the third morning, after yet another sleepless night.

At a look from Pendel, I clamped my mouth shut and paced the floor while Sarah and Tom hurriedly finished their duties and scurried from the room like the hounds of hell were on their heels.

"I am sorry, my lord," Pendel replied when we were alone. He approached me so slowly and carefully it grated on my nerves. "I believe we have at last found something that might work in a shop of goods from the Orient, but, uh, *alterations* needed to be made. The merchant assured me they would be ready today. Tom will go and fetch them as soon as he is done with his duties here, and he will bring them back straightaway."

I took a deep breath and blew it out, trying for calm. I was the one who was out of sorts and being childish and difficult. None of this was Pendel's fault. If I weren't so ill and such a burden, none of this would be necessary at all. He was doing his best for me, the same as he always had.

"Forgive me my ill temper, Pendel. I have not been sleeping well."

"Of course, my lord."

Unflappable and loyal as ever, he held out the tray with my medicine, and for once, I drank it gratefully. I wanted the temporary oblivion it granted. I should have rung for it in the night as well, when the strain and the noises in my head became too much, but I hated the way it made me feel, and I had more pride than sense sometimes.

"I hope to sleep for a time, but do feel free to wake me when the lanterns arrive," I said with as much dignity as I could muster after washing the bitterness down with a swallow of tea.

"I will, my lord. Sleep well."

"Thank you."

I allowed the medicine to draw me under, exhaustion finally catching up with me, and I slept until Pendel knocked sometime in the afternoon. Despite the lingering effects of my medicine, I leapt from my chair the second I heard the key in the lock. At first I saw only Pendel carrying my tea and my heart fell, but then I spotted Tom's wheat-colored curls beyond Pendel's shoulders, and I could hardly wait for Pendel to move out of the way. With an indulgent twist of his wrinkled lips, Pendel stepped to the side, and Tom lumbered toward the fire carrying my heart's desire.

Uncaring of my dignity, I rushed over like it was Christmas morning and I was a child about to be given sweets for the first time. Tom set one lamp on the small table by my chair and the other on the hearth before leaving the room again, I assumed to fill the coal bucket for my fire.

Forgetting my manners, I ignored Pendel completely and ran my hands over the newest additions to my rooms. They certainly were strange little things, squat cylinders on four tiny legs with round flat bonnets on top. The metal scrolled around the cylinders in an ornate vine pattern through which the light could shine but the candle could not be reached. A small door on one side held a lock, obviously a recent addition and at odds with the pretty design. It served as a douse of cold water over my excitement. These were not simply the fashionable oriental curiosities that the papers said were all the rage now with collectors. The addition of the locks more than likely ruined whatever value the lanterns might have had. But despite those flaws, they were mine, and they would chase away the dark. Therefore, they were beautiful in my eyes.

When Tom returned with the coal bucket and began feeding my fire, I stepped away from my inspection of the second lantern on the hearth to give him room. I smiled as the weight that had been pressing on my chest eased and the nagging voice in the back of my mind was finally silenced. "Thank you, Pendel, and you, Tom. I am most pleased with them."

Pendel simply nodded, but Tom jerked and stared at me before ducking his head and mumbling something I couldn't quite catch. I rarely spoke to him, so his reaction should not have been surprising—or irritating—but I was still a little on edge and had to fight to keep from frowning at him.

Sarah had entered while I was lost in my inspection, and once my bed was made, fresh clothes were laid out, my pitcher filled with hot water for washing, and my stove fed, both underservants left.

"Is there anything else, my lord?" Pendel asked as he poured and handed me my tea.

"No, thank you, Pendel."

With a short bow, he was gone too, but this time, I barely heard the lock click. Alone again, I sat in my chair and ran my hands over the cold metal design on the lantern next to me and smiled. My hand never left its surface the entire time I drank my tea and nibbled on sandwiches. I desperately wanted to see them lit, but nights were very long in January, and the gray light outside had not yet turned to black. I didn't want to waste an inch of candle before I had to. I could of course ring to have the candles replaced in the night, but despite the way the underservants looked at me, I was not a cruel or harsh master. I did my best never to make unreasonable demands on any of them.

Eventually, I was able to step away from my lanterns for a time. In the hours before dark, I flitted from one thing to the next, but nothing could hold my attention long. I played a little Chopin on my pianoforte. I tried to read my novel again. I pulled out my watercolors and fussed with a landscape I had started before winter, but the little light that came through my windows was ugly and weak, and even the bright colors of the paints couldn't inspire me.

In the end, I grew desperate enough to venture up to my conservatory garden—such as it was in the middle of winter. My coat, scarf, gloves, and hat were all waiting for me on hooks in the stairwell, but even with them, the cold drove me back to my fire all too soon. Thankfully, Pendel waited with warm stew and a mug of hot chocolate on my return.

"Thank you." The depth of my gratitude as I wrapped my frozen hands around the warm mug must have been plain, because Pendel's thin lips curved slightly, indicating he was pleased.

Tom added coal to the fire as I sank into my chair, and Pendel draped a quilt over my lap, all the while fussing like a mother hen. I bore it stoically, with the dignity expected of a Middleton, though I secretly enjoyed the attention. While Pendel tidied my room, I sipped at my chocolate, not for the first time wishing I could bid Pendel to stay and sit with me for a while. But it was not our way, and he had duties to attend to elsewhere. I would not burden him simply because I was bored and impatient for night to come.

After Pendel left me alone again and I was warmed all the way through by my meal and the chocolate, I was able to settle into my book for a time, but my gaze frequently returned to the lanterns despite my best efforts. By the time the gray mist beyond my window had turned to black, I'd managed to get through a few chapters, but I had also memorized every pit in the metal and every elegantly curved line of the screens.

Pendel and Tom finally returned, and while Tom saw to my fire, Pendel at last asked the question I'd been dying to hear all day. "Shall I light your lanterns for you now, my lord?"

"Yes! Please do!"

I curbed the desire to leap out of my chair at the prospect, but only just barely, and I still managed to spill a bit of my chocolate on the lap quilt in my enthusiasm. Pendel gave me a slight frown as he lifted the heavy key ring from his belt, and Tom lumbered out of the room with his gaze firmly fixed on his boots. I could read Pendel's face better than most, and I thought perhaps his frown was more of concern than censure, but I was never quite certain. Chastened, I set my chocolate aside and folded my hands in my lap as I attempted an air of bored unconcern.

As the first and then the second lantern bloomed with light, I felt an equal blooming in my chest. The shadows and gray-black gloom of my rooms receded, replaced by warm gold scrolling patterns of light across my ceiling and walls. In the flicker of the flame, they danced and writhed, like leafy vines in a breeze, and I was enraptured.

"Beautiful," I whispered.

I had not meant to say the word aloud, but I didn't regret it when Pendel's expression softened. He closed the little doors on the lanterns and locked them, the new keys adding yet more weight to the enormous ring he carried with him at all times, but I tried not to dwell on that.

I was happy in that moment. It would have to be enough.

"Do you have need of anything else, my lord?"

"No. Thank you, Pendel. That will be all."

Drawn to the flickering flames like a moth, I ran my hands over the warming metal, teasing new patterns of light and shadow as I covered and uncovered parts of the design. A droll and disapproving inner voice, sounding a good deal like my mother, told me I was making a fuss over nothing, but I ignored it. Beyond the few unexceptional paintings and sketches I'd produced and whatever arrived in my packets from Mr. Fuller's shop, I had so little that was new in my sanctuary. I marveled at the craftsmanship and skill it must have taken to produce such lovely things.

More and more often the papers spoke of the wonders discovered as Britain's colonies grew in Asia. Collecting delicate china and exotic art was the new done thing for anyone who was anyone. Now I had a bit of the Orient in my rooms, a bit of craftsmanship from thousands of miles away, just like everyone else. It was awe-inspiring to think how far they'd come.

Careful not to upset the candle inside, I carried the second lamp from its place by my chair and set it next to the other on the marble hearth. Undoing Sarah's work from earlier, I pulled the blankets from my bed and created my nest on the floor in front of the stove. Lying on my back, nestled in my blankets, I watched the flickering vines dance across my ceiling for a long time, feeling some measure of peace steal over me until I was nearly moved to tears.

"You feel things too deeply, Arthur. You mustn't take everything so much to heart. It isn't good for your health."

My mother's voice rang in my ears so clear she could have been in the room with me.

I closed my eyes and scrubbed at them with the heels of my palms. She was right, of course. I would not cry over a couple of silly lanterns. I was a grown man now, not a child. If I wanted to be well, I couldn't give in to this flood of emotion inside me, even in the privacy of my rooms. I had to be strong like everyone else.

"I see the lord of the manor has acquired light at last, and what a peculiar light it is."

I swung toward the new voice with such force I nearly upset myself and almost knocked over the lantern closest to me with a carelessly flung elbow. "Fox?"

The man-shaped shadow just beyond the light from the lanterns expelled a dry chuckle. "Yes. That is the name I gave you."

"You came back!" In my excitement, I made no attempt to hide my delight, and my cheeks flamed as Fox chuckled again.

"At least I'm assured of my welcome this time."

"I'm sorry," I murmured, ducking my head. I knew how a gentleman was supposed to behave. Why could I not manage it even once when it counted?

"Don't apologize, Arthur," he said more gravely. "You are a breath of fresh air compared to what I am used to."

My blush deepened at the compliment, and I couldn't think of what to say next. Thankfully, after a long sigh, seemingly filled with meaning—which I could not decipher—Fox broke the silence. "Besides, if I am, as you say, a mere conjuring of your imagination, you have no need to apologize to me for anything, now do you?"

This time I was the one who chuckled. He made a good point. Why should I apologize to a creature of my own making? But good manners were the cornerstone of any gentleman, and I was a gentleman—sorry example of one or no.

"A true gentleman should behave as one no matter the situation he finds himself," I said, lifting my chin, despite the smile trying to force its way to my lips.

"Oh Lord, don't do that. I get enough of that from everyone else."

Grinning like a fool, I searched the shadows but could still see nothing of his face… if he even had one. I hoped he did. The faceless visions were always the most disturbing, and I was truly enjoying our conversation.

"Will you come into the light so I may see you properly?" I asked with some trepidation.

"In a moment. I'd like to keep my air of mystery a little longer. And besides, I haven't finished getting a good look at you."

I shifted uncomfortably. Even knowing he was only a figment of my imagination, I did not like being measured and inevitably found wanting.

I was healthy, at least my body was, but I had a looking glass and had read enough of the gossip rags and novels to know I did not cut a dashing figure. I was not overly tall nor broad shouldered—not like Tom anyway. I was pale in coloring and complexion, and not particularly striking of feature. My cheeks and chin were more cherubic than chiseled, my nose more pert than aquiline. I doubted I would leave any maiden fainting on her couch with a mere smile, even if I'd wanted to.

"Surely you've had plenty of time to see what little there is to see," I complained as the seconds dragged on.

"I fear I shall have to disagree with you there, but as I seem to be making you uncomfortable, I'll leave it for now."

"Thank you," I murmured.

His tone had lost some of its playfulness. I regretted that, but I truly hated being studied.

I sank back into my nest and drew the blankets around my shoulders again, essentially turning my back on him, ignoring the twinge to my conscience. Positioned as I was, he'd have to either come into the light or speak to the back of my head—thus, in my pique, making a lie of my earlier claims to gentlemanly behavior.

Fox remained quiet long enough I feared he'd gone, and I was on the verge of leaping to my feet with an apology when I heard the quiet rustle of cloth and the whisper of soft leather shoes crossing the floorboards.

He had come out of the shadows.

My chest tightened, but I only hesitated a moment before lifting my gaze to him. Standing with an arm casually braced on the back of my chair was the handsomest man I had ever laid eyes on. This was perhaps not a notable accomplishment, given the limited number of men I'd been allowed to see in my life, but my stomach flipped, and my face flushed, regardless.

He was tall. Even from my position on the floor, I could tell he was nearly a match for Tom in height. His frame was lean, outlined as it was beneath a strange black costume that hugged every line of him in a most shocking fashion. The supple black silk that clung to his broad shoulders and hard thighs was bound to his forearms and muscular calves by cords. A broad sash of the same black cinched the costume to his trim waist and supple suede boots covered his feet. I'd never seen or read of anything quite like it.

When I finally had the courage to meet his gaze, I found dark eyes twinkling down at me from beneath arched silver brows. His severe lips were softened by a smile, and not a hint of beard, mustache, or sideburn hid the strong line of his jaw. Thick silver hair crowned his head, making his age difficult to discern, given the scarcity of age lines on his face. For a moment, my fingers itched to know if that hair was as silken as it appeared, and I clenched my hands beneath my blankets, my mind shying away from that desire.

Still, I could not look away. I had made him devastatingly handsome for reasons only my damnably twisted mind could comprehend.

The creases around his mouth and at the corners of his eyes deepened the longer I watched him, but at some point, his eyes narrowed at me and his gaze became speculative rather than amused. His return scrutiny unnerved me enough that I dropped my gaze, and I drew my blankets more tightly around me, seeking comfort.

He moved again, and when I finally found the courage to look up, he'd settled in my chair.

"I wonder if you would mind terribly sharing one of those blankets with me. Your rooms are much warmer than it is beyond that door, but I'm still a bit chilled."

The teasing light still danced in his dark eyes, but his smile of gratitude seemed genuine when I tugged a blanket free of my nest and handed it to him.

"Thank you."

In the ensuing silence, I let my curiosity get the better of my manners.

"Why are you wearing that—that, whatever it is?" I asked, motioning to his strange and unnerving costume.

Fox finished tucking the blanket around his shoulders before he grinned at me. "Do you like it? It's something of my own design, borrowed from costumes and drawings from the Far East. It's surprisingly warm, allows for much freedom of movement, and the silk has a dull sheen that doesn't reflect the light—all very useful in my profession."

"It is quite... unusual."

He chuckled at my tone, his eyes sparkling charmingly in the candlelight. "But you didn't say whether or not you *liked* it," he teased.

My cheeks heated again, and I hoped the low light would hide some of my embarrassment. I didn't understand why the simplest of statements from this man made me blush like a maid. The question had been innocent enough, yet here I was, red-cheeked again. Uncle Oscar and Pendel would be appalled at my lack of aplomb.

"I hardly know what to make of it," I replied with as much tact as I could. "I have never seen its like before."

"Perhaps you would rather I scaled your tower in a dinner jacket and fine trousers instead?"

I frowned at him. "This is hardly a tower."

Fox kicked his legs out toward the fire, slouched against the back of my chair, and waved an indolent hand. "I beg to differ. You didn't have to climb it. This is a fearsome tower, and I have labored mightily—and at great risk I might add—to scale it. The least my fair Rapunzel can do in return is to reward my efforts with a sufficient amount of praise... or a brandy if you have one."

"I am no maiden in a tower, and you, sir, are most definitely no prince," I huffed, my pride stung.

Fox cocked an insolent eyebrow at me, but when I continued to glare, his grin faded. "Forgive me, sir. I was only teasing you. I am very aware that you are no maiden." He chuckled. "And, as you say, I am no prince."

Because of my illness, I often had difficulty deciphering the world of unspoken communication that lay beneath the words men used, but I thought I heard a bitterness underscoring his tone that intrigued me. So often my visions were simple, shallow things that screamed or whispered the same words over and over to me, or said nothing at all, only hovered. I opened my mouth to accept his apology with all the dignity I could muster, but I was silenced by a heavy sound from the hall and a shimmer of white beyond Fox's shoulder.

Thud. Scrape. Thud. Scrape.

It continued, drawing nearer.

Not now. Please go away.

I closed my eyes in irritation, willing the familiar sounds to cease, but they continued, drawing ever nearer until I could feel the vibration of the footfalls through the rug beneath me.

Not. Now.

Opening my eyes again, I turned to Fox, doing my best to pretend nothing was amiss, though my heart had kicked up, and the hairs on the back of my neck had risen. I liked to think my heart raced in anger and impatience, but those footfalls never failed to unnerve me, no matter how many times I'd heard them. I opened my mouth to continue our conversation despite the distraction, but closed it again when I got a good look at Fox's face. His dark eyes were wide and his indolent grin had fallen away completely, his complexion paler. He seemed on the verge of leaping from the chair.

"What is that?" he whispered.

"You can hear it too?" I asked, startled.

Fox leapt from the chair and headed for the door to the conservatory stairs.

"Wait! Where are you going?" I cried.

For the first time since we'd met, Fox looked at me as if I were mad. "I cannot be found here," he hissed, waving frantically in what I guessed was an effort to quiet me.

I struggled out of my nest and hurried to him. "Don't go. No one is there to see you. Please stay."

"No one is there? Then what is that?" Fox insisted, waving a hand to the door that led to the hall and the sounds beyond.

"It's nothing, truly. I—my visions don't normally hear one another. If I'd known, I would have warned you," I continued quickly, insinuating myself between him and the door. I placed my back against it through the drapes, so he couldn't get by me. "It's the same every time, has been for years, the footsteps, the strange scraping. If you were to look in the hall right now, you'd see nothing and no one, I promise you."

The familiar hollow moaning began, reverberating through the walls, and Fox's eyes opened wide enough I could see white all around his dark irises. "A spirit?" he asked in a hushed tone.

His urgency to escape seemed to have subsided, though his skin was still pale in the weak light. I relaxed and stepped away from the door. I even smiled a little. "If that is what you would like to call it. There are stories bandied about that Campden House is haunted. I've heard the servants in the gardens sometimes gossiping with the tradesmen or gardeners, and I believe Pendel had the devil of a time hiring servants in my parents' time, before... well, before my illness and confinement made a full staff unnecessary."

Fox still appeared unnerved as he hesitated by the door. I had a sudden intense urge to reach for his hand to comfort him and draw him back to the fire, but I quashed it. Firstly, it wasn't something a gentleman did with a man he'd just met. I was fairly certain of that. And honestly, I feared this time he might have no substance for me to hold on to, and he might disappear into a cloud of smoke if I tried. With my visions, I never knew what to expect.

The hollow moan turned into a chilling wail as it always did, and I shook my head.

"And they leave you alone up here with that?" he asked, aghast, wrapping his arms around himself.

I moved back to the fire and forced a smile for him that I hoped was soothing. "There are no spirits. Our neighbor, Holland House, has just as many stories told about it, but it's all nonsense—tales for children and servants' gossip. Those sounds are simply another manifestation of my illness. I am the only one who hears or sees them. Pendel or my uncle would have told me if they'd experienced anything of the kind themselves. They take excellent care of me and would not add to my troubles by keeping it from me."

"Are you certain of that?"

I frowned at him, offended for their sake. "What do you mean? Of course they would have told me. They've done everything in their power to help me, to keep me safe and as happy as possible, despite how tiresome I must be."

Fox pursed his lips and eyed the door suspiciously for a few more seconds, but when no other sounds disturbed the quiet night, his shoulders relaxed slightly. "As you say," he murmured, still sounding unconvinced. He slowly made his way back to my chair and pulled the blanket across his shoulders again, all the while casting nervous glances over his shoulder.

I had enjoyed his company thus far, but I did not like the insinuations regarding Pendel or my uncle, so I decided to change the subject. "The noises in the hall won't hurt you. I know them well, and they're always the same—except perhaps for the other night, when you appeared. But that was Tom in the upper hall for some reason I'm still not entirely certain of."

Fox grinned. "He was chasing me, actually. Damned bad luck on my part. I nearly tripped over him on my way to the stairs."

Tom would never have seen you. I chose not to voice that particular thought. There was no need to argue with my delusion.

"And this is what you hear, your hallucinations?" Fox asked into the brief silence.

"Yes." I tried to hold my head high, but speaking of my illness always made me want to shrink away.

"And what do you see?"

That question made me smile, and Fox gave me a puzzled look until his grin suddenly reappeared. "Other than myself, of course," he amended.

I had hoped our conversation would remain light and amusing, but my mind seemed to have other plans. Fox seemed bound and determined to have it out of me. There must have been a reason for that. I wished I knew what it was.

"Not all my visions are as well-formed as you," I began but then blushed as Fox's lip quirked and he raised a single silver brow. "I mean, mostly they flicker at the edges of my sight, or they're a shadow, a darkness within the darkness that neither speaks nor moves, or a diaphanous thing that hovers and then dissipates like smoke."

"And that in the hall? That seemed fairly well-formed at least from what I heard."

I shrugged. "It is nothing. It goes away soon enough."

He seemed to ponder that awhile before he said, "It certainly would've turned my hair white—if it weren't already—but you aren't afraid?"

For my pride, I was tempted to lie, but what would be the point? It seemed silly to put on a brave face when his good opinion would only be my good opinion of myself—meaningless really.

"I used to be. When I was a child, all I knew was fear. I spent many nights cowering and crying. But one can only do that for so long, and I'm no longer a child."

I saw pity in his eyes, and I did not like that, no matter if he were only a part of myself made manifest. He could pity the child I had been, but not the man I was. I lifted my chin and squared my shoulders again. "After a while, I became accustomed to the sounds and the visions. Years of practice and experience have somewhat inured me to them. I can ignore them most of the time. But when I am tired or distressed, it's more difficult, to be sure."

"You're a strong one, aren't you, Arthur Middleton?" he murmured.

Inordinately pleased by that statement, I flushed but still managed to keep my chin high as I shrugged. "I am Lord Campden."

"You are indeed," he replied with only a hint of the wry wit that seemed to color his every word and expression. "Perhaps more worthy of the title than most of the young bucks I see these days—pompous, dissolute, thick, worthless bloody jackanapes that they are."

My mouth fell open at his language and the venom in his tone. "But you said you were a gentleman. Wouldn't you count yourself in that number?"

Fox looked surprised for a moment, but then his lips split in a wide grin. "Oh, certainly. I'm the most worthless of the lot, to be sure. But at least I'm honest about it. I steal outright, rather than running up debts with honest tradesmen I never intend to repay or frittering away my tenants' hard-earned money in gambling hells and opium dens. I only steal from those who can afford it, I assure you. So there you have it. I'm an *honorable* gentleman thief."

He finished with a flourish of his hands and a seated bow, and I couldn't help but laugh. This was what I had hoped for when I'd wished for his return, this playful banter.

"Are you a Robin Hood, then? Do you rob the rich to give to the poor?"

His smile turned devilish as he leaned forward in the chair. "I suppose if one considers the fact that I spend a good deal of the wealth from the items I procure in pubs and bawdy houses in the East End, one might be able to make that connection."

"Oh, you're terrible," I exclaimed laughing and clapping my hands.

His grin broad, Fox settled back in his chair again and chuckled. "If I am, as you say, only a figment of your imagination, then I am only as terrible as you want me to be."

"Hardly," I shot back. "As I said before, my illness has a mind of its own. It isn't as if I want the horrible sounds in the hall or the walking nightmares of my visions. I cannot control them any more than I can control you."

I said it lightly, but Fox's smug grin died despite my tone. "I cannot imagine, Arthur, truly I cannot. I apologize for making light of it and for letting this charade go on too long. You must know I'm not really—"

"Don't do that," I interrupted, my own good humor fading. Before he could say any more, I rushed on. "I like that you tease me, the easy and carefree way you talk to me. I don't have anyone I can speak to like this. Pendel loves me as the master of the hall, but he is my servant and would not bridge that gap for anything. My uncle is the only family I have left, and he cares for me, but I make him uncomfortable, and I know I disappoint him. The only other intercourse I have is with Mr. Fuller at the bookshop, but we only exchange letters. It isn't the same as having a true friend to sit and talk with. I think that's why you're here, really, because I needed a friend, someone to laugh with, someone to tease me and to speak freely with me." Breaking away from the intensity of Fox's gaze, I allowed my eyes to roam the confines of my rooms as if I hadn't memorized ever nick in the floorboards or scratch on the walls years ago. Everything was exactly in its place, just as I needed it to be. "I may never be well enough to leave the confines of these rooms, but I think… I think if I had a friend, someone I could truly talk to, I could bear it." I smiled wryly as I turned back to meet his gaze. "Even if I must surrender to my illness enough to create such a friend for myself."

The smile he gave me in return was gentle but troubled. After a short silence, he said, "If that is truly what you wish, I can hardly deny you. You are unlike anyone I have ever met, young Arthur."

"I should not be surprised to hear that," I replied, regaining more of my good humor. "I hope, for my sake, that is a good thing."

He searched my face for a long time as if memorizing my features before he murmured, "I think it is quite a good thing."

Something in his look made my heart quicken and my stomach flutter. I tried to assure myself it was only the compliment, but I feared it was more.

Why had I made him so devilishly handsome?

"You are unlike any vision I've ever had before, so I suppose we are well matched in that regard."

As I'd hoped, Fox chuckled, and the intensity of his gaze abated. "Well, if I am here to amuse you and make your nights bearable, how about a little of that brandy I mentioned earlier so I can settle in properly?"

I winced as he searched the bookshelves along the walls and the dark corners, probably looking for a decanter. "I'm sorry. I haven't any spirits of any kind, brandy especially."

I made a face when I said that last, and Fox's eyebrows shot up.

"You don't like brandy? I'm not sure I can trust a man who doesn't like brandy," he said with a frown, his eyes glinting merrily.

"I am sorry. My daily medicine is cut with brandy to make it a little more palatable. I don't think I could stand the stuff on its own—too many unpleasant associations."

Fox waved a negligent hand. "Well, there's always whiskey, gin, a fine French wine, sherry, or champagne." He paused with his eyebrows lifted, waiting, but I could only shrug in return. I had not tried most of what he named, only watered wine with my dinner sometimes. "Port? Ale? Cider? Rum? Punch or dainty drinks?" he continued, his tone hopeful. At the shake of my head, he threw up his hands. "What on earth do you drink, then?"

He said it with such bewildered outrage I couldn't help but laugh. "Tea, coffee, hot chocolate, hot milk. In summer I have a little watered wine, or perhaps a cordial or lemonade sometimes."

Fox harrumphed, not looking at all pleased. "This is one of the great houses of Kensington. I did not make it far enough into the house to know for certain, but I would wager my fortune there is an extensive wine cellar, and yet they deprive you, the master of the house, of it entirely? Seems criminal, to my way of thinking. You should at least have a bottle to warm you up of a night, especially if they're going to leave you such a meager fire."

He seemed truly offended for me, but of course he was me—or a part, at any rate. I had not thought myself that discontented. Perhaps I was and had simply become accustomed to my lot, and sunken in melancholia, I hadn't the will to object. I had been listless of late, but I'd attributed it to the dark cold winter and that damnable fog.

"I believe there is a wine cellar," I said absently. "I remember, when my mother and father were alive, they would host stunning parties, and the servants would bring bottle after bottle up. I hid in the kitchens sometimes when nanny was cross with me, or I was dying of curiosity, and I'd see the servants coming up from the cellar."

"Wait, are you telling me you haven't seen the kitchens since you were a child?"

I bit my lip. "No. The… the fever that left me like this happened when I was only ten, and my parents died in a boating accident not long before my fourteenth birthday. I was… *unwell* after that and have been kept to my rooms mostly since."

"And you are how old now?"

"Twenty-four."

Fox leaned forward in his seat, his expression appalled. "Ten years? They've kept you locked up for ten years?"

"For my own good. For my safety and the safety of others," I defended.

"Safety from what?"

Agitated, I shot to my feet and paced by the fire. I thought I had made peace with my lot, but perhaps I'd been fooling myself. My muscles were tense now, and I could feel the pressure starting in my chest as I struggled to keep my breathing calm. "From shame, from embarrassment, from the strain on my nerves. It all gets so much worse when I am agitated. If I remain calm and I am left in peace, I am not overwhelmed by it and I can behave as a gentleman and peer of the realm should. But out there, I-I can't. It's too much. Too much noise. Too many people. Too many expectations and opportunities to fail and disgrace myself."

My scalp stung and when I looked down I found a few wisps of blond hair in my palm, glinting in the wavering light of the lanterns. I folded my arms across my chest and hugged myself as I took a few steadying breaths. When I opened my eyes again, Fox was standing in front of me, his handsome face tight with concern.

"Are you all right? I'm sorry. I didn't mean to upset you."

"I'm well enough," I replied, my voice shaking only a little.

He frowned at me. "Perhaps I should go."

"No! Don't do that." I reached for him, but stopped before I made contact. "Please."

He searched my face again, and eventually he sighed and said, "Forgive me for upsetting you. I spoke out of turn. I don't know you well enough to venture such opinions. But let me say this much. From the little we have spoken, you do not seem so wholly unwell to me, not so much that you would need to be kept to your rooms day and night." He paused, seeming to choose his words carefully, his tone quiet and soothing. "I will take your word for it that going out into the world would cause you undue strain, but I don't see why you cannot have the run of your own house, at the very least."

He stood near enough to me that I imagined I felt the heat from his body, and with it the sweet scents of warm silk and a spice I was unfamiliar with. I inhaled deeply, allowing the warmth and scent to wrap around me like a blanket.

"I-I don't like to be a burden or a bother. I understand that they might feel unsafe with me wandering the halls at all hours, and it's far easier to only have to attend me in one place. Dr. Payne believes a small, ordered environment is best for my peace of mind, and my uncle and my servants have gone to a great deal of effort and expense to see me comfortable here. These were two rooms once that my uncle had combined into one. The glazing in my rooftop conservatory alone cost a fortune, never mind the effort at constructing it and filling it for me…. All this just to make me happy. I don't wish to be ungrateful or difficult."

Fox frowned. "But you're the viscount, are you not? They're your servants. It's your fortune that was spent. I hardly see where that is any kind of burden on anyone."

I grimaced. "I suppose so, though I had little to do with the raising of that fortune or the running of my estate."

Fox chuckled. "So, then, you're like nearly every other young gentleman of my acquaintance in that regard. How perfectly ordinary of you, Arthur."

His levity infected me, and some of the tension left my body. I chuckled with him even as the lonely hollow moan from the hall sounded again, the door rattled in its frame, and the candle fluttered and danced in an icy draft.

"Does that happen often?" Fox asked as he shivered and searched the shadows over his shoulder.

"The noises? Yes, but more so when I'm agitated. I still find it a bit odd that you can hear them too."

Fox frowned contemplatively as he placed his thumb beneath his chin and tapped a finger to his lips. While I watched that finger, mesmerized, he asked, "And you say none of your staff or your uncle has ever heard or seen anything strange in these halls?"

I rolled my eyes at him, flustered by my distraction. "No. My illness isn't contagious."

"But the ghost stories about the house had to have come from somewhere," he pressed.

"Yes, of course. I told you. It's an old house. Just like our neighbor, any pile of an age has a history. Holland has their headless Sir Walter, and we have our lady in white or jealous husband or some such nonsense." I waved an impatient hand before stepping away from him, suddenly needing more space between us. Sinking back into my nest of blankets, I wrapped them around me again in a sudden chill.

Forced to either hover over me or take his seat, Fox did the latter, flopping into it with an exaggerated harrumph. "You know, for a young man with such artistic leanings and a penchant for novels," he said, flipping through the bit of sordid fluff I'd left by the chair with one hand while giving my pianoforte and easel a casual wave with the other. "You seem remarkably skeptical. Are those all your words or your doctor's?"

I clenched my jaw and lifted my chin. "They are mine. The sounds and the visions are symptoms of my illness. That is all. If I'm ever to be well again, I cannot succumb to flights of fancy or fairy stories. I must face the world as it is."

Of course, that statement was completely at odds with the fact that I was surrounded by dozens of novels like the one he held and that I was having this conversation at all, but thankfully Fox didn't throw that in my face.

"But what of spiritualism, the supernatural, heaven and the hereafter?" Fox asked. "The Queen herself has participated in many séances, and she hasn't been locked away. Perhaps your visions aren't some curse or blight, after all. Perhaps you're a gifted medium instead. Did you ever think of that?"

I shook my head and twisted my hands in my lap. "Please don't. I don't wish to speak of it anymore. The joke has gone too far."

"I wasn't joking."

With a sigh, I closed my eyes, clenched my jaw, and stretched the tensing muscles in my neck. Why wouldn't he just leave it alone?

Hoping if I gave in, he might be persuaded to return to lighter topics, I said, "I will explain this once and only once, if you promise to let the subject rest and let us talk of lighter things."

Bargaining with my visions had proved fruitless before, begging even more so. I should have learned my lesson by now, but Fox had proved different in so many ways from those who had come before. When he nodded soberly, I allowed myself to hope.

Unable to hold his gaze any longer, I sought out the play of candlelight and shadow on my walls; the pretty delicate vines still brought me a measure of happiness.

"I was bedridden with a fever when I was ten years old. Ever since, I've heard and seen things that no one else does. You could say a medium does the same, I suppose, but there is more to my illness than that. Since that day, I have also misheard and misinterpreted a great deal more. People would speak and say the strangest things, and when I asked them to repeat themselves, they would say something completely different. Beloved faces would change, become malevolent or simply unreadable. If I was exposed to more than one or two people at a time, I would become confused, overwhelmed, adrift in a sea of expressions and gestures I could not decipher."

Fox remained silent and unmoving, so I took a deep breath and continued, "My mother and father loved me. I knew it in my heart, but

I would have sudden convictions that they were conspiring against me, that everyone was—the doctors, my nanny, the servants. I was so afraid every moment of the day, and angry, and sad, and confused. With time, I managed to gain some measure of control over it and learned to hide the worst from my family. But then my parents died. At first, I did not believe it for weeks. I thought it was some trick by my uncle or some trick of my mind. I had… I had a bad spell after that." I paused, rubbing the scars on one of my wrists through the layers of cloth that hid my shame. "I don't remember much of it. I remember screaming and noises so loud I thought my head might split in two. They told me I was uncontrollable, that I hurt someone, a maid… that I struck her violently and bit her. So you see, I was very ill—*am* very ill. I am not gifted with any miraculous abilities, merely cursed with an affliction that so far has no cure. I cannot be allowed to harm anyone else, and I need the safety and quiet of my rooms if I am ever to be well again. Do you understand now?"

When he didn't say a word, I feared he had disappeared like all the others, but he still sat in my chair, silently regarding me. His dark gaze was filled with pity again, and I had a difficult time meeting it. But I held my chin up, squared my shoulders, and did not turn away.

At last he said, "I'm very sorry, Arthur. You were correct. I didn't fully understand, and perhaps I *cannot* understand. I can't imagine the pain you've endured." He sighed and dragged a hand through his silver hair, rumpling it. "But I can see that you're unhappy here too. You've admitted as much to me already. If I understand you correctly, it has been almost ten years since the episode you speak of, has it not? Don't you think you might have made some progress in that time? From all you've said, I believe you have."

Worrying my lower lip, I shrugged. "I suppose so."

"Then I will believe you when you say you are ill, if you in turn grant that your illness is perhaps not so dire as you fear."

My throat grew tight, and I could only nod my assent.

Fox sighed. "The last time I came here, you said you liked me. Do you still?"

"Yes."

"I said I liked you too, and I meant it. I'm not trying to upset you. I only want to help."

I blew out a shuddering breath and managed a smile for him. "Thank you."

Gazing at me intently, he lifted a hand toward me but then let it fall as he shrugged the blanket up and over his shoulders again. "Right, then. We can leave it at that for now. Why don't we play a game? Do you have any cards?"

Grateful for the reprieve, I clambered to my feet and moved to the table by my chair. Though I rarely played games of patience, I did have a deck of cards tucked away in the drawer. For the next few hours, Fox tried to teach me the games he knew. I made an appallingly poor showing, but Fox was a gracious victor.

"Cheer up," he said after my latest abysmal defeat. "I have far too many years of practice in for you to feel badly about losing—more than I should really. But you're lucky you don't have any coins about you, or I would have had all of them off you in the first half hour."

Trying to be as dignified in defeat as he was in victory, I chuckled as I threw my cards down. "I fear you're right. Luckily I don't have anything to stake."

"I wouldn't say that," Fox rumbled, and when I met his gaze, something unsettling flickered in his eyes.

"What could I possibly have in here to wager that you would want?"

He held my gaze for only a second longer before he turned away, but my breath hitched nonetheless.

His smile was wry, but I didn't have the feeling it was meant for me. "A man can wager any number of things," he murmured before turning back to me. "But you don't have to worry about losing anything to me tonight. I wouldn't take advantage of your innocence."

His eyes seemed to be laughing at something, but I didn't know what. "I never said you would," I replied peevishly, unsettled and uncertain whether I was being laughed at.

"You might not be so sure if you knew me a little better. I am a thief, after all. Stealing is my profession."

"But I haven't got anything to steal, nothing worth anything at any rate... at least, not in this room," I pointed out.

"I beg to differ." His eyes were still dancing with merriment as he gazed at me, and despite the distraction of their beauty, I huffed in frustration.

I was missing something. I knew I was.

I hated that feeling. I remembered it often from my childhood, when the whole world would seem to get a joke and I would be left out because I couldn't understand.

"Well, I'll have to take your word for it, then," I answered, shortly.

"Yes, you will."

His tone was contrite and his smile rueful when I turned back to him, and I lost some of my pique. He gazed at me soberly for a few moments before he sighed and put the cards back in their wooden box. "I should go. The sun will be up all too soon, I'm afraid."

"Must you?"

"Yes, I must."

"You'll come again though, won't you?"

His smile this time held no edge. It was sweet and perhaps a little fond. "I will try."

Chapter Five

Two days and nights passed, during which time I frequently rehashed the entirety of my conversations with Fox. I tried to distract myself with other things, but it was no use. He dominated my thoughts. He'd made me laugh. He'd made me angry. He'd made me happy. He'd frustrated me. He'd fascinated me. He'd unsettled me in a way no one else had, but not in a way I could say was wholly bad. I should have been uneasy that I'd created someone so real, but I wasn't. In fact, I felt lighter and more energized than I had in a long time, particularly when I thought of his return.

Despite my medicine, the cold, and the never-ending fog, I was awake much of those days and anxious to do more than sit reading by my fire. The melancholia I'd suffered from seemed to have fled. I had my lanterns to chase away the dark, and I finally had something to look forward to beyond the endless monotony of my days.

I had hope.

Unfortunately, after the clock in the downstairs hall and Big Ben struck midnight together on the third day, that hope faded significantly. Fox had not come yet again, and I was doomed to another night alone.

I was halfway through consoling myself by playing Chopin's Ballade Number Four when a cold draft made me shiver beneath my fine wool dinner jacket.

"Don't stop playing," Fox said from behind me, and the weight on my heart vanished.

My first impulse was to forget my music and rush to him like an overeager puppy, but I quashed it. Instead I straightened my spine, lifted my chin, and continued playing as if he weren't there, though I couldn't help my smile.

I found it difficult to concentrate on the keys with the weight of his regard on my back, but I did not give in to temptation and glance over my shoulder. Luckily I had chosen a song I knew well and was able to get through it without any mistakes while my mind was obviously elsewhere.

I'd focused my gaze so fixedly on the lantern I'd placed on the piano box that I had to blink away spots when I finally finished and sought him out. My heart in my throat, I searched the shadows until the spots receded and I could at last see his handsome face.

He's only a figment of my imagination. His approbation is only self-flattery.

But I couldn't deny my delight when I saw his smile.

"You are wasted here, Arthur. You should be in a great hall, playing for the delight of hundreds of admirers," he said, beaming at me.

"Oh, good God, no. I'd fall to pieces at even the notion of such a thing."

I laughed even as I blushed, but I spoke only the truth. Me, in a grand hall, in front of hundreds—the idea was laughable. I couldn't even be in a room with more than a few people without my nerves crumbling.

"Perhaps one day," Fox said, dismissing my scoff with a wave of a hand. "I suppose until then, I should be glad to have you all to myself."

I liked the sound of that much better. Forgetting my play at dignity, I hurried over to him.

"Thank you for coming back. I've missed you," I said on impulse, only realizing how silly that sounded after the words had left my mouth.

Fox's silver brows shot up as I put a more appropriate distance between us. But his smile was broad as he said, "I've missed you too, Arthur. You are a ray of sunshine in a dreary world." His smile grew wry, and his eyes glinted devilishly as he continued, "My very own angel in the tower."

"Angel?" I spluttered, my blush deepening. "Oh, for heaven's sake."

"Certainly," he retorted. "You've already told me I can't call you a princess, and just look at the lovely halo your golden hair creates in the lamplight, not to mention the angelic music that issues from your fingers."

I had wanted him to tease me. I had missed our conversations. But this was too much. "Oh *really*," I stammered. "Where on earth do you get such notions? Certainly not from me."

"Where else could they come from if I am what you say I am?" he countered.

His teasing wasn't funny anymore.

"Don't."

I moved farther away and turned my back on him. I straightened my jacket nervously and tugged at my waistcoat and necktie, as they suddenly seemed too tight, even though they'd become rather baggy on my frame in recent months. I'd dressed for company the last three nights, forcing Sarah to press my finer shirts and brush out my best jackets, and now I felt like a fool for taking such pains with my appearance.

Moving to the foot of my bed, I grabbed my dressing gown and pulled it on, feeling exposed and chilled all of a sudden. Fox let out a sigh from much closer behind me than I expected, and I jumped.

"I'm sorry, Arthur. Forgive my teasing. I do like to see the color in your cheeks, but not at the expense of your nerves."

"It's nothing," I lied, stepping around him. "Don't trouble yourself over it. I know you were only teasing. I'm simply not used to it."

"I shouldn't have been so ham-handed about it, though."

I shook my head. If I couldn't even manage a little teasing from one of my visions, how could I ever possibly think I could manage outside these walls?

Raising my chin, I said, "You weren't. This is what gentlemen do with their friends, isn't it? Poke fun at one another?"

The smile he gave me was more of a grimace. "I wasn't so much poking fun at you. I meant what I said, though I suppose I could've dissembled more. But it *is* only the two of us here. I hoped I might dispense with some of that nonsense."

"It isn't nonsense. What you were saying about angels and halos, *that* was nonsense," I replied defensively.

"It wasn't. Your pale hair was quite lovely in the light from the lantern. It was no great stretch of the imagination to draw the comparison."

I frowned and hugged myself, my chest tightening. "You shouldn't say such things."

"Why?"

"Because… because it isn't right. A man shouldn't say those things to another man. It isn't proper."

I couldn't look at him as I moved closer to the hearth, trying to get warm. I was even colder now, despite the extra layer of my dressing gown. I reached for what little heat could be had from the dim coals in the stove, but my hands trembled so much I tucked them back under my arms, not wanting him to see.

Fox was silent for so long behind me, I risked a glance to make sure he was still there. He was, and he didn't appear angry, but the emotion I did see was one I knew well and hated even more—disappointment.

He studied me for a few achingly long moments more before he shook himself and gave me a weak smile. "You're right, of course. We shouldn't say such things. There you are, only asking for a few hours of pleasant company, and here I am, acting the boor. I should confess that I had a little tipple before I came here tonight. Perhaps that is why my manners aren't what they should be." His smile turned wry as he waved a negligent hand in the air and said, "And, of course, as you know, I'm not entirely a good sort of man. You'll have to forgive a little lapse here and there, I'm afraid."

I didn't know what to think. My feelings were in such a muddle, I couldn't bring myself to speak, so I nodded.

His smile fell away. "Would you like me to leave?"

"No." That word at least I could manage. I was not confused on that score.

Seemingly relieved, he took a few steps closer to me. "All right. Then why don't we start the evening over again? You could go back to your piano, and I could sit quietly while you play, and then we could make a fresh start of it. What do you say?"

I had overreacted to a silly bit of teasing, and if I didn't get hold of myself, I would ruin the rest of our night together, and he might not come back again. Instead of replying, I moved to my pianoforte and took a few moments to settle myself, under the guise of arranging my dressing gown more comfortably over the bench.

True to his word, Fox sat quietly while I played another of Chopin's ballades, the soft and lyrical strains soothing me even as my cheeks flamed with the knowledge that he was watching me.

He'd called my hair lovely. He'd called me an angel. No one had ever paid me that kind of compliment before.

Was he thinking the same thoughts now?

Was it truly wrong of him to say so?

I thought it was, but then why did it please me? Why did it make my stomach flutter?

Confused and unsettled, I immersed myself in the music instead of continuing to dwell on it. Fox had said we would begin again. I didn't have to sort through it all now. I would certainly have plenty of time to ponder it when he was gone. I had nothing but time alone to think on such things.

Fox made no sound until the last strains of the melody faded to silence. "That was beautiful," he murmured before he stood and gave me a short bow. "Good evening, Arthur. How are you feeling?"

"Good evening, Fox. I am well enough. I hope you are well also," I replied. Then I laughed at the ridiculousness of it. "This is silly. I'm not so fragile as all that. You need not be so formal. Surely we could find a happy medium somewhere between earlier and this."

I watched in relief as his customary grin split his face. "I'm sure you're right. I just seem damnably adept at upsetting you, and I don't want that."

As we settled by the fire, him into my customary chair, and I into the second that almost never saw use, I took a few moments to struggle for the right words. "You are... you *do* unsettle me. I cannot deny it. But I haven't determined yet if that is good or bad. It's possible you're like my other visions, sent to devil me. Or perhaps you're here because I've been coddled too much." I worried my lip as I pondered that more closely. These thoughts had hounded me often over the last few days. "I think... I think when Pendel, my uncle, and Dr. Payne look at me now, they may only see my limitations. You don't seem to see me that way. You push and you poke at me. You make me question what I may have come to blindly accept. And even if I don't like it, maybe I need it. Perhaps I've grown too comfortable here in my sanctuary."

Fox's deep chuckle broke me out of my contemplation, drawing my gaze back to him. "You may not wish to encourage me like that."

He was smiling at me now, that crooked grin that warned of mischief, and I smiled back feeling steadier than before.

"You're probably right. I shouldn't." I frowned at him in mock severity and wagged a finger at him like Nanny used to do to me. "This isn't encouragement, you understand. This is simply my way of trying to work it all out in my head, to understand why you're here. Why my mind made you this way."

I had meant it to sound teasing, but Fox's smile fell away, and he sighed heavily. When I raised my eyebrows, he shook his head and dropped his chin in his palm, pursing his lips.

"What is it?" I prodded.

"I'd like to ask you something, but I don't want to upset you again."

"Well, now you have to ask it," I laughed, even though my shoulders tensed.

He worried his lower lip for a time before he expelled a breath. "Would it be such a terrible thing if I weren't, in fact, a figment of your imagination… if I were a real, flesh-and-blood man?"

I couldn't hold his gaze. "Yes."

"Why? I'd still be the same man."

"I couldn't talk to you like this if you were real. I'd be too afraid," I whispered.

"Afraid of me?" He sounded truly appalled. "I wouldn't hurt you, Arthur. Surely even after so short an acquaintance you can't believe I would."

I drew in a steadying breath and shifted in my chair. "No. Not like that anyway. I only meant, if you were real, I'd be afraid you were judging me, thinking poorly of me because of my illness. I know I don't always say what I should or behave as I should. I'd be too nervous to speak to you so freely, if I'd be able to say anything at all without bungling it altogether. And I'd be too ashamed of anyone outside my family or my doctor knowing I'm—I'm like this… ashamed of the scandal, of someone finding out."

I tried to hide the signs of my distress, but Fox could obviously see past my weak attempts. He sat back in his seat and lifted a hand in a placating gesture. "All right. All right, Arthur. We won't talk about it anymore. I'm sorry."

Frustrated with myself, I clenched my jaw and shook my head. "You shouldn't apologize. I pushed you to ask it, and it was a simple question. *I'm* sorry I am such a wretch. You see now why I can't be like other men." Unable to sit still, I leapt from my chair and paced in front of the hearth. "My uncle is the only person I see beyond my staff. Did you know I have to time my medicine on the days when he comes to call, so I'm calm enough to meet with him without the worry I'll break into hysterics at the least provocation? My own uncle…. If that isn't pathetic enough to convince you, I don't know what is."

He moved nearer. He was close enough now I could touch him if I wanted, and I wanted. God help me, I wanted. I hugged myself instead.

"You aren't pathetic," Fox murmured. "I see how hard you fight. It isn't your fault." He took another step closer to me, but then growled and moved away. "I wish I had the expertise, the learning to help you better. I can admit I don't truly understand what it must be like for you, but I also don't believe you are as ill as you think, or as your uncle and your doctor think."

I turned to argue with him, but he held up his hand to stay me. "I know I promised to leave it alone after you explained everything to me, but as I said earlier, I'm not the best of men. I lied." His candor startled a weak chuckle out of me, and he grinned at me before sobering again. "I know you believe you are ill, and perhaps you are, but I've seen nothing in my visits that tells me you should be locked up like this. If your doctor is worth the blunt you must have been throwing his way all these years, you should have made *some* progress. From what I've seen and what you've told me of your past, I'd say you have. Perhaps it's time to revisit your treatment… most particularly that *medicine* you keep talking of."

He said those last words with such venom I forgot the rest of my argument entirely. "Why *most particularly* that?"

His stern lips thinned even more. "I know what laudanum is. I know doctors give it out like sweets to children, a *cure-all* for nearly every malady in creation," he spat. "You obviously have never been to an opium house, but I assure you, you wouldn't need to ask that if you had." His gaze became distant and his lips twisted into a parody of a smile. "Now I, of all people, should be the last to preach temperance in anything, but I have been to the dens in the East End." He paused there, and his expression filled with some unnamed sorrow. "I have seen what that poison can do to a man." His gaze focused on me again. "To be dosed every day for years, that can't be good for you. I don't care what benefit your doctor seems to think it holds. There has to be something other than that poison he could give you."

I did not like to see him so distressed. The need to soothe him overwhelmed any anxiety I had for myself, surprising me with its intensity. I smiled wanly and shook my head as I adopted a teasing tone. "First, you tell me I should have a candle at night. Then, I should plunder my wine cellar and roam about my house freely. Now, not only that, but I should do so without the benefit of my medicine." I chuckled. "Next, I suppose you'll tell me to dismiss Dr. Payne altogether, throw open the house, and have a merry party."

Fox didn't blink at the sarcasm, though he did smile a little. "Perhaps you should," he replied entirely too soberly.

I lost a little of my good humor then as I gazed back at his handsome face. "And perhaps you truly are the devil on my shoulder sent to tempt me. I think you might just be a little dangerous, Mr. Fox."

Like the sun after weeks of rain, Fox's grin grew wide and crooked. "Perhaps I am."

We stood staring at each other until my cheeks began to heat again. Clearing my throat, I went to the small table and retrieved my box of cards. "What say I let you trounce me again?"

"All right."

We played for a short while, but I had not improved any, and he beat me far too easily to be in the least entertaining. I simply could not read my opponent's face the way Fox instructed.

"It's all right," he consoled me as I put the cards away again. "You most certainly have many talents I cannot lay claim to. I could never play that instrument as fine as you, for one. Allow me to be better than you at something."

Appeased, I managed a smile and a quiet chuckle. "I'm sure you are better at many things."

"I doubt it," he countered. "But, be that as it may, I think I must be leaving soon."

I wanted to argue, but he'd given me a great deal to think on, and I knew nothing I said could force him to stay. "You'll come again?"

"Yes."

Relieved, I didn't press for more. I walked with him to the door to the conservatory stairs and held the heavy drape aside.

With his hand on the knob, he paused and turned to me. "Arthur, think about what I said earlier. I don't want to upset you, but I don't like to think of you rattling away in here when you don't have to be. I don't like thinking of you taking that poison every day either. Medical science has come such a long way. Surely there are other options for you."

I shifted uneasily, tensing again. Not sure how to answer, I worried my lip and scuffed my slipper on the carpet.

After a brief silence, Fox sighed. "I won't badger you. All I ask is that you think about it, all right?"

I nodded, and then he was gone, a whisper of a draft against my cheek and the faint scent of warm silk and spice all that remained.
Think about it.
As if I could do anything else.

Chapter Six

I slept fitfully that night, feeling as if my rooms had suddenly become that much smaller. Fox hadn't said anything I hadn't felt before, yet hearing it aloud had made the feelings all the more real. I longed to be free of my rooms as much as he seemed to desire it for me. I also wanted to be free of my medicine and how it made me feel. But I had to be healthy in order to achieve any of those things, and Fox by his very presence engendered feelings and desires in me that were the opposite of what a healthy, sane man should have.

Needless to say, I was irritable and out of sorts when Pendel's knock came the following morning. I stayed in my bed and watched in stony silence as the servants performed their tasks, not wanting to unleash any of it upon them.

When Pendel presented me with the tray bearing my medicine, I took the crystal gingerly in my hand. My stomach clenched as I watched the oily substance swirl in the glass, and I couldn't bring it to my lips.

"Poison," Fox had called it, and the word echoed in my ears.

"My lord?" Pendel asked.

Poison.

My mouth filled with sawdust, and my hand shook.

"Are you unwell, my lord?"

I could feel the gazes of the other two servants on me now. I swallowed and swallowed again but could get no moisture in my throat. "I think... I think I'd rather not take my medicine today, Pendel. I fear my stomach won't have it," I croaked.

Pendel frowned. He shot a quick glance at the other two servants, cleared his throat and said, "Should I send for the doctor?"

Despite the sudden stab of fear that question elicited, I managed to place the glass on my night table without incident. Fussing with my bedlinens rather than meeting his gaze, I said, "No. I don't believe that will be necessary. I'm sure it's only a passing thing."

After a brief silence, Pendel dismissed the other servants and closed the door before he returned to my bedside. "My lord," he began carefully, "the doctor was most adamant about you taking your medicine daily and not missing a dose. Perhaps you could try, and if your stomach continues to ail you, I can bring up a posset or a little mint tea and plain toast."

His voice was so gentle and concerned, guilt washed over me, but I could not bring myself to drink the medicine. I would choke on it for certain, or cast it up again.

"No, thank you. I think I'll leave it for today. One day won't make such a difference, I'm sure."

Pendel shifted slightly, the only sign of his agitation. "Perhaps we should at least consult the doctor. I could send Tom with a note and tell him to await a reply. It would only be an hour at most and—"

"No."

If they sent a note, word would get back to my uncle, and that would precipitate not only a visit from the doctor but possibly force Uncle Oscar to make a second visit so soon after the last. I did not want him bothered.

Pendel hovered at my side, his presence grating on my already frayed nerves. I closed my eyes and took a long breath and then another.

I could simply dismiss Pendel and let the chips fall where they may. He wouldn't want to openly defy me, but I was fairly certain the doctor would be calling before the afternoon was out. I couldn't put Pendel in that position. I loved him too well.

Damn.

With a heavy sigh, I reached for the glass, brought it to my lips and choked its contents down. The liquid burned unpleasantly and seemed to get stuck behind my ribs, but I did not vomit.

Another day won't kill me. It's the same medicine I've taken for years.

Clenching my jaw, I handed the glass to Pendel without looking at him and accepted the cup of tea he handed me.

"Thank you, my lord," Pendel said with such relief coloring his gruff voice I couldn't be angry with him.

After draining my teacup to wash the bitterness away, I drew the covers to my chin and settled on my side, staring listlessly at the darkened lanterns on my hearth. The unpleasant torpor settled over me, until my eyes grew too heavy to keep open.

One small victory at a time. I have my pretty lanterns, at least.

When I awoke again, my rooms were dark and quiet. I forced myself from the warmth of my bed, shuffled to my window seat, and drew the heavy green brocade aside. The fog had not relented, making it impossible to guess the hour. I had no clock in my rooms as the incessant ticking drove me mad—well, *madder* I suppose—and with my mind still addled from the laudanum, I hovered with my hand clutched tightly in the drapes, unsure what to do next.

Poison.

My stomach twisted and bile rose in my throat as a lingering bitterness still clung to my palate. My breakfast tray remained untouched from the morning, and I finally dredged up the energy to move to it and pop a wedge of orange in my mouth to remove the taste. Afterward I stared listlessly at the rest of the tray. The tea was now cold, along with the egg and toast, and none of it looked at all appealing.

Shivering in my dressing gown, I moved to the stove. I pumped the bellows, hoping to coax a little heat from the dying coals, but they were as low as my spirits. In the end, I slumped in my chair, pulled my lap quilt over me, and brooded over my failure.

I had tried to assert some independence, some control over my fate, but one word from Pendel about having to face the doctor or my uncle, and I had quit the field. I couldn't blame Pendel. He was only doing as he'd been ordered and as he thought best. My whims could be erratic, my moods more so. I could admit to that.

All the literature and treatises I'd read on the subject of diseases of the mind said the same things—the best prescriptions for those such as myself were rest, quiet, and calm. Laudanum ensured I received all three.

Poison.

Fox had only spoken of overindulgence. I'd read of opium dens in my novels and in the newspapers of course. But it was a very different thing to be prescribed medication under the supervision of a trained physician, wasn't it? But how could I argue that when the truth was, I hated taking the stuff? It tasted awful, and I loathed the way it made me feel. Fox had only given voice to my emotions.

Perhaps if I proved to Pendel, my uncle, and the doctor that I could do without the laudanum, they might listen to me. I'd have a better argument if I could show them. All I had to do was stop taking it for a time without them knowing, and then they'd have no choice but to see the truth. The experiment could be a small one. If I felt my mind slipping and I had more unpleasant spells, then I could simply start taking it again and no one would be the wiser.

It was an excellent plan, surely.

Suddenly energized, I rang for a new tray and devoured the egg, cheese on toast, and hot tea Pendel brought, barely containing my excitement. A few concerned looks from Pendel, despite his obvious pleasure in my renewed appetite, warned me I needed to try harder to mask my feelings, or my scheme would be ended before it began. If Pendel were suspicious, it would be all the harder to deceive him.

Luckily Pendel left not long after, and I didn't need to maintain a calm façade for long. Unfortunately I had the rest of the night to get through without driving myself mad with waiting. Part of me wished Fox would return and help me pass the time, but another part didn't want him to see me until I'd had a chance to implement my plan. I wanted to surprise him. I couldn't wait to see his smile of approval when he found out how far I'd come on my own.

THE FOLLOWING morning, I was awake and in my chair when Pendel and the other servants arrived, still struggling hard to hide my nerves and excitement despite a rather anxious and sleepless night. A slight lift of one eyebrow was the only indication of Pendel's surprise, but he held out the tray with my medicine without comment, and I took it obediently and drained its contents. As always, Pendel had my tea waiting to wash away the bitterness, and I accepted it gratefully. This time, though, instead of drinking, I held the cup to my lips and spit the medicine into it, the cream hiding the addition of the amber liquid. As I set the cup back on the saucer in my hand, with the barest clink of china, I kept my expression bland and nodded my thanks to my oldest and most trusted servant.

Tom and Sarah continued their work, and after what felt like an eternity of picking at my breakfast and pretending to take the occasional sip from my cup, Pendel bid me good day and locked the door behind him. Sitting rigidly in my chair, barely able to breathe, I waited until their steps receded down the hall before rushing to the necessary room and pouring the contents of my cup out. I rinsed it with some of my wash water, and then returned to my chair on wobbly legs to pour myself another cup.

I had mixed feelings at best regarding my success. I was not precisely proud of myself for executing such a deception, but I could not deny a certain sense of accomplishment either. I would not drink that poison anymore, and they would all see I was fine—perhaps even better than fine—without it.

Shrugging off the cobwebs of guilt and shame, I did my exercises twice, and read for a time. When Pendel brought my lunch, I had to pretend to be groggy from sleep. The deception still grated, but I promised myself I wouldn't have to do it for long. In the late afternoon and evening, I grew a bit restless, but I had expected as much. I wasn't used to being awake for so many daylight hours, and I needed to allow for a certain period of adjustment. My agitation was not so pronounced as to be worrisome.

I used the time to write a long letter to Mr. Fuller at the bookshop. It hadn't been very long since I'd received his last packet and letter, and his next packet wasn't due to arrive quite so soon, but I was sure he could forgive me an additional correspondence. He seemed to enjoy our exchanges almost as much as I did. At least I thought he did. One day I hoped to be well enough to meet the man in person to thank him for the pains he'd taken in writing me and selecting the poetry, music, and prose that eased my lonely hours. If my experiment worked, that day might be sooner than anyone expected.

As day progressed into night, I became a little concerned that the restlessness continued into the early hours of morning. I read. I played until my fingers ached. In desperation, I even began a new watercolor—a depiction of a man with laughing dark eyes and thick silver hair. Perhaps I hoped to conjure him with it, like some magician; I don't know. It didn't work, but it kept me busy, even though I couldn't get his features quite right, no matter how many times I tried.

My floor was littered with failed attempts by the time exhaustion finally swamped me. I was careful to pick them all up again before I stumbled to my bed, though, not wanting the servants to see them.

Fatigue dragged heavily upon me when Pendel entered with my tray to start the new day, but I forced myself awake enough to perpetrate the same deception as the day before. Other than a few concerned looks, he left me to myself, and I slept for several more hours even without my dose. I was far from well rested when I finally rose to take my afternoon tea, but at least then I could lay the blame for my lingering lethargy on my medicine with some measure of success.

Much to my disappointment, Fox did not come that night either, and I was forced to while away the hours on my own again. Except this night, not only was I restless, but I had an uneasy feeling in my body, as if I might be on the verge of taking ill. Luckily for my peace of mind, exhaustion claimed me earlier this time, and I slept at least five hours before Pendel arrived with my potion in the morning.

After the third morning without taking my medicine, I woke in the afternoon feeling feverish. I began to fear I had cursed myself with my lie to Pendel about stomach troubles from a few days before, and God was punishing me for my sins. In front of the servants, I hid my discomfort as best I could and lied yet again when Pendel asked if I was feeling unwell.

I dozed fitfully throughout the evening, and by the time Pendel prepared to lock me in for the night, it took all my strength to keep my head held high and to hide my state from his searching gaze. When the lock clicked in place at last, I slumped in my chair and panted. With great effort, I eventually managed to lever myself out of my chair and stumble to my bed.

In the hours that followed, I barely noted that Fox did not come yet again, because I lay curled in a ball in my bed, wracked with the most wretched cramps. I was fevered and nauseated, shaky and weak. As my symptoms only grew worse, I knew I should have rung for Pendel, but I truly did not wish to see Dr. Payne, and I feared their looks of disappointment should my deception be discovered. So I lay in my bed and tossed and turned, trying to find a comfortable position, and when the cramps grew too great, I moaned loudly into my pillows and prayed for sleep to take me.

I don't know how long I lay like that before I heard Fox calling me.

"Arthur? Arthur, what's wrong? Talk to me."

"S-Sorry. I fear I'm not well enough to talk tonight," I panted as another cramp twisted my belly.

"Bloody hell, you're burning up!"

His cool hand on my forehead felt so heavenly, I never wanted it to leave. I tried to reach for it as he withdrew, but another cramp had me clutching my belly instead.

"Has the doctor been called? Do they know what's wrong? Why are you all alone like this?"

Even in my pain, the concern in his voice made me smile. "No doctor. I'll be all right," I gasped. "I'm sure it's just something I ate. By morning I shall be well again."

"The hell you will," he growled.

Before I realized what he was doing, Fox pulled vigorously on the bell rope, and then again for good measure.

"I'd order you to tell them to send for the doctor, but you likely won't have to say a word. If this Pendel cares for you as much as you've said, all he'll need is one look at you and the doctor will be sent for."

I moaned and shook my head. "He'll know, and he'll make me take it again."

"Take what?"

"I don't want to."

"What are you talking of?"

"The medicine. The poison. He'll know if he comes," I gasped.

Fox leaned in, his dark eyes searching my face intently. "The laudanum? You mean you've stopped taking it."

"Like you said." I nodded as his beautiful face swam in my vision.

"Did you speak with the doctor about it?"

"No."

"You simply quit taking it altogether?"

"Yes."

Why is he badgering me so? Can he not see I'm ill?

"Bloody hell. You need to tell him that, Arthur." He swore again and began pacing restlessly next to my bed. "Damn it to hell. This isn't what I meant." He stopped and leaned close to me again. "You can't just stop taking it, you fool. You have to reduce by degrees. I've seen this sickness before. You should have spoken to your doctor first."

I would have argued with him, but I didn't have the strength. When my vision cleared enough to see him again, his mouth was set in a deep frown.

"Arthur—"

Footsteps hurrying down the hall cut him off.

"Ballocks!" he hissed.

"My lord? My lord, is everything all right?"

Keys rattled in the lock as Pendel continued calling for me. My reply died in my throat as I felt the brush of soft lips on my forehead and heard Fox whisper, "Tell him, Arthur."

I turned back, but Fox was gone. I searched every corner in the flickering light from the lanterns, but there was no sign of him, and then I had to close my eyes as the glare from Pendel's oil lamp stabbed daggers into them.

"My lord? Are you ill?"

"'Tis nothing," I panted. "Only a little—"

I clenched my jaw against a wave of nausea as Pendel's concerned faced floated in the narrow view through my slitted eyelids.

"You are not well, my lord. I'm sending for the doctor."

All I could do was moan in response. I was lightheaded, fevered, and racked with pain. I didn't have the strength to object, even if it would have done any good.

I hovered in a purgatory of sheer misery, wishing Fox were there to lay another cooling hand on my forehead—or his lips again—until Pendel returned with a damp cloth for my head and icy water to drink. He left me for a time, and then I heard the sounds of the fire being stirred up and more coals added. I drifted, and when I opened my eyes again, Dr. Payne stood over me like the specter of death in his black frock coat.

"He was ill a few days ago as well?" Dr. Payne asked Pendel.

"He spoke of a slight stomachache, sir, but he hasn't complained of it since then," Pendel replied.

"Has he complained of any symptoms other than the fever?"

Dr. Payne had seen me open my eyes, but he continued to speak to Pendel as if I weren't conscious or I were still a child.

Now I remembered one of the reasons I disliked the man.

"Pendel," I croaked as forcefully as I could muster, purposefully interrupting their conversation. "May I have some more water?"

Pendel hurried to oblige as Dr. Payne at last turned and addressed himself to me. "How are you feeling, my lord?"

I waited until after I sipped from the cup Pendel held for me before answering. "I am a little unwell, but nothing to have troubled you with. I fear Pendel may have been overly concerned."

I was quite proud of myself that I had managed to say so much with only a slight quaver to my voice, but then my belly decided to attempt to tie itself in knots again, almost rejecting the water I'd swallowed, and my sudden curling inward and barely stifled moan exposed my lie.

As I panted through the pain, Dr. Payne removed a stethoscope from his bag and placed it to my chest, the cold metal branding my heated skin through my nightshirt.

"Has anyone else in the house taken ill?" Dr. Payne again addressed his question to Pendel instead of me, but I simply closed my eyes and clenched my jaw.

"No, sir."

"And you all eat the same meal, or was his lordship served something different?"

"Mrs. Peebles prepares meals for all of us."

"Is there something he might've had to drink, anything that is not shared with the staff? Some wine perhaps?"

Even with my eyes closed, I could almost see Pendel stiffening as he replied. "His lordship rarely partakes of wine, per your instructions, sir. His hot chocolate is reserved only for him, but we have all partaken of the milk, and he did not have any this night or last."

"Tell him, Arthur."

I was going to ignore Fox's whisper no matter how many times it sounded in my head, but my gut twisted again, and my resolve crumbled. I was so very tired of hurting. In defeat, I slumped into the icy tangle of my sweat-drenched bedlinens.

"I stopped taking my medicine, Dr. Payne."

When I opened my eyes, I found both men frowning severely at me.

"You what?"

"I know," I continued tiredly. "I should not have done so without consulting you, but I wished to try an experiment."

I spoke more to Pendel than Dr. Payne, but it was Dr. Payne who answered.

"No, indeed, you should not have. Did you know of this, Pendel?"

Pendel regarded me, not the doctor, with his lips clamped tightly shut, but the doctor seemed to read the answer in his silence.

"I see," he said, heaping a great deal of censure and disappointment into only two words.

I cringed in guilt but more from the look in Pendel's eyes than the doctor's words.

Dr. Payne pulled a vial from his bag and administered numerous drops to my water glass, as I'd expected. I took the glass and downed the bitter liquid without complaint, and then closed my eyes.

Pendel and the doctor exchanged a few words, but if any were directed at me, I did not hear them. I heard only a strange buzzing in my ears as the drug slowly stole over me, and then nothing at all until the clatter of the key in the lock woke me the following morning. I said nothing as Pendel held the tray with my medicine out, plied me with tea and broth, and fussed with my bedding. Someone had bundled me into fresh nightclothes and changed my bedlinens in the night, adding to my shame, but I remembered none of it.

As I stared disconsolately at the coals Tom had stirred up in the stove, Pendel continued to hover anxiously over me.

"Is there anything else I might get you, my lord? Perhaps one of your novels?"

"No, thank you, Pendel. Not today."

I wanted to grow irritated with him for hovering and not leaving me in peace, but that required too much energy on my part. My medicine stole over me yet again, and all I wanted was to curl up under my blankets and let the world move on without me.

When I woke again, I was alone, and the gray light of another fog-shrouded day waned with the sunset. I might've allowed myself to slip back into sleep, but for the fact that all the broth and tea and water I'd been given that day had caught up with me. With great effort, I slid from beneath my blankets, donned the dressing gown Pendel had left by my bed, and shuffled to the necessary room. Pendel had left an old chamber pot next to my sickbed, but I absolutely refused to use it. I might be a wreck of a man and a wretched creature at the best of times, but I still had some pride left.

After relieving myself, I managed to shuffle to my chair by the fire. I was out of breath with the effort it took to cross that short distance, and my head swam, but I was able to pull the lap quilt off the back and drape it over me. The coals in the stove had dimmed to a dull orange, and I shivered in the chill. Pendel must have decided not to wake me at teatime, so Tom had not refilled the grate.

I gazed forlornly at the bellpull on the wall, but it seemed such an overwhelming task to reach it that I simply huddled deeper into my chair and pulled the lap quilt tighter around me.

Thankfully, Pendel arrived to check on me before I froze solid in the chair. Upon seeing me awake, he rang for the other servants and soon my fire was cheered up, and I held a cup of hot tea in one hand and a biscuit in the other.

After being wrapped in another quilt and plied with plain toast, tea, and more biscuits, I felt more like myself, and I managed a weak smile for Pendel when he handed me my novel.

"Thank you."

"Of course, my lord. May I say, we were very concerned for you last night. You gave us quite a scare."

I ducked my head. "I know. I'm sorry."

Pendel made a show of pouring more tea before he cleared his throat and said, "Your uncle sent a note to say he would be stopping in to see you tomorrow, to see that you are well."

I gave a purely internal sigh. Of course he would be. Dr. Payne had probably written to him the moment he returned home. Pendel would have waited until morning before he sent his report.

I wanted to send a message of my own stating it was unnecessary for my uncle to trouble himself on my behalf, but it would do no good. He would come, and I would bear the brunt of his disappointment in me.

"It will be good to see him again so soon," I said. Though, in truth, I couldn't dredge up much emotion either way. I was just so tired, so very tired.

Chapter Seven

"Arthur? Arthur, can you hear me? Please, open your eyes, pet."

Fox's voice was strange to me as I struggled to wake. I'd never heard it sound like this before. Was that fear?

"Arthur, please. Tell me they've been taking care of you. They haven't left you here ill and alone again, have they?"

The weight of a warm hand on my neck gave me the strength to shrug off the last bindings of sleep, and I blinked in the darkness. "I'm awake. I'm all right."

The hand on my neck gripped me tighter for only a second before it fell away and left me to shiver in a sudden chill at its loss. Someone had tucked me into bed sometime that afternoon, but I barely remembered it.

"Thank God," Fox exclaimed. "When I came and found that all was dark in your rooms, I feared the worst."

I struggled to sit up, facing Fox's shadow in the darkness. "Dr. Payne ordered more rest, so Pendel didn't light the lamps tonight."

"They sent for the doctor, then? Good."

"I suppose," I replied without much feeling.

Fox let out a long sigh, and when he spoke again, his voice was more like the Fox I was used to—strong, confident. "You sound tired, Arthur. I only came to check on you, to make sure you'd been taken care of. I should probably leave and let you get your rest, as the doctor said."

"No!" I flailed blindly toward his retreating shape, and my hand closed on warm, smooth silk. A strange panic gripped me, and I had a disconcerting feeling that the pervasive fog beyond my windows had settled inside me. I felt as if I was swimming through it as it tried to drag me under, and I held on to his sleeve like a lifeline, certain I would drown without him.

Thump. Scrape. Thump. Scrape.

Fox's arm stiffened beneath my grip.

Not now.

"What *is* that?" he hissed.

A burst of anger fueled by panic pushed through the fog in my head as the shimmering apparition appeared beyond Fox's shoulder. Still clutching his sleeve, I snapped, "I told you. It's nothing. It's my sickness. It's all in my head, all of it! Leave me in peace!" I shouted that last at the door, knowing it would do no good.

Thump. Scrape. Thump. Scrape.

The hollow moaning soon followed, as it always did, and I let go of Fox's sleeve to clamp my hands over my ears, too weakened by my illness to fight. The hairs on the back of my neck stood on end, and I trembled.

"No. No, no, no, no, no. Go away. Please, go away. Please," I begged.

I did not realize I was rocking until a firm grip on my shoulders stilled me.

"Arthur, it's all right. It's all right. It stopped. It stopped now."

After a few cleansing breaths, I forced my eyes open. His face was so close I felt his breath on my cheek. If I leaned forward only a few inches, I could have kissed him.

Flinching away from that thought, I leaned back and closed my eyes again. But when Fox withdrew his hands from my shoulders, I grabbed his wrists before he could get too far.

"Please stay."

He was silent for a time, his muscles tense, but after a long sigh, he relaxed. I released his arms reluctantly as he sat on the edge of my mattress. Feeling his weight next to me calmed and reassured me enough that I could stop shaking and perhaps sound a little less like the madman I was.

"I'm sorry," I said into the heavy silence. "Forgive me. I… as I said before, it always gets worse when I'm… unwell."

"You don't need to apologize." Fox chuckled dryly. "As *I* have said before, if that is what I had to listen to on a nightly basis, I would most certainly go mad—or, well, that is to say—"

I laughed for the first time in what seemed like forever and the oppressive weight on my chest lifted slightly. "It's all right. You can say it. I *am* mad. There is no use denying it. Dr. Payne and my uncle say that I am *unwell*, or taken to my sickbed, to spare the family honor or perhaps my feelings, but the truth remains the same, no matter what it is called."

Fox growled. "Arthur, you know full well I don't believe you are as unwell as you think. I've seen the truly mad on street corners in the East End or through the gates at Bedlam, and you are not they. I have heard the sounds in the hall too, remember? Does that mean I'm mad? I don't believe that I am."

I bit my lip while he spoke, but in the end, I could not help but release a weak chuckle.

"What?" he asked, sounding offended.

"You realize one of my delusions is trying to convince me that I am sane, and it is the world that is mad," I said with another wheezing chuckle.

I could not see his face in the darkness, but I imagined I could feel the weight of his frown as he spoke. "Arthur, enough games. You've touched me. You've felt the weight and solidity of my flesh. Yet you still persist in this belief that I am some sort of vision?"

"You would not be the first," I replied tiredly.

If anything, the weight of his frown seemed to double. "What do you mean? Are you saying your visions have touched you before?"

I shivered and drew my blankets higher. "Yes. Not often, and not for a long time, but yes. I... I don't like to talk about them. They weren't like you. They were not kind, their touch far from comforting. They held me down, swaddled me until I couldn't move, until I feared I wouldn't be able to breathe. Sometimes I would wake and know they were only nightmares, but other times I knew I wasn't dreaming. I know the difference. I do."

I shivered again and had to swallow against the tightening of my throat. Fox's hand settled on my knee, and I closed my eyes to concentrate on the comforting weight of it. Memories did not have the power to hurt me, but my mind could twist them and make them all too real, particularly when I was so weak.

"Oh, Arthur, I am so sorry you had to suffer that, to suffer any of it."

"Thank you."

Another hollow moan broke the now comfortable silence between us, and I drew on what strength I had left to ignore it, but Fox had apparently had enough. His weight left the bed, and I felt the brush of a cool draft on my cheek and heard the rustle of my bed-curtains at his passing.

"Damned fog," he hissed. "If I only had some light to see by, I'd open this bloody door and confront whoever or whatever is out there."

"It's locked," I reminded him tiredly.

"And I'm a thief," he reminded me. "An old lock like this is child's play. I could release it in a thrice, if I only had some damned light. Hell, I'd probably be able to do it by feel alone if I'd brought my tools with me, but I was in such a state when I left to come to you, I managed to forget them."

The door rattled in its frame as if someone had kicked it, and even though the moaning continued, I smiled. "You were worried about me?"

Fox growled as his shadow moved across the room briefly blocking the faint glow of the coals in the stove. "Of course I was worried. Last I saw you were doubled over in pain, obviously quite ill, and locked away with no one to help you. I should've stayed to make sure you were properly looked after and damn the consequences."

Warmth bloomed in my belly at his obvious concern. Even when the moan beyond my door became a wail, my smile didn't dim.

"Hell and damnation!" Fox hissed.

He stopped pacing and stood frozen in front of the hearth, the coals painting the folds of his odd silken garb in splotches of dull orange. "If only I'd remembered my bloody tools." His words held an edge that I did not like, and the warmth inside me slowly died as my chest tightened again.

"It's all right. They're not real. Just ignore the sounds and eventually they go away. Please don't distress yourself," I pleaded, feeling my brief moment of calm and happiness slipping through my fingers.

"It isn't all right. Nothing about this is all right," he insisted hotly. "Although, I believe you're right about one thing. What's going on out there is no spirit. Someone is doing this, and I'm going to find out who and what their game is."

His shadow moved from in front of the hearth to the wall where my bookcases lined every free inch. "Do you have anything I might use to open the door? Something I might reshape? A pocketknife? A broach or pin? A bit of wire?" He rattled off the questions in quick succession as the sound of books being shuffled about and trinkets being knocked over met my ears.

"I... uh, I-I don't think so." I winced at the clink of what was probably one of my delicate china figurines tumbling over.

Every muscle in my body began to tense as he continued his search. I could almost see the wreck he was making of my perfectly ordered shelves, and I couldn't concentrate a jot on what he was saying.

"Come on Arthur, *think*. You must have something here I could use!"

His voice stabbed at me with judgment and disappointment, like everyone else's. The wailing had stopped, but it was replaced once more with the footsteps and scraping outside my door. Strange that it should happen thrice in one night, but I barely noted it beyond the roaring in my ears.

This is wrong. This is all wrong. It's too much.

I flinched at the sound of my chessboard being knocked over in the dark. I screwed my eyes shut, clapped my hands to my ears, and tried unsuccessfully to do my breathing exercises. All I could think about was my ruined bookshelves and the dozens of chess pieces scattered in disarray on the carpet. I had to clamp my mouth shut on a moan of my own.

"Ha! Here we are! These will do nicely."

I couldn't open my eyes to see.

Thump. Scrape. Thump. Scrape.

"Stop. Please, stop," I whispered hoarsely, unable to make my voice any louder.

"I'm going to show you, Arthur. I'm going to prove to you that this isn't all in your head. I should have done this before. I won't let you down this time."

"Please stop. Please."

Finally a rattling at the lock on my door forced its way past the roaring in my ears, and I flung myself from the bed. I knew my room as well in the dark as in the light of day, but I still managed to bang my knee into the chest at the end of my bed in my headlong rush.

"I've almost got it, Arthur. I'll show you."

"No!"

I crashed into Fox. His startled shout was cut off as I landed on him hard and we toppled to the floor in a heap. Something sharp and cold scraped my skin and I grappled for it, tearing it from his hands.

"Stop. Stop. No more," I pleaded. "You shouldn't do that. It's wrong. I have to be here. Only Pendel is allowed to open the door. It's supposed to stay locked. I'm supposed to be here. Everything has its place. The books are supposed to be neatly wrapped and in order on the shelves. The chess pieces have their squares to sit on, always the same before and after a game. I have my place and the servants have theirs. Everything belongs somewhere, and I belong here."

I wasn't making any sense. I was shaking and blabbering, and I couldn't seem to stop either. I wanted to scream at the roaring in my ears and beat at my head and tear my hair, just to make the world stop. I felt I would shake apart into a thousand pieces, and beneath it all was a blackness that threatened to swallow me whole.

"Arthur! Arthur, stop! It's all right. I won't open the door. It's all right. I'm sorry. I'm so very sorry."

The weight of Fox's arms around me, cradling me, not holding me down, reached me better than his words, and I stopped struggling as exhaustion came rushing back in the wake of my hysterics.

Somehow, Fox had moved us until his back was propped against the door and he held me in his lap like a child, but I didn't have the strength for shame. I might've allowed myself to be held like that forever, but for the fact that the floor was hard and cold beneath us, and I had nothing but my nightshirt on. Reluctantly, I moved to stand, and Fox didn't try to stop me. When I was upright, a wave of dizziness swept over me, and I stumbled and had to grip the back of my chair. He was at my side instantly, cupping a palm beneath my elbow. "Come on. Let's get you back into bed."

Like an invalid, I allowed myself to be guided back and tucked beneath the covers. He was silent for a time after he'd settled me in, though he hovered by the side of my bed.

The weight of my shame tripled my exhaustion, and both held me speechless until he said, "Forgive me, Arthur. I was trying to help, but all I seem to do is make things worse for you. I'm no doctor. My stupid bloody pride made me think I knew better. That and my selfishness have done more harm than good. I should never have—"

"Stop. Please," I begged, finally finding my voice. "None of this is your fault. It's *my* madness, *my* illness. Anyone else would never have reacted that way. I know that. And you *have* helped me. Never say otherwise."

The chuckle he let out was bitter and it grated on my ears. "I can't think how."

Struggling against my fatigue, I freed a hand from my blankets and groped blindly until I caught his sleeve, needing the contact and needing him to understand because his words sounded too much like a farewell for my nerves to stand. "You have. Before you came to me, I was sleeping my life away, in a dream, allowing the world to happen to me or to pass me by as it saw fit. I don't know when it happened, but I became complacent. I stopped trying to get better. I stopped thinking about the future and simply let the days pass. You've helped me see that. It's why you're here. Some part of me knows I've taken the coward's way out, and it sent you to remind me of who I am."

Even as I said the words, the truth of them struck me, and I cringed. Releasing Fox's sleeve, I slumped back into my pillows, curling in on myself. But Fox captured my retreating hand between his warm palms and squeezed, halting my retreat as he knelt next to my bed.

"You are too hard on yourself. I've seen some of the battles you face, and you are no coward. A weaker man might have given up a long time ago, but you haven't. You fight every day."

I flinched at his kindness, glad that he could not see the scars on my wrists—a reminder for the rest of my life that I had tried to give up once. I felt as weak now as I had then, and I was terrified of being left alone with my thoughts. Before I could overthink the impulse, I said, "Stay with me tonight. Please. Don't go."

His grip on my hand lessened, but I clutched at him with what strength I had left.

"I can't," he replied. "I can't be found here with you. You must know that."

I didn't want to argue or think about whether he could or could not be found, so I said, "You can leave before dawn, only stay with me for a while."

"You need your rest."

"I'll rest better with you here. I… I want you to hold me… like you did by the door. Just tonight. Please."

I shouldn't ask. It was wrong and weak to need him as much as I did. But on this one night, after I'd already shamed myself with my earlier outburst, what was one more display of weakness?

Tomorrow, I would be stronger. I only had to make it through tonight.

He was silent long enough that my chest grew tight with humiliation. I was on the verge of taking my request back when he released my hand and moved away from me. Clenching my jaw against the pain of rejection,

I said nothing as his steps receded, but then the mattress dipped, and I felt the covers lifted back and weight and warmth slid in next to me from the other side of the bed.

I released a breath I hadn't known I was holding as his hand on my shoulder urged me onto my side, facing away from him, and his body curled against my back. Without a word, he draped a heavy arm across my chest and drew me against his warmth, and I closed my eyes in utter relief and wonder. I wanted to cry.

Before tonight, I had never been held like this in my life, and it was as heavenly as I had always imagined it would be. I had distant memories of being tossed in the air by my father or held in my mother's lap as she or my father read to us by the fire, but they were thin, tenuous things, and the sensation slipped away if I tried too hard to catch it. Since my illness and their deaths, no one touched me or held me anymore. I had no one, nor the hope of anyone with whom I could have that kind of intimacy. Here with Fox, now, I didn't care whether it was real or right. It felt real enough, and I needed it desperately.

I wished that I could've stayed awake longer to enjoy it, but the illness and upset of the last few days caught up to me much too quickly. It felt like only a few seconds had passed before the bed shifted and icy air stung my back.

"Don't go," I croaked plaintively, struggling to free myself from the bonds of sleep. My hand ached from where I still clutched something thin and sharp in my palm, but I dropped whatever it was without looking at it so I could shove the heavy blankets aside.

"I must," he replied, his soft voice tinged with regret. "It's almost dawn. If I don't wish to be seen climbing down from the roof, I need to leave now."

"Promise me you'll come back."

He let out a heavy sigh. I could just make out his shape and the pale sheen of his silver hair in the thin gray light of predawn escaping through the drapes. "I don't think that's a good idea, Arthur."

His words would have sent me into another panic if I hadn't heard the uncertainty in them. "I do. Please. At least allow me the chance to redeem myself and to apologize properly for my appalling behavior last night."

"You have nothing to apologize for," he replied tiredly.

I closed my eyes against the disturbingly cluttered state of my rooms and against the shame of how pathetic I must sound. "*Please*. I need you."

I would beg if necessary.

I felt sure my father and my uncle would have been truly ashamed if they could see me, but they couldn't, and I needed this too much.

I struggled to breathe in the heavy silence that fell between us, but at last I heard a whispered "I promise" before the rustle of heavy curtains falling back into place and the click of a latch reached my ears.

I closed my eyes and pulled the covers over my head to preserve as much of his warmth and his scent as I could. I rolled to face the place where he'd slept and pulled the pillow he'd used close, pressing my face to it as I drifted off to sleep again.

I could be ashamed later.

Chapter Eight

"My lord?"

Pendel's uncertain rasp woke me from a dream that had me flushing in dismay when I opened my eyes to find my butler's craggy face peering down at me. I turned away from his all-too-perceptive study and squirmed beneath my blankets in chagrin, hoping to hide the state of my body. The movement caused something sharp to poke me in the side, distracting me, and I fumbled beneath the linens until I found what had stabbed me and pulled it out.

"Oh dear, my lord, your spectacles," Pendel exclaimed as he took what was left of them from me.

The frame was bent, one of the lenses was cracked, and one of the temples was missing.

"I must've fallen asleep on them," I said with a nervous chuckle.

"The doctor said you should rest," Pendel chided.

I only needed my spectacles when my eyes grew tired from the strain of reading in the dark. But I read on the floor by the fire or in my window seat at night because those were the only places I could find enough light. Pendel was no fool. He would figure that out if he were given the chance. I coughed nervously and shrugged, desperately trying to come up with an excuse for having them in my bed and not in the drawer where they belonged. Luckily Sarah chose that moment to pull the heavy curtains away from the windows, and her gasp and resulting cough had all eyes swinging in her direction.

One look at the state of my room, and I winced and closed my eyes. My bookshelves and chess table were in utter disarray. The drawer of the small table by my chair was on the carpet in front of the hearth, its contents scattered over the floor, including the playing cards. It looked as if a cyclone had run through. When I dredged up the courage to crack my eyes open again, everyone was staring at me, and Pendel's face was stony.

I grimaced in the ensuing silence, not meeting any of their gazes. I didn't know what excuse to make for the mess, but Pendel came to my rescue before I tried.

"Well, don't just stand there gawping. Sarah, Tom, finish your tasks and set to work tidying up," Pendel ordered harshly.

I forced myself to watch as my servants cleaned the mess they thought I'd made, while Pendel supervised in pointed silence. When they'd finished, Pendel dismissed the servants and closed the door behind them before returning to my bedside.

Any lingering aftereffects of my dreams were long gone under the weight of my guilt and shame, and I swallowed my medicine, slid out of bed, and stepped into the dressing gown Pendel held out for me without a single objection.

After taking a few sips of the tea he handed me and attempting to choke down a bit of egg from my tray, I sighed and set my spoon down. I wasn't hungry, and his silent reproach was too much to bear. "I'm sorry for the mess, Pendel. I had a restless night despite my fatigue, and I'm afraid I knocked a few things over, searching for something in the dark. I am better now. You don't have to worry."

The excuse sounded pathetic even to my own ears, but it was the best I could do as my head began to fill with cotton and lassitude stole over me.

"Of course, my lord."

I didn't know if I imagined the rebuke in his tone or not, but I didn't have long to suffer under it. My medicine robbed me of consciousness all too soon in my weakened state.

PENDEL AND my tray were gone when I woke again. I didn't remember his departure or being draped in extra blankets like a feeble old man. Darkness hadn't fallen yet and my window curtains remained open to let in the gray light, depressing as it was. Unwilling to stir from the warmth of my blankets, I gazed about me with a surprising lack of concern or anxiety. Several of my books and baubles had been put back in the wrong places, but beyond that, my room was as it always was. The sharp edge of guilt I'd felt earlier was blunted by the memory of Fox's arms around me while I slept. If he would only visit me every night, I might be content to spend the rest of my days in these rooms, safe and comfortable. I wouldn't have to ask for more. I wouldn't have to fight so hard to be someone I wasn't. I could stay right where I was and be taken care of for the rest of my days.

But no, that wasn't right.

I shook my head to clear the cobwebs still clinging to it, struggling against my lethargy. That was the medicine talking, not me. I could still tell the difference. Couldn't I?

It's poison.

"My lord?"

Pendel's gentle knock made me smile despite the darkness of my thoughts. The man had an uncanny ability to know when I woke. Sometimes I wondered if he could somehow see me through the walls.

"Come."

Keys rattled and the lock clicked. Sarah brought in another tray, and Tom added coal to my fire as always, neither one of them risking a single glance in my direction. When they'd gone, Pendel poured a steaming cup and handed it to me.

"My lord, your uncle has arrived. He would like to come up, when you're ready."

I cocked an eyebrow at that. Uncle Oscar hated this part of the house, but I supposed it made sense. If I were truly unwell in the physical sense rather than my usual state, he would not force me to leave my rooms to see him.

"Shall I fetch him, my lord?"

I sighed and nodded. I might as well get it over with.

Pendel turned to go, but on impulse, I called after him. "Wait."

"My lord?"

"Tell my uncle I will meet him in the library as always. I will come down as soon as I am dressed."

Pendel frowned at me. "My lord, you have been ill. I'm certain Mr. Middleton understands and is more than willing to—"

"But I'm not," I said with as much authority as I could muster while fighting free of my swaddling and attempting to gain my feet. I couldn't fully explain it, but it was suddenly very important to me that I be dressed and out of my bedchamber when I met my uncle. "You may send Tom up to escort me down, if you must, but I will meet him in the library."

To his credit, Pendel only hesitated a moment before he nodded. "Yes, my lord. Shall I send Sarah up with fresh clothes and hot water as well?"

"No. I'll make do with the water in the ewer and the clothes hanging in the wardrobe, thank you."

"As you wish, my lord."

After Pendel closed the door behind him, I slumped against my chair and leaned on it for support. It was pathetic that such a simple thing as exerting my will could drain me as if I'd climbed a mountain. And perhaps it was even more pathetic that my success should feel as exhilarating as if I'd accomplished the very same marvel. But despite my earlier lapse, I'd meant what I said to Fox. I'd taken the coward's way out for too long. I couldn't allow my failure with the medicine to defeat me entirely. I wouldn't be able to face my reflection in the looking glass, or Fox, if I did.

I gave myself a few moments to regain my strength before I shuffled to my washstand and splashed icy water on my face. The shock of it helped clear some of the lingering cobwebs, and I undressed quickly and set to work with the flannel with as much speed and rigor as I could manage, scrubbing away any residue of my illness still clinging to my skin.

Shivering, I moved as quickly as I could on wobbly legs to my wardrobe and withdrew clean undergarments, a shirt, warm stockings, and braces from the drawers. Next I pulled my gray tweed jacket, trousers, and matching waistcoat from the cupboard above. The cut was at best a few seasons out of fashion, but the cloth was warm and still in good condition. My neckcloth gave me some trouble, and by the time I had it righted, I was sweating and feeling as if I needed to lie down for a spell. But my uncle awaited, and if I took too much longer, Pendel would return to check on me, and I might have to go through the whole battle of wills again.

Steeling myself with a few invigorating breaths, I took one last look in the glass mounted to the wardrobe and declared myself presentable. With my chin held high, I went to the door and tried the handle. Even knowing Pendel hadn't used his key when he left earlier, some part of me was surprised when it turned. Such a small thing to be able to open one's own door and step out of one's room, even if Tom's enormous bulk waited in the hall on the other side.

Tom held an oil lamp aloft and stood in silence, though his shoulders appeared tense and he kept shooting nervous glances around him. A flicker of movement to my left caught my eye, but the pale diaphanous thing that floated farther down the hall vanished as soon as I turned. Closing my eyes, I firmed my shoulders and lifted my chin again. When I opened my eyes, Tom still waited quietly, his face unreadable, and I strode past him toward the stairs with as much dignity as I could muster.

In the library, Uncle Oscar reclined by the fire, as always. He rose to meet me and shook my hand, though more gently than was his usual wont.

"Nephew. The doctor wrote to say you were ill. I wish you would've allowed me to come to you. You should be resting."

"I am well enough, Uncle. You've interrupted your busy calendar to see me again so soon. The least I could do was dress and meet you properly." The relief I felt as I lowered myself into the armchair by the fire gave lie to some of my words, but I hated to show any more weakness in front of him.

"You look a little pale, though, my boy."

"I had a brief illness, Uncle, as I'm sure Dr. Payne informed you. But Pendel has taken excellent care of me, and I rested yesterday and more today. I feel sure I'll be better still tomorrow. I'm sorry to have worried you."

After a quiet knock, Sarah brought in the tray. While Pendel poured, Uncle Oscar helped himself to Mrs. Peeble's honey cakes, and I sipped at my tea. Sometimes I wondered if the only reason my uncle visited as often as he did was Mrs. Peeble's cooking, but I would quickly shove such thoughts away as unworthy and ungrateful. I could not imagine what it must be like to have a burden such as me to manage, and to know you would have that burden until the day you died must be a great hardship, one I hoped to alleviate someday.

I searched my uncle's face as he ate. For all its familiarity and likeness to my own and my father's, I feared I could not read it as well as I should. I didn't know him as a man. Our afternoons together had always revolved around me, and today would be no different, if I managed to find the courage to ask for what I wanted.

To hide my nerves, I took another sip from my cup. The journey from my rooms proved I wasn't as well as I'd hoped to be before tackling a difficult conversation, and my courage faltered. I'd already burdened him with worry twice recently over my health. Was it selfish of me to press him again so soon?

We could continue with the useless pleasantries. I could say nothing of my thoughts, and we could play our customary game of chess or discuss the estate until it was time for him to leave.

Or I could stop being a coward and start living my life.

"Uncle?"

"Yes."

"I should like to speak to you about something, if I may."

"What is it?"

I swallowed at the tightness in my throat and pressed on. "I would like to discuss my medicine."

My voice was weaker than I liked, but there was no help for it now. He grimaced, but he didn't look angry. The closest I could come to describing his expression would perhaps be pained, which was almost worse than angry.

He glanced quickly at Pendel before shoving another honey cake in his mouth and chewing vigorously.

Fearing my courage would fail me again if I waited, I plowed on. "I have not had a truly bad spell in a long time... *years* really." I shot a quick glance at Pendel's craggy countenance myself, but I could read nothing in his expression. "I may have had an unsettled night or two, but nothing truly terrible, I think, not like before."

Uncle Oscar shifted his bulk in his seat and cleared his throat. "Pendel, pour me a glass, would you?" he ordered, waving a hand toward the crystal decanters on the sideboard.

"Certainly, sir."

While Pendel did as he was bade, Uncle Oscar worried his lower lip, then sighed, and finally lifted his gaze to mine. His eyes were the same blue that looked out at me from my father's portrait in the hall and back at me from my mirror, but I found no comfort in that now. I folded my hands in my lap to keep from twisting them nervously, or worse, pulling at my hair and ruining the air of calm I struggled to maintain.

"Nephew, I called on Dr. Payne before I came here today. We spoke at length and—oh, good. Thank you, Pendel." He took the glass Pendel offered and downed its amber contents in one go before handing the glass back to him. "Another, if you would."

Without even a blink, Pendel took the glass to the sideboard again as I waited for my uncle to continue. He did, but only after downing half of the second glass Pendel brought him. "As I was saying, I spoke with Payne, and he believes you should continue with your medication as prescribed. He said you'd naturally think you don't need it anymore if you're feeling better, but that you're feeling better only *because* of the medication, as evidenced the other night by your illness when you stopped taking it."

Uncle Oscar's voice had taken on a strange rushed quality as if he were making some sort of practiced speech, and I had to wonder if the words were truly his own or someone else's.

"But that was a physical illness, Uncle. I had a fever and stomachache," I said, but the quaver in my voice upset me even more. I sounded like a child who didn't want to go to bed, and my frustration grew. I clutched my hands together in my lap until they ached and my knuckles turned white. I took a breath and tried again, remembering what Fox had said to me. "Uncle, I will admit stopping my medication without consulting anyone was wrong. I shouldn't have done that. But my reaction was only from quitting it all at once and not stepping back on it by degrees. I should very much like to try again, only more gradually and, of course, with careful monitoring."

Oscar sighed and pinched his brow between his thumb and forefinger. He downed the rest of the contents of his glass and then held it loosely in his hand, staring at it instead of me. "Dr. Payne actually suggested increasing your medication, Arthur. He said that over time, patients can develop a resistance, and the fact that you want to stop taking it is an indication that perhaps it isn't working as well as before and the dosage should be increased."

"No."

I felt the blood drain from my face as I looked back and forth between Pendel and my uncle. The roaring in my ears began again, and all I could do was shake my head. A wisp of white mist shimmered in the corner of the room beyond my uncle's shoulder, but I closed my eyes.

"No."

"Nephew? Nephew, are you taken ill again?"

I heard a rustle of cloth and footsteps before a heavy hand landed on my shoulder. "Pendel, get some water. Nephew?"

"No," I repeated.

More medicine? More poison? Did they want to kill me?

I needed to say something other than that one word, but none would come. With all my strength I fought the rising panic that made me want to throw off the hand on my shoulder, burst out of the chair, and run from the room… and keep running until I collapsed. Even if I had the strength for it, I knew that would only ruin any chance I had of being taken in earnest, but convincing my body of that was a battle. As it was, my heart raced as if I'd already begun running.

"Nephew, Arthur, please drink this."

A glass was held to my lips, and I drank without questioning. Luckily it was only cool water.

"Arthur, don't distress yourself so," Uncle Oscar continued, almost pleading with me. "I told Dr. Payne I didn't think it was necessary to increase your medication … that we could keep it the same and see. We'll keep everything the same. That will be all right, won't it?"

I opened my eyes to find him hovering over me, his forehead pinched and glistening as he glanced nervously back and forth between me and Pendel. The hand that held the water glass to my lips shook so that a few droplets spilled over the side, and I reached out to steady it. His hand was warm and solid beneath my own, and the lines on his face eased when I dredged up a weak nod for him and took the glass from his hand.

I was in no state to argue. Even if I could get the words out, I would only make matters worse. I retained enough sense to know that. "All right, Uncle," I rasped.

His relief was palpable, the smile he gave me so broad I immediately felt the crushing weight of guilt for distressing him so. We were all silent while I took a few moments to calm myself.

Everything would stay the same. Tomorrow would be like yesterday. That wasn't so very terrible, was it?

"D-Do y-you have time for a game?" I asked, by way of apology for my behavior, but I knew his answer before his smile fell away.

"I'm sorry, Nephew. I have appointments this afternoon and an engagement this evening that I must go back to my rooms and dress for. Perhaps on my next visit."

"Of course. Next time."

Uncle Oscar made his excuses and hurried out. I couldn't blame him. My outbursts always made him supremely uncomfortable, as they did everyone, including me. We exchanged good-byes as if nothing untoward had happened, and he left me in Pendel's capable hands, as always.

After his carriage disappeared into the mist, I slogged dutifully back to my room, and as the lock clicked home, I slumped into my chair in a combination of relief and crushing defeat. It hardly seemed possible that only a little more than a week ago I'd been content with my lot, content to while away my days and nights with my books, my music, my garden, and my sketchpad.

But that wasn't exactly true, was it?

I hadn't been content, merely indifferent. Otherwise, Fox's words would not have made such an impression.

I wished for him now. I needed him to make me laugh at myself, to shake me out of my self-pity, and to give me purpose and direction. I hadn't been prepared to hear that Dr. Payne wanted to *increase* my dosage, and though I'd felt well-rested following my night with Fox, I still should have waited until I was stronger before attempting to broach the subject with my uncle.

Now, with another failure looming over me, what little fight I'd had was knocked out of me, and I'd need help getting it back.

Stupid. So stupid.

In my usual mad way, my conversation with my uncle replayed itself over and over in my mind—all the things I could have said and done but didn't. I couldn't distract myself with my sketchpad or my pianoforte. I was too agitated to sleep, and my novel provided no escape from the churning storm inside me. Anxiety and melancholy warred within me, so I spent my nervous energy setting my bookshelves to rights, finishing the work Sarah and Tom had started. By the time Pendel and the other servants arrived with my dinner, I had to use the little strength I had left to hide my state from them, despite finding some measure of calm in handling my books. But Pendel knew me too well to be fooled this time.

"My lord, are you feeling unwell again?"

When am I not?

I shook my head at myself in disgust. Self-preservation, if nothing else, forced me to raise my hand when Pendel stepped closer. If I continued to sulk and brood, he would be forced to send for Dr. Payne again, and I did *not* want that.

Clinging to my pride and the promise I'd extracted from Fox, I managed to dredge a smile from somewhere. "I am well enough, Pendel. Don't fret. Perhaps I am still a little tired from my fever."

"Perhaps we should leave off lighting your lanterns tonight then as well."

"No."

I didn't shout the word, but it was a near thing.

The hand Pendel lifted to signal Tom froze, and he turned to me with his heavy brows lifted high.

"I mean to say, the lanterns won't stop me resting, and if I wake in the night, it will comfort me to have them," I explained, careful to keep my tone moderate. "I don't wish to make another mess like I did last night, fumbling around in the dark."

Pendel frowned, but he inclined his head. "As you wish, my lord."

When I was alone again, I did manage to rest after a time. I watched the play of light my lanterns made on the ceiling and allowed their beauty to soothe me. The lanterns had been a victory, even if I'd failed twice now with my medication. I clung to that victory, and it gave me some hope.

Despite my prayers, Fox did not come to me, but neither did the sounds in the hall, the lady in white, or any other visions. Perhaps they all took pity on me. Or perhaps my illness had given me a short respite. As the quiet hours passed, I was no longer agitated, but I also had no passion to draw or to play. I didn't want to do anything really. I sat in my chair and dozed, occasionally dredging up the energy to open my eyes and watch the lights dance. I should have simply gone to bed, but it seemed sadly empty now. Sarah had changed the bed linens that afternoon, so Fox's scent was no longer there.

Chapter Nine

Over the next few days, I dutifully took my medicine and made as little fuss as possible. I dressed each day in what Sarah brought me. I choked down the food I was given. My rooms remained tidy, and I made no extra work for the servants. I thought Pendel would be pleased by this, but his brows remained drawn in a deep V whenever I saw him.

Then again, perhaps I was misreading his expression. Perhaps I was being oversensitive, and he merely suffered from some sort of stomach malaise. My embarrassing episode in the library and my shameful weakness with Fox had shaken what little confidence I'd gained since Fox had been coming to me, and I began to think perhaps Dr. Payne was right. Perhaps my illness was only getting worse, and the desires plaguing me were a symptom of sinking deeper into madness rather than rising out of it.

Those thoughts only strengthened the longer Fox stayed away. The rational voice in my head told me his continued absence was for the best. My calm and my household had only been disrupted since his arrival. But then I would look at my lanterns, or remember the feel of his arms around me, and an ache would begin in my chest. Weak or not—wrong or not—I would pine for his return. I needed his passion, his anger on my behalf, his wry wit, and his smile. I needed him to quiet the battling voices in my head, to help me make sense of all I was feeling.

I needed *him*.

The third afternoon after my uncle's visit, Dr. Payne came to check on me. I don't know if Pendel sent for him because he was concerned for me or if the good doctor came of his own accord, but I couldn't find much of a will to care either way. After poking and prodding me for a time, while frowning at me a great deal, he lectured me on the necessity of continuing my medication and remaining calm and quiet. I stopped listening halfway through, while I struggled to contain my pique at being scolded like a child. But at least he declared me recovered from my fever, so my uncle and Pendel didn't need to worry on that score anymore.

Still a bit drowsy and muddled from my medication that morning, I simply gritted my teeth and nodded like a simpleton until he finished. I couldn't concentrate enough to argue or reassure the man, but I thought perhaps neither would have mattered to him anyway.

My tiny bit of temper faded to nothing once I was left alone again, and I curled up in my chair beneath my lap quilt and watched the light of another gray afternoon peak and then begin to fade. Loneliness and despondency settled in my bones like the fog outside, and all I did was doze the day away after that. Pendel brought a new packet from Mr. Fuller with my tea, hoping to cheer me, I imagined, and I tried to find some pleasure in the bookseller's letter, but even that seemed pointless. In grasping for something brighter and more beautiful, I had lost the joy in the pleasures I already had. I never should have listened to Fox. I'd let another of my visions fill my head with madness, and now I was paying for it, utterly discontent with an existence I'd made peace with not so long ago. I had no peace now.

Thump. Scrape. Thump. Scrape.

"Oh, go away," I moaned as the sound drew ever nearer and the hairs on the back of my neck rose.

I closed my eyes for fear of what I might see floating in the corner of my room. Of its own accord, my hand sought out the bit of bent wire I'd found in my dressing gown pocket after Fox's last visit. It was the missing temple from my spectacles, and Fox must have left it there for me to find. I should have thrown it away. My broken spectacles had already been replaced. But I'd kept it, and I clung to it now, grasping it tightly enough the metal dug into my palm.

"Someone is doing this, and I'm going to find out who and what their game is."

I stared at the lock on my door as the footfalls and dragging noise receded and the haunting moaning began. Why had I been so terrified of Fox opening the door? I knew he would find nothing on the other side, and I wanted to be free of these rooms, didn't I? I enjoyed going to the library to visit my uncle. I had no fear walking the halls of my house. Why had it been so important that he keep the door closed?

The door rattled and the light from my lanterns flickered in a sudden draft. I clapped my hands over my ears, trying to block out the moaning.

"Arthur?"

"Fox?"

My eyes flew open even as my heart skipped a beat. He stood only a few feet from me. His silver hair was rumpled from the hood he removed, and his black silk costume was as strange as ever, but he looked absolutely perfect, and I could not stop the elation and relief that coursed through me despite my earlier thoughts. I did not try to hide my joy at seeing him, and his answering smile lifted the weight that had been pressing on me for days. Unfortunately that beautiful smile of his only lasted until the moaning began again. Then his eyes widened, and his face grew stony.

"Bloody hell," he swore as he turned from me and took two steps toward the door, but then he froze midstride and turned back to me. "I know it upset you last time," he said, his body tense as a bowstring. "I don't want to do that again, but this has to stop. Please, Arthur, will you allow me to show you?"

The moan changed to a wail, and Fox paled in the wavering light. My stomach knotted with tension, but I swallowed and nodded. He didn't like feeling powerless any more than I did, and with his presence lifting my spirits, I could think beyond my own selfishness. I rather liked the idea that he wished to be my champion, even if he would only be tilting at windmills. Once he saw there was nothing to fight, we could both relax and enjoy our time together again.

"Go ahead."

The smile he gave me warmed me through, and I thought I would sacrifice more than my fears if he would only smile at me like that all the time.

Trying hard to regulate my breathing, I followed him to the door. While I hovered anxiously behind him, he dropped to his knees, pulled a couple of small tools from a thin leather case he drew from his sash, and fitted them into the keyhole. In a startlingly short time, the lock clicked, he turned the knob, and the door swung open.

I gasped, but he showed no sign of hearing it. The moment the door opened, he rushed into the hall searching first up and then down the corridor. I followed a little more slowly, finding it surprisingly difficult to pass through the opening, even though I'd done so many times before. Perhaps it was the absence of the stolid presence of Pendel or Tom's looming bulk that made everything seem so strange and unsettling… and dangerous.

"The sound is coming from over here," Fox called over his shoulder as he hurried farther down the hall, not waiting for me.

Light from my lanterns spilled onto the carpet and over the oak-paneled walls outside my open door, but even so, Fox disappeared into darkness all too quickly. Despite my nerves, I tried to follow him, but the farther I moved down the hall, the more difficult it became. I felt as if I were trudging through mud—like something was holding me back. My feet grew leaden, and whatever it was became thicker and more solid the harder I tried. My chest tightened, and I found it difficult to breathe.

A light behind me made me turn, and the pale apparition hovered at the far end of the hall. This time, she seemed more solid than ever before. I could just make out a pair of ghostly arms beckoning me toward her and dull gray eyes boring into me. A chill ran down my spine, and I froze in place. The sound of a door opening down the hall distracted me, and I whipped around, straining to see through the darkness.

The wailing cut off abruptly, and all was silent until Fox's growl echoed out of one of the rooms. "Where are you? I know you're here. Come out. Show yourself."

I turned back to the apparition, but it had vanished along with the wailing, leaving me alone in the quiet of the hall. Feeling a little dizzy, I braced a hand on the wall and took deep breaths, trying to clear my head. I shouldn't have left my rooms. Things made sense there. Now too much was happening all at once. I was overwhelmed, and the last thing I wanted was for Fox to see me shaking and pathetic yet again.

"Arthur?"

A warm hand cupped the back of my neck, and as I released a breath, strong fingers slid across the fine hairs at my nape, making me shiver for a different reason. He stood so very close to me, his warmth thawing the ice in my veins.

"I'm all right."

I regretted the words immediately when Fox withdrew his hand and stepped back. The look of concern in his eyes changed to puzzlement and what might have been trepidation as he glanced over his shoulder into the darkness from whence he'd come.

"What did you find?" I asked, regaining some of my composure.

"Nothing."

He continued to frown down the hall, and his bewilderment and unease were so reminiscent of my own from years long past, I had to smile. "I already told you that."

He turned his dark gaze back to me, his eyes almost black in the weak light. He frowned at me for only a second more before his lips twisted into a wry smile, and he chuckled weakly. "So you did." Giving himself a shake, he blew out a breath and glanced around us. "Well, now that we're out here, what say we find that wine cellar we spoke of before? Lord knows, I could use a drink right about now."

I tensed again at the prospect of venturing farther from the sanctuary of my rooms, but I struggled hard to hide it. "It will be locked," I said anxiously, the coward in me hoping he would indulge my weakness.

"Lucky for us, I might know a little about opening locks," he countered.

The grin he gave me this time was much more assured, more like the Fox I knew, and my courage grew in its light. His eyes dared me to refuse while his smile said this was just a game—a bit of fun, not a test or something to be feared. After all, what harm would it do to go on a little adventure in my own house?

This could all be a dream, I reasoned. *What harm in letting it play out a little longer?*

Without another word, he stepped around me and headed down the hall toward the stairs. I took a tentative step after him, half expecting the weight from earlier to drag on me, but it was gone. I had no excuse not to follow him. I took another step and another, feeling lighter as I went.

At the top of the stairs, I faltered. The fear of getting caught and having to explain myself to Pendel after all the trouble I'd caused lately clawed at me, freezing me in place. But before it could overwhelm me, my hand was taken in a strong, warm grip.

"Come on," Fox whispered close to my ear. "You know this great Jacobean pile far better than I. I assume the cellar will be near the kitchens, but you'll have to tell me the quickest way there and which doors to unlock."

The warmth of his breath on my cheek and the strength of the hand holding mine made my throat tighten and my heart skip a beat. All I could manage was a jerky nod as he pulled me down the stairs.

Big Ben and the clock in the great hall chimed two as we hurried past the portraits of my ancestors in the pitch-black. Fox was astonishingly surefooted in the unfamiliar darkness, but then he stopped suddenly, and I lumbered into him.

"What is it? Are you all right? Am I asking too much again?" he asked the questions in such rapid succession I hardly had time to answer, especially since he'd taken me by the shoulders and pulled me close to his warmth. "I am sorry. I do tend to just barrel along when given my head, don't I?"

"It's all right. I'm well." As I said the words, I realized they were, for the most part, true. My stomach was tight with nerves, and my breath a bit quick, but I heard no roaring in my ears, and I wasn't wringing my hands or pulling my hair or wallowing in melancholy and shame. Other than him being a little too close for my peace of mind, I was actually having fun. I was giddy—like the child I had once been before the fever, imagining my house was one of the great pyramids of Egypt or the jungles of darkest Africa, ripe for exploration and adventure. How long had it been since I'd had a bit of fun?

"The door to the kitchens is just down there," I whispered, pointing, though Fox could hardly see either my hand or the door.

He could obviously see well enough, because he took off again with me in tow, and moments later, we were through the door and descending the short stone stairs into the kitchens. The fire in the great brick hearth had been banked for the night, but the room was still far warmer than the rest of the house, just as I remembered from illicit childhood ramblings. I moved to the hearth from memory and stirred up the coals with the poker that still hung from the same hook it always had. After using the small bellows and adding a bit of wood, the fire cheered up enough for me to find a taper on the large wooden table that took up most of the center of the room, and I lit it.

Fox was smiling broadly at me when I lifted my gaze to his, and I was ridiculously pleased with myself. His smile made me feel I'd accomplished something far greater than lighting a silly candle.

"Aren't you the bold one, lighting the place up," he teased, his teeth shining brightly in the flickering light.

My cheeks heated, but I rolled my eyes at him. "The servants' rooms don't have hearths for the most part, if I remember correctly. It would take one hell of a commotion to stir me out of a warm bed if I didn't have to, so I doubt any of them will venture forth."

His smile turned just a tad devilish as he took a few steps toward me. "And yet, here you are, out of *your* warm bed."

Something changed in his voice and in the way he looked at me. I couldn't put a name to it, but I had an intense need to swallow, and I couldn't quite catch my breath. This didn't seem like so much of a childish game anymore. The candle flame wavered wildly, until I brought my other hand up to steady it. The move broke whatever tableau had been between us, and I thought, just for a moment, that his smile turned a little sad before he clapped his hands together and rubbed them vigorously.

"What say we have a go at that lock to the cellars, then, shall we? The light will definitely make my job easier."

I nodded mutely and pointed to the door. While I held the candle aloft, Fox removed the leather case from his sash again and set to work. Just as quickly as before I heard a click, and Fox turned the handle.

"I'd tell you these old locks should have been replaced years ago," he said as he took the candle from me and headed down the steps. "But then that would make my job harder next time."

Next time.

I liked the sound of that much more than I should.

The rough wooden steps creaked alarmingly beneath our feet. The air was heavy with damp. Cobwebs caught at our hair and clothes, and in the flickering candlelight, I could see our footprints in the layer of dust on the floor. I shivered in the damp and wrapped my arms around myself as I surveyed the racks of bottles in the flickering light.

"Oh Lord, thou art truly generous and merciful. I think I may have died and gone to heaven," Fox exclaimed as he blew the dust from a bottle and held it up to the candle.

"I am to gather you're pleased?" I teased, forgetting my discomfort.

"Pleased? Do you know what you have here? Some of these bottles predate old Boney himself. After the blight, laying hands on one of these beauties is damned near impossible. In the right hands, this is a treasure, my boy."

His excitement and delight were infectious. His eyes were alight with it. He was beautiful with it, seeming younger somehow. I couldn't look away. I would have gladly given him every bottle in this room if he'd asked.

"Arthur? Are you unwell?"

Flushing at being caught out, I turned away from his searching gaze and stepped to one of the racks. I pulled a bottle out and smoothed my hands over its cool surface, but my eyes didn't see the writing on the paper pasted to it.

"I suppose yours would be the right hands, then, eh?" I forced the words out in what I hoped was a teasing manner, and luckily he either dismissed the strangeness of my behavior or pretended he hadn't noticed, because he went back to his inspection of the racks with a chuckle.

"Perhaps," he said.

That was a benefit to being mad, I supposed. I didn't always have to explain myself.

I set the bottle I held back on the rack and folded my arms, hugging myself against a sudden chill. I had no real experience with wine, so the racks held little interest beyond the obvious pleasure they gave my companion. He seemed positively enthralled. Shadows stretched and writhed across the ceiling and walls as he moved deeper into the darkness, holding the candle over rack after rack. I didn't wish to hover at his elbow, but my mind was beginning to make ominous shapes out of those shadows, and I'd far rather watch him than them, even if he stirred disturbing feelings in me.

"You won't have much time to sample your choice if we spend all night down here," I finally said when the chill and damp and shadows became too much.

Perhaps I was being selfish, but I wanted what was left of my fire, my warm blankets, a comfortable place to sit, and some pleasant conversation. I was also growing increasingly uncomfortable with where my mind traveled as he moved about in his ridiculously unseemly costume, his thighs and arms indecently outlined by the silk.

"You have a point there," he replied with a chuckle. "We'll have other opportunities to plumb the depths of this treasure trove. Until then, I will take these two, and we may retire to your rooms."

My heart pounded faster as we ascended the stairs, feeling exposed by the candle and unsettled by my reactions to him, but his shining eyes and broad smile kept me from succumbing to my nerves completely. When he smiled at me like that, I found it nearly impossible to think of anything else.

Back in my rooms, he had to make do with my hot chocolate mug, for I had no crystal for him to drink from. Unsatisfied with the state of my fire, Fox set to work picking that lock as well, then threw what was left of the coal from the bucket in to cheer it up before settling in my chair and opening a bottle. I dragged the blankets from my bed, handed one to him, and snuggled beneath the others in my usual spot in front of the hearth.

My anxiety receded in the comfort and familiarity of my rooms, and I began to feel extraordinarily pleased with myself. I'd managed a trek through my house unchaperoned, and I hadn't fallen apart even once. Sitting as we were now, I could almost imagine I was any other man, entertaining a friend in front of his fire with a little wine and the last of the biscuits Pendel had brought with my chocolate. Never mind that I was entertaining in my bedchamber, the friend was possibly only a figment of my imagination, and I'd had to steal the wine from my own cellars. I wouldn't let a little thing like the harshness of my reality spoil the moment.

"Now that is heavenly," Fox purred after taking the first swallow from his mug.

My stomach fluttered at the sound, and I shifted uncomfortably. A man's voice shouldn't affect me so, but all I could think about was how much I wished to be back in my bed with him curled around me again.

"Would you care for a game of chess?" I squeaked, lurching from my nest.

Before he could answer, I grabbed my chess table in shaking hands and carried it to the hearth. I kicked my blankets out of the way, set the table between the two chairs, and settled uneasily in the second, a proper distance from my guest.

I could feel the weight of his gaze as he seemed to study me, but I couldn't meet it. "Arthur, are you sure you're well? I didn't put too much strain on you, making you go down to the cellars like that, did I?"

"No. I'm well. I was glad to do it." I forced a smile for him, but his frown did not ease.

"You may tell me if I do anything that upsets you, you know. I can be rather single-minded at times—a bully without even realizing it, I've been told. Sometimes I forget to consider others before plowing ahead. It's all right to remind me."

For the memory of his rapt expression as he viewed my cellar's contents, I would've risked much more than a little discomfort and possible discovery. I would risk even more to have him look at me the same way. It was that desire that was upsetting me, not anything he'd done, but I could hardly admit it.

With a sigh, I shook my head. "You didn't bully me, truly. You helped me. Without you, I never would have attempted such a thing. Now here I sit with a healthy fire, fine wine for the asking, and the knowledge that I can leave the safety and familiarity of my rooms without anyone hovering over me. How could any of that be bad?"

"Is that your way of saying I need to share the wine?" He chuckled as he offered my mug to me. His worried frown was at last replaced with his habitual wry grin, and I basked in it.

I took the mug from him but hesitated to bring it to my lips. I'd had watered wine but rarely in the past. Dr. Payne had advised against anything stronger, given my illness. But Uncle Oscar had a bit of brandy or whiskey on occasion and nothing untoward happened. From what I'd read in my novels, this is what men did. So, if I ever intended to join their ranks, I should learn to do the same—Dr. Payne's instructions be damned.

Fox only smiled encouragingly at me as I held my mug, and I blushed at my skittishness. I lifted the cup and took a tentative sip. The rich and heady flavors burst in exquisite profusion in my mouth. He'd chosen a port, and I chased the sweetness eagerly with my tongue, drawing on my lower lip to ensure none of it escaped.

Fox made a strange noise, but when I glanced at him in question, he cleared his throat and turned his attention to the chess table. "If it pleases you, I'll play. But be warned, I'm a terrible player. Chess isn't my usual kind of game, you see, cards being my preference."

After licking the last of the wine from my lips, I chuckled. "I can't say I'm disappointed to hear it. I should like a chance to get some of my own back. I daresay I can make a better showing at this than I have at cards."

"Only promise me you won't think too ill of me if you trounce me in embarrassingly short order."

"I promise," I replied solemnly, though his grin was infectious and the wine was spreading warmth from my belly all the way up to my cheeks.

I took blacks so he might have the advantage of the opening gambit, but it soon became apparent that he was not displaying false modesty when he spoke of his lack of skill. His moves were aggressive but impulsive. He was overly reckless with his pieces, sacrificing where he didn't need to. Still, the game lasted a good deal longer than it might have, because he continued to refill our cup, and I continued to drink from it.

"Arthur, may I ask you something?" he asked, breaking the comfortable silence that had fallen between us while I struggled to formulate a strategy through the warm haze that had somehow shrouded my thoughts.

"Hmmm?"

"The room I went in earlier, two doors down the hall from here, where the sound came from, whose was it?"

I lifted my gaze from the board and blinked slowly at him as his question sank in. I shrugged. "No one's, that I know of. One of the many guest bedrooms, I suppose. Why?"

He frowned. "Well, it was a very large suite, with a door adjoining what looked like a lady's chambers. In any other house, I would have called it the master's suite. Yet alterations were made to two smaller rooms for you here, instead of setting you up there. It seems odd to me. That's all."

Waving negligently, I managed to slosh a bit of wine onto the back of my hand. Grimacing, I sucked the wine from my skin while he chuckled and took the mug from me. Squinting at him, I tried to think. "No. They can't be the master's chambers. My parents' rooms are on the other side of the house. They rarely used this wing, except for guests, from what I remember." I frowned, trying to grasp at memories that seemed a bit fuzzy and slippery all of a sudden. In the end, I gave up and shrugged again. "I think they chose to convert these rooms for me because it was the best place to install stairs to the roof, and also, I really didn't want to be in my parents' chambers. It seemed wrong somehow."

In truth, I hadn't been in their chambers at all since they'd died. I wondered if Pendel had kept them as they were or if Uncle Oscar had ordered their things removed.

"Well, no matter. I was only curious," he replied, bringing me back to the present and the game.

The clock in the downstairs hall chimed four, but I only noted it absently, saving my attention for the game. I was having a bit of difficulty maintaining the proper level of concentration, and my limbs had pleasant warmth and heaviness, but beyond that I hardly felt any effects at all from the wine. It made me wonder what all that Temperance League fuss was about. Surely something so lovely and mild could hardly be worthy of so much condemnation and disapproval.

Except, when I finally declared checkmate and rose to take the table away, the room spun a bit, and I nearly toppled arse over teakettle, forcing me to admit I might need to reevaluate that opinion.

Fox was at my side at once, his palm under my elbow to steady me. "Perhaps I should take care of that."

"I'm so sorry. I think I may have had too much of that lovely wine," I said, somewhat plaintively.

With a chuckle, he took the table from me and carried it back to its place before returning to my side to guide me back to my chair.

"I think perhaps you may have."

I frowned at him. "You're the one who is supposed to have more experience with these things. You should have warned me."

"Yes, I should have." He grinned down at me, not in the least contrite from what I could see, and I glared at him, though his face had gone a little hazy in the lantern light.

"Just for that, now you have to come tuck me safely into bed," I said.

Appalled, I clapped a hand over my mouth and stared wide-eyed at him as I blushed furiously. Grown men did not ask to be tucked in, particularly by other men. It wasn't done. I knew that.

Fox's thin silver brows nearly reached his hairline as he watched me with a small smile playing about his lips. But inevitably that smile turned devilish again as he said, "Of course, my Lady Rapunzel. A princess's wish is ever my command."

I slapped at the hands that reached for me and scrambled out of my seat. The world spun wildly, and I clutched the back of the chair for balance, but at least I had a barrier between him and me.

"I'm only doing as I was bid," he complained, stalking slowly and gracefully toward me.

"I am *not* a princess," I huffed as I backed away from him. "Forget what I said. It was the wine, obviously."

My heart thumped wildly beneath my breast, and I couldn't think. The urge to run and the urge to stay warred within me. I should be strong, keep my back straight and my chin high, but I so wanted to be weak, just one more time. Sleeping in his arms had been the single most pleasant experience of my life, and I ached to feel it again.

If he was a creature of my own making, no one would ever know if I gave in.

You would know, my conscience nagged.

But I was so tired of fighting. I fought the hallucinations. I fought my impulses and my nerves. I fought the emotions that burst inside me with such intensity they left me breathless. I didn't want to fight anymore. It wasn't fair.

You'll never be well if you give up. You'll never leave this room.

I groaned and wrapped my arms around my stomach as it threatened to toss the wine back up again. I sank to the floor clutching myself and rocking.

Thump. Scrape.

I clutched at my ears and continued to rock, praying the noises would go away. Fox swore and crouched at my side. "Are you ill? What can I do?"

Thump. Scrape.

Fox growled next to me, his body tense, clearly divided between wanting to help me and wanting to confront what was beyond my door. Selfishly I clutched at his sleeve to keep him with me. I knew what he would find if he opened my door—nothing. No one was in the hall. No one was doing this to me. I was doing it to myself, and I needed the one good thing to come out of my illness to stay right where he was.

"Water, please," I croaked.

I released his sleeve as he rose. He returned a moment later with our cup. This time it held only cool water, and I drank it gratefully as the hollow moan began.

"Arthur."

Fox's voice was strained, and he crouched next to me, coiled tight as a spring. In sudden irritation, I waved him away, which he took as permission. His obvious tension was bleeding into me, making it difficult for me to block out the bone-chilling moan that echoed down the hall. He needed to learn for himself that ignoring it was the only option, and I did not have the strength to argue with him about it again.

He had the door open in a thrice and stormed out into the hall as the moan inevitably turned to a wail. I leaned against the back of the chair I'd slumped behind and drank a little more water to settle my stomach.

A door opened down the hall as the wail echoed around me and then was cut off. The silence was soon broken by Fox's copious swearing and the sounds of more doors being opened and closed. A faint bluish light came through my open door from the opposite direction he'd gone, but I closed my eyes against it.

I didn't bother to open them again until he returned to my rooms, flustered and out of breath. The bluish light was gone now, and in the flickering light from the lanterns, his lips were pale and his dark eyes wide as he leaned over me.

"Find anything?" I asked with acid-tinged innocence, feeling drained but a little steadier now that I was on familiar ground again.

"No," he growled back at me. He shivered and looked over his shoulder once before turning his attention back to me. "Are you all right?"

I was so tired of being asked that question.

"Yes." I lifted a hand to him, and he helped me up. For a brief moment, my legs threatened not to support my weight, but I stiffened my spine and locked my knees.

We stood in awkward silence for a few breaths before I cleared my throat and stepped around him. I didn't want to be alone, but I was drunk, shaken, and feeling weak again. If he stayed, I might say or do something I would regret forever.

Fearing my resolve would weaken if I looked at his handsome face, I kept my back to him as I said, "I think I should lie down for a while. I shouldn't have had so much wine when I'm not used to it."

He let out a long sigh behind me. "Yes. You were right. I shouldn't have allowed you to drink so much your first time. I was a poor friend tonight."

"No." My conscience couldn't allow that. "You helped me. You did. I left this room and moved about my own house unchaperoned for the first time in longer than I can remember. You shared your company with me. You showed concern for me. I'm a grown man now, damn it. I may be ill, but I can still make decisions for myself." Lifting my chin, I spun toward him and dredged up a smile. "You are a good friend, and I very much would like you to come back again, but when I'm a bit more clear-headed perhaps."

I really don't want you to leave at all.

He studied me silently for a time before he shook his head. "As you say. Do you still need my help getting into bed?"

I flushed and looked away from him again. "No. I think I can manage on my own now. Thank you."

"Then I should be on my way." He moved to my door and crouched in front of it until I heard the lock click into place again.

I sat on my bed and fought with my weaker impulses while he moved about my room. When I finally dredged up the strength to seek him out, I found him standing near the door to the conservatory stairs. "Sleep well, Arthur."

He said it with such finality, my heart skipped a beat and I rushed to say, "You will come back, won't you?"

The silence between us stretched far too long before I heard him murmur, "I promise."

Then the door clicked shut, the heavy drapes fell back into place, and all was still and quiet again.

Chapter Ten

In the morning, my head was fit for cracking. I had a brief moment of panic when Pendel and the others entered my room, remembering the wine bottles, but a quick glance toward our chairs showed nothing amiss. Fox must have taken the evidence of our adventures with him.

Bless him.

My head ached terribly, and I almost heaved up my medicine, but after a few sips of tea, my stomach settled. Luckily the medicine knocked me out again before I had to feign interest in my breakfast. I never would have made it through choking down even a bit of egg without tossing up my accounts, and then Pendel would've had yet another reason to worry over me.

When I woke in the afternoon, I was ravenous, and my ailments from the morning were completely gone. I was still a bit sluggish as I tore into the meal Pendel delivered, but I actually felt surprisingly good, happy even. Fox's visit had done what I'd hoped, cured me of my loss of faith and my melancholia, with barely a sober word exchanged between us. Because of him, I'd gone on an adventure. I'd had a bit of fun, and nothing terrible had happened as a result. I drank too much wine perhaps, but I hadn't fallen apart. Not only that, but I'd resisted the temptation to beg Fox to stay and comfort me again.

I'd proven Dr. Payne wrong in at least some of his assertions. I was no worse off after a night's indulgence, and I'd managed to keep my head despite the demon alcohol. If he was wrong about that, then perhaps he was wrong about other things. He was only a man. No man was right all the time.

My uncle was due for his regular visit in a few days. He hadn't sent word that he planned to make any alteration to that, despite the unplanned visit he'd had to make. That gave me a few nights to practice and prepare to speak to him again about my medicine. I might be able to get through it this time if I planned what I would say well enough in advance. Fox had done that for me. And if I were very lucky, Fox would come again before my uncle's visit to give me just that little extra push I needed to go through with it.

"Damn and blast," I swore in disgust as I bungled the speech I was preparing yet again. I'd been practicing for days, my uncle's visit was tomorrow, and with each attempt, my confidence diminished a little more.

"Such language, Arthur, really. I'm shocked," Fox chuckled.

I jumped and threw him a halfhearted glare as I tried to get my heart back in my chest. But then I noticed a darkened patch under one of his eyes and another along his jaw. "What happened?" I asked, taking a step toward him before forcing myself to stop.

For a moment, he frowned at me, but then his face split in that wry grin again, and he shrugged. "Nothing to worry about, old chap. I may have run into a spot of trouble the other night with some old acquaintances, but I've had worse."

"You were beaten?" I asked appalled.

"Hardly. I had a little misunderstanding with some of my former acquaintances in the East End. We exchanged a few pleasantries, and then I was on my way."

"Those hardly look like pleasantries."

His expression sobered, and his smile this time was soft. "Don't worry. I'm right as rain, truly. I was more worried about you, after I left you in your cups the other night."

I flushed and rolled my eyes. Clearly he didn't wish to talk about the bruises. "I'm not so fragile as all that. I was fine with a bit of rest. Although I think I'll pour my own wine from now on."

"Perhaps a wise choice. So what has you so frustrated that you would stoop to uttering such profanity?" he asked, as he settled in my chair and regarded me with a crooked smile and quirked eyebrow.

At his reminder, I groaned and flopped into the other chair. "I'm trying to find some way to broach the subject of my medication with my uncle again that won't result in my panicking and bungling the whole affair. I just can't predict what my nerves will do—or I can predict they'll fail me as they always do—and I'm afraid I'll only make matters worse if I keep trying."

"I see," he replied pensively.

I growled my frustration, leapt from my chair, and began pacing again. "The worst of it is, they all still treat me like a child, as if the last ten years hadn't happened and I'm still that broken boy. I know I'm not ready for many things, and I may never be. But you were right. I'm not so unwell as to need to be locked up day and night. I have my spells, and I know I can be unreasonable and embarrassing at times, but I wouldn't hurt anyone. I wouldn't do any real harm. How can I ever get better if I'm never allowed to take even the first tiny steps toward a normal life?"

"I'm glad to hear you say it."

His approving smile warmed me, but I could not allow myself to dwell on it. That way led to the madness I was trying to distance myself from. His smile was given in friendship, nothing more.

"You deserve more," he continued. "Ten years is a long time to pay for one small infraction, if there even was one. I've known men who beat a man nearly to death who didn't serve ten years for the crime."

"Thank you for that." Mollified but still fearing my chances of success were bleak at best, I slumped in my chair and brooded into the hearth. "Now if only I could convince my uncle of that. I stand no chance with Dr. Payne. I know that for a certainty. I just don't know how to get my uncle to listen when I might fall to pieces at any moment. You have no idea how frustrating that is."

"Why don't you write to your uncle, present all your arguments in a letter? You wouldn't have to fear for your nerves, then."

"I'd thought of that, but even as inept as I am at reading faces, I should still like to see his when I broach the subject again. I'd like to have the opportunity to counter, or at least address, his concerns immediately. I fear if I write to him, he will only seek out Dr. Payne before I can make him understand... and my failures recently won't help matters any, I'm sure."

Unable to sit still, I pushed out of the chair and strode back to the looking glass. I fussed with my clothes and my hair, because it gave me something to do, but the same thin, worried face stared back at me as always.

Weak.

It's what my ancestors would have called me.

The weight of Fox's hands on my shoulders made me shiver as I fought the desire to step back into his embrace. I wanted the feeling of his arms around me again, almost more than I wanted to breathe. But it wasn't moral fortitude or pride that kept me still this time. It was fear of rejection, fear of ruining what little good opinion he might have of me and fear of chasing him away for good if I asked too much, particularly when I knew it was wrong.

"You are too hard on yourself," he murmured, giving my shoulders a light shake. "Look how far you've come in only a short time. You cannot expect all of your challenges to disappear overnight, nor beat yourself about the head and shoulders every time you fail to live up to such exacting expectations. Take one small step at a time. Celebrate each little victory and build on it until you can reach the next."

I let out a strangled laugh. "That seems strangely understanding, coming from someone who claims to be a bully charging through life without consideration for anyone else." I lifted my gaze and gave him a wry smile, and he chuckled as I'd hoped he would.

He held my gaze in the mirror for a long time after his laughter died, and my smile fell away too. His hands tightened on my shoulders and my breath stopped. I didn't know what I hoped would happen—or at least I couldn't admit it even to myself—but I couldn't deny my disappointment when he suddenly released his grip and stepped away from me.

"You're absolutely right, of course. I'm horribly inconsistent. You shouldn't listen to a word I say." He laughed, but it sounded forced even to me. Despite his laugh, when he met and held my gaze again, his expression was quite sober. "But I do wish the best for you. I hope you know that. I would see you happy and free to do as you please…. I should like that very much."

My chest tightened with unfamiliar emotion, and I took a step toward him but stopped with one of the chairs between us. My heart beat erratically in my chest as I asked, "Why?"

He frowned, his silver brows drawing together. "Why do I wish to see you happy? I may not be a very good man by society's standards, but I'm not a monster. I'm not without feeling."

He seemed truly offended, and I quickly closed the last few feet between us until I stood mere inches from him. "No, I know that. I only wanted to know why you care so deeply. Why is it so important to you that I leave these rooms?"

He studied my face in silence for a time before he blew out a breath and shook his head. His lips twisted, and his eyes held something almost ugly in their depths. "If I am merely a figment of your imagination, then it is you who cares so deeply about this, isn't it?"

"Don't do that," I ordered shakily, battling my hurt with anger.

His eyes narrowed, and his jaw ticked for a moment before he deflated and turned away from me. "I'm sorry. I warned you, didn't I?" He dropped into his chair again and uncorked the bottle I hadn't seen before. He must have brought it with him. Without looking for a cup, he drank heartily, straight from the neck. For a long time, he sat in silence, brooding into the dying coals of my fire, his jaw tight and the bottle held close.

Part of me feared to push this conversation any further, but another part was so very tired of being afraid.

"You didn't answer my question," I pressed breathlessly. "Why?"

He wiped his hand across his mouth and set the bottle on his knee. Without looking at me, he said, "Because I care for you. Does it have to be more than that? I thought we were friends now, you and I. Friends wish each other well. Friends don't like to see their friends unhappy. And friends try to help where they may. Isn't that enough? Must I have some ulterior motive?"

He sounded so tired all of a sudden that shame stabbed through me. I rushed to him and knelt by the arm of his chair. Taking the hand not holding the bottle in my own, I said, "I'm sorry. You're right. I'm an ungrateful wretch. I wish I could say I'm not myself, but I fear this is how I am, so changeable from one day to the next sometimes I hardly know myself. Forgive me."

He took another long pull from the bottle, then shook his head and gave my hand a squeeze. "There's nothing to forgive." He sighed and gave me a sad smile. "You know who you are. You only speak aloud the feelings and fears all men have but keep hidden. If you remember, it's one of the things I admire about you, how open you are, how genuine. In that regard, you are a far braver man than I."

He took another pull from the bottle while I tried to puzzle out what he meant. I'd held his hand for far longer than was proper, but I couldn't bring myself to let go just yet. The warmth of it in mine made my body ache for the feel of his arms around me again, until I couldn't bear it anymore. I released him and moved to the other chair, putting some distance between us.

He offered me the bottle once I was seated, but I shook my head. "No. I think I learned my lesson last time."

His face softened and his lips quirked. "I shan't let you overindulge again. No need to worry."

"Still, I think I shouldn't for now."

With a shrug, he took another long pull from the bottle while I desperately searched my mind for something to put us back on surer ground. I needed him here with me. I needed his wit, his care—even his provocation. But how far down the path could I go before I couldn't come back again?

Thump. Scrape. Thump. Scrape.

I gritted my teeth and closed my eyes as the hairs on the back of my neck rose. There was my answer.

I wanted to laugh and cry at the same time.

When I opened my eyes again, I found him watching me, his expression uneasy. His shoulders looked tense beneath the silk of his costume, and the tendons in his neck corded as he took another pull from the wine bottle.

"There's nothing there," I assured him tiredly.

He grimaced. "I don't know how you can listen to that, night after night. It sounds as if it's right outside your door."

"Necessity, and all that," I said with forced indifference. "Once you've heard it a few hundred or so times, it loses some of its impact."

His expression said he didn't quite believe me, but he asked, "And you've never seen anything?"

"No."

"But you've never been in the hall when it happened either, correct? You've never been in those rooms?"

"Not that I remember."

He pursed his lips. "Perhaps you might see something where I cannot."

I shivered and shook my head. "I don't think I want to see whatever it is, to be honest."

His lips quirked. "Fair enough."

Thump. Scrape. Thump. Scrape.

Shifting uneasily in his chair, Fox cleared his throat loudly. "Why don't you play for me again, then? Your playing is vastly preferable to that."

His volume increased with each word, until he was practically shouting to be heard over the hollow moan that reverberated through my rooms.

"Such compliments are like to overwhelm me." I forced a laugh, and he smiled.

Hating to see him so uneasy, I quickly moved to the bench and began to play from memory. I chose Beethoven this time, something loud and frantic to drown out the moaning and wailing. It worked. I lost myself in the music, and when I finally reached the end of the piece, the noises from the hall had ceased.

"Thank you, Arthur," Fox murmured.

His voice sounded so downcast, I spun toward him and frowned. "Are you sad?"

I had to be reading his expression wrong. The piece I had played was rousing and angry, if anything, and certainly the noises from the hall had never prompted him to sadness before.

"Maybe a little," he agreed, quietly.

"Why?"

Shaking his head, he waved me off and took another pull from the bottle. "It's nothing. I was reminded of something, that's all, something I once had but lost."

"What?"

"It doesn't matter." He shook himself and sat straighter in his chair. "We're not here to talk about me, now are we? Earlier, you had a concern weighing heavily upon you, and now, I think I just might have come up with a solution."

"A solution? To what?" I squeaked. Had he read my thoughts? Did he know the desires I hid?

"To talking to your uncle, of course."

"Oh. That." Blushing at where my mind had gone, I continued in a slightly more normal voice. "Yes, of course. That. You thought of something?"

"I did. I think you should write down your arguments as I suggested, but instead of posting them, you should simply have them with you when you speak to him next. Then, if your nerves fail you, you can simply hand over the slips of paper." Warming to his subject, he leaned forward in his chair grinning. "You see? It's the perfect solution. I'll help you. We'll both sit down and try to think of every argument he's used in the past or might possibly come up with and write them on separate cards, along with your demands, and you can hand them over as needed, without having to worry about remembering the content when you're flustered. Simple."

My embarrassment forgotten, I pondered it a moment. "I don't know how simple it is, but I'm willing to try."

He beamed at me. His earlier melancholy seemingly forgotten in his excitement, he pushed up from the chair and took my elbow. With his urging, I moved to my small writing desk between the bookcases. Then he carried one of the lanterns over. His excitement was as infectious as always, and my blood thrummed in my veins. Pen and heart in hand, I wrote notes containing all of my wishes down first, including my desire to have free run of my house during the day.

"Why not all the time?" Fox asked, reading over my shoulder.

"You were the one who said I should take things slowly," I reminded him.

"I suppose that's true," he chuckled.

He braced his hands on the back of my chair as he leaned in, and I closed my eyes, savoring his nearness. It was wrong, but I couldn't wish him away. My hand shook, and I had to set the pen aside for fear of making a mess of my remaining paper.

A man could be forgiven a few sinful thoughts as long as he never acted on them, couldn't he? It did not make him wholly irredeemable.

"Arthur?"

"Sorry. I was just thinking if I should add anything," I lied.

Satisfied I'd expressed all of my concerns as well as I might, I then tore the remaining sheaves of blank paper in half to address any arguments my uncle might have. But between my uncle's fears for my health, and his and the doctor's refusal to see me as anything but a child or an invalid, I soon ran out of space to write more.

"Wait, there's a pad over here," Fox said as he moved to my easel and small drawing table in the corner. Before I could stop him, he opened my drawing pad and discovered the dozens of sketches I'd hidden there. I cringed in mortification as he leafed through them, one by one.

After an eternity of silence, he cleared his throat and said, "And here I thought you preferred landscapes to portraits. These are quite good. Yet another talent you possess. Are there any more I should know of?"

Unsure if he meant talents or sketches of him, I could only shake my head, wishing a hole would open beneath me and swallow me. Luckily he didn't ask for any further explanation. He simply removed a few blank sheaves and returned the pad to the drawing table.

"Here you are," he said, handing me the paper, and I gratefully turned back to my work.

He retrieved his bottle from the table by his seat, but when he returned to stand by my shoulder, he put more distance between us than before. I should have been grateful for that, given how distracting his presence could be, but to say I was would have been a lie.

When I finally finished the last of the arguments Fox and I could come up with between us, I set my pen down and rubbed my chilled and aching fingers. He had remained fairly subdued while I worked, only giving quiet advice here and there, and he stepped away from me as soon as I was done, leaving nothing but chill air at my back.

"It won't be long before dawn," he murmured.

"Yes."

"I should go."

I hated those words.

"You'll come back?"

He was silent long enough I stood and took two steps toward him but halted when he lifted somber brown eyes to mine.

"I really do help, truly? I don't make things worse for you?"

He sounded so uncertain, so vulnerable, I blinked at him in surprise. "Of course you don't. I told you before, you've helped me immensely. Who knows how long I would've allowed myself to float in this half life if you hadn't come along to challenge me. Even if nothing comes of this," I said, holding up the papers I'd written, "I'll know I tried. I'll know I didn't give up entirely without a fight. That means the world to me, and it's all thanks to you."

"Thank you. I suppose even a thief and a scoundrel needs a little reassurance from time to time." He laughed and shook his head. "I should go before the wine has me admitting to anything else."

"So you'll come again?" I pressed.

"Yes."

"Promise?"

"I promise." He took a step toward me and looked as if he might say something more, but then he shook his head. "Good night, Arthur."

"Good night."

Chapter Eleven

On that Wednesday, Uncle Oscar arrived at his usual time. Much as I disliked it, my medicine allowed me to pass the morning in relative peace despite my rising anxiety about the coming conversation. By afternoon, however, I had patted the pocket of my jacket where I'd stashed my notes so many times the skin of my palm was chafed and raw and I feared I'd rub a hole in the cloth.

I could do this. I didn't have to speak if my nerves became too much. I could simply hand over the appropriate note and use the time it took him to read it to do my breathing exercises.

My uncle loved me. Pendel loved me. They wanted what was best for me. Even if we could not agree on what that was, they wanted me to be happy too. I had to believe that.

"Uncle," I said, taking his hand and forcing a smile.

"My dearest boy. You're looking hale and healthy, I must say. Wonderful. Wonderful."

I followed him back to our usual seats by the library fire, taking slow breaths and resisting the urge to pat my breast pocket again.

Pendel served the tea like always. Uncle Oscar devoured Mrs. Peeble's sandwiches and apple tarts while I sipped at my tea to ease the butterflies in my stomach and counted my breaths. I studiously turned a blind eye to the flickering bluish light manifesting in the corner of the room.

"Arthur? Are you well?"

God, how I hated those words.

"Of course, Uncle. Why do you ask?"

He grimaced and set his half-eaten tart back on the plate. "I just asked if you'd read anything riveting recently and you've been unusually quiet."

Flustered, I took a sip of my tea and shook my head. "No, nothing of note. Sorry, my mind must have wandered."

He didn't look convinced, but after darting a glance to Pendel, he shrugged and held his teacup out for Pendel to refill. "Good, then. Well, not about the book, but you know...."

He stumbled to a halt, and I smiled sadly. I hated that I made him so uncomfortable. He was the only close family I had left, and I had given him enough grief in this life. Unfortunately I would have to give him more if I ever hoped to be the man he wanted me to be.

It was time. I couldn't put it off any longer.

Lifting my chin and throwing my shoulders back, I drew the stack of notes from my pocket and divided them into two piles on the table between us.

I cleared my throat and settled my shaking hands in my lap. "There are some things I should like to speak to you about, Uncle." I kept my gaze firmly fixed on the papers, for fear seeing his expression would cause me to flounder.

"Arthur, I—"

I held up a hand, still not looking at him or Pendel. "Forgive me, but I need to say this. All I ask is that you hear me out." He was silent, but whether that was due to shock or concern, I didn't know.

After another slow inhale and exhale, I said, "I know you, Dr. Payne, and Pendel only want what you think is best for me. I know you have gone to great trouble and expense to see me content, despite my illness, but...." My mind went blank, and sweat broke out on my forehead. My hand shook as I reached for the cards but steadied when I held them in my grasp. I didn't need to read them—just having them bolstered my courage, as did the bit of bent metal I kept in my waistcoat pocket. Closing my eyes, I pictured Fox's wry grin, and I took another deep breath and pushed on. "The truth is, Uncle, I cannot stay in those rooms for the rest of my life, and I'm sure you don't want that for me either."

Drawing my courage around me, I lifted my gaze to my uncle and then to Pendel. Both men regarded me with wary concern, but it was my uncle who spoke. "Of course not, my boy. When you're well again—"

"I can't get well again, if nothing ever changes." I forced the words past the tightness in my chest, silencing him. Refusing to acknowledge the guilt that stabbed through me at the pained look on his face, I glanced at my notes and pressed on. "I'm in that room day in and day out. I read. I paint. I play. But nothing ever changes. How can I learn how to live in the world and how to behave in society if I'm not given a chance to practice? I'm not saying I'm ready to be seen in society. I wouldn't embarrass you or the family name like that. But I should be allowed to move freely about my own house. I've done nothing in the last several years to warrant such fears for my safety or anyone else's, have I?"

"Dr. Payne said—"

"Dr. Payne isn't the only physician in England or even in London," I interrupted, plowing forward like I imagined Fox would have done. "He's had over ten years to fix me, and he hasn't done so. Perhaps it's time we consult someone else."

I felt fevered. I was sure my cheeks had to be bright red, but I refused to give in to the weakness that threatened to swallow me.

"Arthur," Uncle Oscar said in a conciliatory tone, lifting his hands in a placating gesture, "please don't upset yourself. Perhaps Pendel should go and fetch some of your medicine, just a little to calm you down."

"No."

I didn't shout it, but Pendel froze midstep, and both men remained silent until I dredged up the strength to speak again. "I don't want any medicine," I said calmly and quietly. Drawing on the memory of Fox's firm grip on my shoulders, I sat higher in my seat and held my Uncle's gaze. "You read the papers the same as I, Uncle. You know the dangers of opium, the deaths. Surely in ten years, advances had to have been made in the treatment of my affliction."

Uncle Oscar paled. "I know of some. Dr. Payne has recommended a few, and I've toured some institutions, but you don't want that, do you?"

He's toured institutions?

My throat closed, and I almost lost the death grip I had on my nerves. I fumbled frantically through the stack of notes on the table until I found the one I needed and handed it to him while I struggled to catch my breath.

"What is this?" Oscar asked.

An institution is not a viable treatment option for me. While I concede their reputation may have improved some in recent years, and I know you would seek out only the best for me, I believe such a course would prove disastrous to my health. Any treatments an institution could possibly provide can be acquired here at Campden House without involving others in our private affairs. Furthermore, and to make my feelings on the matter abundantly clear, should anyone press the subject, I will engage the services of a solicitor and drag the whole matter through the courts if necessary.

Fox had insisted I add the last sentence even though it was an empty threat, as I'm sure my uncle knew. I couldn't engage a chimney sweep without his or Pendel's assistance. But Uncle Oscar's dark blond eyebrows shot up to his thinning hairline as he read, just the same.

"Nephew," he said, sounding quite hurt. "There's no need for that, surely. You know I've only tried to do what's best for you. You must know that. I had no idea you were so unhappy. For years you've said nothing of it. And only now, you're having… *troubles* again. Might you concede that your illness may be influencing your decisions?"

He spoke with such care, each word was like a knife of guilt, and I began to doubt myself. Seeking comfort, I took the bent wire from my pocket and clutched it tightly in my palm as I flipped through my notes until I found the one I sought.

I didn't hand this one over to him, but I reviewed it before I spoke, hoping to bolster my flagging confidence. "The return of my *troubles* is more a result of my frustrations and my desire to have some simple freedoms. Yes, I will admit my illness can influence me. It can make me seem irrational sometimes and make me do and say strange things. I can't always trust my mind. But surely you can acknowledge the things I'm asking for are not unreasonable desires for any man. I want to spend my days awake and alert instead of lying senseless. I want the freedom to roam about my own house instead of remaining locked up day and night. I want a chance to improve myself beyond simply not being a bother to anyone. I'm not asking for the world. I only want you to talk to other doctors, to get other opinions. I only want to try to step back slowly on my medicine and see what happens. I only want a chance to leave my rooms, maybe for a little while at first, and then more often as I prove I can be trusted that much and my illness doesn't worsen. I'm not a child anymore, Uncle. I need to at least *try* to be a man, to be Lord Campden."

Pendel shifted restlessly behind my uncle's chair, as if he couldn't keep still. It was the only time I could ever remember him displaying such a lack of aplomb, particularly in my uncle's presence, but I couldn't spare him much attention with so much riding on Uncle

Oscar's response. My nerves were frayed enough without letting Pendel's unease affect me too.

Uncle Oscar searched my face as he worried his lower lip. My heart thudded unpleasantly in my chest, my palm ached where the wire bit into it, and my clothes were clammy with sweat. He stared at me long enough that his gaze grew distant and vacant, as if he weren't looking at me at all. I shivered in my damp clothes and nearly wept when he focused his gaze on me again, because his eyes and face were deeply etched with what I feared could only be sadness and regret.

"You're right, Arthur. Those are desires any man would have," he said, surprising me. "I'm sorry if you felt you couldn't come to me with them sooner. I do want you to be happy, and I want you to be well. But I'm only a simple man. I don't know what to do. I don't know what is best. I couldn't bear it if I chose the wrong thing and you regressed to the state you were in when John and Eleanor died. Or worse.... I... I couldn't bear it."

He looked so much older all of a sudden, but I couldn't turn back now. I'd already said the words.

Following a brief, uncomfortable silence, Oscar sighed and ran a hand over his thinning hair. "I'll send out inquiries for another doctor and think about all you've said. Will that do for now?"

"Yes," I answered, breathlessly. I had a whole stack of other arguments and points I could make, but I was exhausted, and he'd agreed to at least one of my demands. I could save the rest for later. With shaking hands, I tucked my notes back in my breast pocket and returned the wire to my waistcoat. "Thank you."

He nodded. With a tired grunt, he stood and headed for the door. Pendel was there before him and held it open as he passed through. My legs threatened to buckle when I stood to follow, but they grew stronger as I walked. We were a quiet party as we made our way to the front door. Tom hovered anxiously behind me as Pendel produced Uncle Oscar's coat, hat, scarf, and gloves, then opened the front door for him.

On the threshold, Uncle Oscar paused and turned back to me. "I hope you always feel you can talk to me. We're the only family each of us has left now, after all. Be patient with me. We'll figure out what's best."

"Thank you, Uncle." I wanted to leap at him and hug him with all the emotion inside me, but I couldn't in front of the servants, even if Uncle Oscar wouldn't have been scandalized by the very idea.

He tipped his hat to me and to Pendel and then disappeared into the waiting carriage. I almost crumpled where I stood when the fog swallowed his carriage, but I retained enough dignity to make it back to my room before collapsing on my bed in an exhausted heap.

I'd done it.

Chapter Twelve

The room was dark when I woke again. Unsure of the hour, I rang for Pendel, and he arrived with my dinner tray soon after.

"Thank you, Pendel, and thank Mrs. Peebles too. The lamb stew and the mince pies smell absolutely delicious, as always."

"Of course, my lord."

Pendel's demeanor was as formal as ever, but I thought there might have been an approving smile hovering around the corners of his lips. He was pleased, perhaps as pleased as I was with my success that afternoon. I could tell.

After the servants left me alone again with a cheery fire and brightly lit lanterns, I devoured my dinner as if I hadn't eaten in weeks, and the moment every last crumb was gone, I was on my feet prowling my room. I couldn't sit still. I wanted to dance. I wanted to sing. The only thing missing was Fox. Not because I needed his comfort or his ability to distract me for once, but because I was happy and wanted to share that with him, to thank him.

I didn't know what to do with all of the emotion swelling inside me, so I did the only thing I could. I moved to my pianoforte and played and played, pouring everything out through my fingers.

"You seem rather giddy tonight."

I didn't think it possible, but my heart lifted even more. I sprang from my bench and rushed over, skidding to a stop a mere foot from him. "I did it! I didn't break down even once, and Uncle Oscar listened and said he agreed that it was time for a change, and he would think on it awhile and send out inquiries for a new physician. Isn't that wonderful?"

"Think on it? What is there to think on?" he replied, frowning.

I waved a dismissive hand. "I don't mind. I think he actually saw me this time—as a man, not a child, or an invalid, or a burden to be borne. That is enough for now."

His smile was fond as he watched me practically bouncing in front of him. "You're right. I shouldn't belittle your accomplishment." He moved closer to me and placed his warm hand on my neck and squeezed. "Congratulations. I'm very proud of you. In fact, I think a celebration is in order."

He allowed me to lean in to his hand for a brief moment before he removed it. Then he cleared his throat, clapped his hands together, and rubbed them briskly. "I think this calls for a little trip to the wine cellar, don't you?"

"Yes. Let's."

I would not let my nerves ruin this night. I wanted to celebrate. I wanted to run through the halls with Fox and open every door in the house. But for now, I would settle for a trip to the cellar and a small celebration in my rooms, as long as he was with me.

He moved to my door, but before he could kneel in front of the lock, I tugged on his sleeve. "Wait. Will you show me how to do it? Whether Uncle Oscar agrees to my terms or not, it seems a handy thing to know."

He grinned at me. "That it is. Certainly, I can teach you. Hell, these locks are so old and simple, I could have taught you with that bit of wire from your spectacles. With my tools, it should only take a moment."

I pulled the wire from my pocket and offered it to him. "Teach me with this, then, if it's so easy, since I won't have your tools when you're gone."

He lifted an eyebrow, and I felt myself blush that I still carried it, but he only said, "I can bring another set next time I come. I'd give you these, but...." He ran a reverent hand over the small leather case in his palm and smiled sadly at it. "These were a gift, and I'm rather partial to them."

A spike of something I thought might be jealousy ran through me as his eyes took on a faraway look. "It's all right," I said, breaking in on his reverie. "If I learn with this wire, I shan't need a fancy case, and I won't have to explain such a thing being in my rooms if it's discovered. And if I lose this bit of wire, I can always get another from my new spectacles, though Pendel might get a little concerned if I keep breaking them."

"Excellent point," he replied, his smile and dark eyes focused on me again.

After retrieving one of my lamps, I crouched beside him in front of the lock.

"Move the wire around inside until you feel it catch on the bar. It will take a little time for you to know what you're feeling, but really, all you have to do is pull the bar back with the wire and it's done. Like I said, these are painfully outdated and very simple locks. My tools are a little firmer, but mostly unnecessary for this."

It took me longer than it should have, with him beside me—his warmth and his voice sending shivers through me—but I managed it. My sense of accomplishment paled a bit when he stood and stepped away from me, but it was better that way. I couldn't allow his presence to affect me like that.

"Are you coming?" Fox whispered from a few steps down the hall.

I was dithering by the door, lost in my thoughts, when the cellar and another adventure awaited. I rolled my eyes at myself and hurried after him.

The trip to the cellar and back went much faster this time. I let him tackle the lock to that door, not wanting to ruin my wonderful night by being caught out, and we each grabbed a bottle from the racks—though Fox took a great deal more time selecting his than I did mine.

Back in my rooms, he uncorked his bottle and filled two small crystal goblets he'd pilfered from a cupboard in the kitchen on our way back.

"A proper celebration and such a fine vintage deserve proper crystal, I should think. But don't worry. I'll hide them on my way out so they aren't discovered." Smiling broadly at me, he lifted his glass, and at his nod, I did the same. "To Arthur, and living the life he deserves."

I flushed, feeling a bit odd drinking to myself, but downed the contents of my glass nonetheless. He smiled at me with shining eyes as he refilled it. "Now, what say we have some music? We can't have a party without music."

Finding his merriment contagious and not wanting to see it fade in the slightest, I obliged him. This time, I dug through the contents of my bench until I found the scores I'd hidden at the bottom. Mr. Fuller sometimes sent sheets of lowbrow music along with the classics in my packet, writing that he wished to make sure I had access to a well-rounded selection, but Pendel disapproved of such "parlor music" or "music hall tripe," as he called it, so I rarely played it.

Tonight I played the unfamiliar tunes with alacrity if not perfect accuracy. Luckily the melodies were simple, and Fox knew the words to many, singing along in a pleasant, if rough, baritone. I don't know how long I played and drank, but I couldn't remember ever having such a lovely time.

I'd worked up a bit of a sweat, and I was giddy with merriment and wine when he suddenly pulled me from my bench and danced me about the room, laughing and humming the tune I'd been playing. Breathless and a little awkward, I tried to keep up with him, and at last my feet remembered some of the steps to the country dances Nanny had taught me as a young lad. His arm around my side, his free hand clasping mine, we skipped about the room, bumping into furniture and nearly oversetting the second bottle of wine he'd opened. I never wanted it to end, but then I tripped over the corner of the rug and sent us both to the floor in a tumble, laughing breathlessly.

"Shhhh. We don't want to bring the whole house down on us," I gasped.

"Are you all right?"

"Yes. I might have a little bruise on my hip, but nothing to worry about."

I lay sprawled on the carpet in front of the hearth and thought there couldn't be anywhere in the world I'd rather be. I propped myself on my elbows and grinned over at him. He remained reclined on his side not far from me, regarding me with laughing eyes, but that merriment slowly faded as he watched me, and my grin faded in response.

After a breathless eternity where he held my gaze, he cleared his throat and looked away.

"I should go now, Arthur."

"What? Why?"

He rolled away from me and stood, but I came after him before he could get five paces. "Don't go. We were having such a merry time. The sun won't be up for hours. I don't want you to go." I sounded like a petulant child, but I couldn't help it. The night couldn't end yet. It just couldn't.

He sighed and shook his head as if to clear it. "I've had too much wine, Arthur. Please trust me when I say it's better that I go before I do something I shouldn't."

"What shouldn't you do? I don't understand." I hugged myself in a sudden chill, but despite a rising sense of anxiety, I couldn't bring myself to move away from him. He might leave if I gave him more space.

He frowned at me. "I think you do understand. We've been honest with each other thus far, haven't we? At least inasmuch as you'd allow me to. No dissembling, no prevarication, remember?"

I bit my lip and nodded.

He waited for me to say something, but my throat was dry and no words would come. Eventually he growled. "Then I suppose I shall have to be honest for both of us. I've said it before, but you pretended it was a joke, or you became distressed, and I let the matter drop for your sake. Perhaps you don't realize how lovely you are, or the effect you have on me, but I think some part of you must." He sighed and dragged a hand through his silver hair. "I'm not a youth anymore, subject to unbridled passions, but that doesn't mean I'm immune to them either. Seeing you so happy and laughing and beautiful… you take my breath away."

I did take a step back then and shook my head. "You shouldn't say such things," I whispered.

"I know I shouldn't. And that is why I need to leave you now. If we are to remain friends, it's best that I go." I shook my head again in denial, and his sad smile twisted wryly as he took a step toward me. "Remember, Arthur, I'm not the best of men most days. Around you my control seems to abandon me. Add a good deal of wine to that, and if I stay, I'm like to kiss you. We wouldn't want that, now would we, not us proper English gentlemen."

I could barely breathe with the vise gripping my chest. He didn't move closer to me, but he didn't step away either. He was waiting for me to respond again, giving me a chance to deny it, but I couldn't. I didn't know what to feel. A chasm had opened up on all sides of me, and any decision I made would result in a fall.

At length, he nodded and turned to leave, but my hand shot out of its own accord and fisted in the silk of his sleeve.

"Don't go."

Fox sighed and hung his head. "I promise I'll come back again, Arthur. I won't drink so much, and we can go on as we have. Just give me tonight and perhaps tomorrow, and I'll be a better man. I promise."

I should have let him leave, but I couldn't bring myself to release his sleeve. In fact, my hand twisted tighter in the silk. "Do you wish only to kiss me?" I asked breathlessly, surprising myself as much as I appeared to surprise him.

"What?" he asked, searching my face in the flickering light.

"A kiss is not such a terrible thing," I reasoned.

His lips quirked. "No, a kiss is not a terrible thing," he replied slowly. "But I think you know I should like to do a great deal more than kiss you."

I was sure my cheeks had to be scarlet, and I couldn't seem to catch my breath, but I didn't let go of his sleeve as he moved closer to me.

"What do you want from me, Arthur?"

"I don't want you to go."

"But what do you *want*?"

"I want you to be here always, to never leave me."

He gripped my neck and leaned his forehead to mine. "I can't give you that. You know I can't. Not here. Not like this," he whispered into the barest few inches between us, the wine on his breath as intoxicating as what I'd drunk. "Is that all you want from me, my presence and my company? Tell the truth."

"No," I admitted. "But it isn't right to feel this way…. Is it?"

With him standing so close and his hand on my neck, I wasn't so certain of the answer anymore.

Lifting his forehead from mine, he dragged his knuckles down my cheek and held my gaze. "It depends greatly on who you ask, I suppose."

Frowning, I finally forced myself to step back from his drugging touch. "That's hardly an answer."

"What do you want me to say?"

"I want you to tell the truth." I hugged myself and moved closer to the fire. "I'm not so ignorant of the world as you might think. The Church, the law, physicians, they all say what we're speaking of is wrong, *unnatural*. I've seen the trials in the papers. I've read about the scandals. Boulton and Park was not so long ago I don't remember it well."

"They were acquitted of any wrongdoing."

"Not before the scandal killed Lord Clinton."

"I thought the papers said scarlet fever killed Clinton," he replied, his wide eyes and innocent expression telling me he was being deliberately obtuse.

Gritting my teeth, I turned away from him. "I may be mad, but I'm not a fool. Don't treat me like I am." In the silence that followed, I laughed, but it had a brittle, ugly sound. "You know I asked my father about such things once… only once. After my fever, he would sit with me at night and read to me and encourage me to ask him questions. One night, I asked him if I could marry Pendel when I grew up, like he had married Mother. I'd had plenty of time in my sickbed to think on things, you see, and I reasoned that Pendel would make an excellent partner since he seemed so very capable of running the house and didn't really need Mother's help at all. My father was quite *firm* in his rejection of the notion—'scandalized' I suppose I'd have to call it now—and not long after, I was given a lecture on the *natural* order of things from Dr. Payne, as well as receiving a visit from a local parson. My father was uncomfortable with me for a long time." My lips twisted bitterly at the memory, and I rounded on Fox, more confident in my argument now. "So you see, it doesn't matter who you ask, *everyone* says it's wrong."

Instead of baiting me further as I'd expected, he only smiled sadly and said, "Not everyone... but most, yes."

Inexplicably disappointed that he didn't argue with me, I shook my head and turned my back on him again. "It's just another affliction I must bear, yet one more symptom of my diseased mind... as if I needed more."

Sunken in sudden melancholy, I didn't hear him move, but hard hands gripped my shoulders and spun me around to face him. "No. Now that I won't allow." His frown was fierce as he gazed down at me. "Most of the world sees it as depravity—a moral failing. I can't argue that, obviously. You've seen it for yourself. But *I* don't believe it. *I* don't believe it's an illness. I don't believe it's wrong." As if realizing the strength of his grip on me, he relaxed his hands and smoothed them over my shoulders. "I'm sorry. I didn't mean to seem so harsh." Releasing my shoulders, he stepped away from me and began to pace the rug. "It's a sensitive subject for me, and sometimes I get a little carried away.... I had someone, you see, someone who was very dear to me once, and I refuse to let anyone tell me what we had was wrong. No matter what came after, what we had was beautiful and right. To love and care for someone more than you do yourself is never wrong. No one can convince me otherwise."

He spoke more to himself than me and another stab of jealousy ran through me, overwhelming any other feeling with its intensity. "You loved someone? A-Another man?"

"Yes," he replied quietly. "He was my paramour." He studied my face intently as he said this, and I felt heat return to my cheeks. Uncomfortable beneath his regard, I broke away from his scrutiny and let my gaze wander over my room, but like a moth to a flame, I couldn't keep it from returning to him.

Silence stretched between us as I fought with myself.

"You have questions, Arthur. I can see them in your eyes. We're the only ones here. You can ask me anything you wish. You should know that by now."

I could lie and say I was only curious, but I knew the truth. I was jealous, and not out of friendship. I was jealous of a man I'd never met because he'd had something I wanted so desperately. Yet at the same time, I was terrified of what that meant.

"Arthur?"

"You and this man, you spent your days together?"

"And our nights, yes."

"You lived together as man and wife?"

He chuckled. "Not exactly, but near enough, yes. I would have married him if I could."

"But, how?"

His teasing smile turned cautious. "I'm not sure what it is you're asking."

"How did you live together like that? Did you not fear discovery? Scandal? Imprisonment?"

"Oh, well, yes, of course there was a bit of that. We had to be cautious. But it isn't so difficult as you might imagine. We were discreet. In truth, most people have their own lives to lead and enough difficulties of their own they don't have time to meddle in what isn't their affair. It's only the people of our class we needed to worry about, the idle and unhappy elite. I assure you, Arthur, the scandals you see in the papers have more than just moral outrage behind them. No one is ever singled out unless someone has something to gain by it. Ethan and I were both from wealthy families, yes, but not so high that anyone would profit from knocking us down."

He had that fond, faraway look again, but my curiosity managed to temper my jealousy. "What happened?"

He sighed and dragged a hand through his hair. "Perhaps we should leave this conversation for another time, when I'm a little less foxed." His serious expression softened as he chuckled at his own joke.

"Please just tell me."

Ignoring his crystal goblet, he grabbed the remaining open wine bottle and took a long pull from it before collapsing into his chair. He slumped in the seat with his legs outstretched and brooded into the fire for a moment before he murmured, "I failed him. That's what happened."

Unsure what to say, I crouched next to his chair and put my hand over the one he'd rested on the arm. The defeated slump of his shoulders bothered me more than I could say, but I didn't have the slightest idea what I could do to help. Nothing I'd read in all my novels and newspapers had ever prepared me for a conversation like this.

Frustrated and on edge, I struggled to think of something to say, but his nearness was distracting me again, and I wasn't so sure I wanted to fight it anymore.

At length, he sighed, turned the hand beneath mine over, and threaded our fingers together. My breath caught, but he didn't seem to notice. "If you must know," he said, "we were together a long time, from our school days. When we weren't much younger than you are now, we were hellions—spoiled, idle, everything I despise now. We had our allowances from our families, and we spent every penny on drink and entertainment." His dark eyes seemed to clear for a moment as he lifted them to mine. "He was a little like you in some ways—passionate, bright, perhaps a tad mercurial. I came to London first. He was a year behind me at Cambridge. But once he broke free of his obligations, he joined me in the rooms I'd rented, and I introduced him to the myriad pleasures and diversions London had to offer. We indulged in every vice and had a grand time doing it." A smile flickered about his lips and died. "It only took me a few years to grow bored with most of it, and Ethan grew tired of it too, in time… except the one indulgence he could never seem to shake."

"What was that?"

"Can't you guess?"

Realization dawned. "Opium?"

His lips twisted, but I couldn't call it a smile. "Yes. I introduced him to it, you know. I put it in his hands. I thought it a lark. Something to pass the time, like drink or cards. But he couldn't walk away from it like I did. He'd try to stop sometimes, for my sake, but he'd always go back. We fought. I railed at him. I begged him. I nursed him when he was ill from it. But in the end, I failed him."

I frowned and squeezed the hand that still held mine. "I don't understand. How was that your fault? You both indulged. You couldn't have known the effect it would have on him, and you took care of him. You didn't abandon him."

"But there's where you're wrong. I did abandon him."

"I don't believe that."

He barked out a bitter laugh. "I told you I wasn't the best of men."

He took another long pull of wine, and I grew restless, hating the hollow, beaten tinge to his voice. "You have treated me with nothing but care and kindness. I cannot believe you are as bad as you pretend."

The look in his eyes gave me pause. That darkness that sometimes lurked behind them was no longer hiding, and I struggled to hold his gaze.

"And if I were to kiss you right now, would you believe me then?"

He leaned forward, moving his face mere inches from mine, but despite the racing of my heart, I didn't flinch.

He was angry and unhappy. He was testing me. That was all.

"I don't know what to say to that," I answered, taking the coward's way out.

"I think you do."

His heated gaze dropped to my lips when I licked them nervously. The air between us was so close.

"We are alone here, no one to see, no one to hear, no one to judge," he whispered mercilessly. "Tell me what you want, Arthur."

I groaned and closed my eyes against the intensity of his stare. "I want to stop fighting. I want everything I think and feel to not be so wrong."

When I dared open my eyes again, his expression had softened. He released his grip on my hand and cupped my cheek. "I don't think what you feel is wrong."

"I wish I could believe that." My breath caught as he traced his thumb across my cheek.

"Why don't you try to believe it, just for tonight? Step out from under the weight of all that shame and worry and let yourself be happy. You'll be hurting no one."

He was so near I couldn't think for the scent of his skin and the heat of his body. I pressed my cheek into his palm and swayed with the intensity of the need inside me.

"Tell me what you want, and I will do it, whatever it is," he whispered. "I won't push you to do anything you don't ask for."

Closing my eyes, I surrendered and told him my deepest shame. "I want to lie in your arms again, like we did before."

The hand on my cheek twitched, and when I looked to him, his expression was taut. "Arthur, I know you still like to pretend to yourself that I'm a mere conjuring of your imagination, but if that's the case, I'm a weak one. In the state I'm in tonight, I don't think I can give you that without asking more. I don't want to fail you, but I don't know that I can live up to your high opinion of me either."

"What more would you ask?"

He closed his eyes and groaned. "More than I should, I can assure you."

My breath quickened and my body tightened. The choice was mine. He'd promised he would return again no matter what. I would lose nothing if I stuck to the moral high ground. But right and wrong weren't as simple as I'd been led to believe, and just then, I couldn't move away from him even if I'd wanted to.

Taking my courage in both hands, I lifted my chin and said, "As you say, we're the only ones here, so I'll have to be the judge of what constitutes 'more than you should.'"

He blinked at me and then quirked an eyebrow in challenge as the corners of his mouth lifted. I expected some sort of wry rejoinder and braced myself for it, but I was wholly unprepared for him to set the wine bottle down, cup my cheeks in both hands, and place his lips to mine.

I had always imagined a kiss to be a pleasant experience. My novels made it sound so tantalizing and forbidden. Fox's kiss was only the barest brushing of lips, but my novels and my imagination had not done the experience justice. The warm satin of his skin lingered for an endless moment against my own. His scent, the hint of sweet wine on his breath, the heat of his body so close to mine, all combined to hold me rooted to the spot. I didn't even breathe for fear it would end.

"If I were a better man, I'd leave now," he whispered, his mouth still bewitchingly close. "You've read about the world, but you haven't lived in it. How could you possibly know what you really want? Your innocence and inexperience should give an honorable man pause."

I couldn't think. His lips remained only inches from my own. I swayed toward him without conscious thought, but he held me back with the hands still cupping my face.

"Tell me to leave, Arthur. Tell me to go and I will."

"No."

"If I stay, I'm going to kiss you again."

"Yes."

Closing the distance between us, he took my lips again. He plucked at them until I lifted my chin and copied him, kissing him back. The first warm, wet sweep of his tongue on my flesh set my body alight. I opened my mouth, greedy for more. His fingers threaded through my hair until he cupped the back of my skull. Everywhere he touched me tingled and warmed in anticipation of more. As with so many things, sensation overwhelmed me, but I was happy to be so. I surrendered to it, sank into it, not coming back to myself until he broke away from me panting for breath.

He pressed his forehead to mine. "You don't know what you do to me, lovely Arthur."

Even if I'd had the strength to walk away with my principles intact, his broken, raw whisper would've stopped me.

"I think I might," I answered shakily. "If it is anything like what you do to me."

This close, I could not see his expression clearly, but he groaned, drew me to my feet, and tugged me into his embrace. He wrapped strong arms around me and held me to his chest. I was dizzy with sensation, but as I pressed my face into the hollow of his throat, my world righted itself.

How could something so wonderful be wrong? Surely God would not wish me to suffer a life without it. He could not be so cruel after everything else I had been burdened with.

I wrapped my arms around Fox's lean frame and fisted my hands in the silk at his back. I hesitated a moment, keeping distance between our lower bodies, but then he buried his face in my hair, gripped my hips, and drew us together there as well.

My cock throbbed with the first solid press of his thigh against it. My hips jerked forward of their own accord, and I would have drawn back in embarrassment, but he held me still and pressed his own hardness to my belly. My breath caught in my chest, and I clutched at him.

Cradling the back of my head in his palm, he whispered in my ear, "Will you let me give you pleasure?"

My knees were weak, and my body flushed from head to toe. I could not speak for the pounding of my heart, but I nodded.

With a soft moan, he kissed the side of my head, my ear, and then my neck as he slid his hands down to my hips again and encouraged me to ease the ache in my cock against his thigh. As I flexed my hips, he slid his palms lower and gripped my buttocks through the layers of my clothing. I gasped and shivered, and he released me and drew my face between his palms again.

Gazing down at me with a look of concern, he said, "You don't need to be frightened. I would never do anything to hurt you or that you didn't want."

Struggling through the haze of my need, I frowned at him. "I never said you would."

His silver brows shot up for a moment before he grinned and his eyes sparkled wickedly down at me. "No, you didn't."

When I moved to renew our embrace, he stopped me with a hand on my chest. Holding my gaze, he slowly tugged the knot at my throat loose and tossed my neckcloth aside. My breath hitched as the buttons on my waistcoat gave way one by one under his nimble fingers, and then I stopped breathing altogether as he pushed the fabrics aside, undid the top button of my trousers, and drew up my shirt.

His soft fingers against the skin of my belly made me shiver anew, my body aching for more, but my clumsy inexperienced tongue was too afraid to ask for it.

"Fox, I...." Under his questioning gaze, I struggled for the right words, but they failed me. Finally I said, "Could we lie down, do you think? I feel a bit unsteady on my feet."

With a soft smile, he took my hand and led me to my bed. Away from his warmth, the chill of the room crept beneath my shirt and my nipples tightened. I stood nervous and uncertain as he turned down the bed linens. Then he drew me forward, and after removing my jacket and waistcoat, he urged me to lie down. I flushed in shame as he removed my shoes and tucked me beneath the covers as if I were a child, but the heat in his eyes never abated. I forgot my embarrassment altogether as he began to undress himself in front of me.

First, he untied the black silk sash from his waist, setting the small leather tool kit concealed within it on my bedside table. Then he undid the ties binding the silk of his sleeves to his wrists and forearms. At last, he loosened the barely visible ties at the front of his garment and pulled the shirt over his head. He wore no underclothes and as he revealed more of his pale skin in the warm lamplight, I forgot about anything other than my need to drink him in with my eyes and my hands.

His nipples pebbled in the chill air, and a little shocked at my sudden hedonistic urges, I longed to feel them beneath my palms. His grin and heavy-lidded eyes told me he liked me looking at him. But before I could look my fill, he moved to the other side of my bed, pulled off his soft leather boots, and climbed beneath the blankets.

I reached for him as soon as he was near enough, my hands touching his bared flesh for the first time. I couldn't help but wonder at being allowed such liberties with another man's body, but he didn't give me time to fully explore the feeling. He kissed me again, drawing on my lips as if they were a sweet he wished to devour, and I lost myself in the feel of his lips on mine and his hands on my body.

I only came back to myself when his hand slid beneath my undergarments, wrapped around my cock, and freed it from the confines of my trousers. I nearly came off the bed when a jolt of pleasure sang through me. I arched into his fist and moaned, uncaring that I lay with my shirt pushed up beneath my armpits and my trousers open and shoved down, bare to his gaze from my nipples to my cock. I lay sprawled wantonly on my bed linens as he stroked my cock. I could not think beyond the pleasure coursing through my veins or the tension coiling in my belly and my spine. I moaned and panted in abandon as he pushed me closer and closer to the edge of a precipice I feared to go over.

It was too much.

But then he kissed me, swallowing my sounds as he pumped his fist faster and squeezed me, and I couldn't hold on any longer. Arching my back and crying out, I tumbled over that cliff. Stars danced in front of my eyes, and I trembled and gasped through a few last pulses of pleasure before I collapsed to the mattress.

"Give me your hand," he whispered urgently against my cheek.

I complied without conscious thought, and then I felt his hardness in my palm. My senses were far too overwhelmed to fully take in the moment, still dizzy from what he had done to me. He wrapped his hand around mine and moved them as one on his shaft. In reflex more than any skill, I tightened my grip beneath his and allowed him to guide me. He pumped his hips into our combined fists. His hand was damp with sweat and the slick of my spend, and I thanked God that my eyes cleared in time to see his face as he arched into our palms, cried out, and released his own seed. He collapsed against me, his face buried in my neck as he panted, but I could still see the rapture in his expression when I closed my eyes.

Shaken, boneless, and suddenly adrift, I held that picture in my mind as my heart slowed and an ache built in my chest.

"Arthur? Arthur what's wrong?"

Surprised at his tone, I opened my eyes, but his face swam in my vision. I lifted a hand to my cheek and it came away damp. Only then did I realize I was crying. As if the realization opened the floodgates, now I couldn't seem to stop. I sobbed and turned my face away, mortified that he should see me like that, especially after what had just happened.

"Arthur, please tell me what's wrong. You're breaking my heart."

I shook my head. How could I tell him the thousand feelings writhing within me when I didn't understand them all myself?

He hovered over me, obviously distressed, but I couldn't do anything to ease his mind. "Damn and blast! I never should have done this. I'm so sorry. Forgive me. Please forgive me."

"No," I sniffed, forcing the tide back so I could make some sense. "It isn't that. Please don't blame yourself. I'm—it was wonderful, truly. I'm sorry for turning into such a blubbering fool. You should be the one to forgive me."

"Can you tell me? Help me understand?"

I shook my head and forced a weak chuckle. "I would if I understood it. I've never felt anything like this before. I'd say it was only that I'm overwhelmed, but that can't be the whole of it."

Tentatively, as if he feared I might break—and perhaps rightly so—he pressed a hand to my cheek, kissed my brow, and then smoothed my hair. He said nothing, giving me time to collect myself, and I smiled gratefully at him between steadying breaths. Lifting a shaking hand to his breast, I ran it over the soft warmth of his flesh. The turmoil inside me settled a bit as each new feeling separated from the tangle. I struggled to put them into words. "I suppose what I feel most is angry… or sad. I can't quite tell which. Perhaps it's both." I shook my head helplessly.

"So many nights I spent curled beneath these blankets, cold and alone, or in a nest in front of the fire so I would not have to face the empty space beside me on the mattress. I've been so lonely, Fox, you cannot even imagine the depths of it. I was cold to the bones of me, even at the height of summer, longing for something I thought I would and could never have. Hating myself for the feeling." I cupped his cheek and drew my thumb across the softness of his lips. "Now here you are, and we've just done something so wonderful, I want to crow for joy. But the world outside these walls would condemn it as the height of depravity, and I don't know how I am supposed to feel about that."

Unable to say more, I shrugged, my gaze full of pleas I could not voice.

He seemed to understand at least some of it, because he growled and pulled me to his breast. "I don't care about what you're supposed to feel. I only care about what you *do* feel. The world outside these walls isn't always right, Arthur. That's the first thing you'll learn when you're able to experience it. Society is full of folly… but it is ever-changing as well. Only a few short decades ago, I could have been hanged for the kind of loving I've shared with others of our ilk. And today, it results in a mere prison sentence, scandal, and public shaming. You see?" he laughed bitterly. "Such vast improvements in so short a space should be lauded. Only think what the future may hold."

His touch on my cheek was gentle despite the acid in his tone, and I managed a wobbly smile for him.

"You are not sorry for what we did?" he asked, his brows knit, his eyes soft with concern.

"No," I replied, feeling the certainty of that sink in as I said the word.

"No regrets?"

"None," I answered more confidently. I lifted my chin and laid my palm over his hand on my cheek. I could still feel the dampness there, and I brushed irritably at the evidence of my weakness. "However, you may have regrets, being tied to such a pathetic creature as I." Of all the emotions swirling inside me, anger at myself was winning now. I'd ruined a perfectly beautiful moment with my weakness and my nerves.

"Don't say that again," he ordered harshly. He rolled on top of me, straddled my hips, and gave my shoulders a firm shake. "I regret nothing, and you are by no means pathetic. How long will it take before you believe me?"

"I believe you."

"You don't. I know you don't."

"I *am* ill, Fox," I insisted. "You cannot deny that. I may get better. I may not. But this is how I am." I had no idea why it was so important for him to acknowledge that fact right this moment, but I frowned defiantly at him until his scowl fell away and he sighed.

"I know this is how you are. I just don't believe it is so great an obstacle as you think it." He climbed off me and stretched out next to me again. With his chin propped in his palm and his gaze pensive, he said, "I happen to like how you are a great deal, actually." He traced a lazy caress over my chest and down to my belly. I shivered and closed my eyes as he continued to draw patterns on my sensitized skin with his fingertips. "We all have flaws, Arthur. There isn't a soul beyond these walls who is perfect. From childhood we're taught how to act and what to say. We create masks to wear in society. Like papier-mâché, layer by layer we craft them. Then we paint them with respectability. But they only hide our real selves. They aren't who we are. Only the dullest and simplest among us actually becomes the mask."

"What does that make me, then?"

"You, my dear lad, are clever, charming, beautiful, passionate… and stronger than you think. Your mask is gossamer thin. That's all. You hide nothing, and that's wonderful."

I grimaced and lowered my gaze to the palm he'd laid on my chest. "I hide more than you think."

"You don't have to. I don't want you to. I want to see everything you feel."

"But it isn't how things are done outside. I need to learn, Fox. Just like I told my uncle, I can't stay here forever. I have to change some things, or I'll never be well. I'll never be free."

He sighed and moved his palm over my heart. "I know. I want you to have everything you desire, but you don't have to worry about those things when it's only the two of us. That's the beauty of taking a paramour," he said with a grin. "Outside doesn't matter when we're together."

I fiddled with his hand, stroking his fingers, before entwining them with my own. "I'm your paramour now?" I asked tremulously.

"It would appear so," he answered wryly. He was silent for a moment, and then he sighed. "If you really want me to, I can help you with your mask, but I like you better as you are."

I wanted to smile at the pleasure that brought me, but I was still so unsure of so many things. After a long silence, I took a breath and forged ahead. "May I ask what happened with that other man? You said you failed him, that you abandoned him. What did you mean?"

His hand stilled, and when I dredged up the courage to meet his gaze, his dark eyes were pained. "I wasn't there for him when he needed me. I was the one who introduced him to the poison that killed him. I did that. And when he couldn't break free of it, I blamed him and called him weak."

"What happened?"

He hesitated, his jaw clenched.

"Please," I pleaded. "You said you wanted to know everything about me, everything I feel. I only want the same."

His lips quirked. "Did I say that I admired how clever you are? Perhaps I should rethink that."

I glared at him and gave him a shove, and he chuckled and wrestled with me until I was beneath him, my arms held at the wrists and pressed to the pillows above my head.

"You can't distract me forever," I said, fighting a surge of unease.

"I could try."

I laughed breathlessly and shook my head. "Please," I said simply, trying very hard to ignore my body's conflicting responses to our position.

With a sigh, he released me and dropped to the bed next to me again. "All right. I shall tell you this once. Only please don't make me repeat it. Promise?"

"I promise."

"The last time I saw him—Ethan—we had a tremendous row. He'd promised to stop taking that poison again, but by that point I'd lost count of the number of times he'd told that lie. I had already nursed him so many times through the same illness you suffered, in addition to numerous other ailments because he did not have a care for his health when he was in the poison's clutches. He cared for little beyond obtaining more of it really." He blew out a breath. "That night, we were in the middle of a shouting match when Mrs. Bridge, the woman who let us our rooms, arrived with the post—and to kindly ask us to lower our voices. In the respite her interruption brought us, I opened the letter and its contents made me forget anything else. It was from the family's solicitor, you see, informing me of my father's death."

His lips twisted, and I laid a hand on his arm. "I'm sorry."

"Don't be. We were never close. It was the letter enclosed with the one from the solicitor that held more weight, with me at any rate. That one was from my mother and sister, begging me to come home and not just for the funeral. You see, without any of us being the wiser, my father had managed to mortgage our entire estate to the hilt and beyond. Father couldn't touch my allowance as it was in trust since I was the heir, but my mother and sister were in desperate straits, and I was somehow supposed to rush in and rescue the family from ruin, when all I knew how to do was drink and gamble and spend money—as any proper young gentleman."

"What happened?"

He shrugged. "Dutifully I went home. I left Ethan alone, trotted off to help my mother and sister—who hadn't spoken to me beyond a brief letter at Christmas for years—and set about trying to repair the damage that had been done." The eyes he lifted to mine were filled with pain and regret. "I left him. He promised me he would go home to his family for a while. I knew it was a lie, but I was so fed up and angry, I packed and left the next morning without even a proper good-bye." Deep lines etched the corners of his mouth, and he closed his eyes. "While I was dealing with the disaster at home, a friend sent me a letter to say Ethan was gravely ill, but by the time I made it back to London, he was gone. I don't know if he died from the drug or a fever because he hadn't taken care of himself. His family never said. They wouldn't let me near him at the funeral."

"Oh God, I'm so sorry," I whispered, cupping his cheek in my palm. "But I don't see how it was your fault. It sounds as if you did what you could and you had other obligations. Your father had just died, after all. He should have been there for you too."

He shook his head. "I knew he was too weak for me to leave alone, Arthur. Deep down, I knew. I'd sent letters to him at his family home. I told myself the reason I never received a reply was only that he was still angry with me, but I knew he'd never gone home. I told myself I would finish with my family business, and then I could return to London and try again with him—like we had all the time in the world—but I wasn't shocked when I learned of his illness. I loved him, and I failed to be there when he needed me most." He chuckled bitterly. "And here I'm sure you thought I only meant that I was a thief and a rakehell when I told you I wasn't the best of men."

I frowned at him and gave him a little shove. "Despite all evidence to the contrary, you still seem to think quite highly of me. Can't you allow that I might see your worth better than you? Can't you allow that I might see the truth where you don't? My mettle has never been tested like that. I've never had to make a hard choice as you have. I've never done much of anything really. And yet you say you admire me. Perhaps you did make a mistake. I wasn't there. I can't judge that. But I do know how much you've helped me when you didn't have to. That has to count for something. You told me yourself no one beyond these walls is perfect."

He gave me a wry smile and shook his head. "Clever boy, to use my words against me. Perhaps you're right. Perhaps I may make up for past wrongs even now."

Something about his words rang sourly in my ears, and I frowned. "Is that what I am? Am I some sort of penance for you, then?"

I didn't like that thought at all, and I pulled away from him. Tugging at my shirt, I tried to right my clothes, so I was less exposed, less vulnerable, but he cradled my face in his palms, forcing me to stop and lift my gaze to his.

"That's not what I meant." He held my gaze until I stopped struggling. "Yes, when I first came here, I thought I might receive some sort of absolution by helping you, easing your loneliness. But I meant what I said before. You are unlike anyone I've ever met, and I was charmed every minute we spent together. Your sweetness, your talent, the way your mind works, your passions, all of them are refreshing and magnetic. You drew me in. Is it so wrong that I wish to help you even as I admire you?"

I was being silly. Of course he would see me as someone in need of rescue. I was, wasn't I?

I wished I were fully dressed and we were having this conversation standing up instead of lying in my bed, our bodies touching so intimately. Hurt, anger, fear, and need swirled within me, and I couldn't tell what was justified and what was merely a product of all that had come before. Luckily his hands on my face blocked me from reaching for my hair. I couldn't bear him seeing another weakness right now.

Thump. Scrape. Thump. Scrape.

"Oh for God's sake! Go away!" I shouted angrily at the sounds beyond my door.

Fox jerked at my sudden outburst, and for the first time in all the years I'd heard them, the noises simply stopped. I caught the barest glimpse of the silvery apparition out of the corner of my eye, but when I turned to her, she'd vanished as well.

I gawped at the empty space where she'd been and then turned shocked eyes to Fox. "They stopped."

His eyes were wide, but he grinned at my exclamation. "They did."

"They've never done that before. Never. No matter how loudly I screamed at them or how much I begged."

"Perhaps it's an omen of things to come," he replied cautiously, watching me warily as if I might shout at him next.

"Perhaps."

He remained tense next to me and guilt began to push all other feelings aside. I was the one who'd pushed the conversation. He'd given so much and asked little in return. I was insulting his generosity with my confusion and my doubts. He didn't deserve that.

I'd entered wholly uncharted territory tonight. But I needn't ruin what time we had left with my nonsense. I would have plenty of time to think later. I always did.

"Will you hold me for a little while?" I asked.

"Of course."

"I'm sorry."

"For what?"

"All the fuss. Tonight was wonderful. I'm so very grateful you came."

"I'm grateful you allowed me to share it with you," he murmured before kissing my temple.

Like the first time, I curled on my side, and he pressed his body to my back, encircling me in his arms. I closed my eyes and shoved my emotional turmoil to the back of my mind. Even so, I had not thought I would sleep, but he woke me sometime later with a gentle shake.

"I fear I must be leaving, Arthur. Dawn is almost with us."

Biting my lip against a protest, I nodded. He kissed me softly on my brow, my cheek, and my lips before he climbed out of bed. As he put his clothes to rights, he said, "Will you do something for me? I cannot come back tonight—much as I should like to—but I can come tomorrow. Will you squirrel away some extra coal for the fire?"

"Coal?" I asked groggily, unsure I'd heard him right.

"Yes. Take only what you think won't be missed and stash it away."

"Why?"

He finished tying his sash over his shirt and trousers before he knelt at my bedside. In the dying light from my lanterns, he held my chin and kissed me deeply, teasing my lips and tongue until my cock stirred and my arms ached to hold him again. "Because, lovely Arthur, I should like to make this room as warm as possible tomorrow night, so we might do away with all these bothersome clothes and lie in each other's arms as God made us. I want to be able to touch every inch of you and to feel every inch of you on me," he whispered against my lips.

He chuckled at the quiet whimper that escaped me as the images he painted flashed in my mind.

"Oh. All right," I agreed.

Before I could capture his lips again, he moved away. "Until tomorrow, then."

With a whisper of cloth and the click of the door, he was gone. I rolled over and buried my face in the spot he'd vacated, hugging his pillow close. Now I only had two days and a night to wait. It would be agony.

Chapter Thirteen

"May I say, my lord is looking quite well today," Pendel said as he handed me my tea on the second morning after Fox left me.

"Thank you, Pendel. I am feeling quite well." Despite the bitterness of my medicine, I hid a smile behind my cup.

"Your uncle's visit brightened your spirits."

He spoke it as a statement, but I heard the questions in it, and a little of my good cheer faded as I washed the taste away with a sip of my tea. I hadn't received any word from my uncle yet, though I tried to be patient about it. He'd said he needed to think and to send out inquiries. I didn't know how long that should take, but surely more than just a day and a night.

"Yes. I was glad to speak with him as one man to another at last," I replied absently.

"Yes, my lord."

Pendel had seemed happy for me before, but a strange note in his voice caught my attention. Guilt prodded me a little as I realized I hadn't given Pendel an opportunity to speak during my discussion with my uncle. The decisions would affect him as well as me. Pendel disliked change, almost as much as I did. If all went as I hoped, there would be a great many changes in the near future. Add to that all that I was keeping secrets from him, and I was not rewarding his loyalty very well. I should at least make an effort to be kinder to him.

"Thank you, Pendel, for your patience with me and your kindness. I don't know what I would do without you."

He blinked at me a moment, before he smiled ever so slightly and he bowed. "That's very kind of you, my lord. As always, it's a pleasure to serve."

The usual lethargy began to steal over me, and as much as I hated it, I looked forward to the respite from my thoughts. A few hours of oblivion meant I was that much closer to seeing Fox again, and hopefully that much closer to some sort of word from my uncle.

WHEN I woke that afternoon, I secreted away as much extra coal from the bucket as I could without the loss becoming obvious, as I'd done the day before. I had enough of that purloined treasure tucked away in an old chamber pot in my necessary room to keep my fire going most of the night, and I could hardly keep my nervous anticipation in check.

Tonight he would come to me.

My paramour.

I had not thought to ever use such a word—to have such a thing. Somewhere in the back of my mind, I suppose I'd always expected to wed someday, if I were ever well enough. It was what men of my station did. But the concept had never been real to me. Now, I could not foresee a woman ever making me feel like this, and the thought of having to take a wife made me a little queasy. I couldn't imagine doing anything like what we'd done in my bed with anyone but Fox. I couldn't even imagine kissing anyone else.

"You're looking thoughtful," Fox whispered in my ear.

I started and flushed. He'd snuck in without even stirring of the air.

"I was thinking of you."

"I like to hear that." He drew me from my seat and pulled me into his embrace. After a soft, lingering kiss, he said, "What were you thinking?"

"How much I wished you would hurry up and get here," I laughed, my cheeks flushing even warmer.

"Impatient. I like that too," he purred. Pressing a kiss to my jaw and then to my neck, he slid his palms down my back until he cupped my buttocks. "Did you manage to get us some extra coal?"

With his hands on me, squeezing me, and my cock hardening, I could hardly think. I arched against him.

"Arthur?"

"Mmmmm?"

"The coal?"

"Oh, yes. Right. I did. I'll get it."

Moving awkwardly due to the stiffness between my legs, I hurried to the necessary room and retrieved the pot. By the time I returned to the hearth, Fox had the lock undone and the door to the stove open.

"Right," he said as he dumped in most of the contents of the pot. "That should do us nicely. And there's still some in the bucket your servants shouldn't miss, if we're careful." He used the hand bellows on the coals until the heat poured off my fire in heavenly waves, and then he shut the door and stood.

I watched in breathless anticipation as he stalked toward me, undoing the sash at his waist and the ties at his wrists as he went. My hands ached to touch him when he tugged his shirt up and over his head, baring his torso to me.

"Your turn, Arthur," he admonished as I stood frozen, drinking in his beauty.

Clumsily I unbelted my dressing gown and draped it over the back of my chair. I tugged at the knot in the neckcloth I'd taken hours to perfect only a short time ago, and it easily fell away. My evening jacket joined my dressing gown on the back of my chair just as swiftly, but when it came to the buttons on my waistcoat, my fingers no longer seemed to work. Feeling the weight of his stare, my hands shook so much each button took me several tries.

"Allow me," Fox murmured, placing his hand over mine.

He made short work of the buttons, and then all that was left was to remove my falls and tug my shirt free of my trousers. When it too had joined my jacket and gown, I shivered, my nipples hardening. I stepped closer to his heat, and he slid warm palms around my shoulders and pulled me into his embrace again.

Flesh to flesh, I pressed my face to his bare skin and breathed him in, immersing myself in the feel and scent of him.

Fox threaded his fingers through my hair and kissed my temple. "Only a day and a half away from you, and I missed you terribly, my Arthur," he murmured into my hair.

"I missed you too."

Taking my face in his palms, he tilted my head back and recaptured my lips. He held me like that for several long minutes, his lips teasing and encouraging by turns, until I surrendered to the rhythm he set and forgot my nerves. There was nothing in this world beyond the meeting of our lips and his hands on my face.

My lips were swollen and raw when he finally drew away, but I still clutched at him, trying to bring him back for more.

"Come. Let's retire to somewhere a little more comfortable." He took my hand and led me to the bed.

My nerves returned when he reached for the fastenings on my trousers, but I gathered my courage and in one quick move shoved my trousers, my drawers, and my wool stockings down to my ankles. Before I could think better of the idea, I kicked off my slippers, and stepped out of the lot. Holding my breath, I met his gaze. I'd never been fully unclothed with another person as a grown man, at least not when I was in my right senses. I had to screw my courage to the sticking place to keep my head held high.

He didn't leave me there long. He made a strange noise in the back of his throat and stepped close to me again. "So beautiful, my lovely Arthur."

"You truly think I'm beautiful?"

"Oh yes." He moved even closer and pressed his hardness against my hip. "Can you doubt it?"

My hands clutched restlessly at his silk trousers, unsure what to say or do.

"Climb in bed before you freeze solid," he chuckled.

He gave me a gentle shove of encouragement, and I laughed and hurried to comply. This time I quickly moved to the far side of the mattress so he wouldn't have to make the journey around the bed, and I wouldn't miss the opportunity to watch him finish undressing.

He undid two buttons on the sides of his strange costume, toed off his soft suede boots, and untied the bindings at his calves before shoving the whole thing down in one push as I had. He wore no undergarments beneath the silk and my breath caught as my lanterns bathed his bare body in warm, flickering light.

He stood still and allowed me several moments to look my fill before he said, "Do you like what you see?"

"God, yes," I said, and then I blushed and ducked my head.

Chuckling, Fox slid beneath the covers and drew me close. With a knuckle beneath my chin, he lifted my face to his and claimed my lips again. "I told you before, Arthur. I love your honesty, your lack of pretense and affectation."

With the full length of his naked body pressed to mine, I could only nod in response. My blood felt as if it might boil in my veins and my heart beat free of its cage. I never wanted to be anywhere else but in his arms.

Perhaps sensing that I might be a tad overwhelmed and uncertain, Fox placed gentle kisses on my temple, my cheek, and then the tip of my nose. He continued his progress across the other side of my face and my chin before he kissed my lips again.

"There is no right or wrong here, love. You may do as you wish without fear of any judgment from me."

"I hardly know where to start," I answered breathlessly.

"Why don't you touch me?"

Only then realizing I'd left my hands resting uselessly at my sides, I lifted one to his chest and the other to his hip. His heart beat strong and steady beneath my palm, and I let its rhythm soothe me. I had lain with him once before. I shouldn't be so flustered.

I tugged at his hip, and he rolled toward me, bringing our bodies together from shoulders to knees. Fox slid a thigh between mine, and I spread wider to accommodate him. My cock throbbed and my breath quickened at my vulnerability.

Watching my face closely, he brushed my hair from my forehead and then traced the fingers of his other hand down my chest. I shivered and bit my lip as he moved his hand lower, gently caressing my belly but not touching my cock. As his fingers ghosted closer, I closed my eyes and arched my back, begging without words for him to touch me there.

"We can go as slow as you like," Fox murmured. "Last time, I was somewhat impaired with the wine, and I may have rushed you a bit. This time, I'll have better control. Tell me what you want."

"Touch me," I whispered.

He chuckled, and when I opened my eyes, his impish grin had returned. "I am touching you."

"More."

He flattened his palm and slid it over my hip, caressing my flank. "Like this?"

I groaned and squirmed. "You know what I meant," I replied a little petulantly.

He chuckled again and moved his hand back toward my belly, but instead of grasping my cock, he slid his hand farther down and he cupped my ballocks. My cock pulsed, and I spread my legs wider. I surely looked a wanton opening myself for him like this, but his hand on my sac felt better than I would have believed. All the muscles in my thighs and buttocks twitched and spasmed as he lightly tugged and rolled me in his palm.

"There are so many pleasures to be had, Arthur, and I mean to show you all of them eventually. But I think for now I shall ease some of your discomfort."

Fox spread my thighs even farther apart and slid down between them. Uncertain, I held my breath as he moved his arms beneath my thighs and pushed them up until my feet were flat on the mattress. With a wicked grin and a wink, he lowered his head and took the entire length of my cock into his mouth. I gasped and arched my back again, but his arms wrapped around my thighs held me still.

He drew off my member and then slid his mouth back down it again. His tongue drew patterns on my sensitive flesh inside the hot cavern of his mouth, and I moaned and writhed beneath him, unable to control my responses. I had thought his hand on me the height of ecstasy, but it was nothing compared to what he did to me now. I wanted it to last forever, but too soon an urgent pressure built in me.

Freeing one arm from my thigh, he fondled my ballocks again, and it took all my strength not to shout my pleasure and release the dam inside me. Perhaps sensing how close I'd come to losing control, he drew his mouth from me and blew a cool breath across the crown of my cock.

I shivered in delight and clumsily pet his hair and his cheek. Fox turned his face to my palm and pressed a kiss to it as I regained my breath and some of the urgency in my body subsided.

"Shall I continue, or would you like more time?"

How should I answer that?

He rubbed the smoothness of his cheek against my shaft, and I moaned. I clutched at his shoulder and tried to make my gaze convey the pleas I was too embarrassed to give voice to. With a wicked gleam in his eyes, he held my gaze as he ran his tongue lewdly over my flesh, and I caught my breath as my whole body shook in reaction.

"Is this what you want?" he asked, his cheek still pressed to my cock.

"Yes, please."

With a broad smile he took the base of my cock in a firm grip and murmured, "All you ever need do is ask."

Then he took me into the wet heat of his mouth again, and I was adrift in sensation. I lost control in an embarrassingly short time. When my vision cleared and my breath slowed, I found Fox leaning over me with fondness in his eyes. He traced a finger down my cheek, then swept a gentle caress over my throat.

"No tears this time," he said quietly.

I shook my head. "No. I think I might be beyond them. That was… I didn't know such things…." Blushing fiercely, I waved a helpless hand. I had no words.

"I'm glad you liked it," he chuckled.

"I did. Will you teach me?"

He studied my face carefully before responding. "If you're sure you wish to. I've pushed you far beyond where you're comfortable already, even when I promised myself I would take things slowly with you." He shook his head, and his wry grin reappeared. "I seem to forget myself often with regard to you."

I huffed and rolled my eyes. "I'm not made of glass. I may have no experience, and I may have fought with my feelings for a long time, but you made a convincing argument, and honestly, I'm tired of fighting. I've had these yearnings all my life, no matter how I tried to fool myself. This doesn't feel like my illness. My illness makes me unhappy. I'm so very tired of being unhappy. If I can find happiness, and I'm hurting no one in the process, I can't see how that could be wrong. And if I must live a lie to join society, I will. As you've said, I won't be the only one. If what you said of masks is true, then how is my lie so much different from anyone else's?"

"Such a clever boy," he said before he bent and captured my lips.

I tasted my seed on his tongue, but rather than disgust, my belly tightened, and my cock twitched with renewed interest.

"Will you teach me?" I asked again.

"I most certainly will."

He flopped onto his back and drew me over him. My cheeks grew hot at my fumbling, but true to his word, he never judged me harshly or grew impatient with me. I tried to touch him as he touched me, to use my mouth as he had. Though a little unnerved by the intensity with which he watched me, his flushed cheeks, perspiration beaded above his lips and along his brow, and the sounds he made were all the encouragement I needed. I took his guidance and persevered until he arched beneath me and released his seed in my mouth.

I knew it was coming, but I wasn't prepared for the effusion. Much of it spilled from my mouth, but the rapt look he gave me as he swiped his thumb across my chin eased some of my chagrin. He pulled me into his arms and cuddled me close, holding me tightly enough I thought he would never let me go. It was all I'd ever wanted, but didn't know it until I met him.

Chapter Fourteen

Over the following week, and to my great joy, Fox came to me nearly every night. We spent a great deal of time in my bed, but not all. In between exploring each other's bodies in ways I never could have imagined, he would read to me or I to him. He would also tell me stories of his escapades in the notorious East End and his degenerate life of crime. When he asked, I would share some of my sketches or speak of things I'd read in the papers, but I had nothing so colorful as his tales. He never seemed to mind it. In fact he encouraged me to speak freely of every facet of my life, no matter how boring or insignificant it was. When I called him strange, he would only laugh and tackle me into bed again.

One night we even spent a couple of hours by my fire, leafing through my copy of the estate's investments ledger. But when I remarked on how positively boring that had to be for him, he only shook his head and said, "Nothing about you is boring, love. Besides, if you want to practice with that mask we spoke of, and with polite conversation in general, you'll need some of this as well. It's what we gentleman are supposed to do when the ladies leave us to our cigars and port after dinner. We speak of business, politics, and sport, and try to outdo one another with how grand we are."

"You do?"

"Yes, God help us." He chuckled. "If you haven't guessed, I try to avoid such affairs if at all possible—unless I'm seeking out my next house to rob, that is." He waggled his eyebrows, and I laughed. "But, as a viscount, I'm afraid you're doomed to a purgatory of such balls, dinners, and luncheons. Still so certain you want to join society?"

He would tease me like this often, and I would only shake my head at him and roll my eyes, secretly treasuring every moment. When he made the world a joke, it was hard to be afraid of it. I thought perhaps I could face all of it if he were only at my side.

By the end of that week, I was positively vibrating with happiness. Even the sounds and visions that plagued me seemed to have taken a holiday. I was the most content I had ever been. I could hardly contain it when Pendel and the other servants were around. Pendel seemed happy that I was happy, no matter the cause, and though guilt assailed me from time to time when I thought of the deceptions and the secrecy, I was glad to see his happiness.

As I waited for Fox that night, I played some of the bawdy tunes he'd taught me. I'd fed the fire myself with my burgeoning lock picking skills, and the room was as warm and inviting as I could make it. He had promised to come, but the hours from dinner until the rest of the house went to bed always seemed to stretch for an eternity, especially with my body aching for his touch.

"Don't wear your hands out, love. I might need them later."

Grinning from ear to ear, I launched myself from my bench and into his arms. I kissed him until we both had to break away for breath. We tore at each other's clothes and left them in a heap on the floor. Then I dragged him to my bed and pushed him down on it.

"Missed me, eh?"

I jumped on him, sealing our bodies and our mouths together. He held me and petted me, but he was still treating me like spun glass and that wasn't what I craved. I rolled, pulling him on top of me. I dragged my nails down his back and gripped his arse with bruising fingers.

"Please," I whispered.

"Please what?"

I grunted in frustration and writhed against him.

"Tell me what you want," he murmured against my lips, but I could only shake my head.

He was always so careful with me, so tender. I wanted something more tonight, but I didn't know how to put the feeling into words. Blushing furiously, I pleaded with my eyes, and he smiled and dragged his knuckles down my cheek.

"Do you trust me?" he asked.

"Yes."

"Good."

Without another word, Fox slid down my body, gripped the back of my knees and pushed my legs up and out. My cock throbbed against my belly, anticipating what came next, but instead of taking me in his mouth as he'd done before, he slid lower still. Bending me nearly in half, he nuzzled my ballocks and pressed a kiss to the tender skin behind them.

I flushed and shivered in a combination of mortification and need as I felt a trickle of wetness slide along the valley between my buttocks. He sucked one of my ballocks into his mouth and teased it with his tongue as he'd done many other times, but this time he also pressed his thumb to my most private of areas, massaging the entrance to my body at the same time. I moaned and writhed on the bed, unsure whether to pull away or beg for more as my face flamed even hotter in embarrassment.

His thumb remained pressed to that spot, simply rubbing in tantalizing circles while he released my sac and moved back up to press a kiss to the head of my cock.

"All right?" he murmured.

Before I could answer, he sucked my cock into the hot cavern of his mouth, and I had no breath to speak. His fingers teased the wetness that had dribbled to the base of my cock before they withdrew. A moment later, I felt a pressure at the entrance to my body, a moist finger playing along my sensitive skin before pressing slowly inside, and I moaned. The sensation was strange and uncomfortable, but with my cock still in the confines of his mouth, I couldn't find the will to object. In the nights we'd spent together, he'd touched my arse before, but never like this.

One finger became two as he stretched me there, pressing inside and withdrawing again over and over. I thought I might have finally found the will to object to the strangeness of it, but then his fingers brushed something inside me that sent a jolt of pleasure through me. It awakened an ache in me I didn't know I had, and I moaned again and arched my back.

"More," I gasped aloud, uncaring how desperate or wanton I sounded.

Fox chuckled around my cock before releasing it with a lurid wet pop. "Like that, did you? Just wait."

He rose over me, brushed my hair from my damp forehead with his free hand, and then pressed a kiss to it. All the while his other fingers remained inside me moving, stretching, rubbing that place within me that threatened to drive me mad.

"I want to put my cock here," he whispered, as he gave the fingers in me a twist. "Will you let me?"

My crown dripped a steady stream of moisture on my belly, and I could hardly think for the ache. "Yes. Anything," I gasped.

He withdrew his fingers, leaving me feeling empty for the space of a few breaths, but then I heard him spit and felt pressure of a different kind.

"Breathe, love. Push back. Relax and invite me in."

The pressure became discomfort, and I feared what he wanted would be impossible. I didn't know if I could even do as he asked, but I tried. I pushed back, and when I feared I might be torn asunder, my body gave way at last and the head of his cock breached me. I gasped, and he petted me and placed kisses all over my face.

"Sweet, love. That's it." He moaned and slowly pressed farther inside me.

The discomfort eased a bit after that, and I thought I might feel the first twinges of pleasure again as he moved. The ache he inspired in me lessened, replaced by a fullness I'd never experienced before, but then he pressed my legs closer to my chest and curled over me, and suddenly I couldn't breathe. He was too close, the air between us stifling. His weight began to feel as if it was crushing me, and a familiar panic began to rise. I was trapped beneath him. I couldn't move.

Shaking and gasping for air, I pushed weakly at his chest, but he only captured one of hands and placed a kiss in my palm as he moved inside me.

"No," I wheezed. "Stop."

I'd barely managed above a whisper, but Fox froze above me. "Arthur? What is it? What's wrong?"

"Stop. I can't breathe. Please. Get off me."

He moved off me at once, and I rolled from the bed and stood clinging to one of the bedposts as I fought for breath.

"Tell me what to do. What can I do?"

He hovered behind me but didn't try to touch me.

"Just give me a moment, please," I gasped.

I clamped my eyes closed tight and shivered as my heart beat frantically in my chest. He remained a silent, solid presence at my back, and eventually I could breathe again, and my limbs stopped shaking.

I was not held down. I was not trapped.

A flicker of bluish light illuminated the corner by the window when I opened my eyes, and I closed them again and clenched my jaw. I had ruined a beautiful moment with my madness yet again, and the lady in white only served to remind me of how little progress I'd actually made.

"I'm sorry," I whispered around the lump in my throat.

"You don't have anything to be sorry for, love. Can I do anything?"

He was always so understanding. I didn't deserve it.

I ducked my head in shame and whispered, "Will you hold me?"

He took a step toward me but then hesitated. "Are you sure?"

"Yes. The spell has passed, I think."

He wrapped me in his arms, and I pressed my cheek to his shoulder. "I'm sorry," I repeated against his skin, and he clutched me tighter to his breast.

"Don't be. It was my fault. I pushed again. I should be the one to apologize, not you."

I could feel my cheeks heat in more than shame now, and I shook my head. "It wasn't that. I… I liked what you did, truly." I squirmed in mortification. It didn't seem proper to speak aloud of such things, but I couldn't have him blaming himself. "It was only being held down that became too much… not the other."

"But I've been on top of you before, and you didn't seem to mind then."

I grimaced. "I know. But isn't it one of the benefits of being a madman that I don't always have to make sense?"

The words burned like acid in my mouth despite my weak attempt at a chuckle, and he gave my shoulders a little shake. "Don't."

He held me like that until we were both shivering from the chill air. I knew he had to be freezing, but still he held me and would probably continue to do so until his arse was frostbitten. "Come on. Let's get back in bed before we catch our deaths."

He allowed me to draw him beneath the covers, and then I curled against his side and pillowed my head on his breast. Shame and guilt warred inside me, choking off anything I might have said, but he held me and ran soothing fingers through my hair until I drowsed in his embrace.

At length he murmured, "Don't beat yourself up, love. Give yourself time to heal. I promise I'll understand whenever you say you aren't ready for something."

"But what if I want to be ready? What if I'm tired of waiting?" I groused. "Besides, I thought you admired my impatience."

As I'd hoped, he chuckled, the sound resonating through his chest beneath my cheek. "Not when it's with yourself. I'm here. I'll be back tomorrow and as often as I can. Take as long as you need. You're recovering from a very long illness. You can't expect to become well overnight."

"I know. And I suppose I don't mind it so much really, most of the time. But when I ruin a perfectly wonderful moment for no good reason, I can't help feeling ashamed. I can't help wishing I were someone else."

He grunted and shook me again. "You shouldn't. I, for one, don't want you to be anyone else, nor do I think you have any reason to be ashamed."

I clutched him tighter. "You know, you're the only person who has ever even suggested to me that my illness might be a gift instead of a curse? And while I still don't believe that, it was kind of you to say nonetheless. You see me differently from everyone else. You allow me to see myself differently, and I want you to know how much I treasure that, even when it's hard for me to see any progress at all."

Taking my hand in his, he kissed it and then pressed it to his cheek. "I see you as you are. The people in your life have done you a disservice in more ways than I can count, but teaching you to hate who you are is by far the worst. As I told you before, the men and women you so desperately wish to emulate are not so perfect as you were led to believe. Many of them couldn't hold a candle to you, in my opinion. They backbite, they drink, and they gamble. They're nasty to one another and don't care a jot for anything or anyone beyond their own little worlds. They believe themselves superior, and yet they prove every day how inferior they truly are. They run up debts with good, hardworking people without an ounce of sympathy for the pain they cause, always leaving a mess behind for others to clean up. You are none of those things, love."

His entire body had tensed beneath me, and I placed a soothing hand on his breast.

"You're speaking of your father now, aren't you?" I guessed.

He settled beneath my hand and let out a quiet chuckle. "Yes, I am. But he is only one of many, I assure you. The gentry hang on to their stately homes, their lands, and their treasures, whilst spending monies they don't have on things they don't need, all for the sake of appearances, to impress people they don't even like. Does that make any sense whatsoever? Is it any wonder I decided to relieve them of some of their baubles and redistribute them within the public at large?"

I grinned at his airy tone. "And of course you didn't benefit in the slightest from this most generous undertaking."

"Perhaps a little," he grinned. "But if it helps, I sold most of my own family's treasures before I turned to thieving other people's."

"Did you?" I asked, all jesting aside.

His smile fell away, and he nodded. "All but the family house in Kent. My mother and sister still reside there, though I had to sell off much of our land and strip the house of anything truly valuable to satisfy my father's creditors. My sister has a dowry, should she choose to marry, and both my mother and sister have generous allowances, but the tradesmen in the town have instructions to only extend credit so far before they're cut off. Mother was mortified at first, of course, but I think she's got used to it by now. And now that I'm thinking of starting a new trade of sorts, I might be able to extend their allowances in the not so distant future."

"What new trade would that be?"

"Why speculating, of course. You think I asked after your uncle's ledger for my love of tables and columns?"

At my look of surprise, he laughed and wrestled me onto my back until he was looming over me, straddling my hips. He was careful not to hold me down any more than that, and this time I felt no twinge of panic.

"You're using my uncle's journal?"

He shrugged. "Only taking his advice. I hope you don't mind. But you said yourself he had a masterful head for business, so I am investing where he invests."

"He isn't always successful," I felt compelled to say. "You should take care with it."

"Oh, I know. I'm being careful—not putting all my eggs in one basket and all that. And I can always go back to thieving if nothing comes of it. I simply have more motivation to pursue a respectable career now. I wouldn't want my paramour to be ashamed of me, would I?"

I rolled my eyes at him. "I don't care a jot about your respectability, and you know it. But I do like the idea of you being more careful and not coming to me with any more bruises." I traced a finger down his chin where the discoloration had all but disappeared. "I'd rather not read about you in the papers someday either."

He bent and kissed me sweetly. "Don't worry. That's why I'm making every effort to mend my ways. Yours is the only house I intend to break into from now on. And as soon as my investments begin to pay dividends, and I can set myself up as an honest man of business, you and I can begin discussing our future together—where we'll live, who our friends will be, holidays we'll take together. We both just need a little time, that's all. Your uncle will find you a new doctor, a better doctor— or two or three, or however many it takes to obtain the best treatment for you. Then I'll come calling in my finest jacket and trousers, you'll introduce me as a friend you met at the club or some such nonsense, and we'll sit down to tea together in the drawing room like the respectable gentlemen we are. We'll spend our days walking or riding in the park and nights at the theater...."

I closed my eyes and imagined all of it as he continued to paint lovely pictures of our life together. I wanted it so badly, and the fact that he wanted any of it with me warmed me to my toes. I could see it, our future together, and it was beautiful.

Chapter Fifteen

The following morning, I was irrepressibly giddy. I had hope for a life beyond these walls. I had something to strive for. Any moment, I felt sure my uncle would send word he'd found a new doctor for me. Soon I could begin weaning off my medicine, and the world Fox spoke of would be within reach.

My panic the night before was only a small setback in the grand scheme of things. It could be overcome. Even the oppressive fog outside my windows seemed a little lighter than it had been, and I could almost imagine the faint outline of the sun above the clouds.

I devoured my breakfast with alacrity. I'd taken my medicine as always, but my joy seemed to burn through it in almost no time at all, leaving me with the rest of the day to fill. I didn't mind. I did my exercises three times that afternoon, practicing my forms until I had to wash and change into fresh clothes. After lunch, I played and played, singing loudly, uncaring if Pendel found the bawdy tunes distasteful. I even braved the cold and spent time tidying my rooftop garden in preparation for the spring that I was certain was only a few short weeks away. The sleeping plants gave me hope for what was to come instead of depressing me as they usually did. Nothing could dent my spirits.

With so much unaccustomed activity, I should have been tired by the time the sun set, but I was still restless with an insatiable need to be doing something. I thought I might pen a letter to Mr. Fuller, or perhaps one to my uncle, but eventually decided against it. I didn't want to make a nuisance of myself just because I couldn't sit still.

That night following dinner, my restless meandering eventually drew me to my door. I had a few hours before Fox would come, so perhaps I would go on a little adventure. He would be proud of me when I told him of it, and I needed to prove to myself I could do it on my own.

I crouched by the lock, fished the bent wire out of my pocket, and twisted it in the opening until I felt the bar release. The hall beyond was dark and empty, not a sound apart from the odd creaks and pops of the old house and not a single one of my visions to bar my way. I took that as a good omen.

I had no aim as I left my rooms. My lanterns were too heavy to carry with me, but I managed to find a taper in a sconce at the top of the main stairs, and after carrying it back to my rooms to light it, I began my journey again.

I quietly opened doors and peered down dark corridors, creeping on tiptoe through my house in no particular direction. It had been a long time since I'd walked many of these halls, and they were at once familiar and strange to me. I ran my hands over fine wood tables, picture frames, and vases, thinking of all Fox's family had been forced to give up and hardly able to grasp that all of this was mine now. As a child, I knew it all belonged to my parents. They were so grand in my memories—my father tall and imposing, but still kind, my mother elegant and slight but still obviously the ruler of her domain. Seeing it all as a grown man, and knowing the responsibility for it rested on my shoulders was a bit daunting. I didn't have to think of such things if I were ill. I could stay in my rooms all day and read and drink my tea, and none of that weight would fall on me, but only because they all thought me too weak to bear it. This was the legacy my father had bestowed on me. If I wanted to call myself Campden, with all the pride that entailed, I couldn't shirk my responsibilities unless I had no other choice—not and be able to look at my reflection in the glass every day.

As always, thoughts of my parents gave me both pain and pleasure. I missed them terribly, even after all these years, but the memories from my childhood still brought me comfort. On impulse, I stopped my idle wanderings and moved with purpose across the gallery to the east wing of the house—to their rooms.

Unlike the west wing where I spent my time and the servants visited daily, a hush lay over this part of the house, as if even the air itself was draped in white cotton. Nothing stirred in the corners of my vision. Nothing broke the heavy silence or disturbed the cobwebs except my slightly labored breaths.

I paused outside the door to the master's suite, reluctant to disturb that silence. But as the eerie quiet began to weigh on me, I forced myself to turn the handle. I'd come all this way. It seemed silly to back out now.

Beneath the white linen cloths draped over everything, my father's rooms were much as I remembered them. His massive canopied Tudor bed still held court along the far wall, the red velvet corner drapes tied back, just as they'd been the last time I'd seen the room. Mother had always hated the décor of this room, but Father would not hear of changing it. A stab of sadness went through me as I took it all in. The room felt so empty and oppressive without my father's warmth to fill the space.

I stepped farther into the room, bringing my candle up to illuminate the dark recesses. It reflected off the carved oak-paneled walls and ceiling, making the wood gleam, but was swallowed by the empty hearth. Particles glittered in the air when I trailed a finger down the dust-filled creases of the velvet drapes, but soon even they fell away and all was still again.

With a sigh, I turned and headed for the adjoining door to my mother's rooms. As dark and rich as my father's rooms were, my mother's were the exact opposite. Brilliant yellow-papered walls towered above white wainscoting. An array of yellow, cream, and pale blue florals adorned her rugs, bedding, and drapery. The furniture was so delicate the chairs looked as if their legs would collapse if anyone actually sat in them, and despite the profusion of white cloth covering most of it, the room was less oppressive.

Her silver brush and comb still rested on her dressing table, along with her perfumes and powders—all of it covered in a thin layer of dust despite the cloth I'd lifted out of the way. I wondered if her dresses still hung in the wardrobe, but I hesitated to look. I'd rather imagine they were still there, waiting for her, than know the truth.

I trailed a wistful finger over the soft bristles of her brush and delicate ivory of her comb. Her looking glass only reflected my gaunt pale specter, not her vibrant brown eyes and rosy cheeks, though I suppose I had a little more color in my cheeks recently. Turning away from it, I tucked her comb into my pocket before wandering over to her secretary. I could still picture her in her favorite fawn-colored day dress, sitting right here, writing her letters. The writing desk in my rooms wasn't as fine as this one, and as I lifted the drape from it, I fought a small internal battle over whether I should order Pendel to swap them out. Part of me wanted to leave the room just as it was for the sake of my memories, but rationally such notions were silly. My memories did not change, and leaving all this to rot made no sense at all. One day soon I'd have the full run of this house. Why shouldn't I begin to make changes?

I set the candle on the top of the desk, then removed the drape from the chair and sat. After lowering the writing surface, I ran my palm over the smooth inset wood and traced loving fingers over the carved drawer fronts, little cubbies, and slots. Perhaps, like the comb, it would do me good to have a little part of her in my rooms. As a child, I was never allowed to touch her things, but I thought she would be happy to see me use them now.

With a small smile, I stood and went about putting the desk back to rights, but when I closed the front panel, a piece of paper slid through the gap between the hinges of the writing surface and floated to the floor. After replacing the dust cloth, I retrieved the paper and held it up to the light. The unfinished letter was in my mother's hand, dated the twenty-fifth of March, 1870, barely a fortnight before she died, and my heart swelled a little that I would have a chance to read some of her last words.

> *My dearest Portia,*
>
> *Ages have passed since we were last together, and you must know how keenly I feel your absence. I am desperate for your companionship and the loving support you have shown me throughout our lives, dear sister, but most especially now, for I don't know what to do.*
>
> *After a long winter, we are at last in Town again. As always, my dear husband insists on us staying in this horror of a house. He knows how much I dislike the place, but he absolutely refuses to find us other smarter lodgings in a more fashionable neighborhood.*
>
> *You of all people know how many parties I have hosted to try and cheer the place up, but it does no good. Ghosts from the past cling to it like a heavy shroud against all my efforts. With enough diversions, I might have been able to bear it even so, but my dear husband insisted on bringing Arthur with us from the country, and no matter my pleas, he would not be gainsaid.*
>
> *Dear sister, you are the only one into whose kindness and discretion I might trust my greatest joy and my deepest shame without fear of censure or that my words will travel beyond your ears. I simply must tell someone. After many years of trying in vain, I am at last*

with child. I can finally bring my husband that happiness he has so often wished, but in doing so I must at last admit to him my failure as well.

Only you can understand how much it pains me to confess it, but I have failed to keep my promise to him. I cannot love Arthur as a mother should. I have tried, dearest. You know how I've tried. He was such a beautiful baby, sweet, tractable, barely ever fractious. But as he grows, I see more and more of his father in him, in his strangeness, and it frightens me.

But how can I tell my husband I will not have Arthur near our child? How can I tell him I have failed in the one task he demanded of me, when he has given me so much care and happiness? The thought fills me with dread even as I should be overflowing with joy for the child I'm bringing into the world, but I can see no other way. John will simply have to understand.

In a few days' time, we leave for France, a holiday for just the two of us, while Arthur is to spend time with his uncle. Somehow, I must find the courage to share my news and my feelings with my husband, but without you there to hold my hand, I fear I may lack the courage.

The letter ended there. It was unsigned and obviously not posted, so my mother must have intended to add more. I stared at the familiar delicate lines and swirls until they blurred before my eyes. When my hand began to shake, I closed my eyes and crumpled the letter in my palm. My knuckles showed white and popped with the force of my grip, but I barely noted it.

I cannot love Arthur as a mother should.

... I will not have Arthur near our child....

I clenched my jaw and tried my breathing exercises, but the roaring in my ears grew steadily louder. My chest constricted so much I gasped for air, and my heart beat against the cage of my ribs like a trapped bird.

My hand went slack and the crumpled paper fell to the floor. The small clicks it made as it bounced on the waxed wood might as well have been a horn sounding the start of the hunt, for I took off as if the hounds of hell were chasing me. I remembered nothing of my flight back to my rooms except the feeling that if I stopped running, even for a moment, I would collapse on the spot. Shaking and light-headed, I barely managed to close my door before I crumpled to the floor. With my knees drawn to my chest, I rocked where I fell, as tears slid unchecked down my cheeks.

My mother didn't love me. What did she mean she was at last with child? All the nights spent in her lap by the fire while my father read to us were a lie. It was all a lie. Or perhaps I had only imagined those nights. Perhaps it had all been a hallucination, and I couldn't trust my memory of anything. Were any of my memories real?

I felt fevered, and every inch of my body ached.

If my own mother couldn't love me, how could I expect anyone else to? Did Uncle Oscar feel the same? Did my father? Did Pendel? Was I only some distasteful burden that they all had to bear? Was I so strange she could disavow any connection to me?

I couldn't think. The roaring in my ears blotted anything else out. I could only feel, and what I felt was like a knife had been thrust between my ribs. I opened my eyes, hoping the order and familiarity of my room might soothe me, but the shimmer of a ghostly apparition only a few feet away, reaching for me, forced a strangled yelp from my throat, and I closed my eyes.

"Go away," I gasped against the vise around my chest as icy fingers brushed my cheeks.

Thump. Scrape. Thump. Scrape.

"No!" I screamed this time. "Go away! Leave me alone!"

But the sounds continued, drawing nearer to my door.

I moaned and clapped my hands over my ears, but another whisper-soft brush of cool air on my cheek shocked me into opening my eyes. The white apparition was right next to me now, her face almost human as it shifted and wavered in my gaze.

"No!" I shrieked. I threw my hand out to keep it away, but my fingers only slid through the misty thing. I shivered at the chill and shot to my feet.

I skittered around the apparition and put several feet between us. Grabbing the first thing I could find, I threw the lantern that rested on the table between my chairs at it. The heavy metal went right through the creature and crashed into the door. The candle inside guttered out. Then the hollow moan replaced the thump and scrape from the hall, and I lost all sense and reason.

"No!" I shouted over and over again as I threw anything I could get my hands on at the door. My denials and the satisfying crashes of splintering furniture and shattering china blotted out any other sound until Pendel's concerned shouts reached me through the haze of anger and pain.

"My lord! My lord! What is happening? Are you hurt?"

Keys rattled in the lock.

Heaving in breaths like a bellows, I let my hands fall to my sides, and only then did Pendel peek around the edge of the door. As I had feared would happen during my mad dash from my mother's rooms, the moment I stopped what I was doing, the world went black.

I must have collapsed, because the next thing I remembered was Tom lifting me and depositing me gently on my bed.

"My lord? What is it? What's wrong?"

Pendel's concerned visage hovered over me, his dark brows drawn so far down they almost met in the middle. Tom's eyes were wide and frightened.

"It's a lie. It's all a lie," I moaned.

"What is a lie? I don't understand," Pendel replied.

"It's all a lie," I repeated. I hadn't meant to say it again, but when I closed my eyes and tried once more to explain myself, those were the only words that would leave my mouth.

I whimpered, as heavy footsteps thundered from the room only to return a few moments later. When I opened my eyes again, Pendel held a glass for me while Tom hovered nervously behind him, breathing heavily. I swallowed the bitter liquid gladly, aching for the oblivion it might give, no matter how temporary. I thought I might shake apart or my throat might close so I couldn't take a breath. My head pounded, and sweat prickled all over my body.

"Tom, go and collect Dr. Payne. Don't come back without him. I'll have a message for you to wire to his lordship's uncle when you return."

"Yes, sir."

As always, I tried to take some solace in Pendel's stalwart presence at my bedside, while my head filled with cotton and my limbs grew heavy. But the tightness in my chest persisted, and I tossed and turned fretfully for a long time. By the time Dr. Payne arrived to give me another dose, I had been reduced to a pathetic whimpering lump, my limbs now far too heavy to move, but my anxiety still too strong to let me seek the oblivion of sleep.

As if I were an invalid, Tom had to lift me into a sitting position to down the second dose Dr. Payne prepared. I choked and coughed as the bitter liquid hit my throat. I suppose I managed to swallow enough to please the doctor, because he instructed Tom to lower me again and draw my blankets over me.

Hushed whispers haunted me as I slipped into darkness. I resisted the current as it dragged me under, wanting to hear what they were saying, but it was no use, and I quickly lost the battle.

Chapter Sixteen

When I woke again, my uncle sat at my bedside. I blinked at him in the harsh light from the oil lamp on my nightstand, struggling to make sense of his presence through the thick fog that still clung to my mind.

"Uncle?" I croaked.

Startled out of a doze, he jerked his chin up and rubbed his eyes. "Arthur? How are you feeling, my boy?"

He spoke each word quietly and with such care that I frowned at him.

"Why are you here? What's the matter?" I asked, my stomach twisting with a dread I couldn't name.

He blinked at me for a moment, seeming at a loss. Then his gaze darted to the side and back to me. "I received a wire last night, and I took the first train. You don't remember?"

I frowned at him and searched my memory. My heart beat faster as a wave of nerves swept over me, but it was only when I caught a glimpse of the state of my rooms beyond my uncle's shoulder that I understood why.

No attempt had been made to clear up the disaster I'd made of my perfectly ordered space, probably so my uncle and the doctor could witness it. A couple of small pieces of furniture lay in splinters. Shards of my little bits of china statuary glinted in the flickering light. My precious books lay in tumbled disarray on their shelves and scattered on the floor, along with my chess set. As the memories flooded back, so did my fear and heartache.

I turned wide eyes back to my uncle as emotion clogged my throat. What would he do? Was it all a lie? If I could not trust his love for me, who could I trust?

"Was it all a lie?" My strangled whisper was barely audible over the pounding in my ears.

"Was what a lie?" Oscar asked, his eyes widening in alarm.

I could not imagine how mad I must appear, and the thought only made my struggle for control harder.

"Th-The letter," I croaked. "M-Mother's room. The *letter*."

I'd left it there, crumpled on the floor.

Uncle Oscar frowned at me and shook his head, his mounting confusion and concern evident in every line of his face. Eyes just like mine, and just like my father's, pleaded with me to make sense, to get hold of myself, to be sane. I moaned and pulled at my hair. The storm of my emotions swallowed my reason, and the bloody medicine made it too hard to think.

"It was all a lie. It was all a lie. It was all a lie. The letter. Mother's room," I gasped between breaths.

I couldn't stop. I had to make myself understood, but I could barely breathe, let alone make sense.

"Bring Dr. Payne," my uncle called out to my closed door, and I moaned and began rocking on the bed.

"No, no, no, no, no."

The medicine wasn't helping. It was poison. I couldn't be helpless. I'd lost a whole night and a day. Had Fox come? Had they turned him away?

I had to think.

Dr. Payne arrived soon enough that he must have been somewhere in the house. As always, Pendel held a glass of oily liquid out to me. In addition to my uncle, Dr. Payne, and Pendel hovering over me, Tom stood by the door, wringing his hands and looking thoroughly unhappy, and I knew what would happen if I refused to take my medicine: I would be forced to take it. In my state, I wouldn't be able to convince them I didn't need it, so with a resigned whimper, I took the medicine into my mouth.

In sudden inspiration, I turned away from them, curled into a ball, and spit it into the bedlinens. The cool liquid seeped into my nightshirt as well as the linens beneath me as I closed my eyes, gritted my teeth, and tried to concentrate only on my breathing.

Breathe in. One, two, three. Breathe out. One, two, three.

"That should calm him for a while longer and help him sleep. I gave him a heavier dose this time than I did this morning," Dr. Payne said. "Perhaps when he wakes again, he'll be in a better state."

"Yes."

The exhaustion and resignation in that one word from my uncle tore at my heart, but I kept my jaw locked and my eyes tightly closed.

"Come, sir, let's let him sleep, and perhaps we might speak in the library?"

"All right."

Uncle Oscar grunted, and a moment later, they moved away from me. I didn't dare shift a muscle, until I heard the door close and the lock click into place.

My breathing exercises had helped calm some of the storm inside me, but fear still clung to me, and my heart still raced. My legs would barely support my weight when I stumbled out of bed, and I had to cling to my bed-curtains for support until I stopped wobbling and my head cleared. Tom had put extra coal in my stove, but I still shivered in the draft, the damp patches on my nightshirt turning icy. After drawing on my dressing gown and slippers, I crept to the door and listened. The sound of footsteps receded down the hall along with the thin thread of lamplight beneath my door. When all was silent and dark again, I fumbled with the bit of wire in my dressing gown pocket and crouched by the lock.

I could not trust any of them now. I had to know what Dr. Payne wished to discuss with my uncle. My hand shook so much that I had to do more breathing exercises before I could finally free the bar in the lock. My heart beat a frantic tattoo as I slipped from my rooms toward the stairs.

The hall outside the library was empty when I reached the ground floor and snuck a peek around the corner. A single lantern rested on the hall table, casting wavering light on the ceiling, but no one was there to guard it. Unsure if Tom, Sarah, or Pendel might return any moment, I rushed down the hall as quietly as I could and stole into the billiard room adjacent to the library.

Voices carried clearly through the adjoining door, but I couldn't quite understand them at first, due to the thumping of my heart. I held my breath and gripped the wood trim around the lintel so tightly my knuckles popped, willing the pounding in my ears away.

"No. Absolutely not. We've had this conversation before, sir, and you know my feelings on the subject." Uncle Oscar's voice came and went as if he were pacing. A moment later, I heard the clink of crystal and the splash of liquid in a glass.

"Of course, sir, and I do understand your feelings. Truly, when we were young, such places well earned their reputations. But so much has changed now. We have entered a new age of science and discovery.

New treatments are being invented every day, and patients are given the utmost care, day and night."

"I won't ship him off to an institution. I won't leave him amongst strangers."

My uncle's words comforted me, but his voice didn't hold as much conviction as I would've liked.

"They will be strange to him for a time, yes. But he will come to know them. Sir, to be frank, his violent outbursts are quite concerning. I agreed that he should stay at home, despite my reservations, as long as he seemed calm and content here. But his actions and rebellions of late tell a different story. And now this scene upstairs, wrecking his rooms, speaks of a return to the violence we've seen before. I fear his medication is no longer working, and without new treatments, he may only get worse. Should he not be in more capable hands than a few untrained servants and an occasional visit from myself? Should he not be with skilled physicians, nurses, and attendants who can monitor his progress day and night and employ the most modern of treatments available—treatments like the electric therapies and water therapies that I cannot administer here?"

My knuckles ached and my fingernails dug into the finely carved wood as I struggled to take even breaths. The longer the silence beyond the door stretched, the harder I prayed that my uncle would speak, would shout at the doctor and tell him he was wrong—cast him out of this house—but he didn't.

"Mr. Middleton, I know your feelings on the subject," Dr. Payne continued, "but we must think of what's best for Lord Campden. At least allow me to send out a few inquiries. We might set up an appointment to tour some of the more exclusive retreats, so you might see for yourself they are professional medical facilities of the highest caliber."

No, no, no, no.

I heard another clink of crystal and splash in a glass before my uncle sighed and said, "I will think on it."

I backed away from the door shaking my head in denial and disbelief. He wouldn't. He couldn't. I would refuse to go. They couldn't make me if I refused. My uncle would have to have me declared unfit in order to force me.

He would never do that. Would he?

I didn't know anymore.

Suddenly dizzy, I gripped the edge of the billiard table, doubled over, and heaved. Only a little spittle fell to the floor. Stumbling to the door, it took me three tries to turn the knob because my hand shook so badly.

A murmur of voices continued from the library, but I could not listen anymore. I hurried to the stairs but skidded to a halt when the white woman appeared on the first landing above me, hovering in front of the portrait of my father. Wrapping my arms tightly around myself I silently willed her to go away. If I had to be plagued by a vision, why couldn't it be Fox? Why wasn't he here? I needed him badly.

She hovered on the landing, unmoving, her form more solid than ever, her boney arms outstretched to me but not beckoning. Instead she seemed to be warning me away, blocking my path.

"Go away. Please go away," I whispered, tears burning my eyes. I was held together by the most tenuous of threads. I could not bear much more. I needed to think. I needed to calm myself. If I could only reach my rooms, I could sit for a while. I'd gain control of myself again. I knew I could. Then I would write my arguments for my uncle, as I'd done before, and I would convince him that Dr. Payne was wrong. I had to.

Voices echoing down the hall finally broke the tableau between me and the apparition. The doors to the kitchens opened followed by footsteps and the clink and rattle of trays. In a panic, I closed my eyes and rushed the stairs. A shiver ran down my spine as I passed through something thicker than mist and colder than death. I stumbled, but I did not stop my headlong flight. Breathing heavily and running on tiptoe, I nearly crashed into a table when I skidded to a halt at the entrance to my hall.

Frozen in horror, I could only stare and gasp for breath at the scene in front of me.

Thump. Scrape. Thump. Scrape.

A shadow in the shape of a man dragging something backward down the hall lurched past the door to my rooms, accompanied by the sounds I'd heard a thousand times before. Oily blackness stained the hall carpet in its wake, glistening wetly in the faint light coming from beneath my door. As it passed through the small rectangle of light across the carpet, the thing the shadow dragged resolved itself into the shape of a woman in a white dressing gown. The woman's gown was covered in more dark stains and a charm bracelet glittered in the light as it scraped across the wood floor beyond the carpet. A pathetic whimper escaped my lips as I stood transfixed.

I might have stayed there forever, frozen in fear, but I felt a tug at my arm. I looked down, and a boney hand clutched at my sleeve. Stumbling back in horror, I fell to the floor and scrambled backward across the hall carpet. After what I'd seen, I expected to find my hands covered in the wetness, but they were dry and the wool beneath me was unblemished.

"Oh, God. Oh, God."

The white woman moved toward me again, and I crawled the last few feet to my door, shoved it open, and quickly pushed it closed behind me. With shaking hands, I fumbled with my bent wire in the lock, though why I bothered I couldn't say. It wasn't as if a locked door had ever stopped any of the apparitions before, but I locked it anyway.

Fear of discovery in this state was the only thing that kept me from joining in when the wailing down the hall began. I collapsed to the floor with my back against the door, hugged myself and rocked in place. Small pathetic sounds escaped my tightly clamped lips, but I couldn't stop them.

When a heavy hand landed on my shoulder, I did cry out and nearly shot out of my skin, but then I turned and found Fox's concerned brown eyes looking down at me. With a desperate cry, I launched myself into his arms, dragging him to his knees.

"Arthur? What is it? What's wrong?"

"Tell me you're real. Please, tell me you're real."

"I'm real, love. I always have been. What's happened?"

I could only shake my head and cling to him. He hissed, and I felt sure I could hear his ribs creak, but I could not ease my grip. He was the only solid thing I had right now.

Despite the discomfort he must have been in, he held on to me and petted my hair. "You're all right now. I'm here. Tell me what's wrong. I came last night, but I heard men in your rooms, and I couldn't get close to you without being discovered. What happened?"

I let out a feeble little moan and clutched him tighter.

"What can I do?" he wheezed.

"Take me out of here," I finally choked out.

"What?" I allowed him to draw back enough to search my face.

"Take me away. Take me someplace quiet. I just cannot be here any longer. Please. Take me with you, anywhere."

My words calmed me some. It made sense. Everything, every feeling, every overwhelming sensation and emotion resided in this house. If I weren't here, if I had some distance, I could think what to do next. I didn't even care about the thrill of anxiety that shot through me at the thought of venturing beyond these walls. These walls had betrayed me. As long as Fox was with me, I would feel safe. He was the only one left that I truly trusted.

"Get dressed," he ordered as he untangled himself from my embrace and drew me to my feet.

With his help, I stumbled to my wardrobe and pulled out my clothes. I dressed hurriedly, fumbling with the buttons until he had to help me with that as well. After he retrieved my coat, scarf, and gloves from the stairwell to the roof, I tugged them on and followed him to the hall door. He dropped to his knees and undid the lock infinitely faster than I had managed. Then he stood and offered his hand to me, but I hesitated.

"Have you changed your mind?" he asked, frowning.

"Why aren't we going up to the roof?" I searched the darkness beyond his shoulder, terrified of what I might see.

"You can't climb down the way I do, not in the dark. I won't risk it. How many people are in the house?"

"Dr. Payne, my uncle, Pendel, and three other servants."

"Do you know where they are likely to be?"

"They were in the library and the kitchens only a few moments ago."

He arched a brow in surprise, but before I could explain, he shook his head. "Will anyone be coming to check on you?"

"No. I don't think so. They think me still drugged."

His face darkened, but he made no comment. After a quick glance into the hall, he offered his hand to me again. "Come on. We should be able to sneak out if we're quick about it. If we hear anyone coming, we can duck into one of the rooms."

Closing my eyes against what I feared I'd see in the hall, I allowed him to drag me behind him. When he paused at the top of the stairs, I opened my eyes but didn't look back. My heart pounded in fear and anxiety, but we encountered no one.

The front door had blessedly been left unlocked, and for the first time in over ten years, I simply walked out of my house and into the fog-shrouded night.

It was terrifying and exhilarating all at once. If not for Fox's hand pulling me along behind him, I might've turned to stone on the front lawn, but he didn't give me time to think or to panic. He urged me onward until we stopped by a small stand of bushes at the edge of Campden's grounds. From the shadows, he drew a greatcoat, hat, gloves, and boots and donned them after tugging off his soft leather shoes. I caught a brief glimpse of him in the weak light of a gas streetlamp despite the foggy darkness, and the figure he cut distracted me from my nerves. I'd never seen him in proper clothes before, but in the state I was in, I couldn't comment on it. All I could do was blink stupidly at him.

As soon as his strange clothes were covered and his shoes stashed in his coat pockets, he grabbed my hand and dragged me away again. I was lost in moments as we ran through the mist-shrouded streets until we reached a wide thoroughfare where carriages and people suddenly appeared out of the gloom. Music and light spilled from closely crowded buildings, but before I became overwhelmed, Fox draped my arm over his, drew me to his side, and started walking as if we were on a Sunday stroll in the park.

Despite the hour and the dense fog, carriages and other couples passed by us with dizzying frequency. I closed my eyes and kept them that way, trusting Fox to lead me. If I imagined it were a dream, the panic did not rise in my chest, and I could keep putting one foot calmly in front of the other, as if I belonged there.

"Not long now," he murmured.

When I glanced at him, he gave me a reassuring smile, and I tried to return it. He raised his free hand and whistled at a passing carriage, and the horse slowed to a stop not far away.

"Where to, guv?" an old man in a battered coat and bowler hat called as soon as we stepped up to his carriage.

"Pimlico, please."

The driver took the coin Fox offered, gave him a broad, gap-toothed smile, and tipped his hat. "Right ye are, sirs."

After helping me inside the carriage, Fox climbed in next to me and tapped the roof. The coach lurched forward, and I swallowed and closed my eyes. I'd been barely more than thirteen the last time I'd ridden in a carriage.

"Are you all right?"

I clenched my teeth and nodded.

"It's only a few miles. We'll be there soon enough at this time of night," he murmured, squeezing my hand.

He understood. Of course he understood.

"I'll stir up the fire and add plenty of coal," he continued. "I'll tuck you in my bed, under soft blankets, and keep you close all night."

He pulled me against his side as he murmured more soft endearments and comforting promises, and if not for the bouncing and lurching of the carriage over the cobbled streets, I might've slumped against him and dozed off. My burst of courage fueled by desperation was rapidly wearing thin. My feet were damp and ached from running in shoes that were never meant to splash through icy puddles. I felt wrung out and old. All I wanted was to crawl into the haven Fox described and never come out again. A dam of emotion threatened to burst inside me, and I shivered and clung to him, uncaring of the shame I knew I'd feel later.

An eternity of bumping and jostling later, Fox shook me out of my stupor and stepped down from the carriage.

"Here we are, Arthur. Come on, only a little farther and you can rest."

As he tossed the driver another coin, I dragged my weary bones from the seat and down to the street. The row of white townhouses in front of us was quiet and dark. The mist-shrouded street was empty but for us and a few gas streetlamps obscured by the fog. I couldn't see much beyond the weak halo of light from the lamp closest to us, but the houses looked clean and respectable, if not overly large or lavish.

I followed Fox through an iron gate and up the stairs to the third door in from the corner.

"We'll have to be quiet. I let the apartments on the third floor. Mrs. Trotman knows I come in at all hours, but I'd rather her not know you're here, at least for the present," he whispered to me as he pulled a set of keys from his coat pocket and unlocked the door.

We tiptoed up the stairs, Fox showing me which loose boards to avoid. I had to concentrate so hard on each step that I was completely exhausted by the time we reached the top. He fitted a key in the lock of another door without a sound—impressive in the darkness—and a moment later ushered me through before closing and bolting the door behind us.

While I shivered near the door, he struck a match and lit a gas lamp on the wall, and then an oil lamp on a table, flooding the room with light.

"It isn't grand, but Mrs. Trotman has installed all the modern amenities as they've become available—gas lamps, piped water in the necessary. My rooms are hot as the devil in summer, but they're also the warmest in winter." As he spoke, he knelt in front of a parlor stove, stirred up the banked coals inside and added more. After a few pumps of the hand bellows, the fire cheered up, and I moved to it gratefully as I blinked sleepily at my surroundings.

His rooms weren't grand, as he'd said, but they were tidy and comfortable. He had a sitting area by the stove, a small dining table by the windows, and a writing desk along one wall. Of most interest to me was the door on the far side of the room that I hoped led to a bedchamber.

"Let's get you out of those damp things and into bed." My smile must have been a pathetic thing to behold for he chuckled as he drew my coat from my shoulders. "You'll feel better once you've rested."

With relief, I collapsed onto his bed as soon as he'd finished helping me undress. Tired as I was, I made no objection when he pulled a soft cotton nightshirt over my head and tucked me in like a child. Only when he made to leave me, I found the energy to protest. "Where are you going?"

"Only to see to the fire and the lamps. I'll be back soon."

Struggling to stay awake, I listened as he bustled about in the other room. When he returned, he carried the oil lamp in one hand and a bottle in the other. He'd taken off his coat and boots and stripped to the waist, and for a moment, I allowed myself to forget all my troubles and simply admire his beauty. His lean torso glowed in the lamplight, his chest and arms wiry with muscle, and his stomach flat despite the silver of his hair. I reached for him, but he handed me the bottle instead.

"Drink."

"What is it?"

I didn't mean to sound suspicious, but I'd had about enough of potions and medicine.

"It's only sherry."

He set the lamp on the nightstand, and then bent to undo the ties at his calves and remove his silk trousers. I uncorked the bottle and downed a swallow.

"I thought we both could use a little drink," he said. His usual wry smile held a hint of caution as he searched my face. After taking the bottle and downing a hefty swallow, he handed it back to me and slid in beside me.

"I shan't need much," I said around a yawn. "I'm so tired all of a sudden."

He took the bottle from me again and pulled me against his chest. Burying my face in his shoulder, I finally allowed myself to relax and forget the events of the day. I was asleep in moments.

Chapter Seventeen

When I woke the next morning, the sun was shining through the window curtains, but the light was wrong. It came from the wrong direction, and the curtains were the wrong color. Blinking the sleep from my eyes, a strange room came into focus, and my heart skipped a beat. Panic swelled in me as I searched for anything familiar. In my distress, I must have let out a sound, because Fox came through the door and strode quickly to my bedside.

"It's all right, Arthur. I'm here."

"Fox? Where am I?"

"My rooms. Don't you remember?"

After taking a few steadying breaths, the night before came back to me. It was real. I had left my house and everything I knew behind.

What have I done?

"Arthur?"

He knelt by the bed and gripped my shoulders, distracting me from the rising tide of emotion that threatened to swamp me.

"You're all right. You're safe here with me. You won't have to do anything you don't want to. And I'm here for you, whatever you need."

His eyes were actually a lovely, warm shade of brown with hints of gold streaked through them. I'd never seen them in daylight before. They were breathtaking, beautiful. *He* was beautiful, and he was here for me.

Forcing the rest from my mind, I cupped his cheeks and kissed him desperately. He stiffened slightly but soon wrapped his arms around my shoulders and kissed me back.

I broke away only to catch my breath, and he held me close and scattered teasing kisses across my face and neck until I couldn't help but laugh.

"I'm here," I said wonderingly.

"Yes, you are."

"And you're here."

"I am."

I shook my head and blew out a breath. "I can't believe it. I left."

"You did." He grinned broadly, probably relieved that I wasn't going to fall apart on him just yet. Then he touched my cheek and brushed my hair from my forehead. "Can you tell me what happened?" he asked cautiously. "Why were your rooms in such a state? Did someone hurt you?"

My cheeks flamed at what he must have thought, finding me collapsed on the floor and weeping as the wreckage of my rooms lay about me. I drew in a shaky breath, but I hardly knew where to start.

After several moments when I could say nothing, he shook his head. "It doesn't matter. You're here now. You don't need to say anything. I shouldn't be bullying you before you've even had your breakfast. You must be starving."

I wanted to object as he drew away from me and pulled clothes from his wardrobe, but my stomach chose that instant to remind me just how long it had been since I'd last eaten.

"I'll see what I can drag out of Bette, Mrs. Trotman's cook. She can usually be charmed into fixing me something, no matter how late it is. I'll be back as soon as I can."

Anxious now that I'd been left alone, I climbed out from under the covers and pulled on the dressing gown Fox had left at the foot of the bed. To distract myself, I wandered to the windows in the main room and drew back the curtains.

I hadn't been mistaken. The relentless fog had finally lifted, and weak winter sunlight touched my skin as I lifted my face to it, but the cacophony from the street below soon drew my attention. Carriages, carts, animals, and people of all walks of life going about their daily business swarmed beneath the window. I hadn't seen that many people in more than ten years, and I quickly stepped away from the window and hugged myself. I was not prepared for so many. I didn't know if I would ever be prepared for it. Shivering, I moved closer to the stove. Fox had obviously tended it already, but I could not resist the novelty of simply opening the grate and adding coals to it at will. It gave me something to do other than panic at the situation my rashness had landed me in.

I had to focus on the positive. I could do anything I pleased. I could light the gas lamp on the wall. If I had the courage, I could step outside and walk the streets of London as any gentleman. I could go see the plays I'd read about. I could go to a bookshop and simply browse for hours. I could find an open field and run until my legs failed me.

I was free.

Except I wasn't truly free, was I? I couldn't even look at a street full of people without my nerves starting to fray and my breath growing short. What made me think I could take a stroll down the sidewalk or even *enter* a bookshop without panicking and making a spectacle of myself?

Glumly I surveyed the confines of Fox's apartments. This would only be a replacement for my rooms at Campden House—that is, if Fox didn't grow tired of me and my foolishness, which I felt certain he would eventually. My own mother had—

The rattle of a tray and the click of the lock made me jump. To my relief, Fox pushed the door open and bent to retrieve a tray from the floor. "Will you get the door?" he asked, and I hurried to close and bolt it behind him as he carried a heaping tray of food inside. "I knew Bette wouldn't let me down. A little kiss on the cheek and gushing compliments for her cooking, and we have a tray of eggs and sausages, warm bread and jam, and coffee and tea. I didn't know which you'd prefer."

Beaming at me, he set the tray on the small table by the windows, and I took the seat he offered me. Suddenly ravenous, I dug into the meal with relish. Halfway through my plate, the world did not seem so terrifying and overwhelming as it had only a few minutes before. It was amazing how a full belly could change a man's outlook.

I was with Fox. He was here to help. I wasn't alone, and he understood how hard this was for me. This was real. He was real. He had to be.

"Thank you," I said with as much feeling as I could imbue those two words.

He seemed to know I meant more than just the food, and he took my hand in his across the table. "You are most welcome, lovely Arthur."

Forcing myself to hold his gaze, I cleared my throat and swallowed. "You asked before what happened. I think I can tell you now."

"Only if you want to. I make no demands on you."

"I know. You've been extraordinarily kind. I honestly don't know what I would've done without you these past weeks." He squeezed my hand and the warmth and approval in his smile gave me the courage to continue. "I've been so happy the last few nights. You've made me very happy. And after you talked of the future we might have together, I felt like I could conquer the world. The night before last, I picked the lock on my door and left my rooms to prove to myself I could do it on my own." I took a breath and blew it out. "I was in a... a *nostalgic* mood, I suppose. After a while, I started thinking about my mother and father, and I decided to go see their rooms for the first time in years." Curling my free hand into a fist, I broke from his gaze and worried my lip. "They were much as I remembered them. Nothing had been removed, only draped to protect the furniture. Before I left to return to my rooms, I decided to open my mother's secretary, thinking I might ask Pendel to exchange it for the one in my rooms, and that's when I found the last letter my mother wrote, a letter to her sister, unfinished and never posted." He remained silent while I took a moment to work through the remembered pain, and I squeezed his hand in gratitude. "In it, she told my aunt she never loved me. That she was with child and didn't know how to tell my father she wouldn't have me near her new baby.... My own mother couldn't trust me near my baby sister or brother for fear of what I might do. She thought me that broken, that diseased."

"Is it possible you misunderstood her meaning?" he interjected gently.

I shook my head, clinging to the hand that still held mine. Losing the battle against the tide of my emotions, I closed my eyes as I felt a single tear slide down my cheek. I clenched my jaw even harder and fought for control. "I paraphrased, but the words were much the same. She did not love me. She 'could not love me as a mother should.' Those were her words exactly. Hard to misinterpret that, don't you think?"

"Oh, Arthur, I'm so sorry."

"What if none of my family ever loved me? What if my 'strangeness' as she called it made me somehow unlovable? My uncle always told me how much my parents loved me. Pendel always told me. They lied. And if they were lying about that, what other lies have they told me?" I felt that panicked tightness in my chest again, swelling to cut off my air, and I fought it down, counting out my breaths. "I have happy memories of my mother and father, but what if they're a lie too? What if I can't trust any of my memories from before my fever, or any of my memories at all?"

"Come here, love. Come back to bed."

He tugged at my hand, and I rose and followed him without resistance. Once he'd tucked me beneath the blankets again, he kicked off his shoes, slid in beside me, and gathered me against his chest. I closed my eyes and buried my face between his throat and the pillow, trying to draw his warmth inside me and hide from the rest of the world.

He was the first to break the silence. "I can't pretend to know what you're feeling, but I do know a little about the loss of parental affection." A soft chuckle vibrated through his chest. "Though in my case, there was never very much to begin with, as is the case with most of the members of our class. Such things aren't encouraged, you see…. You know, if your mother was with child, I've heard ladies can become a bit overwrought during such times. Perhaps she was only experiencing a temporary sort of hysteria due to her condition, and she didn't mean a word of it. That's why the letter was never sent."

I tightened my grip on him and breathed him in, trying to see the sense in his words, wishing I could believe them.

He pressed a kiss to my hair and entwined our legs, allowing me to get as close to him as I could. "But even if she meant what she said," he continued softly, "it doesn't precisely follow that the rest of your family doesn't love you, or that you're unlovable. You've told me time and again how your uncle and butler care for you. And I know for a fact you are loveable, Arthur, because I love you."

I jolted and pulled back until I could see his face. "You love me?"

The smile he gave me as he pushed my hair away from my face and cradled my cheek was so gentle, a lump rose in my throat. "Of course I do. How could I not?" he murmured.

I could think of a thousand reasons why he shouldn't, but I wasn't going to argue with him. "I love you too, so much," I whispered before I kissed him with every bit of feeling I possessed. "Touch me. Help me forget."

"Are you sure?"

"God, yes."

I was still wearing the dressing gown, so it took a bit of awkward fumbling to remove it and my borrowed nightshirt. And despite my unreasoning objections, Fox had to leave the bed entirely to divest himself of his clothes. But then he was naked and in my arms again, and my world was as it should be.

He kissed and caressed me everywhere he could reach, but I was frantic with want. I needed more. "I want you inside me again," I begged.

He stiffened in my arms and searched my face. "I don't think that's—"

"I do," I interrupted. "Please. I want to feel you everywhere at once. I want to be so full of you I can't think or feel anything else. I want to be yours utterly and completely."

When he still hesitated, I wrapped a hand around the back of his neck and the other around his waist. I rolled on my back, drawing him on top of me. "Make me yours."

His smile was as crooked as ever, but I could tell my words pleased him by the heat in his eyes as he said, "You're already mine, as I am yours. But if you want me to make you forget the rest of the world exists, I gladly accept that challenge."

My heart beat frantically, unsure if I should've been more careful about what I wished for. But then he slid down my body, nestled between my legs, and took my cock in his mouth, and my fears and the rest of the world disappeared.

He brought me to the brink over and over with his mouth and hands, until I shook with frustrated need. Then, at last, he slipped a wet finger inside me, and I ground down on it begging for more.

"Hold on, love," he growled, and a moment later he withdrew from me completely.

I whined in confusion, as he moved away and fumbled in the drawer of his bedside table, but then he returned and pressed himself along my side. "Roll over," he ordered breathlessly.

At his urging, I reluctantly moved to my side, facing away from him. I didn't like this position much, as I couldn't reach him easily. But then he pressed his full length to my back, bit my shoulder, and slid two slippery fingers inside me, and I forgot about any awkwardness or discomfort on my part.

"I'll stop whenever you need," he whispered as he opened me.

I didn't want him to stop anything, ever. Arching my back, I lifted my leg, spreading myself for him, and with a quiet groan, he withdrew his fingers from me and pressed his crown to my opening. I caught my breath as he pressed slowly inside me and a familiar discomfort built and then vanished.

Unlike last time, my cursed illness did nothing to ruin the pleasant fullness as my body stretched to accommodate him, and when he began to move inside me, the ache turned to utter bliss. His strokes in me were slow and gentle. He kissed along my shoulder, my neck, my jaw, and my cheek as he moved in me, and I had never felt so cherished in my life.

"You're so lovely, my Arthur, so sweet. You hold me so tight inside you, as if you were made for me, and I for you," his whispered against my skin.

I wanted to weep at his words. I was full to near bursting, but still it was not enough. I pushed back seeking more, the pressure inside me almost unbearable. With a grunt, he obliged me, increasing the force and speed of his thrusts as I gripped my aching cock and stroked myself until I teetered on the edge of the precipice. Reaching behind me with my free hand, I gripped the back of his neck, holding him as close to me as I could. He buried his face in my hair and whispered, "I love you," and I cried out and spilled my seed over my fist. My entire body tightened as wave after wave of pleasure washed over me, and he continued to move.

Utterly spent, I slumped to the mattress like a marionette whose strings had been cut, and Fox thrust twice more and spilled his seed inside me. We both moaned as the warmth spread in me, and he gathered me tightly in his arms and held me as if he'd never let me go. I fell asleep with a feeling that the world was not so frightening or painful as I'd feared. As long as I had Fox, I'd be all right.

Chapter Eighteen

"Arthur? Arthur, love, will you wake a little for me?"

"Mmmm?"

Fox chuckled, and I smiled without opening my eyes. I was warm and happy, curled against his side, and I didn't want to move.

"I need to go out for a little while, and I didn't want you to wake and find me gone."

Like a douse of cold water, his words made me open my eyes, lift my head from his shoulder, and frown at him. "Where are you going?"

"I need to go to the markets and get provisions for us. I have almost nothing to eat or drink here. Bette will provide some meals, but we'll be on our own sometimes, and I've only paid for one person. We'll need more than that, if we're going to stay in for a few days while you get settled."

I didn't like being left alone, but the thought of accompanying him to a crowded market started a thrill of panic in my stomach and chest. I swallowed and nodded at his questioning glance, and his lips curved slightly. "I'll try not to be gone too long, but there's something else I have to get, and I don't know how long it will take me to find it in the strength you'll need."

"What?"

"Your laudanum."

I scowled and tried to pull away from him, but he held on. "You know I have to, Arthur. You don't want to spend another night of fever and cramps, do you?"

"No," I admitted begrudgingly.

"I'll be here to help. You'll decide how and when to take it, but you can't just stop. It has to be a process. You know that."

Reluctantly I nodded, and he placed a kiss on my forehead before releasing me and climbing out of bed. "Since the Pharmacy Act, I can't just pop into any corner shop and pick up what you'll need. I'll have to check the chemists' shops, so I'll need to go a little farther afield than the local market. I'll be back as soon as I can. I promise."

I bit my lip to keep from voicing any of the myriad reservations I had. He was right. I needed the laudanum, and we both needed the food and drink. All of these things made sense, but as usual, my heart didn't want to be rational.

Swallowing my fear, I nodded and tried to smile for him. When he'd finished dressing, he sat on the edge of the bed, bent, and kissed me. "I'll be back soon, with enough supplies to keep us for a week. Help yourself to anything you want here. There isn't much, but I do have a few books you might not have read. And when I get back, we can spend as long as you need here, and we'll talk everything through."

He kissed me once more before putting on his shoes and leaving the room. After a few moments, he was back in the doorway. "I won't lock you in, but you may want to bolt the door after I leave. I've told Mrs. Trotman to leave off attendance for the time being, so you shouldn't be disturbed, but just in case." At my nod, he smiled. "See you soon, love."

I DID all right for a time. After throwing the bolt on the outer door, I snuggled back into the warmth of his blankets, surrounded by his scent, and reveled in the memory of at last being able to wake up in his arms, knowing I could spend as much time with him as I pleased. But eventually my solitude, the strangeness of my surroundings, and the constant noise from the street wore on my nerves. Despite my best efforts to stave it off with logic, worry settled in my stomach—unpleasant and all too familiar—driving me from the bed, desperate for a distraction.

I reluctantly dressed in my soiled clothes from the night before, but after that I didn't know what to do with myself. Fox's rooms held little to divert me. He had no piano, no drawing supplies, and I didn't think I could settle enough to read, even if any of his books caught my interest. I had far too much swirling around in my head from the past few days. Far too much had happened, and the only thing that had helped thus far was Fox.

I needed him too badly. I couldn't conceive of stepping beyond the door to his apartments on my own. I had no money, no one I could depend on but him. I didn't even know where I was.

What if something happened to him? What if he never came back? *What if...? What if...? What if...?*

Growling in frustration at the endless refrain in my head, I paced the confines of the main room until I feared wearing a hole in the carpets. I had to be stronger. I had to become well. I could no longer pretend even to myself that Fox was not real. It had been easier to continue with the simple fantasy than face the overwhelming complexity of the truth. Especially if it meant admitting Fox was only a man, not a bottomless well of kindness and compassion. If I didn't conquer this madness inside me, I would eventually drain him dry, as Ethan had done.

Where is he? Why is it taking so long?

When I finally heard the knock on the door, I'd worked myself into such a state, I could hardly breathe. I ran for the latch, threw the bolt, and yanked open the door. Luckily it was Fox on the other side, because I hadn't even thought to check.

He breezed through, carrying an enormous basket of food and wrapped parcels, and I closed and bolted the door behind him. After setting his burden on the table by the window, he turned to me with a happy smile, but it faded quickly when I joined him.

"What's wrong?" he asked.

I shook my head and threw myself into his arms. "Nothing."

"It can't be nothing to put you in such a state," he murmured into my hair.

"It can," I contradicted miserably.

He sighed and hugged me tighter. "You've been through a lot. Give yourself time. I intend to give you as much as you need."

I nodded, already feeling my nerves settling, now that he was back and I was no longer alone with my thoughts.

"Did something happen?" he asked.

"You weren't here."

It sounded even sillier when I admitted it out loud, but he continued to hold me. Just when I thought my heart had settled, a knock on the door made me jump and set it racing again.

"Don't worry," Fox whispered, "I couldn't carry everything I bought, so I paid a boy to bring the rest round." He placed a kiss to my temple and set me away from him. "Go hide in the bedroom, and I'll see to him."

After the boy left, I joined Fox in the main room again, feeling a bit more in control of my emotions. He was removing packages from the basket and arranging them on the table.

"Do you want to tell me what happened?" he asked quietly.

"Nothing happened. It was just my stupid nerves getting the better of me. I'm sorry."

He stopped what he was doing and regarded me soberly. "I've told you, you don't need to apologize, particularly for missing me. And you have every right to be nervous. You're in a strange place, outside of your rooms for the first time in over ten years. It's perfectly understandable for anyone to be nervous under the circumstances. I wouldn't have left you today if I'd had a choice. But now we have plenty of provisions to keep us for the next several days, and we can stay in together as long as you need."

"Thank you."

"Don't thank me. I finally have you all to myself. I'm a *very* happy man."

AFTER SPENDING most of the afternoon indulging in carnal delights, we lay cuddled together beneath the blankets as the sun dropped below the rooftops. He seemed content to doze in my arms, and I wished I could relax enough to do the same, but some unpleasant business still needed to be addressed, and I couldn't put it off much longer. It wouldn't be fair to Fox to force him to bring it up again.

Lifting my head from his chest, I propped my chin on the back of my hand and regarded him soberly. "Were you able to get the laudanum?"

"Yes," he answered without opening his eyes.

I sighed and continued reluctantly. "I should probably take some. Dr. Payne said he gave me a heavy dose yesterday morning, but I haven't had any since."

"Do you want me to get it?"

"Not really." I chuckled. "But I should."

He gave me a small smile and a peck on the lips, then disentangled himself from me and hurried from the room. He returned with the sherry, a small bottle of clear liquid, and a crystal cordial glass and handed them to me, before sliding in beside me again, his naked flesh chilled from even that short time out of bed.

"Try cutting back just a little. Don't try to reduce the dose too fast," he murmured, but he left the rest to me.

I had no means to measure with any accuracy, but judging by the doses I'd seen Dr. Payne pour for me in the past, I filled the cordial glass with as close an approximation as I could. As usual, I fell asleep shortly after swallowing the vile stuff and chasing it with a bit of sherry, but Fox was still next to me when I woke again, and my heart swelled with joy despite the cotton around my thoughts.

"You're still here," I murmured stupidly.

"I am. You can trust me. I intend to be here as often as possible from now on."

"I do trust you. I followed you, didn't I?"

He hugged me to his side and smiled. "You did. I have to admit I was surprised you asked. I would've gladly taken you from there sooner, but I thought the outside world terrified you too much."

I sighed and snuggled deeper in the blankets, pressing my cheek to his chest. "It did. It *does*, but the house was beginning to terrify me too. I couldn't stay any longer. Too much had happened. I haven't told you the whole of it yet."

"Will you tell me now?"

In fits and starts, I explained about my episode in my rooms, cringing at my loss of control and the memory of the destruction I'd wrought. I didn't even want to think about what I'd broken beyond repair.

"You know, you don't need to be embarrassed there," he murmured into the silence between us. "Any man might have done the same. We all have to let off a little steam now and again, or we'll boil over. You don't have a club to go to, but I assure you, that's half the reason they exist. I would imagine you haven't been allowed to let off any steam in a very long time."

I was sure what I'd done was a good deal more than letting off a little steam, but his words and his laugh eased some of the tension in me, at least until I continued with the rest of my tale. When I reached the part where I needed to describe the conversation I'd overheard between my uncle and Dr. Payne, my throat tightened again, and he pulled me closer.

"I won't let that happen to you, no matter what," he said, pressing kisses to my hair. "You have my word on that. If we have to start over someplace new, someplace far away, and never let your uncle know where you are, we will."

The thought of never seeing Uncle Oscar again, or Pendel, pained me. I didn't want that if it could possibly be avoided, but the truth was

I had no idea what to do with my life now. I hadn't thought beyond the next hour, let alone the next day or week or year.

The silence stretched between us, and I hesitated to tell him the rest, but I didn't want any secrets between us.

"There's more," I murmured. "You remember the sounds you chased down the hall?"

"Yes."

"Well, I was wrong. There was something to see after all. I came upon it in my mad dash back to my rooms from the billiard room." Swallowing against the sudden constriction in my chest, I tried to describe the horrible scene I'd witnessed in the hall.

"Oh good God, no wonder you were in a state. I can't even imagine how awful that must've been, how terrifying… and on top of everything else."

With some distance from it, and being wrapped tightly in Fox's arms, the memory didn't petrify quite as badly as it had, but I still shivered in his embrace.

"You were right to leave," he continued. "I don't understand what's happening in that house, but it isn't all your imagination. I heard what you did, even if I never saw anything. It isn't all in your mind."

And because I wanted it so badly, I chose to believe him. The reality I had in front of me was far superior to anything I'd had for as long as I could remember, superior to anything waiting for me back there. It had to be enough.

Chapter Nineteen

Over the next week, Fox never left my side for more than a few minutes at a time. He occasionally had to go down for a tray from the kitchens or more coal for the fire, but that was as far as he ventured. We stayed tucked up in his rooms, feasting on the cheeses, bread, sausages, and wine he'd bought for us, in addition to Bette's fine cooking, which was almost as good as Mrs. Peebles's. We talked of everything and nothing. We explored our new passion often, whiling away many an hour in his bed or tangled together on his couch in front of the stove.

I could still hear the dizzying swirl of activity just beyond the windows, but cradled in his arms, secure in his affection, the panic rarely surfaced beyond a twinge here and there. My favorite times, other than when we were making love, were when he would speak to me of our future together, when we would dream of our life. My heart soared every time he mentioned finding us other apartments—somewhere a little quieter and big enough for a pianoforte, for my sake. In my more giddy moments, I waxed poetic along with him, dreaming of all the places we might holiday together—France and Spain and Italy. I could almost believe I was capable of such things, particularly with his unflagging confidence in me bolstering my courage. He believed in me, and therefore, I believed in myself.

The only time my happiness was threatened was when I thought of those I'd left behind. Did Pendel or my uncle miss me? Did they worry, or were they relieved to no longer be burdened with me? Every day with Fox made me more certain I didn't want to go back to that house, and I could never go back to the way things had been, but I also hated to think I might have caused them any pain at my abrupt departure.

Sometimes, in the quiet of the night or the lethargic hours after taking my medicine, I would decide to write to them, explaining my absence. But then Fox would wrap himself around me, or he would begin teasing me and start me laughing, and I'd forget again. It was so much easier to remain safe and warm in his arms and dream about the future than to face the disaster I'd left behind me.

It was the coward's way out and unworthy of a gentleman, but I took it all the same. I wanted our idyll to last forever and the world outside our little rooms to disappear, but a knock on the door on Friday evening brought reality crashing back in.

"Who's there?" Fox called.

"Mrs. Trotman, sir."

Fox groaned quietly and began disentangling himself from me. "A moment, please," he called out.

I rolled off him so he could climb free of the couch.

"Go in the other room. I'll get rid of her," he whispered, and I hurried into the bedchamber but left the door open a crack so I could hear.

I heard him draw the bolt back and open the door. "Good afternoon, Mrs. Trotman. To what do I owe the pleasure?"

"'Tis after the first of the month, sir. Your rent's past due, and you owe an accounting for the extra rations you've been charmin' out of Bette. I've added the tally to your bill," she sniffed.

Her voice grated on me, and I could almost picture the sour expression that went with it. My stomach clenched in anxiety but also a little outrage that she should dare speak to him like that—awful woman.

"Certainly, Mrs. Trotman, of course. But I fear I don't have the funds on me at this very instant."

"I thought you might not, seein' as how you haven't left your rooms for a week."

Her words seemed filled with meaning, but I couldn't fathom what she meant by them, other than a general air of suspicion and accusation.

"I've been a bit under the weather, what with the cold and all," he replied far more pleasantly than I would have in his place. "Forgive my tardiness with the rents. I shall have it to you soon."

"Best see you do, sir. I'm not running a charity house, and I don't like you gents taking advantage of Bette's kind nature, neither."

"Certainly, madam. Good afternoon."

His tone was stiffer that time, and I silently cheered him on. When I heard him close the door and throw the bolt, I rejoined him in the main room, expecting to share in his outrage at the woman's cheek, but the look on his face stopped me. Instead of seeming angry, he looked worried, and my stomach knotted in response.

"What's wrong?"

He took one look at me and his face softened. "Nothing. I was just hoping to put this off a little while longer, but I'm afraid I can't anymore."

"Put what off?"

"Between my mother and sister, the house in Kent, and my recent change in profession, I'm a little light on ready cash at the moment. I can put off some creditors with promises, but Mrs. Trotman is a shrewd old spinster. Pound notes in her hand is the only language she speaks. I won't be able to put her off for long before she sends for the bailiffs."

I cringed, fully aware how far out of my depth this sort of thing was. "What should we do?"

He closed the distance between us and hugged me close. "It's nothing to worry about. We'll be fine. I have, shall we say, a reserve of items from my former trade stashed away in the East End. I can sell what's left, and we'll be flush long enough for my new investments to begin paying out. I just didn't want to have to leave you alone again so soon. I'm not sure how long it will take me."

"Oh." I tensed, my whole body rejecting the idea of being left alone again to fret and worry. "Let me go with you," I said in a rush.

"What?"

I pulled back enough to meet his gaze. "I'm coming with you."

"No, you're not. It's not safe."

"Exactly why I should come. Let's do it now, tonight. It'll be easier in the dark. There won't be as many people about," I pressed.

"Arthur, no. You don't know what you're saying. The thought of leaving these apartments still frightens you. The East End will be a hundred times worse."

I lifted my chin stubbornly. "If it is that bad, it's no place for you either, which is why I can't let you go alone. What if something happened to you? What if you just disappeared and never came back again? I won't sit here alone and worry when I can be with you. I can do it. I swear. I won't let you down."

I wasn't exactly sure of any of that, but the doubt in his eyes got my back up. I had something to prove to both of us. Not to mention the thought of rattling around these rooms again, agonizing over everything that could go wrong, sounded a hundred times worse than anything I might encounter out there by his side.

He stepped away from me and pursed his lips. "I don't think this is a good idea, Arthur."

"But you won't stop me?"

After a few moments in which we regarded each other in stubborn silence, his lips curved slightly, and he shook his head. "As if I could stop you from doing anything you really wanted. You'll be a force to be reckoned with, one of these days when you're done with that medicine and fully well again. I only hope you won't ride roughshod over me when that day comes."

I rolled my eyes at him and laughed. "Hardly. So what do we do?"

With a sigh, he stepped around me and headed for the bedchamber. "First, we need to get dressed. My clothes will be long on you, but ill-fitting clothes will only work to our advantage in the East End."

The clothes he pulled from his wardrobe were old and worn, with patches at the elbows and knees. The set he handed me was indeed too long in the trousers and jacket sleeves, but I rolled the cuffs and stuffed newspaper in the pair of shabby boots he handed me.

"You don't want to be conspicuously overdressed in that part of Town. The less attention we draw, the better," he explained.

He examined me after we'd both finished and grunted in what I hoped was approval before pulling a wool cap low over my eyes. "Come on."

He still sounded out of sorts, but I chose to ignore it. I refused to let him go alone, no matter his wishes or the panicked twisting in my stomach as we snuck down the stairs and out of the house.

"We'll need to go a ways before we'll find a cab willing to take us to the East End at night."

The sun had set only a short while ago, so the streets still held more activity than I was comfortable with, but I kept my head down and followed closely on his heels, doing my breathing exercises and pretending that everything else didn't exist. The crowds grew thicker as we went, the buildings piled on top of one another like blocks. Light and music spilled out of several of them, the tunes familiar enough that I moved my fingers in time with the music to give my hands something to do beyond wringing them or pulling my hair.

Eventually Fox took my arm and quickened his pace until we stopped abruptly, and he whistled. Like coming out of a dream, I lifted my head and blinked as a carriage came into focus. Fox was having some sort of discussion with the driver, but I didn't hear much of it. Then he stuffed me in the carriage and climbed in after me, and as the contraption lurched forward, he closed the door, cutting us off from the rest of the world.

"He'll only take us as far as Bishop's Gate," he grumbled. "We'll have to go the rest of the way on foot. Are you all right?"

"Yes. I'm fine."

"You're sure? I can tell him to turn around and come back by myself."

"I'm *fine*," I insisted through gritted teeth.

"All right." He sighed once and then fell silent as the horses' hooves clopped on the pavers and the carriage jostled and bounced.

I won't let him down. I won't let me down. I can do this. It's nothing but a carriage ride in the city. It will all be over soon.

I repeated the words over and over in my head, and then, at last, the carriage stopped and Fox stepped out. I followed, but before I took a single step away from the carriage, a wave of stench assaulted me, forcing me to pull my borrowed scarf over my face.

"What is that?"

"Wind's comin' from the southeast tonight," the driver chuckled. "Welcome to the East End, sirs."

The driver laughed again, though it ended on a cough, and after a crack of his whip, the carriage lurched forward and disappeared into the night.

"It's a thousand times worse in summer," Fox murmured. "Come on. The sooner we get done, the sooner we can go home."

He took my hand and dragged me along behind him through twisting streets filled with detritus as I held the scarf to my mouth. Shapes huddled in doorways, women called to us from alleyways, but Fox didn't slow. I was very grateful for the borrowed boots as we splashed through puddles of I knew not what. I had a feeling I would want to throw them away, along with my borrowed clothes, as soon as we returned home.

The half-moon above provided the only light for much of our journey, but I supposed I should have been grateful not to see the place in the light of day. The paucity of streetlamps or anything else resembling civilization gave our journey a dreamlike quality—well, perhaps more a nightmare—that actually helped me keep a handle on my nerves. No one was there to judge me or find me strange. No one would know who I was, and therefore I had no standards to fail to live up to.

When the whole world seems mad, a madman is as sane as anyone.

My feet ached, and I had the beginning of blisters by the time Fox stopped behind a seemingly deserted shamble that looked much like all the rest. He unlocked the outer door and led us up a crumbling staircase to the second floor, where he unlocked another door and stepped inside.

Weak moonlight filtered through the filthy windows, illuminating the shapes of a single table, chair, and cot. The room was empty beyond that, and I squinted into the shadows in confusion.

"Why are we here?" I whispered.

"You'll see."

He moved to the cot and dragged it away from the wall. He crouched where the bed had been and lifted a few loose floorboards. From the space beneath, he withdrew a small sack that clinked when he tucked it under his arm.

"All right. Let's go."

"Aren't you going to replace the boards?" I asked as I followed him out.

"No. I won't be coming back here again. Let the next fellow make use of it."

He led the way back into the warren of streets, and I stuck to his side like a burr. I had no idea if this was the way we'd come or not, and I didn't care. I only wanted to be free of this horrible place and back in our comfortable little rooms again. It felt like we traveled miles before we finally stopped in an alley in what seemed a slightly more pleasant area. The streets were cleaner here at least, and there were more streetlamps to break up the dark.

"An associate of mine owns a shop here. I'll try to get him to buy the lot tonight. He'll probably cheat me out of half its worth, but I'll be glad to be done with it," he murmured.

After a quick look up and down the street, Fox stepped into the open, and I followed him across the street. We'd almost made it to the back door of a shop, when it opened and four men spilled out. The moment they spotted us, they froze.

"Hell and damnation," Fox whispered under his breath.

"Well, look 'oo we 'ave 'ere, boys. If it ain't the very bloke we been askin' after."

A man as big as Tom, standing to the right of the one who spoke, rubbed a rag stained with dark splotches over his knuckles and dropped it to the dirty cobbles, as they all chuckled.

"Boggs, ye were lookin' fer me? If I'da known, I woulda come to call," Fox replied. His voice held that strange accent he'd used the night we met, and his tone seemed oddly cheerful, given the tension in the air—or perhaps I was misreading things.

He stepped in front of me, blocking my view of the others, and his shoulders were definitely tense.

"Where ye been, Barker? We've missed ye," the one who'd spoken before said.

"When I tell you to, you run," Fox whispered over his shoulder. I wanted to argue or ask what was happening, but he turned back to the four in front of us. "I been round, 'ere and there."

"After our last discussion, I woulda thought ye'd learnt yer lesson 'bout steppin' out on our little arrangement. Ye don' do business in the End without we get our cut of the ream swag. Ye know that."

Over Fox's shoulder, I saw the group of them take a step closer to us. Fox held out his hands in a placating gesture. "Gents, don' be so 'ard. Ye gave me a good thump last time, an' I needed a bit a rest to recover, that's all. I got yer message loud an' clear. I ain't done no business since."

"What's that, then?" the spokesman asked, pointing at the sack Fox held.

"Just some bits and bobs left over is all. I'da sent along yer cut. I swear to ye."

The men took another few steps closer.

"Run!" Fox yelled.

He tossed the sack at the men and gave my shoulder a shove to get me moving. I nearly tripped over my feet in my haste, but when I heard a grunt behind me, I skidded to a halt in the street. A quick glance behind me told me Fox was no longer there, and in the faint moonlight, I saw shapes writhing in the alley from where we'd come.

"Go!" Fox yelled from the pile before I heard more grunts and swearing.

My heart raced, and ice ran through my veins. I could barely breathe, but I would not run. Instead I turned and dashed back at the tangle of men as fast as my feet would carry, plowing into the whole lot at full speed. I thudded into hard bone and muscle and crashed to the ground, the impact stunning me for a moment. I couldn't hear beyond the roaring in my ears, and my vision narrowed to the glint of Fox's silver hair in the moonlight as he struggled with the others. I'd never been taught how to box or anything of the kind, but panic and desperation took over my body, and I flailed about with my fists, leaping on the nearest man.

After the first blow landed on my jaw, I could hear a strange, almost inhuman howling, and I realized it was coming from me as I kicked and swung blindly and with all my might at the men around me like the madman I was. But then a sharp pain exploded across the back of my head, and my world went black.

Chapter Twenty

"Arthur? Arthur can you hear me?"

I knew that voice.

Why was it so hard to open my eyes?

"Arthur?" the voice was more excited that time. It seemed relieved.

My eyelids finally broke apart, but I flinched away from the bright light streaming through my windows. "The curtains," I croaked.

"Tom, the curtains," Pendel ordered, and soon the room was blessedly darker.

"Thank you," I rasped.

I blinked a few times until my room came into focus. Pendel hovered at the foot of my bed, and one of my chairs had been dragged next to the bed for Uncle Oscar.

"What are you doing here?" I asked my uncle.

"Oh lad, you can't know how happy I am to hear your voice."

I frowned at him. He sounded as if he were almost in tears. I didn't think I'd ever heard him like this before.

I tried to sit up, but pain stabbed through my skull and almost every other part of my body, and I moaned.

"Lie still, Arthur. You've been badly beaten and suffered a lengthy fever. Tom, fetch the doctor."

I groaned again. Dr. Payne was the last person I wanted to see.

"What happened?" I asked.

"You'll have to tell us, lad," Uncle Oscar replied. "You were missing for a week before constables found you near to death in Limehouse. We'd had men searching for you all over London."

"Searching?" And then it hit me all at once, and I struggled to sit up. "Oh God, Fox! Where is he? Is he all right?"

Uncle Oscar held me down with very little effort. I was weak as a baby, and even that little expense of energy had my head spinning. I collapsed back to the mattress with a groan. "Please, is he all right?"

"Is who all right?"

"Fox."

Uncle Oscar frowned and shook his head. "I'm sorry, Arthur. I don't understand. But please, calm yourself. You've had a terrible fever, on top of everything else. You'll injure yourself, if you don't lie still."

"But I have to find him," I cried weakly. My chest ached with every indrawn breath. "I have to know if he's all right."

I tried to sit up again as I began to cough, and Uncle Oscar huffed in relief as someone entered the room. "Oh good. Dr. Stuart, please can you help?"

A man I didn't recognize stepped up to the side of my bed and smiled at me. "I see you're finally awake. That's good news."

Surprised, I quit struggling, and eventually my cough subsided after the new man handed me a glass of water to sip on. He was a little taller than my uncle but thin as a reed. He looked as if a stiff breeze might blow him over. His lively green eyes peered at me over a pair of rectangular spectacles, and his black hair was slicked back with pomade, adding to a beetle-like first impression. But the smile he gave me was cheery enough, more pleasant than what I'd come to expect from a doctor.

"I have to find Fox," I insisted weakly.

"What is Fox?" Dr. Stuart asked, never taking his eyes off me.

"He's a man," I forced out, though I could feel my throat tightening in my anxiety and desperation.

The doctor looked to my uncle and Pendel, but both men shrugged, watching me with wary concern. I closed my eyes and tried to count my breaths. I'd never get anywhere if I couldn't be coherent, and I had to find Fox.

"Lord Campden." I opened my eyes to find Dr. Stuart had moved closer. "We're all here to help. You want to find someone, is that correct?"

"Yes."

"This person's name is Fox?"

I blew out a breath and nodded.

"We'll help you if we can, but we're going to need more information, all right?"

"Yes."

"Is Fox a friend?"

"Yes. He helped me. He's the one I stayed with this past week." The doctor's calm manner and soothing voice helped, and the constriction in my chest eased.

"Where was this?"

"It was, uh—" I desperately searched my mind for the names. "—Pimlico. He told the driver Pimlico. His apartments…. M-Mrs. Trotman's apartments in Pimlico."

To my relief, he took out a notepad and wrote the information down.

"Do you have a street name or house number?"

"No," I replied, feeling my spirits sink. "I don't know. I… it was the third house from the corner, and his rooms were on the third floor. But I don't know if he'll be there. We weren't there when this happened. We… we were in the East End."

"Can you tell us what happened, my lord?"

I clenched my hands in my lap, trying to get hold of myself. After a deep breath, I took a little time to consider how much information I should give. "He had some *business* there, and I accompanied him, but we were set upon by four men. I was hit on the back of the head, and I don't remember anything more." I lifted a hand to the small swelling at the base of my skull and winced. "He was there, though, with me. He had to have been hurt too. He never would've left me there. I know he wouldn't."

"Nephew, how did you even—" Uncle Oscar began, but the new doctor cut him off.

"Sir, I think it best we address his primary concerns first. We can get to the rest later."

Uncle Oscar's brows drew down, and he pursed his lips but waved a hand for the doctor to continue.

"My lord, you were saying."

"That's it. That's all I remember." I worried my lip at how feeble that sounded, how inadequate. I hadn't even tried to find out Fox's real name. I was utterly useless.

"Well, perhaps he was taken to a hospital nearby or some such. Can you give us a description of this man?"

"Yes," I replied breathlessly, struggling to sit up again. "He's tall, lean. He has silver hair and brown eyes. He's a gentleman, but he would've been dressed much like you found me."

"You were found stripped of nearly every stitch, Arthur," Uncle Oscar said quietly. "The constables thought you dead when they first came upon you."

At the strain in his voice, I looked closely at him and was dismayed by what I saw. If I'd thought he'd looked older the last time I saw him, it was nothing to how haggard he appeared now. Dark circles bloomed beneath his bloodshot eyes. His skin was sallow and paper thin. He looked as if he hadn't slept in days, and a quick glance at Pendel showed him much the same. My breath hitched, and crushing guilt mingled with my panic over Fox.

"All right, well, we have something to go on at least," the doctor broke in, distracting me. "I'm sure your uncle can set his detectives on the case, and they'll do everything they can to find your friend."

At a pointed look from the doctor, Uncle Oscar nodded at Pendel, but before he could leave, a thought occurred to me. "Wait! My sketchpad. I drew his likeness. They aren't perfect, but they might help."

Pendel brought my sketchpad to me and despite the furious blush that stained my cheeks, I handed over several of my drawings. Good, solid Pendel didn't even raise an eyebrow. He simply took the drawings and the slip of paper the doctor tore from his pad and left.

I was so relieved someone at least was listening to me, I slumped back into my pillows and sighed. "Thank you."

Dr. Stuart's smile bloomed across his elfin face, transforming him from beetle to a somewhat attractive young man again. "Of course, my lord. And now that we're doing all we can for your friend, I think it best if you get some more rest. You're a long way from being recovered from that fever and cough."

I didn't want to rest. I wanted to find Fox, but even the little I'd done since waking had left me utterly exhausted, and my breath rattled in my chest alarmingly. I had little choice. I wouldn't even make it down the stairs in the state I was in.

At my reluctant nod, both the doctor and Uncle Oscar smiled. "Good," Dr. Stuart said. "Rest for a bit, and we'll send you up some broth and tea in a little while."

I opened my mouth to order them to keep me informed of the investigation, but the doctor smiled and lifted a hand. "Don't worry. As soon as we hear anything, we'll let you know. Rest now."

THE FOLLOWING morning, I was restless, frustrated, and angry at my weakness. I had enough strength to lie awake and fret and worry, but not enough to get out of bed and do anything about it. Pendel and my uncle and the rest of the servants were only trying to take care of me and help me get better, but I had to expend precious energy to keep from snapping at them in my distress.

When Uncle Oscar and Dr. Stuart came into my room late that morning, my heart skipped a beat, and I sat up straight in the bed. One good look at the regret stamped all over their faces made me slump back again in disappointment.

"I'm sorry, Nephew. We have men searching every hospital in London, and we sent others to Pimlico to find this Mrs. Trotman's apartments, but we've heard nothing as yet," Uncle Oscar said as he took his seat next to my bed again.

I clenched my jaw and nodded. They were doing what they could; railing at them would be totally unfair. I wanted to rail at something, though. I wanted to scream and carry on and throw things. I supposed it was a good thing I didn't have the strength for any of that, or they really would lock me up and throw away the key.

"It seems you're a little stronger today," Dr. Stuart said as he moved between us, took my arm, and held his fingers to my wrist. "Your pulse is stronger. How are your lungs?"

"A little better, I think."

"Good." He sat on the edge of my mattress and smiled at me, and I returned it weakly. "If you're up to it, your uncle and I would like to speak to you about a few things."

Uncle Oscar shifted uncomfortably from foot to foot at the end of my bed, and I closed my eyes and nodded. I would have to do it eventually, and anything was better than being left alone to agonize over Fox. They couldn't cart me off to an institution in the state I was in now. I had a little time before they'd risk taking me out in the cold.

I hoped.

"All right, then," Dr. Stuart continued. "First I think we need to make sure you realize you aren't in any trouble, my lord. No one is blaming you or censuring you."

I blinked at the man in surprise. A quick glance at my uncle showed him nodding and smiling encouragingly from the chair beside my bed.

"You aren't angry with me?" I asked Uncle Oscar directly.

"No, lad. Only concerned."

We sat in silence for a few breaths, staring at each other before Dr. Stuart broke in. "Your uncle is concerned that whatever made you leave the house in the first place might make you run off again, once you're able. Therefore, we thought it best that we address any concerns *you* might have straightaway to avoid any confusion."

"All right."

"Will you tell us what happened?" Dr. Stuart prodded.

Both men seemed open and encouraging as they waited for me, but I hardly knew where to start. After all I'd gone through, I was right back where I'd started, tucked up in my rooms again, at the mercy of those around me. Some of what I had to relate was so fantastical, I knew they wouldn't believe me. They'd think me madder than ever.

Clenching my fists in my lap, I worried my lip as I tried to fight through my emotions.

"You're obviously upset, my lord," Dr. Stuart said gently. "And that's perfectly understandable. You've been through a lot of late. Why don't we start with what you're feeling right now? Can you tell us that?"

"I'm afraid," I admitted ashamedly.

"What are you afraid of?"

"I'm afraid you'll think me mad. I'm afraid you'll lock me up and throw away the key."

Uncle Oscar made a pained sound in his throat, but Dr. Stuart lifted a hand to stay him. "No one is going to lock you up or send you away, no matter what you tell us. You have my word as a physician and your uncle's word as well. Doesn't he?" he asked, turning to Uncle Oscar.

"Yes. I promise, Arthur, no institutions."

"How can I believe you?" I asked. "I heard you and Dr. Payne that night, Uncle. I heard you talking about visiting facilities."

He flinched under my accusatory glare and shook his head. "I won't. I promise. I won't even entertain the thought. That's why I hired Dr. Stuart here. Despite his obvious youth, he's been all over the world researching medicines and techniques. He is not a proponent of such places. He believes in a one-on-one approach, with as much inclusion of the family as possible."

"And no locking me in my rooms?" I asked breathlessly.

Uncle Oscar shot a quick glance at Dr. Stuart, and at a nod from the man, he nodded too. "No more," he agreed.

"And what about the medicine Dr. Payne prescribed?" I asked, pushing my luck.

Dr. Stuart answered, "If you mean the laudanum, I believe we are all in agreement it should only be used in an emergency, and only if there is a concern you might do harm to yourself. I gave you only small amounts during your fever, to help with your cough, but I should like to keep dosages to the barest minimum from here on out, and hopefully wean you off it entirely in the future."

I blew out a breath and had to hold back tears of relief. I finally had someone who would listen to me. I hardly knew what to do with myself.

"Does that help with your fears, my lord?"

"Yes. Thank you."

"Do you think you could tell us something of what happened now? Perhaps you might start with what happened in your rooms the day before you left."

I hadn't really looked at my rooms yet. Everything that could be put back had been, almost in the same place. There were a few pieces of furniture and trinkets missing, probably broken beyond repair, and my books weren't in their proper order, but someone had gone through a lot of trouble on my behalf.

Worrying my lower lip, I ignored the stab of pain in my chest and turned to my uncle. "I... I left my rooms that night and went to my parents' bedchambers, where I found a letter from my mother."

If anything, Uncle Oscar looked paler, and he couldn't hold my gaze. "Yes. We found it crumpled on the floor in her room when we searched the house for you," he murmured.

"You read it?"

"Yes, I read it."

"And?"

Uncle Oscar shook his head, and he still wouldn't look at me. "Perhaps we shouldn't talk about this just yet. You're still—"

"No," I interrupted, cutting off not only my uncle but also whatever Dr. Stuart had been about to say. Both men turned wide eyes to me at the harshness in my tone, but I didn't care. Imagining it was Fox at my back instead of just a pile of pillows, I gathered my courage and my strength and put as much of both into my voice as I could manage. "If you want me to tell you all my secrets, you will do me the courtesy of reciprocating. I'm not as weak as you imagine me, at least not anymore. I won't be treated like a child or an invalid. I won't be dismissed or coddled."

A coughing fit came on me again, ruining the effect somewhat. When it subsided, I found my uncle regarding me silently, as myriad emotions played across his face. Dr. Stuart, on the other hand, only smiled encouragingly and nodded. "Of course, my lord. I'm glad to hear it."

He seemed an odd sort of man, even from my limited experience, but I liked him. He was perhaps a little young for a physician, but that might work in my favor.

"Tell me, Uncle," I ordered, before my nerve and strength abandoned me again. "Was it all a lie? Did she ever love me? Did my father? Do you?"

Uncle Oscar's head snapped up at those final questions, and his pale cheeks flushed an affronted crimson. "Of course I love you, Nephew. You're the only family I have. Can you doubt my love for you? After all these years?"

I shook my head as guilt once again stabbed through me. "I'm sorry," I whispered. "I didn't know what to think after I read the letter. I always believed my mother loved me also, but she didn't. She said so herself."

His expression softened. "Your mother did love you, very much."

"That's not true. Don't lie to me."

"Perhaps we should take a moment to—" Dr. Stuart began, but Uncle Oscar held up a hand, silencing him.

"Dr. Stuart, I've engaged you for the well-being of my nephew, therefore I believe you should stay, but I need your solemn word nothing that is said here will leave this room."

I'd never heard my uncle so severe and commanding. He seemed somehow larger, all of a sudden, and I blinked at him in surprise as the doctor said, "You have my word as a physician. You can count on my utmost discretion, of course."

With a curt nod, Uncle Oscar rose from his seat and tugged on the bell pull. Pendel must have been close, because he knocked and opened the door only seconds later.

"Yes, sir?"

"I need a drink, Pendel. Bring the bottle."

"Yes, sir."

Pendel disappeared, and Uncle Oscar returned to my bedside and sank wearily into the chair.

Pendel must have sent Tom running for it, because he returned far too quickly for him to have made it to the library and back at his age and not have been gasping for breath.

"Send the rest of the servants downstairs, and come back and close the door," Uncle Oscar said to Pendel after downing half the contents of his tumbler. While Pendel did as he was bade, Uncle Oscar dragged a hand down his face and then took another drink.

Dr. Stuart simply sat quietly and calmly through all of this, while I was nearly ready to shake out of my skin. "*Uncle*," I prodded.

He nodded and let out a long sigh. "There are things about this family only a very few know. We thought it best not to tell you, but maybe we were wrong. I don't know anymore. Your mother loved you, Arthur. She loved you with all her heart and soul. I can't stand the thought of you believing otherwise. The woman who wrote that letter was not your mother."

"What?" I asked stupidly. "I know my mother's hand, Uncle. Even after all these years, I would recognize it anywhere."

Would he try to convince me I'd imagined it, that my illness had made me see something that wasn't there?

I fisted my hands in my lap to keep from pulling my hair.

"That isn't what I'm saying." Uncle Oscar shot a quick glance at Pendel before returning his gaze to me. "I'm saying the woman you knew as your mother... wasn't."

My breath quickened. I searched his face for some sign he was joking. Dr. Stuart looked as shocked as I felt, but Pendel's face held only sorrow. That look convinced me my uncle was telling the truth.

"*I am at last with child,*" the letter had said, but at the time I'd refused to acknowledge what that meant.

"I don't understand," I replied helplessly. "Why?"

Uncle Oscar lifted his empty glass, and Pendel refilled it. "I suppose I need to start at the beginning for that, if you're sure you want to know."

"I'm sure," I gritted out, not sure at all.

After downing another swallow, he nodded wearily, as if he'd thought as much. "My father, your grandfather, had three sons, not two. The eldest was Herbert, then the man you knew as your father, John, and me. Everyone adored Herbert, or Bertie as we called him. Everywhere he went, people followed. Even as a child, he was the life of every party, the captain of every fantasy pirate ship, the leader of every adventure. As the eldest and the heir, one would expect as much, but it was more than that. He was a force of nature." He took another swallow from his glass and sighed deeply. "But Bertie wasn't always a joy to be around. Those of us who knew him best saw a darker side to him when he flew into his rages or couldn't be coaxed out of bed for days at a time. I didn't learn about it until much later, but after an incident at school when Bertie was fifteen, Father sent him away to a *retreat* for six months without telling John and me." He spat the word "retreat" out like it was poison on his tongue. "Bertie was never the same after that. He settled into a respectable life at home. He took over the management of the estate, as Father wanted, and we saw him on our holidays from school, but the light was gone from his eyes. After Father died, Bertie inherited the title and married Hyacinth, and some of that spark returned. She was also a force to be reckoned with, and he seemed truly happy for a time, especially when their son was born." He lifted his gaze to mine and held it until I nodded that I understood him.

I was that son. Bertie and Hyacinth were my real mother and father, and perhaps it was the shock, but I had no idea how I should feel about that.

"What happened?" I prodded, fairly certain I wouldn't like the answer.

"They died, and John and his wife, Eleanor, agreed to raise you as their own," he answered simply.

I growled, anger beginning to replace shock. "That can't be all. Otherwise why the charade? Why keep it a secret?"

Uncle Oscar sighed. "Bertie wasn't well, Arthur, like you're not always well. Do you understand? We thought it best you didn't know, that you thought it was something brought on by a fever rather than the family curse. Bertie wasn't the only one, you see. There are stories in the family."

"Oh."

How stupid of me not to have put that together. My father was mad. Therefore I was born mad too. I turned away from them and hugged myself, but a quiet clearing of someone's throat drew my attention.

Dr. Stuart regarded me with sympathetic eyes. "If I may interject here, I for one do not believe in curses. Perhaps your father did pass along an illness of sorts to you. Such things have been proven to occur. It could also be that your illness may have been triggered by a fever. We don't have all the answers yet. But that doesn't mean it can't be cured with the proper treatments. There's no reason to lose hope."

I gave him a watery smile in gratitude, and he gave an awkward nod.

I took a few calming breaths as I tried to work through all I'd been told so far. Something else still bothered me about my uncle's explanation, but I couldn't quite put a finger on it. I was on the verge of asking him more, when I spotted a wisp of bluish light beyond Pendel's shoulder, and the questions died in my throat.

I blanched and closed my eyes, praying she didn't become any more solid or come any closer. I knew what followed her appearances, and now that I had a picture in my mind to accompany the sounds in the hall, I wasn't sure I could stand to hear them again. This was why I'd never wanted to come back to Campden House.

"Arthur? What's wrong?"

"My lord?"

"Lord Campden?"

All three men in the room spoke at once, but I could only shake my head.

Go away. Please, go away.

"Lord Campden, what is it?" Dr. Stuart asked as he placed his hand on my shoulder and squeezed.

I latched onto the solidity of that touch, wishing it were Fox's. "She's here. One of my visions, my hallucinations, is here again," I whispered shakily.

"You see her now?"

"Yes."

"Describe her to me."

My eyes flew open, and I blinked at the doctor in surprise. No one had ever asked me that before except Fox. "Sometimes she's easier to make out than others. I can't really see her face, except for her eyes. She's in a long flowing white gown that writhes and sways as if in a breeze, and she glows with a bluish white light no matter the time of day or night."

"You've seen her before?"

"Yes."

"And what does she do? Does she talk to you?"

"No. Most of the time, she doesn't do anything really, though the last few times she's touched me, and it was awful—a cold, shivery feeling, as if someone were walking on my grave."

He blinked at me over his spectacles, but his expression remained merely curious, with no censure or fear. "Have you ever tried to talk to her?"

Now I was the one who looked at him like he was mad. "Of course not, other than to tell her to go away. She never speaks."

"But she frightens you?" he pressed.

I looked to my uncle and Pendel, who were both surveying the room uneasily, and I wondered if they thought that was as stupid a question as I did. But then I took a breath and blew it out and tried to think past my emotions. Dr. Stuart was trying to help, and he was distracting me, which was a good thing.

"It isn't her, precisely, that frightens me. More what she represents in terms of my illness… and what follows."

"And what is it that follows?" he persisted.

I covered my face with my hands. "The noises in the hall. For years I've heard them. Always the same, terrible noises that make the hair on the back of my neck stand on end, no matter how hard I try to ignore them or blot them out."

"Do you hear them often?"

"Too often for my liking," I replied acidly.

"Well, yes, of course. That I can understand." I seemed to have flustered him at last, but he rallied quickly. "Did you hear them the night you left?"

I groaned. *Why must he persist in badgering me?*

"All right, yes, I heard them," I replied with a huff. "But it wasn't the sound. It was what I *saw* that was the final straw."

"What did you see?" he pressed.

I supposed this would be the real test of whether they would keep their promises to me.

"I saw a man dragging a woman in a white dressing gown backward down the hall. Leaving a smear of blood on the carpet in their wake," I said, holding his gaze and daring him to judge me, but Dr. Stuart's eyebrows only rose slightly as he continued to peer at me quizzically through his spectacles.

"I see," he murmured quietly.

When I gathered the courage to gauge my uncle's reaction, I found him staring at me with his mouth hanging open. His face was white as a sheet and so was Pendel's.

"That's not possible," Uncle Oscar gasped. "You couldn't possibly remember. You were barely more than a babe in arms." He hugged himself and cast a nervous glance toward the door.

"Remember what, Uncle?" I asked, my heart beginning to race.

He shook his head. "No. It's not possible."

Pendel moved behind my uncle's chair, and for the first time ever, I saw him lay a hand on Uncle Oscar's shoulder. "Sir. Are you all right? Can I get you a glass of water?"

Uncle Oscar lifted his tumbler in a shaking hand, and Pendel took it and filled it once more with whisky from the decanter. My uncle downed the contents of his glass in a single gulp before setting the tumbler on my bedside table. After dragging a shaking hand down his face, he lifted his gaze to me. "You say you saw this the other night?"

"Yes," I whispered. "But I've heard the sounds for years."

"What sounds?"

"The thump of halting footsteps, the scrape of a charm bracelet along the floor, a long haunting moan, and then an anguished wail that cuts off abruptly… always the same."

He swallowed as more color leached from his skin. "A charm bracelet?"

I nodded. "I didn't know what it was until I saw it the other night. It was the first time I'd ever seen what made the noises. What's going on, Uncle? What does this mean?"

"He gave her that on their first wedding anniversary," he whispered.

When my uncle dropped his head into his hands and groaned, Pendel stepped forward and cleared his throat. "I believe Mr. Middleton thinks you weren't having a vision, my lord. I think he believes you're remembering something that happened, something we would all like to forget. It was a terrible night for everyone."

"What happened?" When Pendel hesitated, I clenched my teeth. "Someone is going to tell me what's going on," I insisted, despite the fatigue and anxiety clawing at me and the persistent ache in my lungs.

"It's all right, Pendel. I should be the one," Uncle Oscar said wearily. He lifted bloodshot blue eyes to mine and sighed. "I didn't want to tell you any of this, Nephew, because I feared what the knowledge might do to your health… and because I wanted to forget. I wanted to remember Bertie and Hyacinth in happier times, not as I last saw them. But if you insist, I will tell you, only I beg you not to make me speak of this again." At my nod, he continued, "The night your real parents died, there was a terrible storm. Hyacinth was pregnant with her second child, and she went into premature labor. The winds and the rain were so strong we couldn't risk trying to get her to a hospital. We sent for the doctor, but there was nothing he could do. She lost the baby, but worse than that, the doctor couldn't stop the bleeding. I did everything I could to keep Bertie calm while we waited in the library, to keep him away while the doctor did his work, but… he loved your mother so very much, you see. He wouldn't be kept from her." He paused for a moment and turned away. When he lifted his gaze to mine again, his eyes glistened, and his lips curved into a tremulous smile. "Your mother was a very strong woman, Arthur. She kept Bertie in line. She kept him, and this house, and the whole family together. She knew she was dying, and she knew your father wouldn't be able to stand it, so she sent for you first, to say good-bye."

I closed my eyes on a wave of sadness, desperately searching my memory for any of this, but there was nothing.

"I'd stopped Bertie from charging upstairs several times already, but the last time, there was no stopping him. Your father was not a large man, smaller than you are now, but he pushed me aside as if I weighed nothing and dashed up the stairs. I followed on his heels as closely as I could and nearly ran into you and your nanny in the hall. The ruckus your father made drew every servant in the house, and while I tried to get everyone away and back downstairs to give your parents their privacy, your mother died. I knew the moment of her passing because of the sound Bertie made. I'll never forget that sound." He shivered, and I did the same. "When I turned back… well, it was just as you described. They'd locked the adjoining door to the lady's chambers during her pregnancy. I won't go into unseemly detail as to the reason. But Bertie must have wanted her in the master's chambers where they'd spent nearly every night together since their marriage, so he had to take her through the hall. By the time I had everyone away, he'd bolted the door against us."

Uncle Oscar stopped there, seemingly unable to continue, and Pendel stepped forward again. "I was downstairs with the other servants when I heard the shot," he said somberly. "We raced upstairs, but in the time it took us to batter down the door, your father… your father was gone too." He paused for a moment before rallying again. "Mr. and Mrs. Middleton were sent for, and it was decided they would claim you as their own. If you'll pardon my impertinence, my lord, I would like to assure you that your uncle John loved you like a son, no matter what you read in that letter."

"My lord?"

Dr. Stuart's voice startled me. He'd been quiet so long I'd almost forgotten he was there.

"Yes."

"This is a lot for anyone to take in. It's all right if you're upset or angry. Such feelings are perfectly natural."

"To tell you the truth, Doctor, I don't know what I am right now," I replied wearily. My head was spinning with so many things, and I wished to God that Fox was there. I needed him so badly right now. I had a sudden strong craving for the oblivion my medicine would grant me, but I shoved it away. I wouldn't go down that road again. "I think I just need some time alone, if you please." All three men exchanged glances, and I sighed. "I won't do anything terrible. I promise. I can hardly climb out of this bed on my own in my present state."

At a nod from the doctor, Pendel helped my uncle out of his chair and walked with him to the door. Dr. Stuart paused at the foot of my bed and turned back to me. "In my travels throughout the East, I've come across a few practices that help me when I'm feeling overwhelmed, or when I need to think things through. It may seem silly at first, but I'd like you to try something for me."

"I really don't—"

"Just promise me you'll try it, and I'll leave you alone."

"All right. What is it?"

"I want you to close your eyes and lie down flat on your bed. Then tense and relax every muscle in your body, one at a time, starting with each of your toes—first on your right foot, and then your left—then up through your legs, your torso, your fingers and arms and so on. Take the time to do each one slowly and carefully and don't think about anything but that as you do it. If you get through the whole thing, I promise you, you'll feel better than you do now. Can you do that for me?"

"I gave you my word," I replied a bit grumpily, but thankfully, he didn't take my ill manners personally. He simply smiled and tipped his head to me before leaving the room and closing the door behind him.

I listened carefully, but I never heard the lock.

Though my mind was awhirl with a kaleidoscope of thoughts and feelings, I had given my word, so I stretched out flat on my mattress and tried to make my weak and aching muscles do as I'd been instructed. I fell asleep before I'd finished with the fingers on my left hand.

Chapter Twenty-One

I STARTLED awake sometime in the night. Praying it had been a particular sound that had woken me, I held my breath and strained my ears for the click of a door, the telltale rustling of the drapes, or the creak of the stairs from the roof, but I heard nothing. Disappointed, I slumped back onto my mattress and stared at the shadowed canopy above my bed. Someone had been in to tend my fire, and the weak orange glow reached all but the deepest recesses there.

Pendel had told me, since my fever, they'd taken it in turns to keep my fire fed throughout the night, and extra blankets had been heaped on my bed. I found the added weight almost smothering, but I shouldn't complain. I was warm and well cared for. Who knew if Fox had the same? He had no family in London, no one to take care of him. He could be alone and ill in an alley somewhere, and I was too weak to go and find him.

I growled in frustration, but a fit of coughing took me, until I gasped for breath and my head pounded. I couldn't think like that. If I did, I'd drive myself madder than I already was.

Except, perhaps I wasn't as mad as I feared.

After all the revelations that afternoon, I didn't know what to think anymore. I didn't know if Dr. Stuart had intended to send me to sleep with his little exercise, but the respite had helped. I wasn't so overwhelmed. I could think about some of it rationally, though my emotions threatened to get the better of me if I peered too closely at them.

I wasn't the son of John and Eleanor. I was the son of Herbert and Hyacinth. I was still the heir, so that much hadn't changed. But my father had been a madman who'd taken his own life. I rubbed at the scars on my own wrists in agitation. Like father, like son.

I struggled from beneath the weight of my blankets and swung my legs over the edge of my mattress. The action took all my strength, and I was left there for a time, panting and coughing, while I waited for my head to stop spinning. I was so damnably weak, but I couldn't lie abed forever while Fox could be suffering somewhere alone.

With the aid of my bedpost, the chair next to my bed, and the table in front of my fire, I hobbled to the other chair still by the hearth. I collapsed into it with a gasp of relief and more coughing, and I was sweating by the time I pulled the lap quilt from the back of the chair and draped it over myself. I'd made progress, though, even if the likelihood of my making it back to my bed unaided was slim to none. The entire situation brought back unpleasant memories from the night I'd slit my wrists after my parents' accident—or at least the people I'd thought were my parents. Like now, I'd been weak as a baby, and everyone had hovered over me. Uncle Oscar had looked just as haggard then as he did now, perhaps even more so. Seeing me like this must have brought back terrible memories for him as well.

I closed my eyes and took a slow, deep breath, hoping to avoid another coughing fit. My poor uncle, he'd been put through so much. I'd put him through even more, ending up just like my father despite his efforts. I didn't want to be, but Eleanor, my second mother, had been right. I did feel things too deeply. I couldn't always be trusted with my own welfare, not when things became too much and I was overwhelmed. I would always be a burden to someone.

"You are a breath of fresh air compared to what I am used to."

I'd had someone who loved me for who I was—warts and all—and I'd lost him.

A flicker of blue-white light in the corner of the room caught my eye, and I sighed. Steeling myself, I lifted my chin and faced her head-on. I refused to be afraid anymore, of her or what came after. Knowing the truth helped immensely. The horror in the hall was only a memory—whether mine or the house's—of my grieving father on the worst night of his life… the last night of his life.

"What do you want from me?" I whispered.

The apparition only hovered there, its substance swaying in that unknown breeze. Though it didn't move any closer, I flinched when it reached for me. Her hand was the only clearly defined part of her, but unlike in the hall, it seemed softer, less skeletal, and she merely held it in front of her, palm up in a sort of beseeching gesture.

"I don't understand. I'm sorry." I felt an overwhelming sadness for the creature now. She had to have something to do with the tragedy that had occurred in this house, because the noises always followed her appearance in my rooms. I listened for them now with a sort of melancholy resignation, but I heard nothing but the wind rattling the shutters outside my windows.

The silent tableau between us stretched too long, and eventually, I blew out a frustrated breath, shoved the quilt aside, and levered myself out of the chair. Bracing a hand on the little table next to me, I took a halting step toward her. "I don't know what you want. I don't know how to help you, or even if I can," I rasped.

She turned her outstretched hand and curled her fingers as if she were cupping someone's cheek, and as her wrist solidified, I recognized the charm bracelet encircling it.

"Hyacinth? Mother?" I gasped.

Her countenance shifted in and out of definition as it always did, but I thought perhaps she smiled.

"Are you my mother? Is that why you're here?"

I received no answer, but I hadn't really expected to. In all the years she'd appeared to me, she'd never made a sound. My knees wobbled with the effort of keeping upright, but I locked them and held on to the table with all my strength.

"If you are my mother, and you loved me as Uncle Oscar said you did, then I can only guess you were trying to help me? Was that it? Were you trying to stop me from seeing what I did? Were you trying to comfort me after? I'm sorry I didn't understand."

A tear slid down my cheek unchecked as she shifted and fluttered soundlessly. She was only a shadow, not real in any logical sense of the word, but she deserved to be at peace, not trapped in this indeterminate existence.

"You don't have to worry. Uncle Oscar told me everything. I know it all, and I'm not afraid anymore... well, not of anything in this house, at any rate. I still have a long way to go, but perhaps not as far as I'd feared, and I have help. I'm loved."

She seemed to be fading with each word I spoke, but before I lost her shape altogether, she lifted her fingers to where her lips should have been, and then disappeared.

"Good-bye," I whispered.

All fell quiet and dark after that, and I slumped back into my chair, coughing and struggling to breathe.

I MUST'VE fallen asleep, because the next thing I knew, Pendel was hovering over me, frowning.

"My lord shouldn't be out of bed so soon," he chastised as he directed Tom to half drag, half carry me back to my bed.

After being plied with my watered medicine and broth and some toast, I slept again until Pendel brought Dr. Stuart in some time later.

"Pendel here tells me you were out of bed last night," he said, frowning at me. "I admire your eagerness to get well, but you really shouldn't push yourself too hard just yet."

Ignoring his censure, I asked, "Is there any word from the detectives?"

His face softened, and he shook his head. "I'm sorry. Your uncle will have more details on their investigation, but from what I can tell, they've found no trace of your friend." He looked to Pendel for confirmation, and at his nod, my spirits fell.

I'd already asked that morning. I'd just hoped a few hours might've made a difference. I growled my frustration rather than letting any of them see my heartbreak, and Dr. Stuart nodded. "I understand your anger at feeling helpless, my lord. But if you push too hard too soon, you may have a relapse, and you won't be able to help your friend for even longer."

He made sense, but I didn't have to like him for it.

"What am I to do, then?" I asked testily.

"Get better. Your uncle has hired a dozen strapping men to search the hospitals and to seek out the apartments you spoke of. Trust them to do their jobs. I'm sure your friend wouldn't like to think you neglected your health for his sake."

Fox would be angry if I ruined my health searching for him, but that was small comfort when all I could do was lie in bed all day and worry. I'd take his anger. I'd take anything, if it meant he was here with me.

"I'll do my best," I agreed reluctantly, and Dr. Stuart smiled.

"Excellent, and now that your fine Pendel here has seen to your body for this morning, I think it might be time for us to move on to your mind for a time."

I narrowed my eyes at him. "How will you do that?"

He smiled at me. "Nothing terrible, I assure you. But your uncle hired me from the profusion of medical professionals in this great city of ours because of my keen interest in diseases of the mind… and my somewhat unorthodox approach to the same." He blushed, showing his youth for a moment, but then he threw his thin shoulders back, cleared his throat, and adjusted his spectacles. "My methods are a blending of innovations from this country and the Continent... and even as far as the East Indies. I'm constantly keeping apprised of the latest discoveries, but I also include ancient wisdoms in my treatments. Centuries of trial and error shouldn't be dismissed out of hand, despite the fact that they may have arisen in primitive cultures. There are many close-minded individuals who believe such teachings are superstition and nonsense, but I've found a number of mental exercises and medicinal teas, particularly among the *kabirajes*, or village healers, in Bangladesh—and elsewhere in Asia—to be quite effective." He glanced at me and flushed again. "Forgive me. This work is a passion of mine, and I tend to get a little carried away in my defense of it. At any rate, when you're well enough, we will incorporate fresh air and physical exercise into your daily routine again. I believe your Dr. Payne had you on a regimen of sorts before, and I see no reason to stop. But until then, we shall begin with some talking therapy sessions between the two of us, and I should like to prescribe a medicinal tea of my own devising for you to take in the afternoons, if you're amenable?"

I had no real idea what he meant, but his energy and enthusiasm were infectious. What he proposed didn't involve an institution, laudanum, or anything as unpleasant as some of the therapies I'd read about, so I saw no harm in agreeing to try.

Other than missing Fox, I had everything I'd truly been hoping for. I wasn't locked away anymore, I was weaning off the laudanum, and I seemed to have a doctor who wanted to take a more active role in my treatment. Strange as he was, I felt sure that if Dr. Stuart's methods failed to work, he would be open to trying something else until he'd exhausted all resources.

I had hope in that much.

It almost made Fox's absence bearable.

Chapter Twenty-Two

After two months with no word of Fox, I began to lose hope. Each time we received a message from the detectives, my spirits would lift and then crash down when the news was still the same—no sign of him could be found anywhere.

My health improved daily, and with Dr. Stuart's sessions and his teas, I rarely had visions anymore. The sounds in the hall had ceased altogether, and my mother never materialized again. Perhaps they had all only been memories, as my uncle and Pendel believed, and now that I understood them, I didn't need them anymore. Or perhaps as Fox had hinted once, the spirits of Campden House had been laid to rest. Either way, I was left in peace for the most part, beyond a shadow or two that moved on their own or the odd movement in the corner of my eye. I would've said that my mind was healthier for it, but for the ever-increasing melancholy I experienced because of Fox's loss.

No one at any of the hospitals in London had seen or heard of him. The detectives had found Mrs. Trotman's apartment house, but according to her, the man in the third floor apartment hadn't returned, though men had come to collect his things.

Mrs. Trotman had given the detectives a name, Robert Tremblay, but only when they'd handed over twenty pounds. That news had sent my spirits soaring, because we finally had a name. But after trying the hospitals again and sending the detectives off to Kent—where I'd remembered Fox's mother and sister still lived—I'd learned it wasn't his real name. At least, no one knew of a Robert Tremblay whose widowed mother and sister lived together in a great house that had recently sold off most of its land, despite the detectives swearing they'd asked every shopkeeper, innkeeper, and publican in the county. They had learned of a widowed gentlewoman and her daughter living in a house that matched that description, but the family name hadn't been Tremblay, and when the detectives had called on the place, it had been packed up and empty.

In an effort to lift my spirits and distract myself, I moved my rooms to the second floor of the west wing. Uncle Oscar came often, trying to cheer me up. And my weekly sessions with Dr. Stuart had me feeling stronger and surer of myself, but nothing could ease the emptiness inside me when I thought of Fox. I went through the motions with everyone. I built that papier-mâché mask Fox had spoken of, and put on a brave face for my uncle, Pendel, and the doctor, but I wasn't sure anymore why I bothered.

Before Fox, my only ambitions had been to be well enough someday to assume the full responsibilities of my title, to make my uncle proud, and to no longer be a burden. But I'd never honestly believed it possible, so I'd never planned for anything beyond that. I feared that what lay beyond my lofty goal wouldn't measure up to what I'd lost. It hardly seemed worth it, except I didn't want to disappoint the people who'd worked so hard for me.

I'm sure my uncle thought Fox another figment of my imagination, though he humored me and continued to pay the detectives. As the weeks dragged on, I began to doubt myself. I feared I'd banished Fox along with my other visions, but that was too painful to contemplate, and it couldn't be right. I could never have dreamed up so much, and I had been gone from this house for a full week—not even my uncle denied that.

In an effort to improve my spirits—with Dr. Stuart's approval—I added a daily walk outdoors to my regimen in late March. I started small, with a few turns around the gardens at Campden House, but as my confidence grew and my strength returned, I ventured farther afield. My lungs weren't fully recovered yet, and Pendel and Uncle Oscar still worried about me, so Tom accompanied me whenever I left the grounds, though he kept a decent distance to respect my privacy.

The wonders of Kensington Gardens, and Hyde Park beyond, were only a short walk from the house, and I spent many a day wandering the paths, despite the lingering dreariness of winter. I spoke to no one on my walks, although I tipped my hat and nodded to passersby as if I were like any other gentleman on his daily stroll. Luckily no one tried to talk to me. I don't know what I would've done if they had. I wasn't ready for that yet.

ON THE first Saturday in April, the sun rose bright and warm, easing some of my usual melancholy. It had rained heavily for the two days prior, so I'd been forced by my fragile health to stay indoors. Now almost desperate for the distraction, I rang for my boots and coat and hat immediately following breakfast, and I was kitted out and striding across the front lawn before Tom made it out the door to come after me.

I didn't have to worry about slowing my pace for Tom, though. The man was enormous, his stride nearly twice the length of mine, and he caught up to me easily. I wouldn't be winning any footraces in the near future, at any rate. I mostly ambled along and frequently had to avail myself of a bench to catch my breath.

I was restless after too long indoors, so once I'd passed through the gardens, I took the bridge over the Serpentine into Hyde Park to continue my walk. The distance was ambitious, and I probably needed to rest before the return trip home, but Tom seemed content to be out of the house as well, so I decided to keep going.

On the far side of the bridge, I began to regret my impulsiveness. My chest hurt and my legs felt a little unsteady. When I spotted a bench nearby, I set off for it without hesitation, despite the fact that it was occupied and I might have to make polite conversation with a stranger. As I drew close, sunlight reflected off a lock of silver beneath the man's charcoal top hat, and I froze in my tracks. I must have stopped breathing altogether, because a sudden desperate intake of breath set me coughing.

The man on the bench turned at the sound, and I stumbled toward him, wheezing. "Fox?"

He frowned at me. "I'm sorry?"

"Fox, it's me. Arthur. Don't you know me?" I gasped between coughs.

He looked confused. "I'm sorry, I don't—here now, come sit down and catch your breath before you fall over."

He rose from the bench and took my elbow. His steps were awkward and stiff, and I noticed a cane hooked over his arm. Tom rushed to us, but I waved him off. "I'm all right," I rasped. "Just a bit of a shock. I'll be fine in a moment."

The look Tom gave Fox was not at all friendly, but he stepped back.

"I'm afraid I don't have any water to offer you," Fox said as he reclaimed his seat next to me on the bench.

I swallowed a few times until the fit subsided, my cheeks flushing in embarrassment. I searched his face but saw no signs of recognition, and my heart constricted.

He didn't know me. How could he not know me?

"Fox?"

He frowned in confusion again and shook his head. "I'm sorry. I don't know—"

"Robert Tremblay?" I tried.

I saw a spark of recognition at that, and a hint of caution as he glanced back and forth between Tom and me. "I know that name," he replied cautiously, "but I'm sorry, I don't know you."

Breathing through the whirlwind of emotions inside me, I studied his face intently. This was my Fox. He couldn't be anyone else. I couldn't have dreamed it all. Too many things had happened. I knew Mrs. Trotman and her apartment house. I'd been beaten and left for dead in the East End. I never would have left my rooms without Fox. I never would have known how to pick the locks or had money to hail a cab to such places.

I clenched my jaw to keep it from quivering as I tried to make sense of it all. "You really don't remember me?"

He lifted a hand and rubbed his temple as if it pained him. "I'm sorry. I've been ill recently, and I seemed to have lost a bit of time before I woke in hospital. You say you know me, though?"

"Yes."

"How do you know the name Robert Tremblay?"

"It was the name you gave Mrs. Trotman, the woman you let your rooms from in Pimlico."

Some of the wariness eased from his expression, and he nodded. "Yes. A bit of a ruse there, I'm afraid.... Didn't want the family to be able to find me, though our lawyer knows that name in case he needed to get a message to me. I lost that place, fell behind in the rents while I was ill, and the woman is not, shall we say, *forgiving*."

"We had men looking for you."

"We?" he asked, wariness returning.

"My uncle and I. I-I was worried about you. I feared the worst."

Something in my expression must have conveyed my feelings because his face softened. "I'm sorry to have worried you. I spent some time with my mother and sister, and I've only recently come back to Town."

The dam of emotions threatened to break and drown me in loss, but I clenched my jaw and lifted my chin. He didn't remember me, but he was still Fox, still as handsome and charming as ever. I knew him, and he had loved me for who I was, even when I didn't love myself. I was better now. Perhaps I could make him remember. There was a chance, if I didn't give up.

Stifling my fear and disappointment, I took a breath and stiffened my spine. "I'm sorry. Where are my manners?" I said with forced cheerfulness. "I'm Arthur Middleton, Viscount Campden."

I held out a hand that only shook a little, and Fox took it. "Mr. Dorian Reynard, at your service, my lord."

Acutely aware of Tom hovering behind me, I only held his hand a little longer than was proper, and Fox—*Dorian*—quirked an eyebrow at me.

Clearing my throat, and hoping my blush wasn't too obvious, I said, "Well, Mr. Dorian Reynard, do you have time to take tea with me this afternoon? It's only a short walk beyond Kensington Gardens to my house, and I should dearly love to renew our acquaintance."

He studied me for a time before his lip quirked in that wry grin I knew so well. "I believe I do, Lord Campden. Thank you for the invitation."

"You may call me Arthur," I murmured.

THE WALK back to Campden House took an eternity. Neither of us had recovered from our illnesses, and we had to stop often, but I didn't mind in the slightest. With Tom behind us, I couldn't talk of anything important, but we managed to fall into easy conversation about the weather and how lovely the gardens would be in only a few short weeks. Much of the time, we didn't talk at all, given that I needed to conserve my breath for the exertion, but Fox stayed by my side, a warm, solid presence, and my heart rejoiced. He was alive.

True to form, Pendel didn't bat an eyelash at the company, although I thought I might've seen a pleased smile playing at the corners of his mouth. He had us settled in front of a cheery fire in the back parlor, and he and Mrs. Peebles pulled together a tray of sandwiches and cakes with no warning at all. I'd have to go down and thank her personally when I had the chance.

"Thank you, Pendel."

Pendel bowed a little deeper than usual, and the smile he gave me was almost cheery. "Of course, my lord."

He backed out of the room and closed the door behind him, cutting us off from prying eyes. I was certain Tom would inform them I'd found my Fox, and I could only guess at the speculation that would be going on belowstairs.

"So, Arthur, now that we're alone, will you tell me how it is you know me?"

He rested casually against the back of the couch, with his legs crossed and his teacup held negligently in one hand, but I could tell he wasn't as relaxed as he appeared. He grimaced every so often when he moved, and though he kept the side of his head angled away from me, I'd seen the crescent-shaped scar above his ear when he removed his hat. Someone had shaved away his lovely silver hair around the spot, and it hadn't grown back yet.

My heart squeezed at the thought of all that pain, and I couldn't help but lean toward him on the couch, though I'd put a respectable distance between is when I sat down.

"We met here," I replied. "You told me you came to rob me."

"What?"

He nearly spilled his tea when he jolted, and I was sorry for that, but we'd had no secrets before—well, perhaps except for his name.

"You came to rob me," I repeated. "At least that's what you said. But you changed your mind when you came into my rooms and we started talking."

Seeming to have regained a little of his composure, I saw the beginnings of one of his wry grins as he regarded me. "You're a forthright one, aren't you?"

"We had no secrets before, and I'm not very good at dissembling, I'm afraid."

"Oh good. I get enough of that everywhere else."

His grin was in full bloom now, and I smiled too, remembering a similar conversation we'd had.

"God only knows what all I did in the months I lost," he continued, "but the more we talk, the more I'm beginning to think I deeply regret what I can't remember."

My body flushed at the huskiness in his voice, but I maintained control of myself. "I can't speak to all of it, only the time we spent together."

"And what did we do?" he pressed.

"You came to visit me in my rooms upstairs. You took pity on me and kept me company… eased my loneliness."

His grin faded a bit as his brows drew down in confusion. "Why would I need to take pity on you?"

I flushed for an entirely different reason and squirmed in my seat. I could lie to him. We could start anew. But I didn't want to lie, and I was not so recovered he wouldn't notice something off about me eventually. I might as well get it over with.

"I'm unwell, and not only in body. I was kept in my rooms for my own good, you see. I now believe it was the wrong thing to do, but I didn't know it then. When you first arrived, I thought you a delusion, like many I'd had before, and you humored me rather than upset me. You came back night after night, despite all that. We talked and played games. You helped me more than you could possibly know, even when I'm sure you could have had better company elsewhere. You did say you liked my playing on the pianoforte, though. That was one thing I could do for you in return for your kindness… that and my wine cellar."

I chuckled, but he didn't smile. His silver brows drew together as his gaze grew remote. "I remember a dream I've had a few times now of a tower and an angel and the most heavenly music… a golden-haired angel."

His gaze focused back on me as he said the last, and I smiled as my heart fluttered. "You called me an angel once. I was quite cross with you over it, as I recall."

"You shouldn't have been. I'm sure I meant it as a compliment."

He looked at me so intently my heart sped.

"I really want to kiss you right now," I whispered.

For the space of a few breaths, he appeared taken aback as he blinked at me, but then that wonderful grin spread across his lips. He shot a glance toward the door before leaning closer to me. "I may be many things, but I'm no fool. How could I possibly refuse an offer like that from someone as lovely as you?"

With a quick glance of my own to make sure the door was still closed, I set my cup aside and slid across the space between us. From the moment I'd seen him in the park, I'd positively ached to touch him, so much that my hands shook as I reached for him now. Cradling his jaw in my palms I leaned in and took his lips. It started as a gentle brush, but that first taste of him after so long made me ravenous. I moaned and deepened the kiss, pushing until he opened for me.

Several long minutes later, we broke apart, both of us panting for air, but I only allowed a few inches between us.

"Good Lord," he gasped. "If it was all like that, I think I might kill to get those memories back."

I laughed breathlessly, closed my eyes, and pressed my forehead to his. I was shaking all over, and all I wanted was to be completely wrapped up in him, to feel him everywhere.

"So, young Arthur, tell me, did we do more than just kiss?" he murmured into the intimate space between us.

His voice had gone even huskier, and I shivered. "Yes. We spent many nights together here as well as an entire week in your bed in Pimlico…well, we spent some time on your furniture too, and once on the floor, but…."

He laughed loudly and shook his head as he studied me. "You are a breath of fresh air for a weary soul. This morning when I stepped out of my apartments, I had no idea I would be so fortunate. Surely fate has smiled on me at last."

"And me." I traced the curve of his cheek with my fingertips.

His expression sobered, but he still had that wicked glint in his eyes I knew so well. "Perhaps we should reenact this week you speak of to jog my memory."

His crooked grin was back in full force, and I was lost. I could do this. I could woo him and show him all I'd learned. "That sounds like an excellent idea. But I'm afraid we can't do it here. The servants don't know about me. I'm not certain how they'll react after everything else I've put them through. Do you have rooms somewhere close?"

"Yes, I took rooms at a house on Half Moon Street, finer than those in Pimlico, now that my prospects have somewhat improved."

I smiled. "Yes, Uncle Oscar's choices of investments proved to be advantageous as always. I've been following their progress."

"Uncle Oscar?"

"My uncle. You went through my ledger and said you were going to follow his advice and speculate, so you wouldn't have to do that other occupation any longer."

His smile grew sheepish, and he shook his head. "I knew I couldn't have managed it on my own. That's one mystery solved, at any rate. I suppose I owe your uncle a debt of gratitude. With my investments and selling the house in Kent, I'm set for life."

"You sold your house?"

"My sister is getting married to a well-to-do young gentleman, and my mother intends to go with her. They spend most of their time in the north of England these days, now that they no longer have to care for me, so we've packed the place up. It made no sense to keep it. I certainly don't intend to live there.... But enough of that for now. We have more important things to discuss, like how long it will take to find us a carriage to my rooms."

Despite his injuries, he scrambled quickly off the couch and limped for the door, and with a surprised chuckle, I chased after him.

Pendel waited a short distance down the hall, and I stopped grinning long enough to put my mask back in place. "Mr. Reynard and I are going out for the evening, Pendel. Will you fetch our things?"

Pendel hesitated a moment, a slight frown and lift of his brows the only betrayal of his surprise, but then he nodded. "Yes, my lord. Should I send Tom with you?"

As giddy as I was, I felt I could conquer the world. The last thing I wanted was Tom tagging along after us. "No. That won't be necessary. Will you send him to fetch a carriage for us, though?"

Poor Pendel's forehead pinched a little, but he waved Tom over and sent him off. Fox and I pulled on our coats and outer things while we waited, but before he opened the door for us, Pendel drew me aside. "I don't mean to be impertinent, my lord, but are you certain you wish to go out alone?"

"I won't be alone. I'll be with Fox," I whispered. "It's him, Pendel. It's really him. He's alive. It appears we're both a little worse for wear, but he's alive. I know him. I trust him. He's my friend." At Pendel's reluctant nod, I continued, "Mr. Reynard's rooms are on Half Moon Street. If our evening runs too late, I'll stay there. Don't wait up. I'll send word if I won't be back by tea tomorrow. I promise."

His jaw ticked, but he nodded again. "Yes, my lord."

"It's all right, Pendel," I assured him. "I'm so happy right now I could burst. Be happy for me."

"I am, my lord."

His lips curved ever so slightly, though his brow remained wrinkled, and I nearly bounced away from him when I heard the carriage pull up the drive.

Pendel held the door for us, and then gave the driver the street and paid him. As we pulled away, Pendel tipped his head, while a frowning Tom loomed behind him.

"Should I be jealous?" Fox asked when I couldn't see them anymore.

I'd been concentrating on my breathing to keep the old anxiety at bay, so the question caught me completely off guard. "What?"

His lip twisted, and he jerked his head in the direction we'd come from. "Should I be jealous of the big one?"

"How do you mean?"

"The man was staring daggers at me all day. Is there something between you?"

I blinked at him a moment, and then I frowned. "Me and Tom? Don't be absurd. Where would you get that idea?"

He rolled his eyes. "I don't think it's absurd, given the looks I received from the man. But if you say I have nothing to worry about, then I'll let the matter drop."

This was an entirely new experience for me, and I probably shouldn't have enjoyed it as much as I did. "Are you jealous?"

He shrugged, looking supremely uncomfortable and possibly a little confused. "Maybe a little," he replied begrudgingly. "I've never been one to share. I suppose I'm too selfish." After a brief pause he shook himself. "Though perhaps I have no right to such things."

As much as I liked the thought that he could still be jealous, I didn't like the sullen twist to his lips or the narrowing of his lovely brown eyes. "You've nothing to worry about. You're the only man I've ever shared such intimacies with."

"Am I?"

"Yes."

He smiled and relaxed against the bench again, his crooked grin blooming anew. "Good."

Chapter Twenty-Three

Fox seemed to have a strange penchant for third-floor apartments. By the time we reached his rooms, we were both perspiring and panting as if we'd run a mile. A quick survey of my surroundings as he ushered me through the door showed he hadn't changed in his choice of décor. If anything his apartments were even more barren and austere than the last. Nothing in the room even hinted at the passionate and colorful man I knew.

I hovered anxiously by his side as he hung our hats and coats on the stand by the door, but when he finished, he only threw me an uncertain smile, stepped around me, and moved to the fireplace to stir up the coals in the grate. Fisting my hands at my sides to keep from reaching for my hair in a sudden spate of nerves, I took a few cautious steps after him. He'd seemed so confident before we left Campden House, so much like the Fox I knew, but the man who rose and turned to me searched my face uncertainly and made no attempt to close the distance between us.

"Fox—I mean, Dorian? Is something wrong?"

He grimaced and shook his head. "I've always been rather impetuous, ruled by my whims, but now I've got you here, I'm at a bit of a loss. You have me at a disadvantage, I'm afraid. I wish I could remember all that transpired between us."

"I know you don't remember me, and perhaps it's too much to ask for you to put your trust in me so soon, but I do know you. I know your heart. I know your kindness and generosity." He winced and I couldn't help but take a few steps toward him. "Deny it all you want, but I've seen it. I've seen the goodness in you as well as the pain. We shared a great deal with each other, good and bad, despite our short acquaintance. I know all about your family, what drove you to the life you led, and I know about Ethan and the guilt you carry."

He jolted at the name and gaped at me. "You do?"

"Yes. We had few secrets between us." I took another step toward him. "It's because of you I'm no longer a slave to the same poison that took him from you. Unlike Ethan, I was under a doctor's care, but the result might have been much the same for me if you hadn't appeared. It's because of you I'm now free to discover how I may fit in this world, how I'm able to leave my house and find what joy I can. You did that for me. Believe me, when I talk of your kindnesses, I speak from experience."

His expression softened. "I have a feeling you are the one being kind. I may not remember these past months, but I know myself, and I'm no magician, nor am I any kind of saint."

Unable to hold back any longer, I closed the last few inches between us and dragged my knuckles down his cheek. "I know you," I whispered. "Believe me. Please."

I'd rarely ever taken the lead in our encounters, but he seemed so fragile and so lost. For once, he needed me. Taking my courage in both hands, I pressed a kiss to his jaw, his cheek, and then his lips. When he opened for me, I took the kiss deeper. I gripped the back of his neck and sucked on his tongue. He moaned and pressed his body to mine. He fisted his hands in my jacket and kissed me back with all the fire I knew he possessed, and I smiled against his lips. This was my Fox.

We only broke apart to catch our breaths, but he pressed his forehead to mine as if he didn't want any space between us.

"I know you," I whispered again, instead of the three words I desperately wanted to say.

His forehead moved against mine as he shook his head. "I'm not the man I was," he murmured hoarsely. "My memories and my damned leg are only part of what I've lost. My balance is shot, even when I'm standing still. I become confused sometimes, particularly when the damned headaches start, and the doctors say I may never recover from all of it. Even if I was the hero you claim, I'm not anymore." He huffed out a breath and pulled back enough to hold my gaze. With a rueful smile, he continued, "My baser nature is screaming at me to shut my mouth and take whatever you're willing to offer, but you said we had few secrets between us, and I like the thought of that very much. You paint me with such glowing strokes, I hate to disappoint."

Not so long ago I had forced him to hear and acknowledge all my defects. I understood his need better than anyone.

"In these past months I prayed every moment of every day that God would see you safe and returned to me. You don't remember what we were to each other. You don't remember how you accepted me, *cared for* me, even at my worst, but I do. God saw fit to answer my prayers, and I will thank him for the gift he has given me every day until I die, whether or not you regain any of what you've lost."

His answering smile was almost painfully sweet as he shook his head and searched my face with wondering eyes. "I don't think I've ever met anyone quite like you."

"I know."

I kissed him then, hard enough to forgo any further argument. I shoved his jacket from his shoulders before fumbling with the buttons on his waistcoat. Taking my lead, he kissed me back with equal fervor while he applied his deft and agile fingers to my jacket and waistcoat. Once we'd managed to undo each other's neckties, collar buttons, and cufflinks, we drew apart only long enough to drag our shirts over our heads before coming together again. In his ardor, his passion-darkened eyes no longer held any trepidation or hesitation, and I basked in their heat and reveled in the strength of his hands on me.

He leaned on me heavily as we limped and stumbled our way into his bedchamber. Refusing to allow any embarrassment or uncertainty to creep back into his eyes, I pushed him onto the mattress and climbed on top of him, careful to avoid his injured leg. I kissed him until all the tension left his body. I climbed off him only long enough to divest us of our shoes and the last of our clothing, and then I urged him under the blankets before sliding in beside him.

In the waning afternoon light, I felt his gaze on my nakedness for the first time since my illness, and uncertainty of my own crept in. I was a good deal thinner now than I had been. But his hands and his lips had lost none of their urgency, and I soon forgot my fears and surrendered to my need. I hadn't had him in my arms for what felt like an eternity. All those days and nights of anguish and longing and fear came crashing down on me, and I ravaged his mouth and throat and clutched at every bit of skin I could reach, desperate to reassure myself he was solid and real and mine again. A sob escaped me as I buried my face against his neck and trembled with the strength of my feelings.

"Arthur? What's wrong?"

"I'm sorry. I just—you have no idea how much I've missed you."

He tightened his arms around me, but he remained silent. I couldn't blame him. What could he say? He didn't know me. He couldn't have missed me. If I didn't pull myself together, I'd send him running in the opposite direction before I even had a chance to woo him back.

To end the awkward silence between us, I lifted up and kissed him again. I trailed kisses down his throat and over his chest, paying homage to his nipples and then sliding lower. He moaned and threaded his fingers through my hair when I finally took his member in my mouth, and I hummed my approval as I drew him in until his cockhead bumped the back of my throat. My still-healing lungs objected to the rigorous activity, but I suppressed the threatening cough and pressed on. I would show him the strength of my longing through deed rather than word. I would use everything he'd taught me to prove how well I knew him, how much I loved him still.

He writhed and arched beneath me as I laved and sucked him deep into my throat. I cradled his sac in my palm and squeezed with just the amount of pressure he liked as I bobbed my head. When he cried his pleasure and released his seed, I drank down every drop and held him in my mouth until the last of the tremors left his body. As he sank into the mattress panting for breath, I crawled up and cuddled against his side. He lifted a shaking hand to my cheek and smiled at me, but he seemed to be struggling to keep his eyes open. I took his hand in mine and kissed his palm.

"It's been a long day for both of us. Sleep. I'll be here when you wake."

He opened his mouth, possibly to argue with me, but then seemed to think better of it.

"I'm sorry," he murmured.

"Don't be."

He curled on his side and his breathing evened out in slumber. My cock ached with need, but the exertion had taken its toll on me as well, and I was more than content to cuddle against his back, press my face into his hair, and allow sleep to take me.

The sun had set when he woke me with a kiss. Seemingly determined to make up for falling asleep on me, despite my assurances he had nothing to apologize for, he spent what felt like hours relearning every inch of my body, bringing me to brink over and over with his hands and his mouth.

"Please," I begged.

With a chuckle, he rose over me. "Please what?"

I dragged him down for a lengthy kiss. He rested his elbows beside my head and draped his full length over me, pressing his hardness against my own. I ground against him and clutched at him. "Please. I need you. I want you inside me again. I want to feel you everywhere."

He drew back and searched my face. "Are you certain?"

I smiled at the echoes of the past. "God, yes."

With an almost pained moan, he burrowed his hands beneath me and gripped my arse. I lifted my legs to cradle him between my thighs and thrust against him. My own moans of pleasure at the exquisite friction were cut short when he swore and scrambled from the bed.

"Give me a moment," he said as he limped hurriedly to a wardrobe in the corner of the room. He panted heavily as he rifled through the drawers, and threw clothing in all directions. "Oh, thank the Lord."

Then he climbed on top of me again, brandishing a crystal vial. "I was afraid this might not have made the journey from my old apartments, and I've had no cause or desire to procure a replacement since my return to Town."

I didn't have a chance to form a reply other than to gasp as he slid a slippery finger inside me. He was patient and gentle in his ministrations. I had no doubt that he'd believed my assurances that he was the only one. But I'd been so long without him, I didn't care a jot for any discomfort I might experience. I couldn't wait any longer.

"I need you inside me. Please."

His withdrew his fingers, and then he rose over me and pressed his crown to my entrance. Struggling with my impatience, I did not rush him as he filled me ever so slowly and carefully. When at last he was fully seated inside me, we both exhaled deeply. I wrapped my arms around his shoulders and drew him closer to me as I hooked my heels beneath his buttocks.

Thankfully, the unreasoning fear that had plagued me before didn't rise this time to cast a pall over the moment. I whispered a silent prayer of gratitude for that, then all other thoughts were obliterated by the joy of having him inside me again as he began to move.

Neither of us lasted long, but given the sad state we were in, I wasn't surprised. A wave of ecstasy crashed over me shortly after he cried out and filled me with his seed. We both collapsed, and I finally succumbed to the fit of coughing I'd been fighting the entire time.

"Are you all right?" he managed between gasps of his own.

I chuckled, which set off another brief episode of coughing. "Yes. I'm perfect but for the lingering weakness in my lungs and everywhere else. We make a fine pair don't we?"

He gave a rasping laugh in return. "Yes."

Too exhausted to tend the fire or anything else, we curled together beneath the mound of blankets on his bed. I closed my eyes and breathed him in until sleep stole over me again.

I WOKE to find Fox reclining beside me with his cheek propped on his palm, watching me. His expression was strangely unreadable, and a small frisson of anxiety moved through me.

"Good morning," I murmured hesitantly, as if it were more of a question than a statement.

His lips curved gently. "Good morning."

"Is something wrong?"

"No."

If he'd meant that to be reassuring, he'd missed the mark entirely.

"Are you hungry?" he asked, breaking the awkward silence that had fallen between us.

"A little."

"It's well past the hour breakfast is served in the parlor, but I think I may be able to charm a tray out of Mrs. Porter, the cook. She's taken me under her ample wing to some extent since I moved in. I think she feels sorry for me, crippled as I am."

I opened my mouth to argue that he was not crippled or in need of anyone's pity, but the chiming of the Great Bell in the distance cut me off. When the eleventh bell rang, I winced.

"I didn't realize it was so late. I should be getting home. I'm sure Pendel will be frantic by now."

He frowned. "I thought we were going to reenact our week together."

"I want to. Believe me, there's nothing I'd like better. But I have standing appointments with my doctor, and I've already put my uncle and Pendel through enough worry for a lifetime. I can't simply disappear for an entire week again."

"I suppose you have a point there. Do you have time for breakfast at least?"

After worrying my lip I shook my head. "I'll need to bathe and dress before Dr. Stuart's visit. I should go home."

With a resigned sigh, he nodded and threw off our blankets. We both rose unsteadily and gathered our discarded clothing. We helped each other dress, exchanging shy smiles and tender touches all the while. My clothes were wrinkled and soiled from spending a night on the floor, and I winced, imagining the look on Pendel's face when he saw me.

As a clear sign of how distracted I was by my companion, I didn't experience any anxiety at being in a strange place, nor even notice the cacophony from the street outside until Fox opened the door to his apartments for me. Then the reality of my predicament set in, and I froze on the threshold.

"Arthur?"

I shook my head mutely, struggling with fear and shame.

"Arthur, what is it?"

The weight of his hand on my shoulder eased some of the panic in me, and I took a deep breath and then another. "I'm sorry. I-I don't know how to get home from here."

"There isn't a driver in London who'd turn down an opportunity to take Lord Campden home," he replied chuckling.

I shifted uncomfortably and grimaced, my gaze firmly riveted on my shoes. "I've never hired a carriage before. I don't precisely know how you go about finding one."

"Oh."

His voice held no condemnation, only surprise, and some of my mortification eased.

"Give me a moment to make myself a little more presentable and we'll go down together," he said.

I stepped back with a sigh of relief, and he closed the door again. Once he'd finished pulling on his jacket and combed his hair and mine, he grabbed his cane and led the way. The streets outside were worryingly crowded in the late morning, and I kept close to his side, praying no one would speak to me.

He waved down a carriage with surprising speed, and after giving the man in the box my direction, handed me up. I wished I could think of something clever to say by way of parting, but I was near to bursting with conflicting emotions. Embarrassment at my helplessness, regret for leaving him, anxiousness to be back in the quiet and safety of my house, and joy that I had him back in my life at long last threatened to crack the fragile mask I'd managed to build. I could only stare mutely at him as he stepped back to the curb and smiled reassuringly at me.

He seemed to understand. His eyes were warm as he tipped his hat to me. But just as the driver snapped the reins and the contraption jerked forward, his smile fell away, his brows drew down, and he lunged forward again.

"Promise me I'll see you again," he called urgently as we began to move away.

"I promise. Tonight. Dinner. Come to the house." I threw out the invitation recklessly, but his answering grin made any concerns I might've had fade to nothing. Pendel and Mrs. Peebles would forgive the late notice, and perhaps Uncle Oscar would be pleased when he learned I was entertaining a guest.

Chapter Twenty-Four

My reunion with Fox dominated my talking session with Dr. Stuart. The inquisitive little man peppered me with questions, and I struggled a great deal to keep the extent of my joy contained. I hadn't shared the intimacy or the nature of our friendship with anyone, not even the good doctor. Dr. Stuart was kind, patient, and had proved himself open to new ideas, new ways of thinking, but I dared not take the chance, particularly as I could harm more than myself if the information ever made it beyond our meetings. I wanted to tell him everything, but even with his assurances of confidentiality, I couldn't trust him with that much.

Dr. Stuart lingered long past our usual hour. Perhaps he hoped Fox would arrive early for our dinner and he'd have the opportunity to take Fox's measure. But as the minutes dragged on, eventually even Dr. Stuart's boundless curiosity had to surrender to the dictates of convention and propriety, and he bid me good afternoon without receiving any satisfaction.

The hours between the doctor's departure and Fox's arrival were interminable. I had to resort to nearly all of my old methods of distraction to contain my excitement and stave off my fears that he wouldn't come. My most recent novel and a half-finished sketch of the front lawn lay discarded on a table by the window in the front parlor, and I was a few measures into my third Mozart concerto when I finally heard the carriage arrive.

My fingers faltered a moment on the keys, but I persevered. Fox had always liked my playing, and I fully intended to use every weapon in my limited arsenal to regain his admiration and regard. Perhaps my music might help him remember something also, but I'd wait to try Chopin or the tavern songs until the servants had gone to bed for the night.

I nodded and tried to control my breathing when Pendel knocked and introduced my guest, but I didn't stop playing. Pendel retreated and closed the door behind him, and Fox moved closer. The last few measures took all of my strength and concentration with him so near, but I managed to get through them. Tucking my fingers in my lap so he wouldn't see them shake, I turned to him and smiled, but my breath caught at the rapt expression on his face.

"That was beautiful, truly beautiful," he murmured huskily. His aspect was so similar to the first time he'd come upon me playing, my body flushed, and my heart ached with a combination of joy and pain.

"Thank you."

With a sigh, he broke his gaze from mine and limped to the window overlooking the front lawn. I trailed behind him but stopped a few feet away, unable to read his disposition.

After an awkward silence, Fox huffed out a quiet chuckle and said, "At every turn you show me what a remarkable young man you are, Arthur. I'm not quite sure why…." He took a deep breath and blew it out. "The last several months haven't been easy for me. I'm not accustomed to being dependent on anyone. Returning home and having to entrust my care into the uncertain affections of my mother and sister, as well as having my body and mind fail me at every turn, was a blow to my pride." He continued to stare into the darkness rather than look at me. "Even returning to Town and taking rooms of my own again did little to alleviate that state. I quickly realized how few of the people I might've once called friend that I was willing to have see me in this state, or that I could trust to lean on in my weakness. I've been quite lost, you see, praying for God to show me some direction to take now that I've left my old life behind… or it left me behind. I'm not sure which."

While I struggled for a response, uncertain if he even wanted one, he lifted my sketchpad from the table next to him and held it up to the gas lamp to the left of the window. "This is yours, isn't it?"

"Yes."

He smiled and traced a finger over some of the pencil lines. "I found several drawings like this in my belongings when I unpacked. I knew I couldn't have done them. They show too much skill and imagination, and there's a likeness of me among them that's far too flattering."

"I drew it the week we spent together. It's how I see you."

He shook his head before turning this gaze to mine. "Yesterday in the park, I was feeling quite sorry for myself. I sat on that bench for a long time, trying to dredge up the strength to return to my empty apartments. Then an angel dropped in my lap, invited me to tea, and kissed me, and ever since I've been struggling to believe my luck. I feel as if I'm in a dream, and at any moment, I'll wake broken and alone again."

He turned back to the dark window, his jaw clenched so tight the muscles popped. Unable to hold back any longer, I stepped close and took his face in my palms, forcing him to look at me.

"You aren't dreaming, and you certainly aren't broken. If you will only put a little trust in me, I'll prove it to you."

His lips curved slightly, but whatever he would've said was lost when a knock on the door forced me to jerk away from him.

"Dinner is served, my lord."

AS IF our earlier conversation had never happened, Fox flirted with me and teased me throughout our meal, much as he had in our first days together, and I flushed and stammered back at him as I had done before, despite all that had come between. He seemed more his old self, and whether that was only for my benefit or he'd let go of some of his melancholy, I didn't question it.

After dinner we returned to the parlor, and he asked me to play for him again. I sent Pendel to his bed, assuring him I could take care of our guest, and then I moved to the pianoforte while Fox took his glass of sherry and settled into a chair by the fire. With the servants in bed, I played Chopin for him, pouring all my feelings into the notes.

He remained a silent audience, but when I moved to begin a third sonata, he said, "I want you to tell me everything you remember of our time together, down to the smallest detail. I want to know all of it."

I turned to face him and worried my lip. "All of it? Now?"

"Yes. Now. Everything. Good or bad. Start from the night we met, and don't leave anything out."

In a spate of nerves, I moved to the sideboard and poured myself a sherry. I immediately regretted downing half the contents in one swallow as it set off a coughing fit, but I refilled the glass almost to the brim anyway before moving to the chair across from Fox's.

"Every detail could take some time," I hedged.

"I don't mind. If you need a rest, we can always begin where you left off next time we're together."

With a sigh of resignation and another sip for courage, I began. In fits and starts, I told him as much as I could remember, and he only occasionally interrupted me with questions. I only truly faltered when I had to speak of the noises in the hall and the spirits of Campden House.

I had to skip to the end of my tale to explain all of that to him, about my mother and the night my parents died, and my glass was empty by the time I finished. A little afraid of his reaction, I quickly rose to refill it, in desperate need of more fortification.

"Extraordinary. So were they real, these spirits, or only a memory?"

"I don't know."

"But you say I heard them too?"

His glass was empty as well when I turned back to him, so I brought the decanter with me and set it next to him before I returned to my seat.

"Yes."

"Yet no one else has heard or seen anything?"

Shifting uncomfortably I shrugged. "You are the only one to ever say anything to me about it. I suppose there are rumors about the house, of course, but any house of an age has those."

"Rumors have a start somewhere," he murmured almost to himself. He downed the contents of his glass, took the decanter from me, and refilled it again before grinning at me. "There are scandalous rumors of a gypsy somewhere back in a never-mentioned branch of my family tree. Perhaps they're true as well, and I inherited a trickle of gypsy magic that allowed me to pierce the veil just a little."

I couldn't tell if he was teasing me again, but some of my tension eased, and I returned his smile.

After another sip of his drink, he set the glass aside and propped his chin in his palm as he regarded me with a softer smile. "Or perhaps—if I'm the hero you paint me—your spirits wanted me to hear them."

"Perhaps," I murmured. I seemed to be having a difficult time keeping my eyes open as my anxiety slowly bled away, and I had to struggle to remember what we were talking of.

"You look tired. I think perhaps I've asked enough of you for now. I should bid you good night."

I struggled to my feet as Fox rose gracefully and reached for his cane. I didn't want him to go, but I couldn't think of an excuse for him to stay, and I was quite drowsy all of a sudden.

"You'll call again?"

He stepped close to me and took my lips in a gentle kiss. "As often as you wish. You need only send word. And you're welcome to call on me anytime, night or day."

I wanted to go with him, but I'd already sent Pendel away, and I feared how Pendel and my uncle would feel or what they might think if I spent another night away so soon. I had entered strange new waters, and I feared I would need to tread carefully from now on.

I found his coat, hat, and gloves by the front door, but once he'd put them on, I was at a loss. "Should I wake Tom to find you a carriage?" I asked.

"No. Sweet Arthur, you've given me much to ponder tonight, and a little fresh air will do me good. I'll walk until I find one."

"You're sure?"

"Yes. I'm not as broken as all that. I can still manage a short walk on my own."

I winced and would have tried an apology, but he took me in his arms and kissed me until my head spun, and afterward, I could only gape at him while he disappeared into the night.

After closing and bolting the door, I somehow managed to put out the lamps and make my unsteady way up to bed. I still had no head for drink. I needed to try to remember that.

As I'd anticipated, by the end of the week, my uncle sent word he was coming to Town and to expect him for dinner. Fox didn't even blink an eyelash when we met for a walk in the park and I broke the news. I told him he didn't have to come, but he insisted and arrived early, impeccably turned out and head held high.

The three of us shared an awkward meal together. Our conversation was somewhat stilted and painful to start. I didn't know what to say, and my uncle wasn't exactly a garrulous man at the best of times. Thankfully, Fox had no such difficulties. He remarked on a broad range of topics while we ate, until he came upon a few that sparked my uncle's interests, namely speculating and fishing, and from then on kept my uncle talking until Uncle Oscar took his leave.

When Pendel finally closed the door behind him, leaving me alone in the library with Fox, I collapsed into one of the chairs by the fire with an exhausted sigh. Propriety and breeding had forced Uncle Oscar to leave unasked most of the questions I felt sure he had, but the weight of them had hung heavily in the room. Eventually we would need to come up with a more convincing story than the pathetic lie I'd invented about stumbling into Fox on the street and being offered asylum in his home to explain our meeting, but with Fox's easy charm we'd managed to put it off for another night at the very least.

"I'm sorry, but there was no avoiding it once Pendel sent him word," I said as soon as Fox joined me by the fire.

He took a sip of his sherry and waved a dismissive hand. "Don't worry. I rather liked him, actually. Besides, given he's the author of my current success and obviously very dear to you, I could hardly do anything but."

"Thank you."

He lifted his glass to me before draining the rest of its contents. After setting it aside, he pushed himself out of his chair and moved in front of me. He pulled me up, drew me close, and kissed me softly. "Can you come back with me tonight?"

With deep regret, I shook my head. "I can't."

Against my better judgment, I'd already spent a second night with him in the course of one week, and even I, with my limited experiences, knew we had to be more circumspect than that or risk suspicion and discovery.

He placed a kiss on the corner of my mouth and then another on my jaw before he moved down and nibbled my neck. "Well, perhaps I could stay here, then," he murmured quietly between teasing nips to my earlobe. "Your servants could set me up somewhere close to your rooms, and I'd make sure to be back in my own bed before dawn."

I moaned and leaned into his body. As had happened earlier in the week, I couldn't think beyond the sweet torture of his lips and teeth and tongue. I shouldn't say yes. I should show more caution.

"I could pretend my leg is paining me or I've had too much drink to make the journey back to my apartments," he whispered before nuzzling the sensitive skin beneath my ear. His hands roamed my body, and my cock ached for his touch.

With a herculean display of restraint, I stepped back, held him at arm's length, and attempted a severe frown. "We shouldn't."

With a sigh, his devilish grin slipped from his face, and he nodded. "We probably shouldn't."

"At least, not this early in the evening," I wavered.

One of his silver brows quirked, and his grin returned.

With a nod, he stepped away from me, took his seat again, and kept a safe distance between us while I waited for my blush to fade. Then I rang for Pendel and ordered a fire in the parlor. I could play for him for a while, and then perhaps we'd try a game of chess or cards.

He managed to keep his hands to himself, mostly, over the next few hours while I played and we sang the songs he'd taught me. I thought I heard a rustle outside the parlor door sometimes, whenever I stopped playing, but I chose to ignore it. If someone were there, they'd only hear two friends amusing themselves. If I were imagining things again, I'd wait to see if it got any worse before addressing it with Dr. Stuart. I didn't have to be afraid anymore. I had Fox. I had Dr. Stuart and my uncle and Pendel. I had hope for the future and shoulders to lean on if I faltered. I had someone who needed me in return. And I had time to learn to navigate the world that had been opened to me.

"What shall we sing next?" Fox asked when I'd let the silence go on too long.

"Let's go to bed," I offered instead.

His elegant silver brows rose, and he grinned. "So you'll let me stay, then?"

"Yes. I want you to."

After a quick glance toward the closed door, he pulled me from my bench and kissed me soundly. But just as suddenly as he'd kissed me, he broke his lips from mine and pulled me into a crushing hug. He held me like that in silence for several long breaths before he said in a subdued voice, "You know you're going to have to be the voice of reason between us, don't you? I'm afraid I won't be much help there at all."

"I'll try."

"I feel as if I can't get enough of your company. I don't know if it's my memories and feelings returning or just you, but I think of you every minute of the day. I can understand how we came to be so close in so short a time before, because falling for you now is so terrifyingly effortless."

His voice shook with emotion, and I squeezed him back as hard as he'd held me. "It doesn't have to be terrifying."

"But it is. Don't you see? I've always been reckless, heedless of the damage I left in my wake. I'm the reason we were in the East End. It's my fault you were hurt. You said so yourself. I need you to keep me in check. You mustn't let me bully you into recklessness again."

"I'll try my best, but it isn't bullying when I want it just as much." With effort I broke away from his embrace and moved to the mantel. After taking a few breaths to settle my pounding heart, I said, "Still, you have a point. We're no longer tucked away in the dark, behind locked doors. We must have a care for our surroundings. We must show restraint and not give in to our passions too often."

"Just not tonight?" he qualified.

I could hear his grin returning, and I couldn't fight my answering smile.

"Not tonight," I agreed.

ROWAN MCALLISTER is a woman who doesn't so much create as recreate, taking things ignored and overlooked and hopefully making them into something magical and mortal. She believes it's all in how you look at it. In addition to a continuing love affair with words, she creates art out of fabric, metal, wood, stone, and any other interesting scraps of life she can get her hands on. Everything is simply one perspective change and a little bit of effort away from becoming a work of art that is both beautiful and functional. She lives in the woods, on the very edge of suburbia—where civilization drops off and nature takes over—sharing her home with her patient, loving, and grounded husband, her super sweet hairball of a cat, and a mythological beast masquerading as a dog. Her chosen family is made up of a madcap collection of people from many different walks of life, all of whom act as her muses in so many ways, and she would be lost without them.

E-mail: rowanmcallister10@gmail.com
Facebook: www.facebook.com/rowanmcallister10
Twitter: @RowanMcallister

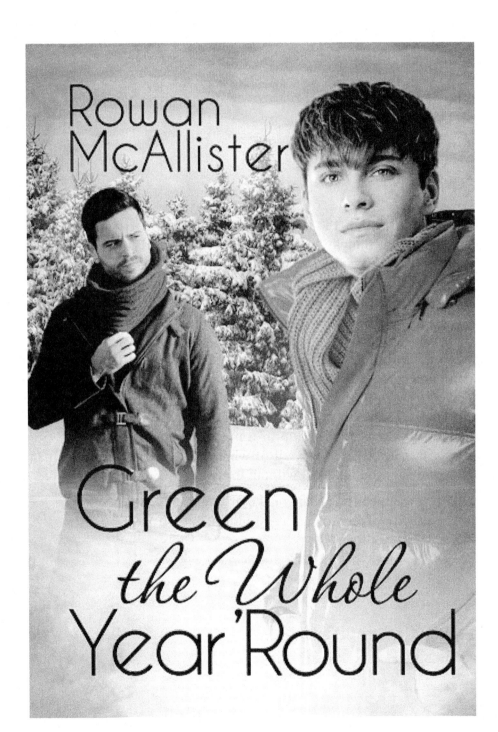

Couples counselor Ted Freeman is still reeling six months after his partner left him. He desperately hopes a week of peace and quiet at a quaint mountain cabin will be just what he needs to regain his personal and professional confidence.

Neil Kelly is a computer programmer who just got promoted to full time and is celebrating over Christmas by going on his first real grown-up vacation at the Cabins in the Pines Inn. When he runs into Ted, his longtime crush, Neil can't believe his luck, and he vows to do whatever it takes to make Ted see him as something other than the dork next door.

Neil wasn't part of Ted's plan for the holidays, but he might turn out to be exactly what Ted needs.

www.dreamspinnerpress.com

When Nathan Seward wakes up in a cheap hotel with a stranger, unable to remember the night before, unscrupulous plots and clandestine schemes are the furthest thing from his mind. True, he's in Houston to bid on his biggest contract yet, one that will put his software development company on the map, but he's the underdog at the table, not one of the big players. Unfortunately someone out there sees him as a threat and isn't above drugging and blackmailing him to put him out of the running. Luckily for Nathan, the man in bed next to him couldn't be further removed from the corporate world.

Tim Conrad is scraping the bottom of the barrel. He left college during his freshman year to take care of his dying mother, and life and lack of money prevented him going back. Now twenty-seven, his dreams are long buried, and he's scraping by with dead-end jobs and couch surfing because he can't afford a place of his own.

As Nathan tries to run damage control and figure out what the hell happened to him, he and Tim discover a connection neither was looking for, as well as dreams they've both forgotten.

www.dreamspinnerpress.com

Can a pickup line from a stranger completely change the way an ordinary man sees himself?

Adrian wouldn't have thought so, but after an ugly breakup where his self-esteem took a serious beating, he's willing to try just about anything to repair the damage… even return to a secluded bar in rural Maryland and the intriguing stranger whose words have been on his mind since they met.

Biker, bouncer, bartender, and tattoo artist, Wyatt is a rolling stone. After fifteen years, he is tired of a life on the run, but he isn't sure he knows how to do anything else or if he has anything besides a physical relationship to offer.

What's supposed to be a one-off turns into another and another, and the relationship looks promising until the mob and the FBI come knocking on Adrian's door.

www.dreamspinnerpress.com

Elemental Harmony: Book One

When absentminded video game developer Jay Thurson impulsively follows his intuition westward, he never expects his rideshare to turn out to be a gun-toting madman. In an act of desperation, Jay turns to the gift he's long neglected and feared for help and leaps from the moving car on a dark and deserted back country road.

Running for his life leads him to the doorstep of Adam Grauwacke, a roadside nursery owner and sometime vegetable farmer, whose affinity for the earth goes far beyond having a green thumb. Adam's world is ordered and predictable, dependable and safe, but despite having his dream farm and business, he's always felt something's missing. When he welcomes Jay into his home, life seems to click for both men, and together they explore their gifts and their attraction.

But harmony has no value if it is easily won, and a crazed gunman and volatile ex might be their end if Jay and Adam can't learn to trust the strength of their bond.

www.dreamspinnerpress.com

FOR **MORE** OF THE **BEST GAY** ROMANCE

dreamspinnerpress.com